Awakening

Some rules should never be broken...

Paj Vang

<u>Content Warning</u>

This book contains references to suicide, sex, arranged marriage, violence, foul language, abuse and assault, emotional manipulation, generational trauma, death, and depression.

Special thanks to Danielle Lowary and Lily Szafas. I could not have done this without you two always looking out for me in every way!

Special thanks to Yajminuu and Darlene Vang. Your quick reading and thoughtful feedback helped me shape this story into what it's become!

To the reader: may this story be the escape you need for just a little while.

The Shaman and I Series

By Paj Vang

Book 1: Chosen Bride

A reluctant girl. A grieving shaman.
A destiny neither wanted.

Book 2: Awakening

Love deepens. Powers rise.

Book 3: Sacrifice

When protecting the one you love means sacrifice.

Book 4: Bound *(Coming Soon)*

Memories fade. Souls disappear. Love remains.

Preface

The Hmong culture and its practice of shamanism are very real. For thousands of years, shamans have helped heal the sick through traditional practices such as herbal medicine. When necessary, they also commune with spirits and gods.

For readers unfamiliar with the culture, I would like to explain a few concepts mentioned throughout the story.

Shee Yee is considered the first Hmong shaman, though the mythology surrounding him in this series is entirely fictional and created for the story.

Soul-calling is a common Hmong practice performed when someone is believed to be traumatized, ill, frightened, or spiritually lost. Soul locks are necklaces worn to help protect and keep the soul safe. Protection bracelets are also commonly worn to ward off evil spirits.

Shamans use tools such as split horns, hoop rattles, swords, and finger bells to help them enter, navigate, and protect themselves within the spirit world.

No one chooses to become a shaman; according to tradition, shamans are chosen by special spirit guides. These gifts may manifest through physical or mental illness, and in some cases, the more a person resists this calling, the worse their condition becomes. Many people have reported experiencing healing only after accepting their role as a shaman.

In Hmong spiritual belief, spirits can sometimes be appeased or persuaded to help through offerings such as money, food, or gifts. In certain rituals, the soul of an animal may be exchanged in an attempt to recover the soul of a loved one.

In Book 2, there is a ritual involving the "slave spirit." This is a rarely practiced and deeply dangerous ritual, typically performed only to save someone who is dying. The slave spirit is said to travel where even a shaman's spirit guides refuse to go—and it may leave the shaman there. Because of this risk, many shamans consider it a serious warning sign.

Touso would certainly disapprove.

Although all the characters in this series are fictional, their struggles and emotions are universal. Mossy Cha views aspects of Hmong culture as a burden against her own desires. Touso struggles with grief and the loss of a loved one. Cindy Thao and Alang Vang carry deep pessimism shaped by abuse. Kai Khang is seen as a rebel because he believes change is necessary and beneficial. Pahoua and Lihue love their children deeply, yet express that love in ways that unintentionally create conflict. Throughout the story, there is a strong emphasis on how personal experiences and the people around us shape who we become.

The Hmong culture is rich with tradition, yet many aspects of it remain mysterious. I hope this information helps you better understand the world and themes within the story.

With love,
Paj Vang

Character Legend

CLAN NAMES
KHANG - CANG
CHA – CHAW
THAO – TOW
XIONG – SONG
MOUA – MOO-A
HER – HER
VANG - VANG

MAIN PROTAGONISTS
MOSSY AKA MO (MAW) CHA
TOUSO (TOO-SO)
AKA TUB XOB (TOO-SAW) KHANG

MAIN ANTAGONISTS
DU YONG – DOO-YONG
DYLAN REED
SENG VANG
ALANG (AH-LENG) VANG
CHEWY (CHOO-WEE) THAO

MOSSY'S FAMILY
BLIA CHA
KENG CHA
SHENGMII (SHENG-MEE) CHA
ALLEN CHA
CHENG CHA

MOSSY'S EXTENDED FAMILY
MAY KHANG
YER KHANG
SARAH KHANG
THAI (TY) KHANG

TOUSO'S FAMILY
LIHUE (LEE-HOO) KHANG
PAHOUA (PAH-HOO-AH) KHANG
BAO (BOW) KHANG
FUECHI (FOO-CHEE) KHANG
WANG MENG (WA-MENG) KHANG
PADEE (PAH-DEE) KHANG

MOSSY'S FRIENDS
EVA GARCIA
CINDY THAO

SHAMAN CLUB OWNERS
KOU (KOO) HER
YING HER

Prologue

uechi Khang was scared. He told his mama exactly this as she tucked him into bed. Nia kissed him on the top of the head and smiled.

"What's there to be scared about, baby?"

Fuechi answered, "Bad Man! Bad Man is coming, Mama!"

Nia frowned. It wasn't the first time her son had mentioned the "Bad Man." Their apartment was on the third floor, with all the doors and windows securely locked. Unless the Bad Man could scale walls like Spider-Man, it would be nearly impossible for anyone to break into their home.

"Baby, what does this Bad Man look like? Have I met him?" she asked.

Fuechi shook his head. "Bad Man has long hair—and looks like Uncle Marx at church!"

"You mean he wears a suit?" Nia tapped her chin thoughtfully.

Marx was one of Kai's closest friends, and Fuechi often sat with him during Sunday services. On those mornings, the local music mogul exchanged his designer jumpsuits for tailored suits, a more sophisticated look that contrasted sharply with his colored locks and flashy gold teeth.

Fuechi nodded. "Sometimes."

"Sometimes?" Nia furrowed her brows.

"Sometimes Bad Man is a snake monster."

Something about those words sent a chill up her spine.

Finally, she said, "No one's getting in here, sweetheart." She walked to the large window and gave it a firm push to prove her point. "See? It's locked."

Next, she opened the closet door and made a show of peering inside. The small space, barely three feet wide and two feet deep, was just large enough to fit Fuechi's clothes on two bars. Nia could touch the back wall without stepping inside. Nothing could hide in that closet without being seen.

Lately, Fuechi had insisted the door stay closed.

"It comes from there," he had said a few days earlier. "Bad Man always comes from there!"

"No one's hiding. It's just you and me, baby."

"Bad Man is coming for Fuechi!" he insisted.

"Not on my watch." She tried to smile, though her son still looked unconvinced. "I'll sit here with you until you fall asleep. I promise no one will hurt you."

Fuechi sighed. His mama didn't see the things he saw. For a long time, she thought Ling was just an imaginary friend. It was only after Uncle Touso explained that she finally believed. Fuechi wondered if Uncle Touso saw the Bad Man, too.

Awakening

The boy yawned. He hadn't napped in days and often cried before bedtime. Fuechi missed his father, but she didn't understand why he was seeing things.

"Mama, you stay," he whispered.

She promised, "I'll be right here."

Nia was relieved when he finally closed his eyes and smiled when the soft snoring began. Fuechi snored like his daddy. She used to threaten she'd make him sleep on the couch, but now, he'd do anything to hear that sound again.

Wiping tears from her eyes, Nia stood and went to close the closet. She was still thinking of her late husband when something rattled inside. Nia narrowed her eyes and listened—then jumped when the noise came again.

It sounded like nails scratching against the wall.

Mice! Nia cursed under her breath.

Creaky floors and thin walls were common with cheap rent and old buildings, but she wouldn't tolerate pests. The thought of mice crawling in the cabinets and surfaces she and Fuechi used made her skin crawl.

Frustrated, she knelt to search for holes along the wall. She'd try to seal them until speaking to the landlord in the morning.

Distracted, Nia didn't notice the gray hand emerging from the sea of clothes above her head. Long, black nails hovered over her braids... and yanked!

Nia yelped as she fell backward. She rubbed a tender spot where a braid hung loosely at the base. She stared into the closet with its neatly hung clothes and toy boxes, but couldn't see what could have snagged her hair.

She glanced at Fuechi, who was fixated on the closet lately as he rambled about the Bad Man. Maybe if she let him decorate the door with stickers, it'd feel less scary.

It was just mice, after all.

With a sigh, she carefully closed the closet door and snuck out of the room.

A little after his mama left, Fuechi felt a tug at the foot of the bed. He opened his eyes to see Ling beside him. He hadn't seen Ling since his Uncle Touso banished him.

"Ling! What are you doing here?" Fuechi asked, rubbing his tired eyes.

Ling placed a tiny finger against his lips.

"What's wrong?" Fuechi sat up and frowned.

Before Ling could answer, there was a change in the room. A prickle of goosebumps crawled up his spine as he recognized what was happening.

He was back.

The walls seemed to shrink around him, making Fuechi feel like a bird trapped in a cage. A heavy chill spread throughout the room like soldiers surrounding their target. Fuechi gasped and slid quickly under the blanket. He was startled to feel another body curled up next to him. Fortunately, it was only Ling.

"Bad Man is coming!" Fuechi whispered.

Again, Ling pushed a finger to his lips, urging him to stay quiet. The ghost had seen the dark one moving through the underworld. Usually, the demon carried a mood of indifference. He ate souls the way one might breathe air—without effort or care. Tonight, however, he was noticeably agitated.

Awakening

Du Yong, the Bad Man, slipped from door to door and realm to realm, leaving a trail of burnt embers across the ground. The evidence of his fury was everywhere, so much so that he couldn't keep his preferred shell of a gentleman. Ling didn't know why the evil lord was angry, but he was headed toward Fuechi.

Ling was a master at teleporting, which he'd used to protect Fuechi in the past. Now, he hoped to get to him before the demon did. Like Ling, Du Yong knew Fuechi was special.

Fuechi was his friend, and he wouldn't let anything hurt him. But a ghost was no match for a demon. Their only chance was to run. He'd reached Fuechi only seconds before the Bad Man's arrival. Now, they hid under the blanket together.

What now? Fuechi's golden-brown eyes widened in fear.

Cold hands wrapped around his own and squeezed.

Ling wants Fuechi to follow?

Ling nodded.

Where?

When the ghost glanced at the closet, Fuechi knew the answer.

The demon was after Fuechi's soul. The only way to avoid being eaten by him was to run away and hide in the vast underworld. A soul that couldn't be found couldn't be eaten. This was why Ling had come—to take him away for the ultimate game of hide-and-seek.

As Fuechi hesitated, the room grew very hot, and his heart leaped to his throat. The closet door flew open, crashing against the thin wall. Then, something heavy slithered across the room.

The scent of sulfur and decay made Fuechi nauseous.

"Come out, come out, wherever you are," the demon purred from the foot of the bed. "I've come to play."

Fuechi's little feet burned from the heat of the demon's proximity.

Du Yong said, "Your daddy was a bad boy. He didn't want to play with me. But you'll play with me, won't you?"

Fuechi caught his breath. His daddy had been gone for a long time. Did the Bad Man know where to find him? This curiosity was almost enough to make Fuechi peek from under the blanket.

Almost.

"Your Uncle Touso is a bad boy, too." This time, the demon growled, and Fuechi could tell he was angry. His serpent tail whipped and crashed against the leg of the bed, nearly toppling Fuechi and Ling onto the floor. "He thinks he's safe, but he's a fool. I will have his soul soon enough!"

Uncle Touso! When Fuechi's heart cried out this time, he almost heard his uncle's soul replying. But he was too far away.

"You won't be like them, will you?" the demon asked, sounding sad. "You'll come out to play like a good little boy?"

Slowly, the blanket fell from Fuechi's head. The fingers against his shoulder were so gentle that he nearly confused it for tenderness. But a creature like Du Yong did not know tenderness—only trickery! He was reminded of this truth as he opened his eyes.

Du Yong grinned, revealing razor-sharp teeth in the darkness.

"You'll let me eat you like a good little boy?" The demon cackled horribly.

As Du Yong closed in on Fuechi, claws reaching for his throat, Ling leaped out from under the covers and struck the demon across the face.

Awakening

Du Yong let loose a deafening scream. Ling clung to the demon as he stumbled backward—hoping to buy Fuechi time. But the little ghost knew he was no match for the powerful demon.

Fuechi jumped out of bed and headed straight for the closet. His mama always thought Fuechi was making up stories, but the closet was a door to a different world. Things came out of the door, and things returned through it.

Ling had shown him many times.

Now, his cold hand slipped around his own. Just as Du Yong reached them, Fuechi and Ling leaped into the dark abyss inside the closet.

The last thing they heard was Du Yong shrieking.

It was the scream that awoke Nia. She nearly fell over twice, running toward Fuechi's room. But when she thrust open the door and found him sleeping quietly in bed, she sighed in relief. Even so, she rechecked the window to ensure it was locked and peeped around the corner before stopping beside her son's bed. Everything was exactly as she'd left it.

Almost. She frowned at the sight of the open closet. She closed it…hadn't she?

Nia shook her head. She was scaring herself for no reason. Of course, Fuechi was safe! It must have been a dream. He was sound asleep underneath the blanket, exactly where she'd left him.

Rubbing her elbow and shins, Nia touched his face. He was warm. *Too warm.*

"Hey, baby, are you okay?" She touched his shoulder, but he didn't move. "Fuechi, wake up."

Nia's heart raced. Something was wrong.

She cried, "Baby, wake up!"

As a strange breeze brushed her skin, she turned toward the closet. Fuechi's clothes wavered, and she thought she heard: *"Mama..."*

Dylan Reed rolled the snack cart down the hallway, offering the nurses an easy, practiced smile. Some blushed. A few giggled. The handsome son of Dr. Reed had that effect on people.

But the moment he passed them, the smile slipped. His expression hardened into a scowl as he checked his watch, then his phone.

Nothing.

He muttered a curse under his breath, then flashed another quick smile at a passing nursing assistant. When she tried to speak with him, he pretended not to hear and turned sharply down the corner.

Room 511 stood empty. He slipped inside and shut the door behind him, dialing Mossy again.

It rang.

No answer.

His jaw tightened. He ended the call and immediately dialed another number.

"Hey, Ev," he said, voice low. "Have you heard anything?"

Awakening

Sometime during the night, Mossy had taken her father's car and never returned. Her phone kept ringing, unanswered. It wasn't like her—Mossy was responsible, careful. Eva had first assumed she was with Dylan, but a quick call proved otherwise.

"Not yet," Eva said now.

"She's been gone all night." Dylan kept his voice steady with effort. "Where could she have gone?"

Silence stretched between them, heavy and uneasy. The same thought lingered unspoken—there was only one other place she might be. Dylan's eyes burned, a flicker of yellow slipping through his frustration.

Eva didn't notice. She promised to call if she heard anything.

Dylan muttered something like a thank you and ended the call. Then he drove his fist into the wall.

"Who's there?"

The voice came from behind him—a woman's, thick with the weight of recent tears.

Dylan looked up sharply. His job was to move through the rooms with snacks and drinks, sometimes keeping a patient company while family stepped out. He usually knew which rooms were occupied.

Room 511 was supposed to be empty.

"Who's there?" The voice came behind the privacy curtain at the back of the room.

Dylan straightened. "I'm sorry. I didn't know anyone was here."

A woman with long black braids leaned her head into the doorway, hastily wiping at her tears. "It's okay," she said, voice uneven. "He can't hear you anyway. He can't hear a thing."

Something in her grief tugged at Dylan. She felt familiar, though he couldn't place why—until his gaze shifted to the patient lying beneath the covers.

"Hey… I think I know you." Dylan stepped closer, staring at the boy. He could still remember the feel of small arms wrapped tightly around his neck. He glanced back at her. "We met at the theater."

Nia studied the pale blue scrubs and the blond hair falling into eyes that looked dark green in the dim light. Too young to be a nurse.

"I remember," she said at last. "Small world." She smiled, though it didn't reach her eyes. "What's your name?"

"Dylan."

"I'm Nia." She turned toward the bed. "And this is Fuechi. He really liked you."

Dylan looked at the boy. Warm, but pale. Alive… yet dim, as if something essential had gone quiet. He wasn't a doctor, but the thing inside him recognized it instantly—something was missing.

"What happened?" he asked.

Nia studied him suspiciously at first. But something in his genuine concern finally softened her hesitation.

Dylan couldn't look away from Fuechi.

"We don't know," she said at last. "I put him to bed like any other night. Later, I thought I heard a scream… but when I found him, he was like this. Just sleeping." Her voice trembled. "He hasn't woken up since. The doctors still don't know what's wrong."

When her voice broke again, Dylan fought the sudden urge to comfort her. The Thing inside him churned—restless, unsettled. It wasn't used to feeling anything beyond anger, yet for this woman and her son, something like sympathy surfaced.

His gaze dropped to Fuechi's wrist, catching on a familiar red-and-white twist bracelet, then lifted to the name tag.

"What's wrong?" Nia asked as he gently took the boy's wrist.

Dylan looked up. "That last name… who's his father?"

Nia frowned. "Why do you ask?"

"Fuechi's Hmong, isn't he?"

Her suspicion sharpened. "How did you know?"

"What else happened before he fell asleep last night?" Dylan asked. He stepped closer, close enough for her to catch the faint trace of his musky cologne.

Nia hesitated, then answered, "He was scared. Kept crying about a bad man. I stayed with him until he fell asleep."

Dylan swore under his breath.

"What's going on? What do you know?" she pressed.

He rested his hand lightly on the boy's forehead and murmured something too soft for her to hear. Then he straightened.

"The doctors can't help him."

Nia's breath caught. "What do you mean?"

"He needs help," Dylan said, steady now, "but you won't find it here."

"Then where?" Her voice trembled on the edge of breaking.

Dylan held her gaze. "Whatever's happening… he needs a Hmong shaman."

Nia leaped up from the chair. "He can't leave. They're still running tests on him—"

"He's not safe here!" Dylan's explosion surprised them both.

Nia straightened in surprise. Slowly, she said, "I think you need to leave."

"Nia—"

"No!" Her voice cut sharply across the room. "Fuechi needs doctors. I don't know who you think you are coming in here—"

"The Bad Man wears a suit."

Nia froze.

"Sometimes, he's a snake—am I right?"

She wanted to scream and tell him to leave. Everything he was saying sounded crazy. But as her eyes fell upon her baby boy, her heart fell. There was no denying that something was wrong.

And somehow, Dylan knew about the Bad Man.

"How did you know?" she whispered.

"I've seen him. The doctors can't help Fuechi. The longer you wait, the worse it will get."

"What am I supposed to do?" She shook her head helplessly.

"Do you know his father's people? Do they have a shaman?" he asked.

Nia considered this question before nodding. "His uncle is a shaman."

Kai was always secretive about his family and determined to keep them apart. Lately, however, their livelihood seemed dependent upon this estranged family.

"I know this doesn't make sense, Nia, but trust me. You need to get Fuechi to him," Dylan insisted.

"But they'll never let us leave while he's like this!" she exclaimed.

"You let me handle that." His blue-green eyes flashed a strange color as he walked to the front of the room.

"What are you going to do?"

"I'm just going to organize the snack cart," he answered. She watched with confusion as he tossed containers to the floor.

Finally, Nia pulled out her phone. "I'll call his Uncle Touso."

She didn't notice when Dylan's back went rigid.

"He isn't picking up, but I know where they live," she said as she hurried to collect their belongings. If the doctors didn't have answers, they had no choice but to find them somewhere else.

Dylan kept his gaze on Fuechi. He should have seen the similarities, especially with the eyes. He did not doubt that the boy also shared his father and uncle's fate.

If Mossy was with Touso, she was also in danger.

"I'll help you," he said, emptying the food cart with new energy.

A while later, Dylan Reed walked out of room 511 with the snack cart, whistling a happy tune. He stopped by the nurses' station and offered each a cup of coffee with the best cafeteria muffins he chose "especially" for them.

As they giggled and fawned over him, Nia Johnson walked by unnoticed and hit the elevator button. Once she slipped through the stairwell exit, Dylan winked at the ladies and pushed the cart into the open elevator.

"See you later, ladies. I must report to the boss before I can enjoy the rest of my weekend," he said, mustering a most sorrowful expression.

"You call us if that father of yours gives you trouble!" A nurse with short red curls smiled as she bit into one of his treats.

Dylan saluted as the elevator closed.

Exiting the first floor, he promptly pushed the cart past the employee-only doors. He waved at staff coming out of the break room and parked the cart near the only exit to the outside world. He made a show of removing the trash bag, followed by some grumbling about parents and child labor laws.

Everyone laughed because they knew his father. When he was finally alone, Dylan carefully pulled Fuechi from the cart. He stared at the sleeping child who had most certainly lost his soul, and he prayed it wasn't too late.

As soon as he heard the roar of a car, Dylan ran outside with Fuechi tucked safely against his chest.

"Good timing," he said as Nia thrust the door open from inside.

Nia shrugged, but her lips turned proudly. "We drive fast in this family."

Soon, the engine roared as they headed straight toward the home of Touso Khang.

Chapter 1

The family gathered in the living room, the air thick with tension. Pahoua and Bao were visibly upset, while Lihue stood apart, his expression caught somewhere between grief and anger. At the center of it all sat a woman and child.

Mossy stopped so abruptly that her hand slipped from Touso's grip. Her eyes immediately locked onto the woman's black braids and butterfly tattoos.

It was the woman from the movie theater…and the little boy who looked eerily like the man Mossy was about to marry.

She stared at him now, limp in his mother's arms, his eyes closed. Something about his complexion was wrong.

Very wrong.

"Moss."

It was a voice she never expected to hear in the Khang house, and Mossy gasped as Dylan Reed stepped out from the shadows. This time, she didn't miss the swirl of yellow smoke that filled his blue-green eyes.

Chee, the most discerning of her spirit guides, leaped into the air and circled Dylan. Beneath the shadow of his rice hat, he studied the newcomer, taking in everything from the blue scrubs to the strange glow of his energy.

The human pretended not to notice him, but Chee saw the way Dylan narrowed his gaze and lifted his chest.

Chee pulled out his spear—

"No!" Mossy's voice broke through like a sharp command, and Chee disappeared instantly.

Her heart beat loudly against her chest as she watched Dylan, ready to move if he acted strangely. But the yellow smoke was gone from his eyes.

"Moss! What are you doing here? I've been calling you all morning!"

When he rushed toward her, Touso pulled Mossy behind him. It happened so quickly, Mossy nearly tripped over her own feet.

"You're not welcome here," she heard him say.

Dylan's face twisted into a scowl. "I'd get out of the way if I were you."

Touso smirked as his spirit guides swirled around Dylan. But just as it happened at the Thao house, their ferocity faded into confusion. The spirits whispered among themselves in low, uneasy voices—words Touso couldn't understand.

When Kong, the fiercest of his spirit guides—a war general in his previous life—motioned for the others to stand down, it was Touso's turn to be puzzled.

Why were they acting so strangely?

He almost jumped when Mossy touched the hand still gripped around her arm. She said, "It's okay."

"He doesn't belong here," Touso said, gently releasing her.

She studied Dylan's hospital scrubs and asked, "How did you find me?"

"I've been worried about you," Dylan said instead of answering her question. "Why didn't you call back? Are you okay?"

"Mossy is no longer your concern," said Touso.

"Oh, yeah? And who exactly do you think you are?" Dylan took a step forward, prompting Touso to do the same.

"I don't think you're ready to find out, kid," Touso said evenly.

"Stop it! Both of you!" Mossy threw herself between the two men. "Touso—I can speak for myself! Dylan, what are you doing here?"

"It's because of me." Nia surprised them all when she spoke. Adjusting Fuechi on her lap, she met each of their eyes. "I asked him to help us. I'm sorry for showing up like this, but Fuechi needs help. I didn't know what else to do."

Bao hugged Nia and whispered comforting words while Pahoua stroked her grandson's head. Across the room, Lihue looked furious, muttering something about irresponsible children.

Mossy couldn't look away from the child, who lay limp in his mother's arms. Finally, she turned to Touso and asked, "Who are they?"

When he rested his chin against the top of her head, she inhaled his familiar sandalwood scent and prayed for an answer she could accept.

"This is my sister-in-law, Nia, and my nephew, Fuechi. Turns out I'm not the last son after all."

Her relief was immediate—and obvious.

Mossy blushed when Touso arched a brow.

"Touso will do whatever it takes to care for his family, especially Fuechi," Bao had explained.

Now, she understood. If Touso wasn't the last son, then Fuechi was also cursed.

"Why didn't you say anything before?" she gasped.

"You run pretty fast," Touso said with a smile.

Mossy shook her head with regret. "Glad you don't give up easily."

"Not in this lifetime," he promised, gazing at her in a way that brought a fresh wave of heat to her cheeks.

Finally, she turned her attention back to Nia and her son. Fuechi hadn't stirred since they arrived.

"What happened to him?"

Nia clutched Fuechi tighter as tears slid down her face. "I don't know. It was just like any other night. I read him a story and tucked him into bed. Then I heard him screaming." Her voice broke. "I ran back to his room, and he was still there—still tucked safely in bed where I left him—but he wouldn't wake up."

She looked desperately between them.

"The doctors have run all kinds of tests, but they can't find anything wrong with Fuechi. Dylan said the doctors can't help him— that he needs a shaman." Her expression crumpled with fear. "Why does he need a shaman?"

"Because his soul is missing," Dylan answered.

He stood behind Mossy, his blue-green eyes glued to the boy in Nia's arms. His family was Catholic, but he didn't practice. Dylan volunteered at the hospital while his parents attended Sunday service.

Hearing him speak of missing souls was most definitely out of character.

"What do you know about souls?" Touso demanded.

"I googled it," Dylan replied.

"Hey, you two, this isn't the time," Bao snapped, but her frown softened as Nia released Fuechi into her arms.

"He's right," Pahoua said, glancing at Dylan. "There's something wrong, and it's not in the medical books. How long has he been like this?"

Nia said, "I put him to bed around 8 p.m."

"This Bad Man—what can you tell us about him?" Lihue asked, speaking for the first time.

Nia hesitated, looking briefly toward Dylan. She said, "Fuechi describes a man who sometimes turns into a snake monster. Sounds crazy, right?"

"Mom…" Bao turned anxiously to her mother.

Pahoua closed her eyes. With Touso uniting with his chosen bride, they thought their troubles were over. A young grandson facing the same dangers was horrifying. Poor Fuechi must have been so afraid!

Touso paced the room, glancing between the photo of Kai and his nephew. His frustration stirred a breeze that caught everyone's attention. He had promised to protect Fuechi and failed!

As Mossy caught his gaze, they both realized Du Yong had come for Fuechi because he couldn't have Touso.

"What's going on?" Nia asked when she noticed the strange look on their faces.

Touso said, "We don't have much time. I need to see if I can find him."

"Find him?" Nia repeated. "What are you talking about?"

"Nia." Pahoua was careful as she asked, "Didn't Kai tell you anything about himself or his family?"

Nia stared at her husband's mother. Kai had always refused to speak about his family, almost as if their lives depended on their two worlds never colliding. He said his family would never accept Nia and Fuechi because of old rules.

Still, he would disappear for days at a time to attend "family business." Then one day, he never returned.

Nia studied Lihue, who refused to meet her gaze. With a heavy heart, she shook her head.

"In this family, we are all shamans, and Kai was the strongest," Pahoua explained. "He never told you about the curse? Didn't you see how sick he had become?"

"Curse?" she repeated, her eyes bright with tears. "He just kept saying it was a bad stomach bug. He refused to go see a doctor."

Bao was noticeably agitated as she watched Nia cry. Even in death, her big brother continued to cause havoc. *He was so irresponsible!*

Kai had asked Bao to help take care of his family, and she appeared on Nia's doorstep the day he died. Bao was the one who consoled her when their world fell apart. Worst of all, Nia and Fuechi couldn't attend the funeral because of how this secret would affect their parents.

Their hearts were broken all over again.

"Kai was a shaman. It's a common practice in our culture. Only a few are chosen, but our family has been chosen since the beginning. Shamans heal things that doctors don't understand," Pahoua explained while fighting her own sorrow.

"Like Ling," Nia said, turning to look at Touso. "You sent a ghost away from Fuechi."

Pahoua gawked at her children, who looked away because they felt her sense of betrayal. She said, "Shamans fight the evil things that endanger human souls. But our family, our lineage of shamans, faces a curse."

"This sounds crazy. What curse?" Nia demanded.

Because Pahoua was struggling, Mossy said, "There's a demon that wants them dead. It's the same demon that took Kai and the same one that has probably taken Fuechi."

Nia leaped to her feet and glared at Dylan. She asked, "Is this the kind of help you're talking about?"

"Nia—" Dylan began.

"No!" Nia snapped, losing control of her emotions. "Okay—maybe there was a ghost messing with Fuechi. Maybe Touso was able to exorcise him—or whatever! But my baby is sick. You said these people could help, and they're talking about demons and curses! I need to go—my son and I need to get back to the hospital where everything makes some goddamn sense!"

When Nia wouldn't stop pacing the room, Dylan grabbed her by the shoulders. "Nia! Get it together. You know there's something odd going on here. The Bad Man! Remember, the Bad Man is a snake monster. Your son told you this! How does everyone seem to know what this thing looks like? Forget what's normal. There isn't time for logic!"

Everyone stared at Dylan and Nia in surprise, especially when she didn't shake him off.

"A snake monster," she repeated, then scowled at a portrait of Kai. "Damn you, Kai. What have you gotten after our baby?"

Her emotions vacillated between disbelief, contempt, and sadness. Then she collapsed onto the couch and wept. Dylan was careful not to touch her again.

"What do we do now?" she asked, wiping the tears from her eyes. Nia had never cried so much, and she was exhausted.

"I have to go into the spirit world and find him." Touso had been listening a few feet away and now stood to leave.

Mossy hurried to his side. She touched his arm and searched his face, her expression anxious.

"Are you sure that's safe? After what happened last night?" she demanded. Now Mossy was the one struggling to keep her emotions in check. She remembered him surrounded by vampires and shuddered. "What if that's exactly what he wants?"

"I have to try." Once again, his golden-brown eyes glanced between Fuechi and his brother's photo. Kai seemed to glare at him from the frame. *You promised!* "I promised to keep Fuechi safe."

"I'll prepare the altar," Lihue said, leaving without looking at anyone. For weeks, he'd mourned the loss of his oldest son. Now, he struggled between feelings of betrayal and new grief over a grandchild he didn't know.

Mossy watched Lihue in dismay. This morning, his aura had glowed with renewed strength. It wavered and flickered until the glow was no more than a dull trace. As he walked away, Mossy met Pahoua's eyes.

She saw it, too! Without a word, Touso's mother got up and followed her husband.

Awakening

Bao resumed her role as Nia and Fuechi's caretaker. She placed her nephew back into Nia's arms and set off to prepare them some nourishment before the ritual began. It usually took time to prepare, but the Khangs lived in seclusion for a reason. In the back of the property, they kept hens and hogs. The pantry was full of joss paper. They had everything needed to perform the ritual.

Mossy turned to look at Dylan, whose sharp gaze remained on the woman and child. He looked different. She couldn't pinpoint exactly what, but he wasn't the same. Dylan was cool and carefree. The way he grabbed Nia and talked about souls—he seemed like someone else. He must have felt her watching him because he turned.

"Moss," he said, moving toward her. "I swear I didn't know you'd be here."

Mossy asked, "How did you know—about his soul?"

Dylan enjoyed sports and fast cars. He laughed at every horror movie they'd ever watched together. He didn't believe in things like ghosts and demons. She dared even to say Dylan didn't believe in God. He poked fun at Deloris for praying before every meal and family outing. Religion was the only source of contention between stepmother and son. Lost souls would have been the last thing on his radar.

Dylan ran nervous fingers through his blond hair. "I just remembered what you told me about Thai. When I saw Fuechi's last name, I thought maybe he needed the same intervention."

Mossy was unconvinced. Pao and Chee reappeared and now leaned against the wall behind Dylan. Pao rolled his slender eyes while Chee tapped anxiously against the shaft of his spear. Her spirit guides were just as skeptical.

She said, "Thank you for helping Nia and Fuechi, but I think it's time for you to leave."

"Moss—" he protested.

"Let him stay." Touso surprised them both with this answer. He appeared behind Mossy, meeting Dylan's stern expression. "We need to do this now, and none of the relatives will be able to get here quickly enough. My father is too fragile—I need someone strong enough to watch my back."

A shaman had special assistants to watch out for him as he traveled the spirit world, especially if it required leaping on the bench or riding a flying horse. Blinded by the veil, there was always the risk of falling, so helpers needed to be quick and strong. Lihue was in no condition to physically support him.

"How about it, Dylan? Can you watch my back?" Touso asked.

"Why me?" Dylan's brows furrowed suspiciously.

He shrugged and said, "You're already here."

Dylan was silent for a long time. He sympathized with Nia and Fuechi, but he had come for Mossy. Helping Touso was the last thing on his mind. When Touso kept looking at Mossy, a sly grin turned on his face. Dylan strolled over to Mossy and ran long fingers up her bare shoulder. The room grew instantly warmer as Touso glowered.

"I'll stay—if Mossy wants me to," Dylan offered.

Mossy's dark eyes rounded in surprise when his hand paused on her face, and she gasped when he lifted her hand to his lips. The room felt like someone had lit a fire to every wall, and Mossy stood frozen.

"Cool!" Touso exclaimed louder than necessary and turned to leave. "I'll go get ready. When my parents return, they'll tell you what to do."

Dylan's blue-green eyes flashed with satisfaction as Touso disappeared from the room.

Mossy glared at him. "What are you doing?"

Dylan feigned innocence. "What? I can't kiss my girl—"

"Stop!" Mossy was overwhelmed with exasperation. She parted her mouth to say something more but changed her mind. Shaking her head, she turned and ran after Touso.

Dylan watched after her. Despite the smile on his face, his eyes simmered with a dark golden glow. His ears perked at the uncanny sounds echoing from the darkest corners of the home. Dylan was losing ground, and *they* all knew it. He was going to have to pick up his game.

"You came here for the girl." It was a simple comment, and Dylan turned to face Nia. She was holding Fuechi again while Bao prepared a meal. But instead of being angry, Nia only smiled.

"I'm sorry." Dylan's expression was sincere for the first time since arriving. He didn't try to explain, and Nia didn't ask.

She shrugged. "Don't be. Kai had terrible game, too."

Dylan was instantly defensive. "Excuse me? Did you miss what I just did there?"

"You just pissed him off." Nia giggled before turning serious. "When did you two break up?"

"Who says we broke up?"

"Boy, please." She smirked.

When they arrived at their home, Mossy was with Touso. When he left the room, she ran after him without looking back. Whoever Dylan was to her, she was over it.

"Mossy will come back to me," Dylan insisted.

Nia studied him with empathy. She knew love, and she knew heartbreak. Touso looked at Mossy the way Kai had looked at Nia. Dylan didn't stand a chance.

"You're a nice guy, Dylan," she said. "I'm guessing you only came here for Mossy, but I'm still grateful for the help."

Dylan's gaze fell upon the boy in her arms. Once upon a time, the same child looked at him with bright eyes and hugged him without hesitation. It was hard to see him without that same light.

"He's a good kid and will come back to us. Don't worry," he said quietly.

"Be happy."

"Sorry?" He looked confused.

"It was something Fuechi's dad used to say." Nia smiled as she thought of her late husband. "Don't worry, be happy. He believed good things were coming no matter how bad things got."

"I'm sorry about your loss." Dylan studied the portrait of a smiling man with copper blond hair. He looked like an older—more colorful version of Touso. A modest black shirt barely hid the blue koi tattoos along his neck. In the morning sun, his light brown eyes seemed alive through the glass frame. "You lucked out. He looks like he was the smart brother."

Nia chuckled. "He was something else." Then she looked at him with sad eyes. "If you really love her, give her space."

They didn't know each other, but breaking out of a hospital together somehow made them closer than strangers. For this reason, she felt sorry for him.

"I can't do that," Dylan said as he looked away.

"All right." Nia sighed. Her only experience with the Khang family was Kai, and she pitied the fool who was reckless enough to mess with him. She was sure Touso Khang was no different. "I guess you better prepare yourself for battle, too!"

"I intend to," he said quietly.

As Nia returned her attention to Fuechi, Dylan closed his eyes. The moans and growls had grown louder, vibrating at a pitch beyond human hearing.

Outside the Khang house, the birds perched along the roof suddenly scattered into the sky. A cat stalking a lone mouse froze mid-step, ears twitching, before bolting into the shadows. Even the rooster Lihue released that morning stopped pecking at a patch of greens when violent convulsions overtook it. Moments later, it collapsed onto the ground.

When Dylan opened his eyes again, they burned a fiery yellow. If he gave up now, worse things would follow.

Touso was abnormally dismissive, refusing to turn as she called his name. She finally grabbed his hand. "Touso—wait! Where are you going?"

"To get ready," he answered without looking at her.

"Are you sure about this?" she asked. It was unusual to enlist someone from outside the culture—let alone anyone without experience. "Dylan won't know what to do!"

"Are you worried about him or me?" He turned to look at her for the first time.

Confused by the change in his mood, she searched his face for an explanation.

"Who are you worried about, Mossy?" Touso asked again. He reached to caress the side of her face that Dylan had touched. Dark blue flames simmered in his eyes.

Her expression turned into disbelief. *He was jealous!*

She backed away as Touso closed in, trapping her in a part of the house that was unnaturally dark. Her heart raced as the heat from his body pushed against her.

"Who?" The question tickled her lips while his hands rested on her waist. From head to toe, her flesh prickled and screamed.

"I—of course, I'm worried about you!" she gasped.

Mossy froze in surprise when his mouth brushed across her own, gently nipping at her bottom lip with his teeth. Heated golden eyes watched to see what she would do. When she responded by tugging at his waistband, the gentleness of their embrace quickly turned ravenous. Touso wrapped his strong arms around her body and pulled her close. But when his hands traveled up her long skirt to caress the bare flesh of her hips, she remembered herself and pulled away.

It was all happening too quickly. She said, "We can't!"

"Mossy," Touso whispered her name with agony. "What are you doing to me?"

She looked at him, only to be taken aback by what she saw—fear.

"You don't have to be afraid." She was no longer talking about the ritual and rested her hand over his heart. "I'm here."

Gradually, the blue fire in his eyes faded, replaced by a much warmer, familiar color. Touso rested his forehead against her own. "I'm sorry."

"Don't be," she replied, gingerly caressing his neck. "Of course, I'm worried about you. I want you to be safe. Are you sure Dylan can help you?"

"He's already here, and I want to keep him close."

Mossy frowned. He never ceased to surprise her. One moment, he was enraged with jealousy. Next, he was determined to keep the reason for that jealousy close at hand.

"Why?" she asked when he seemed content to leave her befuddled.

"My dad is too weak to do it. Everyone else is too far away—" he started to explain.

"But I could watch you," Mossy offered quickly. She had seen her cousins and uncles do it so many times. If the purpose was to protect him, that was already her job.

"You could," he said, smiling in a way that melted her heart. "But I want him to do it."

"But why?" She frowned with confusion.

He said, "Because there's something wrong with Dylan Reed, and I want to see what happens when he's around the gong and the rattle."

The gong and rattle served as both a call and warning to spirits. When spirit guides heard these sounds, they knew it was time to work. Evil spirits who heard them took it as a warning to stay away—or run. Mossy didn't understand how any of this was related to Dylan Reed.

What did Touso expect to find?

"I want you to be careful around him," he said, his expression turning stern.

Confused, she searched his eyes. "Touso, just tell me what's going on."

"How did he know about the snake monster?" he asked.

Dylan couldn't know unless... Her mind turned with memories of smoky yellow eyes and Dylan holding a thrashing Chewy against the wall.

No! Mossy refused to believe it.

"I don't like the guy for many reasons, but we need to know what we're dealing with. Promise me you'll be careful," Touso repeated.

Mossy was at a loss for words. Her life was so ordinary up until recently. She missed complaining about homework and chores. She longed for the days when hiding a secret boyfriend was her only problem. Everything was different now, but she couldn't fathom that Dylan was anything but a normal guy she always adored.

"I'll be careful," she promised when Touso continued to stare at her.

When her compliance was rewarded with a kiss, she blushed.

"I wish today was different," he said, lips trailing down her neck. "I wish we had more time…"

And more privacy.

As his mother's voice cut through the air, Touso groaned and dropped his chin in defeat.

"Duty calls," Mossy said with a grin. She asked, "Are you sure you want to do this?"

They both knew what was waiting for him on the other side, but Touso nodded.

"Then I'll be with you every step of the way," she promised.

"I know," Touso said with a smile.

She was his chosen bride.

Chapter 2

The first phase of the ritual was to discover what had happened to Fuechi. Lihue returned carrying a basket stuffed with joss paper while Pahoua crouched beside a large clay pot, blowing the charcoal until orange flames flickered to life. Heat rolled through the room, carrying the bitter scent of smoke and incense.

A long wooden bench had been placed before the altar. Bao moved quietly around it, checking each item one by one. She refilled the cups of water until they trembled at the brim, lit fresh incense sticks, and pressed several eggs into bowls of uncooked rice in case the spirits arrived hungry.

When she finished, she glanced toward her father.

Lihue sat near the altar with his head lowered, folding strips of joss paper into perfect squares. The paper cracked sharply beneath his fingers. Fold after fold. Stack after stack.

Bao hesitated before walking over.

"Dad," she asked softly, "are you okay?"

Lihue reached for another sheet. His fingers pressed so hard against the crease that the paper ripped straight down the middle.

The room fell quiet except for the hiss of burning incense.

He never looked up.

"We were going to tell you both," Bao said quickly. "We were just waiting for the right time."

Lihue let out a bitter laugh under his breath.

"What kind of children keep secrets like this from their parents?"

The words struck Bao harder than a slap. She was his only daughter, the youngest, and the closest to him. And she had betrayed him.

"Kai didn't think you would understand! The two of you just fought all the time."

"Did that mean I loved him any less?" Lihue didn't have the energy to fight. Instead, he turned to look at the small boy lying on the couch with his mother. "Your brother died because he didn't follow the rules. This child will suffer for the same reason. You all should have known better!"

"We thought he was too young…" Bao dropped her gaze shamefully.

Du Yong had never gone after a child. They were usually too weak for his grand tastes. His targets were always those with active spirit guides—chosen ones who had taken time to build powerful energy. Fuechi was either very special or very unlucky.

"If your brother were here right now—dead or alive, I'd give him a good beating!" Their father shook an angry finger at his son's smiling portrait. Then he whirled around to face Bao. "Remember this as a lesson, my daughter. There are terrible consequences for secrets. That child may not survive."

Bao glanced at Nia, who continued to rock little Fuechi as though it might coax him out of slumber. The ham sandwich she'd made for her remained untouched.

As Lihue and Bao watched over the mother and child, Pahoua approached the young man standing by the window. He was gazing outside, focused on something no one else could see. She took this time to consider him. He had a strange energy about him for someone who looked so ordinary. There was a tautness to his flesh and a glow about his body. There was also a wall.

The seer in her could not see his future or past. But she knew her son disapproved of Dylan's relationship with Mossy Cha. Still, she felt relief that Touso's bond with his chosen bride was strong.

"We live out here because it's peaceful," she said. When he didn't respond, she continued. "Sometimes, you run into lost spirits, but like kids, you just send them home."

"Things are never what they should be," he replied.

Her attempt at lightheartedness went over his head, but Pahoua didn't let that dissuade her. Years of raising Touso had taught her how to coax the spirit out of the introverted child.

"Your name is Dylan, right?"

"Yeah."

"Touso said you'd be helping with the ritual?" When he only nodded, she sighed and glanced at the pair in the living room. Nia had fallen asleep with Fuechi in her arms. "Thank you for helping Nia and Fuechi. He's our only grandchild."

"Strange that it's the first time you've met him." Dylan turned to face her for the first time.

"It's a shame." Pahoua didn't falter. Years of raising a rebel had taught her patience. "Kai and his father had a difficult relationship. This secret is the fruit of that challenge."

"But you're his mother. Why didn't he tell you?"

Pahoua narrowed her eyes. He was particularly personal for a stranger. "I don't know. But he knew I loved him. Whatever he decided, he felt it was right, and I won't waste time judging him or anyone else for it."

When she frowned, Pahoua reminded Dylan of Touso. But her tone was firm and soft in a way only mothers could express.

"Did you know Kai?"

"No. Just Fuechi. But I hear he's a lot like his father. He's a great kid."

He heard a choking sound and was surprised to find the older woman stifling tears with a hand. Feeling guilty, he said, "I'm sorry, Mrs. Khang. I didn't mean to upset you."

When Pahoua looked up, her eyes were bright with tears. But more than just sadness, there was joy. "Fuechi is a blessing we don't deserve! We are all incredibly happy to meet him and must save him at any cost!"

Dylan nodded. Regardless of his feelings about Touso, he cared about the little boy. When Fuechi hugged him at the movie theater, it was the first time The Thing felt any emotion. It was a curious feeling that made him more helpful than he would have otherwise chosen to be.

"Whatever you need," Dylan promised.

Paj Vang

Pahoua guided Dylan to the altar. "It's simple, really. You'll know when Touso enters the spirit world because his body will start jumping. Some liken it to dancing. But on the other side, he'll be riding a horse into the spirit world to find Fuechi. Touso's father will handle the gong to keep the portal clear of evil spirits, but someone must watch Touso to ensure he doesn't fall."

"How will I know when he needs me?" Dylan glanced between the wooden bench and Pahoua.

"You'll know. He'll be falling!"

"This could be fun."

Pahoua chuckled. "You're a little mischievous, but you'll do well!"

Dylan was startled when she ruffled his hair. It was a strangely maternal gesture, and he wondered if she was this way with everyone or if she was toying with his mind. Did she know what he was? But as Pahoua returned to stoking the coals, her body relaxed and expression peaceful, he knew the seer couldn't see.

All these thoughts disappeared as Mossy returned to the room. She had changed out the yellow dress for something more practical but still looked pretty in a simple T-shirt and jeans. Bao was taller and a little fuller around the hips and chest, but the usually form-fitting clothes on Mossy fit just right. She avoided his gaze as she greeted the others. Eventually, she made her way toward his direction because Pahoua was standing next to him.

"How's my son doing?" Pahoua asked with a smile.

"He's fine." As Mossy spoke, her eyes flickered briefly toward Dylan. To her relief, he stayed quiet. "He's almost ready."

"Good." Pahoua gestured for her to join her on the ground. "When the ritual starts, this will be your job, *Nyab*."

Awakening

Mossy's heart skipped excitedly when Pahoua referred to her as "daughter-in-law." She was already considered part of the Khang family.

She glanced over the basket of ghost money with curiosity.

Pahoua smiled and said, "This will be a good lesson for you, Mossy. One day, you will also search for souls, and you must know what to do."

"How will I know?" she asked.

"The spirits will choose one of us to become your official mentor, and that person will be responsible for teaching you everything you need to know," Pahoua replied.

Mossy frowned. "How do they do that?"

Pahoua gestured at the sword by the altar. "That sword has been in our family for centuries. It guides us in everything, including who will teach whom. Lihue has mentored Bao and Touso. I was chosen to teach Kai, and soon, we will learn who will teach you."

Mossy parted her mouth in awe. *Things just kept getting stranger.*

"For now, I'll tell you what to do!" Pahoua offered. "It starts with the movements. When his father hits the gong, he will start jumping. As he travels further into the spirit world on his flying horse, it will seem erratic. Eventually, his movements will slow. You may not understand him, but you'll get a sense that he's talking to someone, usually negotiating for answers. Pay attention to his tone and his gestures. When it's urgent, you'll hear it. He'll need you to burn something to help him get past certain spirits and gates. Each one will have a different price, and you keep burning until his tone and movements relax. But sometimes, there will be disagreements that can turn into battles."

Pahoua rested her eyes on Dylan and continued, "When this happens, his body will jerk and jump even more violently. It'll be up to you, Dylan, to ensure he doesn't fall. Any disturbances here can be deadly in both realms!"

There was a long pause as Mossy and Dylan looked at one another. He was her first love. She saw flashes of herself and Dylan laughing together. He usually held her too long before letting her go home. She could still feel the tenderness of his touch on the different parts of her body... Ironically, they were working together to help her future husband now.

"We must work together to ensure Touso and Fuechi return safely," Pahoua spoke with quiet determination.

After a few more words, she went to check on her daughter and husband. Then Dylan turned to Mossy with a scowl. "You're one of them? What does that mean?"

For a moment, she was speechless. Then she said, "I have spirit guides. I'll be a shaman just like them."

"This is ridiculous!" Dylan snapped. "What are you doing here? This isn't you, Moss!"

Mossy frowned. "I don't understand it either, Dylan. But this is the way it has to be. I'm sorry. This was not the way I wanted things to end."

There was a long pause before he met her gaze. "End? Who says this is the end?"

Mossy blinked in confusion.

"I'm going to help him because I want to help the kid." The intensity of his voice was scathing. "But if you think I'm going to let this go, you're wrong, Mossy. We belong together. When did you forget that?"

"Dylan—"

"Mossy, he's dangerous! Listen—I know I was a dumbass before prom. I get that you're pissed off. But this—Do you really know what you're doing? Right now, we're about to help this guy play with spirits—or worse. Is this really the life you want?" Dylan realized his fingers were digging into her shoulders, and he quickly let her go.

Mossy hesitated before she said, "I don't know, but things are different now. Please, just be careful with him."

Dylan inhaled sharply, feeling agitated to the soul. But in the end, he nodded. He would be helpful—this time.

Touso returned to the room, dressed in a loose black shirt and trousers. He winked at Mossy as he took his place by the altar. While Lihue and Touso discussed the plan, Pahoua and Bao guided Nia and Fuechi to a chair nearby.

Nia was tempted to run away with her son, but she did her best to remain calm because these were the people that Kai loved the most. If she couldn't be safe with them, she didn't know where else to go.

Touso walked to the front door, where two live chickens rested beside a bowl of uncooked rice. With these offerings prepared for hungry spirits, Touso began swinging the hoop rattle. He chanted, "Fuechi Khang, come home where you belong."

He hit one side of the door frame three times with the split horns and repeated it on the other.

"What's he doing?" Mossy asked.

Pahoua whispered, "The door is the way home. Knocking on the door calls the soul to come home. If it's nearby, it'll follow the sound.

If not, then he'll throw the horns to find out more answers from the spirits."

To their dismay, Touso cast the split horns onto the ground.

"Is Fuechi's soul really gone?" he asked.

The horns fell in uniform, pointing away from each other.

Touso sighed. *It was definitely gone.*

He tossed it again, wanting to know how far the soul had traveled. This time, one-half of the horns fell further away. Touso stiffened. Fuechi was farther than he should have been and would soon be somewhere he couldn't return from.

The last time the shaman tossed the horns, the portal to the other side opened. Touso turned and leaped gracefully onto the bench to begin his journey.

"You ready?" He arched a skeptical brow at Dylan, who stood within an arm's reach.

Dylan shrugged and said, "That depends. Do you feel lucky?"

Touso smirked, but his expression relaxed when a soft hand touched his own.

Mossy said, "Don't mess around in there, or I'll come after you."

"Yes, ma'am," he replied, saluting her with his free hand.

She stepped back as Touso flipped the red veil over his face. His father hit the gong and ordered the spirits to open the door. As Touso swung the hoop rattle, a powerful glow emerged from his figure. Spirit guides swirled around his body until his soul lifted. As it did, Touso began singing.

He greeted the spirit guides and asked for their help, then provided them with specific instructions. The rest of the words he spoke were meant to anchor his soul to the body. Souls were distractable and prone to wander. To prevent this, Touso constantly spoke of his purpose and reminded the spirit guides to watch his back so that evil could not surprise him. This constant narration also enabled his assistants to help him.

Hmong words gradually became inflections that sounded Mandarin. Soon, Mossy didn't recognize the language at all, but Touso never faltered as the foreign words flowed from his mouth.

It didn't take long for something to happen. He paused and slowed his dance on top of the bench but kept speaking.

Pahoua noticed the frown on Mossy's face and said, "Some shamans repeat the chants taught to them by their masters. Others follow the language spoken by their spirit guides. Everyone is different. Touso has many guides and may speak many languages. Eventually, you'll learn this, too."

"They want money!" Mossy gasped and quickly grabbed papers from the basket. After tossing them into the fire, she looked anxiously at Pahoua. "They also want his horse!"

"You can understand?" Pahoua stared at her in amazement.

Mossy nodded. At first, it was confusing, but then it became as clear as the English language. It took time for rising shamans to learn the language of their spirit guides, and it was even more challenging to understand those who belonged to another. The fact that she learned so quickly was a testament to Mossy's abilities.

"Here—burn this." Pahoua sifted through the basket and handed her a piece with intricately cut lines.

Joss paper could become any currency the spirits desired—money, jewelry, clothes, and even animals. One only had to know how to fold and cut them correctly. The basket was full of intricate designs representative of every object of desire.

Mossy tossed many of the same pieces into the fire and grimaced when Pahoua raised a brow. She said, "Just in case!"

With the provision of a team of horses, courtesy of the chosen bride, Touso's journey returned to a casual banter with the spirits. Mossy glanced at Dylan, whom she had worried wouldn't take his job seriously. But he was attentive and never let his eyes wander from the shaman.

Touso's journey remained relatively smooth, with Mossy quickly burning paper before any disputes began. Some of the spirits only wanted attention. One of the new gate guards was a teenager who passed away in the late nineties and didn't care about money.

She missed modern music!

Mossy felt Touso's disgruntled resignation when the spirit asked for a rendition of the Backstreet Boys' "As Long as You Love Me." She loved Nick Carter and asked specifically for his solo. It was the only time during the ritual that Touso spoke in English. Even Dylan cocked his eyebrows in bemusement as Touso began a soft ballad. Mossy stifled a giggle, making a mental note to ask for an encore later.

It was after passing the young spirit guard that Touso abruptly grunted in pain. When he violently swung the rattle, everyone knew he was under attack. In a panic, Mossy threw a handful of ghost money into the fire and looked desperately at Pahoua.

"Not all entities can be bought," she said as her son twisted in pain.

"What's happening?" Nia asked.

Awakening

"He's being attacked!" Bao gasped as Touso collapsed onto the ground.

With each passing second, Lihue hit the gong louder and more urgently. At the same time, Mossy felt a familiar explosion from inside her head and staggered in front of the altar. Her body trembled and began to glow.

The sword from the Khang altar rose from its vase and spun quickly in the air. Mossy lifted her eyes just in time to see it point at Pahoua. It began turning again until it pointed at Mossy. Then, it fell to the ground, balancing perfectly at the blade's tip.

"What's happening?" Mossy asked, eyes wide with fear.

Pahoua answered, "The spirits have spoken. I'll be your teacher from now on!"

Mossy was struck with pain so sharp that she fell to her knees. Soon, her spirit guides soared all around her. Even Kalia had answered the call. Mossy doubled over in agony as the dragon spirit glided around the room. It felt like her soul was being ripped from her body.

Pahoua grasped her by the shoulders and said, "I know you're scared, but you must stop fighting them. They're taking you to him— Touso needs you!"

You must accept us, Mossy! Gowli's words came back to her like a gentle breeze. *We are you, and you are us...*

With immense effort, Mossy relaxed her body. As soon as she did, her spirit guides lifted her soul away. Dylan tried to reach her but fell beside Touso, curling in pain. The last thing she saw was Dylan convulsing, his eyes glowing yellow like fireworks on the fourth of July. Everyone was shouting and screaming, and then her world went black.

Chapter 3

Six months ago...

Daisy Vang was born "lucky." The youngest and only daughter of seven children, her parents spoiled her. She went to school with the best lunches, and her mother dressed her in the latest styles. Even her shoes remained shiny on the cloudiest day. She was also smart.

By the time she was twenty-five, Daisy was the successful business owner of a fashion boutique in Downtown Sacramento. She increased her popularity by posting daily social media content on how to look fabulous with simple looks. Daisy thrived on attention and power. She learned to expect she could get whatever she wanted, which was why it was so confusing when she couldn't.

Daisy began to have nightmares. She had visions of a ghostly woman watching over her. Always, the hair was long and stringy, brushing over Daisy's face as she slept. The creature whispered things that she couldn't understand. Sometimes, she saw something else: a man in a suit watching her from a dark corner.

"It's almost time, Daisy..." he'd say.

"Time? For what?" she'd ask.

"Time for you to join me!" As he laughed, she'd awake, screaming at the top of her lungs.

It began happening all the time. Soon, the sparkle in her eyes waned, and her bright face faded to a dull pallor. She stopped tending to her store and lost touch with her followers. Daisy didn't want to see anyone. Instead, she stayed in her room, refusing to look around because of the shadows that followed her everywhere!

It was her older brother, Alang, that usually found her in this state. He'd quickly throw red beans in each corner and assure her she was safe. No one was affectionate in their family, but he'd sit by her until she felt better. They were the youngest and shared a deeper bond as a result. So, when Daisy needed help, Alang came through. But she could tell by the tight line of his mouth that he was afraid for her.

Finally, her father came to visit.

"I've had a vision, and I know what's wrong," Seng Vang said, looking grave.

Daisy snickered. Her father was a shaman who did readings and seances for a living. He lied if it meant clients would pay extra money. To strangers, he was cold and manipulative. He wasn't much better to family.

"Let me guess... I'm becoming a spinster, and I must get married to heal this sickness of the soul!"

She didn't understand why marriage continued to be so important for the Hmong. All her brothers, except Alang, were married with children. They weren't concerned for him, but Daisy was a daughter and already twenty-five years old. Her expiration date was long overdue.

"Yes," her father answered.

At first, she laughed, but the expression on his long face quickly sobered her mood. She shouted, "You're kidding! Dad, that's so lame. This is America. You can't just marry me off like livestock."

"This isn't a joke, Daisy. We have spirit guides that can't be denied," he said.

"If you're asking me to join the family business, Dad, the answer is 'No.'" She crossed her arms defiantly.

He constantly ordered her brother around for the purpose of business. Daisy preferred giving commands rather than obeying them. One could say she was her father's daughter.

Seng's expression made her uneasy when he said, "If it were only that simple. I knew the day you were born that something bad would happen."

"Gee, thanks for the vote of confidence," said Daisy with a roll of her eyes.

Her father wasn't easy, but he had always favored his daughter. He showed this by leaving her alone and letting her do as she pleased.

"You're a chosen bride. You've heard the legend. Demons don't forget the ones who cross them, and Du Yong promised to come back for all the sons of Shee Yee. He can eat every single last one of those bastards, as far as I'm concerned—but if you're a chosen bride, he'll come after you, too."

Daisy frowned. She didn't partake in her family's shaman practices but had grown up learning all the traditions and stories. Despite being a modern woman, she believed some rumors were true. Being haunted by spirits was no coincidence. Even now, she avoided the dark entity hiding in the corner of her room.

"What can I do?" All traces of laughter left her eyes.

"What else can you do? Your spirit guides are frantic because they know what's coming, and you're so goddamn negligent that you haven't been listening. No wonder you're sick! You'll marry that damn Khang boy if only to protect yourself," her father replied.

"Who are you talking about?" Daisy arched a curious brow.

"Kai Khang."

Daisy parted her mouth in shock. Her father abhorred that family. He spoke of Kai Khang and his father with blatant distaste. He never explained why, but Daisy understood the nature of the game; anyone more powerful was a threat, and the Khangs had a strong reputation for being just that—powerful.

Her father's resignation was once again another unusual gesture of love. While he saved words of affection for the weak, he was willing to swallow his ego to protect his only daughter. For this reason, Daisy saved any sarcasm she might have otherwise used. Alang always said Daisy was the only one who could look at their father sideways and live. But no matter his character, their father was right about one thing: Daisy had been chosen to become Kai's bride.

Daisy was beautiful. Traditional mothers praised her pearl-like complexion and long black hair. It draped lovingly over her slender figure like dark silk. Meanwhile, their sons ogled the curves of that same figure, wondering what was beneath the designer pieces that covered it. Daisy could have anything she wanted simply by turning up the charm. That changed the day Kai and his father arrived at their home.

Paj Vang

The eldest Khang son towered over the others, his copper-blond mullet making him impossible to miss. The clean fade along the sides of his head sharpened his jaw and made the tension in his face even more obvious. He didn't smile or say a word as he sat beside his father.

Koi tattoos curled along his arm and up his neck, the ink seeming to shift as he turned to face Seng and Alang Vang.

Kai sneered at the beverages on the coffee table, a traditional gesture of welcome. They had never been friendly with Seng's family. Necromancers were slippery snakes who sold secrets from the dead. He couldn't count the number of times he rescued someone after falling for one of their schemes. There was a price to pay for anything given, and Seng never gave what he should to keep his clients safe.

"Let's get this over with." Kai yawned as though bored. "Why are we here?"

"Lihue, fatherhood must be a struggle. Your son still has no respect for elders." Seng's sharp gaze met with the older Khang.

"Forgive him. He lacks grace but makes up for it in other ways." Lihue said, his gentle smile never reaching his eyes.

"I hope so, especially if we're to become family," Seng remarked.

"You're kidding, right?" Kai laughed. He looked at them all like they'd gone insane. "Did you start drinking before we got here, old man?"

"It would certainly make this insanity more tolerable," quipped Alang.

Kai narrowed his eyes at the youngest Vang son, usually the quietest among them. Alang was quick and intelligent, handling most of his father's shady and legitimate businesses. He rarely spoke while his father was in the room, but any words were short and scathing. Alang was quick to defend his family, no matter what.

It made him a good son but a dangerous adversary.

"It's a miserable moment for all of us. Let's cut to the chase and be done."

Alang and Kai stared at one another, eyes blazing.

"Daisy, come meet the Khangs," said Seng.

Kai turned in surprise when a beautiful woman walked into the room. Daisy Vang was long and graceful, like a ballerina. But what he studied was the paleness of her complexion and the shadows underneath her eyes. No makeup could hide the strain of a troubled soul.

As she sat down, the energy in the room shifted. His spirit guides emerged, whispering and pointing. They soared around Daisy as though they couldn't believe what they saw. Even as he resisted, Kai felt the connection.

"Your family has been cursed, and it seems the fates have tied us together." Seng glanced at his daughter, who sat silently by his side. "The spirits have been coming to my daughter because they know she's his chosen bride. I doubt it's going any better on your end, Kai."

Seng rested his sharp eyes on the young Khang shaman. For all his bravado, Kai wasn't sleeping very much either. There was a hollowness to his cheeks and a dullness to his energy that trained spiritualists couldn't miss.

"This is not happening." Kai was on his feet, and for a moment, his father feared he might storm out. He was relieved when his son stood in one place, even as he scowled at the people around him.

Daisy wasn't used to anyone looking at her with distaste, and she flinched when those glaring golden eyes touched her. Kai Khang was furious about their shared fate. Even so, she couldn't help feeling drawn to him. The shadows that had been following her disappeared. It was clear that apart they were both vulnerable, but together... Daisy frowned.

What the hell was his problem? He should have felt as much relief as she did.

Lihue said, "You know there is no choice. Our ancestors have always chosen our brides. It is the only way to make sure we survive the curse."

"That's bullshit!" Kai's energy rattled the room, causing the blinds to shift against the large windows. "There is no way that my bride is a necromancer!"

This blatant assault on their livelihood sent all the Vangs to their feet.

"You disrespectful brat!" Seng swore loudly.

"Once again, the Khangs think they're too good for the rest of us." Alang's tone was even as he narrowed his gaze. "If I could burn that connection or cut it up with a sword, believe me—I would. I begged my father to let Du Yong take you. That's getting rid of two monsters, as far as I'm concerned."

Kai and Alang faced each other. Kai was taller, but Alang stood firm. He disliked the Khang family as much as his father did for different reasons. Seng didn't like them because they were powerful. Alang didn't like them because they were arrogant, and he refused to bow.

"That's enough!" Lihue rarely raised his voice in public, but his tone was firm. "Sit down, Kai. Your stubbornness won't get you out of this one. The spirits have spoken. If you want to live, you'll shut your mouth and follow the rules for the first time in your life!"

Lihue was a proud man who preferred to keep family troubles private, but he was running out of patience. Kai's obstinacy was going to get him killed. While Kai never disclosed how much he suffered, Lihue knew. His energy was waning by the day.

"Khang shamans marry their chosen brides," he repeated. "There is no choice."

"There is always a choice." Kai glanced at Daisy with a frown. "I'd rather die than live life as a prisoner."

It was shocking when Lihue slapped him. Daisy and her mom gasped while Seng and Alang sneered.

"You fool! Why must everything be so hard with you?" Lihue demanded.

Daisy's flesh burned as though she had been slapped herself. She touched her face tentatively as she raised her eyes to the young Khang shaman. He surprised her by laughing.

"I'm the fool, am I?" Kai shook his head. "You'll never know how much I wish you were right." With those words, he turned and walked out of the Vang residence.

Daisy Vang was furious. She was angry that her father and brother didn't try harder to reason with Kai. She was irritated that the Khang shaman was so stubborn. As soon as Kai stepped out the door, the dark shadows came rushing back. In her mind, Daisy heard the man in the suit laughing. Unable to stand it any longer, she ran after him.

"Daisy! Stop!" Pang shouted after her. Young ladies didn't chase men!

"He's in trouble now." Seng grinned as his daughter disappeared through the front door. When Lihue arched a brow, he added, "Of all my children, she's the most like me."

"Maniacal and unscrupulous?" Lihue smirked.

"She doesn't take no for an answer." Seng's eyes flashed dangerously.

When Kai got to his father's black sedan, and he didn't have the keys, he cursed. He should have driven his own car. There was never a good reason to visit a necromancer's home, and this was the worst outcome he could have imagined. As his spirit guides complained all around him, Kai warned them to cease their racket. He was pissed off at them, too. Of all the people in the world, it had to be the daughter of necromancers!

"Hey, you!" Daisy's long legs carried her quickly across the lawn. If Kai heard her, he didn't bother to respond. It only enraged her. "I'm talking to you, asshole!"

"Go home, little girl." Kai didn't bother to turn around. "I don't care what the spirits say—it isn't happening."

"Little girl?" Daisy almost choked on the words as she glared at him. "I'm a grown-ass woman!"

But he was no longer paying any attention to her. Instead, Kai was checking messages on his phone. Daisy surprised him when she cut to the front and jabbed a finger into his chest. "What they say is true, isn't it? You're an egotistical and selfish prick!"

"Whoa!" Kai's eyes sparkled with amusement as Daisy scowled at him. "Watch out. The infamous Vang anger is showing."

Awakening

There weren't very many clans in the Hmong culture, and each had a reputation. The Vangs were known for their beautiful men and women, but also infamous for their cantankerous nature. Quick to anger and retaliation, these were not people to displease.

Daisy ignored him. She grabbed his hand, forcing him to pay attention. "Don't you feel different at all? Alone, we're weak, but together—don't you feel the peace?"

Instantly, Kai felt their spirit guides drawing them together. They whispered and lectured him about the right thing to do.

Protect…

Chosen…

It is the only way…

For a moment, he was lost in her beautiful eyes and saw a flash of their future: a traditional Hmong wedding with many white blessing strings, a honeymoon in Hawaii where they laughed and danced all night, and children running along the beachside.

None of it was meant to be.

Holding his wrist when most men would have feared looking at him, Kai knew she was brave, like a chosen bride should be. He relented enough to say, "I feel it, but I'm sorry, Daisy. You and I are not meant to be."

"How can you say that?" Daisy demanded, searching his eyes in bewilderment. "I've never wanted anything to do with this shaman stuff! But even I know that when the spirits speak, we must listen. The more we fight, the more painful it will be—and it hurts!"

"Pain is certain, suffering is optional," Kai quoted a Buddhist proverb. "I have already chosen a different path, Daisy."

He pulled a locket from underneath his shirt. In it was a picture of a young woman and a child. At first, Daisy was confused. Then realization dawned.

He had a family.

Daisy gasped and said, "This isn't right. You're supposed to be with your chosen bride. You're supposed to be with me!"

"I'm supposed to put an end to this curse," Kai said, his eyes hardening. "I'm sorry for the pain this will cause you, but we can't keep hiding behind the chosen brides."

Daisy shook her head. "My father and brother are right about you—you're arrogant. You really believe you can end an ancient curse?"

"I can't, but I know someone who can," he replied quietly.

She stared at him as if he'd lost his mind, but she was fearful as she said, "What am I supposed to do?"

Kai pulled several strands of hair from the back of his head. She watched in confusion as he twisted the golden strands around a pair of red and white strings.

"You never know when a blessing is needed." Kai always kept a handful of strings in his pocket in case of an emergency. Daisy pulled away when he attempted to tie the strings around her wrist. "Come on, Daisy—this is the least I can do. This hair carries whatever strength I have left and will protect you."

"So, now you're worried about me?" Daisy laughed bitterly. "You're unbelievable, Kai Khang. All you had to do was marry me, and we'd both be safe."

Kai looked frustrated as he said, "No one should be tied to anyone because of fear!"

"But I'm scared!" Daisy screamed. When she began crying, Kai drew her into his arms and felt her anxiety. "They're always watching me, Kai. They won't leave me alone. Please don't do this!"

She clung to him, burying her face in his chest. Anyone who saw them then would have assumed they were longtime lovers, but it wasn't meant to be. If he married his chosen bride, they would both be safe, but it wouldn't end the curse.

Kai couldn't bear the idea of Du Yong terrorizing his son or others down the line and would accept any pain to make sure it never happened. He'd sacrifice it all to save his son.

He said, "I can't be with you, Daisy. Please. Just let me tie this for you."

Daisy shoved him so hard that he almost fell and glared. "Fuck you! You want to be a damn hero—go for it. But more likely, I'll see you in hell. These things are coming for both of us, and there's nothing you'll be able to do."

Someone was headed toward them: it was his father. Before Kai could say anything else, Daisy was already running away.

When Lihue arrived at the car, he asked, "What have you done?"

"What I had to do," Kai answered, curling his fingers around the string in his hand.

Daisy threw a glass cup across the room. As it splintered against the wall, she targeted the innocent desk by the window. She pushed all the papers and photo frames off the surface. When that wasn't enough, Daisy threw her laptop onto the ground. Something about how it shattered made her feel better, and she continued breaking everything within reach. The sound of her wrath continued for so long that it was a while before she heard the voices from the other side of her door.

"Daisy, are you okay?" Her mother, Pang, asked as she turned the doorknob. "Let me in."

"Go away!" Daisy threw a pillow against the door.

"Daisy, don't blame yourself," said Alang, who was usually the only one who could calm her. "The Khangs are snobs and don't deserve you. Open the door. We'll figure this out together."

She sank to the floor as the strength left her legs. Nobody understood. Daisy stared blankly at a mirror, averting her gaze from the shadow creeping from the perimeter of the frame.

If Kai Khang didn't want her, nothing would keep them away.

He's right… It was a terrifying, familiar voice. He doesn't deserve you.

She gasped as something brushed against her face.

The Khangs have always been arrogant and presumptuous, putting their nose where it doesn't belong! They think only of themselves. They seek glory over responsibility.

Daisy's heart raced as shadows swirled all around her. Her fledgling spirit guides shrank back in fear.

You're too good for him, Daisy. Who is he to reject you?

She wrapped her palms over her ears. The voice sounded as though it was just behind her.

You are his chosen bride. He should respect you, but what did he do? He didn't just reject you—he had a baby with another woman!

Daisy shook her head. The voice was digging into her mind, trying to taint her soul.

He doesn't care about you. Instead, he laughs at your pain!

"Stop—stop talking!" Daisy curled into a ball on the ground.

"Daisy?" Pang sounded alarmed.

"Daisy—open the door!" Alang shook the doorknob, trying to get in.

Daisy couldn't hear any of them. She was focused on the man in the dark suit. He was sitting beside her now, gently caressing the side of her head.

"Kai Khang is selfish." Du Yong removed a strand of hair from her eyes. "He thinks of only himself. You were ready to do your duty as his chosen bride, but he laughed at you—he chose someone else and made you an even bigger fool. Does he even care that you're suffering?"

Daisy's tears dried as a new fury broiled within her heart.

"No, he doesn't care. You begged him, and he refused. But I know how to make him regret it." Du Yong ran a long finger down the side of her cheek. "I can give you the power to ensure he and his family suffer."

Daisy shook her head.

"Why should you care? His family deserves to die. They will toss aside anything and everyone so long as their precious lineage exists!" Du Yong spoke furiously. "He left you to suffer alone, Daisy Vang. Should he get away with that?"

"No!" She was angry as she thought about Kai and his family. He didn't care about her, and she was tired of feeling scared of the shadows.

"You don't have to be scared, Daisy. We're not here to hurt you. We only want you to join us. I want to give you all the power in the world." Du Yong was gentle, stroking her shoulders like a paternal figure.

Daisy looked at the monster for the first time. "I won't have to be afraid anymore?"

"You will bring fear to the souls of all men," Du Yong promised.

"And he'll suffer?" Daisy burned with the memory of Kai Khang sneering at her.

"As you please."

There was a long pause as Daisy considered what this meant. She was a necromancer's daughter and a chosen bride. The men who were supposed to protect her had failed. She was tired of fearing for her life and knew the shadows would never stop unless something changed. Daisy Vang was a businesswoman who only placed her bets on the best odds. Slowly, a deep red light began to simmer in the pupils of her eyes.

Du Yong grinned. "You will be the most powerful and will never need the protection of another man again! Are you ready to join us, Daisy?"

The necromancer's daughter—the scorned bride looked into the face of evil. "Yes."

Du Yong released a thundering laugh. All the items Daisy had thrown on the floor lifted and flew around the room. The shadows creeping in every corner dulled, and she was no longer afraid. When

Du Yong extended his hand to her, she readily accepted. As she walked into his embrace, Daisy was no longer a daughter, a sister, or a bride.

She realized that she'd seen this moment happen many times. Her first and only shaman premonition was of the ghost woman, who was none other than her future self. Instead of becoming a shaman, Daisy would become queen of the most unholy beings… the *poj ntxoog*, a succubus: an entity whose only purpose was to rip out the souls of men.

It was too late when Alang finally broke through the door. His beloved sister was curled up on the floor with a dreamy expression. Unfortunately, she was also cold and dead.

Present time…

"Sarah, I told you—I'm fine!" Thai Khang was exasperated.

His sister wasn't home from college yet, but she was already on his case. She continued ranting as he threw his book bag onto the desk. He glanced at the calendar, noted the date with the big red circle, and frowned.

Just a few more days before she could yell at him in person.

"Since when did you get so goddamn superstitious?" Sarah demanded.

He could almost picture her yanking at her hair in frustration. Sarah had an undeniable flair for drama and wasn't happy about his engagement. He could barely get in a word as she continued ranting. More and more, he understood why his parents let their eldest attend college so far away.

"Look, sis, I'm sorry if I'm too Hmong for you," Thai murmured. "But I'm telling you—this is the real deal. I haven't had a single nightmare since Sheng came into my life!"

"Don't even say her name," Sarah retorted with irritation. "It just makes this delusion sound more ludicrous."

"It's not—you don't understand!" Thai released an angry growl. Nobody understood. "If you could just see the things that I see—feel the things that I do… Sarah, this world isn't what you think it is."

Sarah opened her mouth to speak again but stopped when her brother began sobbing. Anger turned to concern as she asked, "What's wrong? Tell me."

Thai was fine now, but he had been sick for a long time. It was increasingly clear to Sarah how much the illness had impacted his mind. He was her baby brother. If she had to protect anyone, it was him—but she didn't understand these new problems.

Thai whispered, "I told you—it's a curse. Sheng is the only one who can protect me!"

"You don't even know her!" Sarah shouted, wanting to reach through the phone and shake him. "Curses aren't real, Thai. Shamans aren't real, either. Give them enough money, and they'll tell you whatever you want. Don't give them what they want, and they'll make sure you pay more! Why are you falling for this crap?"

"Did you talk to Mossy about this 'crap'? You heard she's going to marry the shaman who did my ritual," Thai asked.

Sarah inhaled sharply. Mossy and Sarah had different temperaments, but they always shared similar beliefs. Neither were very connected with their Hmong identities, but things had changed in Sarah's absence.

Awakening

Mossy and Thai had lost their minds.

Thai was only fifteen years old, and Mossy wasn't much older. Marriage should have been the last thing on their minds. The people she loved most were being brainwashed by tradition and superstition.

Mossy surprised her most of all. She was supposed to start a new life soon, but was marrying instead. What was she thinking?

Sarah said, "I'll be home soon! I don't know what kind of crazy water you all are drinking up there, but we'll figure this out when I get home. Just please, don't do anything stupid."

Like getting married.

"Do you hear me?" she demanded again.

"Fine, whatever," Thai grumbled.

It was useless to argue. The wheels were already in motion. When Sarah returned, she would become the maid of honor whether she wanted to or not.

After Sarah hung up, Thai headed into the shower and was careful not to disturb the bracelet around his wrist. It was a protection string woven from black cloth and strands of Sheng's equally dark hair. Alang had promised it would protect him against Du Yong until the wedding was over.

"He can't see you because the chosen bride hides you," Alang had explained. "That's why they're special."

As Thai closed his eyes, he thought of his chosen bride. She had barely spoken a word since they met, but he didn't mind. She was pretty and would protect him, which was enough. But he was so happy that he never noticed the stranger things—like how she never blinked and stared endlessly at nothing.

Paj Vang

The black bracelet was supposed to protect him from bad dreams, but its real purpose was to keep his spirit guides away. Now, nothing stirred or buzzed in his chest when it came.

As Thai fell asleep, a shadowy figure emerged from the corner of the room. It floated until it reached the side of the bed. Then it bent and hovered its pale, gaunt face over his own.

As a human, Daisy was beautiful. As a ghost, she was ghastly. Her silky hair now hung like moldy straw. Her pearly white complexion was sullen and gray. Hollow black eyes fixated on the teenager, wishing he would wake so she could hear him scream. Instead, he slept, and she moved in.

He was already dreaming of his chosen bride and smelled quite delicious when he was happy. Sheng smiled at him and beckoned him closer. As he leaned in to kiss her, the Succubus Queen pried his mouth open and opened her own. He never suspected this dreamy kiss was with a malicious creature draining his soul.

Chapter 4

If Mossy didn't understand the importance of a flying horse before, she learned the moment she was dropped abruptly onto the ground. Spirit guides weren't designed for smooth riding. Mossy toppled several times down a small hill before stopping against a tree.

Groaning, she wondered why there were always so many trees in the spirit world. This time, the lone palm tree was in the middle of a seemingly ordinary neighborhood. It looked like a typical Sacramento subdivision with Mediterranean-style homes. The sidewalks were neat, with perfectly trimmed bushes and tall palm trees. The only thing amiss was the dark and gloomy atmosphere. All thoughts ceased as she heard a roar.

Touso! Mossy quickly scrambled to her feet.

It felt like déjà vu as she found him battling a vicious creature nearby. They faced each other in the middle of the road.

Phim Nyu Vais! In all the legends, the beast was vicious and insatiable. It targeted people walking alone in the woods. Once a prey was selected, there was no stopping until blood coated the ground. The horrid beast was described as an animal that stood tall like a man.

No one survived an encounter with the beast—something that couldn't feel pain didn't go down quickly. In Sacramento, the legendary monster was a pit bull, snarling and snapping its razor-sharp teeth. Currently, it towered over Touso on long hind legs. The shaman leaped high, striking either side of its massive body with his feet, before bringing the sword down to its neck. The dog monster screamed and tossed him aside.

In the distance, Touso heard the frantic banging of the gong. Something was wrong, and his father was trying to bring him home. It was difficult to think of much else as the beast reached for him with jagged claws. It had come from nowhere, nearly sinking its teeth into his arm before his spirit guides pushed him out of harm's way. Now, Kong and his soldiers fought the creature as Touso gathered himself. He stepped forward to swing his sword but stopped short when a pair of hands gripped his arm. Touso nearly hit Mossy as he turned.

"Mossy! What are you doing here?" His eyes furrowed in confusion.

She hastily dragged him from the road. "What do you think? You already know what happens when you're in danger. Come on—we need to go! Where is it?"

"Where is what?"

"Your flying horse!"

"Are you talking about Neng?" Touso studied her as she searched the sky.

Neng? Mossy tossed him a strange expression. While she suspected Touso wasn't the most creative person, this was disappointing. Neng was the simple Hmong word for "horse."

"Don't look at me like that. That's his name!" His tone was defensive. One didn't name their flying horse any more than they could name their spirit guides. Then he pointed to the distant horizon. "He's coming! We need to hurry."

At first, it was just a tiny object in the sky. As it got closer, Mossy gasped. Neng wasn't just a horse but a magnificent creature with a copper-red coat. Balls of fire finished off the ends of long and powerful legs. A blond mane waved marvelously across the gray sky as he raced toward them.

Just as she and Touso turned to run in that direction, Mossy fell. A pair of claws caught her ankles and yanked her to the ground. She screamed as the beast dragged her away.

"Mossy!" Touso shouted in horror.

When the beast glanced up, its grin was chilling. These monsters hungered for human flesh, but they craved female humans more than anything. Women disappeared all the time for no reason, and it was difficult to place blame on a monster that shouldn't exist.

As the beast climbed over Mossy's body, Touso feared he would tear right through her. What happened next was much worse. The creature slung a heavy chain over her head. A moment later, a red jewel glistened maliciously at her chest.

The Hmong wore amulets to keep their souls safe. This was a dark amulet designed to lock down spirit guides. Now, Mossy's guides couldn't help her.

Paj Vang

It was a trap! Touso realized they'd been expecting her to come. Mossy's struggle was fruitless as the creature carried her away.

"No!" Touso ran toward her, but more beasts leaped out to block him.

They snarled and snapped their long jaws, daring him to make the first move. He felt a familiar burning sensation as Kong and the other spirit guides appeared to battle the beasts. Soon, weapons clashing against fur and flesh filled the air.

He moved quickly—kicking, spinning, and thrusting his blade at every step. Before long, Touso was drenched in blood. But each time he brought down the sword, more creatures rushed in to push him further away. Touso had never felt more helpless than when the pack leader disappeared with his bride.

Chapter 5

As Dylan Reed fell, brilliant swirls of energy surrounded him. Some whispered. Others cried. The rest chattered with excitement. Mystical faces peeked at him before vanishing in the light. Invisible fingers poked and prodded his ribs in disbelief. Finally, the spirits embraced him so tightly that he thought they would carry him away. Instead, they disappeared, and Dylan hit a tree branch before crashing onto the ground.

Dylan rolled onto his back and stared at the black sky. There were no stars in this world. The horizon seemed woven from smoke and ash. The only light came from the moon, but even this was a façade.

Dylan heard a gong playing faintly across the sky. Lihue would continue playing until they all found a way to return. Abruptly, he sat up, hoping to find Mossy nearby, but she was nowhere in sight.

It was an abandoned amusement park. Dylan had fallen just beyond the entrance. The tree and the grass had hurt upon impact, but now he was thankful. He was just a few feet from the concrete pavement that made up the rest of the park. As Dylan glanced around, seeing the small airplane rides and the carousel behind them, he realized it was Funderland! At least, it was a version of it.

The spirit world had many levels, and the one seen most often looked very much like where they came from. But everything in this world was just a shade darker and gloomier. Even the expressions on the carousel horses seemed more sinister, with mouths that turned up maniacally.

It was believed that spirits retreat to the place they loved most during life. The ghosts that humans reportedly saw were spirits enjoying those memories. Dylan didn't understand why he was in Funderland. The Thing certainly had no attachment to such a place! There were footsteps, followed by childish giggles. The amusement park looked empty, but he was not alone.

Something ran across the yard. Dylan whirled around just in time to see a pale little boy disappear onto the carousel. Seconds later, another boy with a braided bun ran after him. His eyes were bright, and a happy grin spread across his face. It was a sharp contrast against the dark environment. *Fuechi!*

A large yellow school bus pulled up to the entrance. He narrowed his eyes at the unusually calm children inside. He sensed evil. As they turned their heads to peer out the window, their hungry eyes glowed red. They pressed pale faces and palms against the glass.

It was a gift and a curse to be chosen for the shaman's life. A strong shaman could heal and vanquish most evils that tortured men. Dylan's energy was so strong that most spirits knew to steer clear. But a new shaman, like a child, was vulnerable. Only the strongest of evil could make a human see them. Those with shaman gifts could already see. It made them easier to prey upon, and their inexperience made them even easier to catch.

Fuechi was just a child. He should have been free from this burden, but his father's blood was too strong. Shaman energy was already leaking from his soul. This glowing yellow mist left a trail of breadcrumbs for hungry monsters to follow. Dylan stiffened as the chorus of whispering started all around him. Bright lights appeared and disappeared, forcing him to tear his eyes away from the school bus.

Danger!

Get him!

Run!

Whatever beings gave voice to these words, they seemed to be on his side. As the bus door opened, Dylan turned and ran toward the carousel.

Strange forces were clearly at work. The carousel was spinning, alive with music and lights. When Dylan arrived at the platform, the boys sat on two parallel horse figurines. They laughed and chatted like all was well. But when the pale one saw him, he narrowed his dark gaze. He mumbled something to Fuechi, who glanced over at Dylan.

"Fuechi!" Dylan hoped he recognized him, but Fuechi seemed afraid as he slid off his horse. Within seconds, he and the other boy were running again. "Wait!"

They neither turned nor listened. Then, joining hands, the boys leaped off the spinning platform and dashed for the grass ahead. When he heard a train's engine, Dylan instantly knew their plans. The boys intended to hop aboard to achieve a quick getaway.

The clinking of metal gates and shuffling feet had him momentarily distracted. The zombie children were stumbling through the amusement park's entrance, following the misty yellow trail toward the carousel.

By the time Dylan returned his attention to the boys, they were already on the train.

He ran after them.

It was this movement that stirred the zombie children to quicken their pace. Their little eyes twitched, and their mouths curled into a snarl as they gave chase.

The train followed an endless cycle around the park. Their best hope was to get to the other side, away from the little monsters chasing them. As their hunger intensified, the shuffles came faster, with some already jogging. Dylan was sure they would soon be at a full sprint.

The boys leaped off as the train rounded the corner. Fuechi was surprisingly agile, landing gracefully on his little feet before following his friend into the maze.

Dylan wondered what significance Funderland had for him. The hay maze was a seasonal attraction that the amusement park put up in the fall. Back at home, spring was yet to end.

They were there because this place was special to him.

Distracted by these thoughts, Dylan didn't notice that the zombies had stopped chasing the child to follow *him*. On the train, Fuechi's shaman scent was lost in the wind. But the horde locked quickly onto Dylan's misty trail.

No matter how fast he ran, he couldn't hide what he was or how he smelled. In the spirit world, everything craved life. As he disappeared into the straw maze, the ravenous horde started to run.

"Fuechi!" Dylan shouted as the boys dashed around the corner.

Awakening

The hay maze was usually stacked short so that parents could easily track their children. But this particular structure was taller than Dylan remembered.

Eventually, he came to a split in the maze. In frustration, he listened closely for any sound. If there was anything, it was drowned out by the growling of the zombies behind him.

His chest burned again. Soon, several orbs floated all around him. They were different colors, and sometimes, he caught glimpses of faces.

Right. Turn Right!

Without hesitation, Dylan followed.

Left!

Left again!

Almost there...

Finally, he heard Fuechi's voice.

"Ling, Fuechi is tired! Can we go home now?"

If Ling responded, it wasn't in words that could be heard.

When Dylan came around the corner, he found the boys hiding behind a bench. It was a dead end, but the wooden seat stood before a peculiar Black Door floating just above the ground. Wherever it led, Dylan was sure it wasn't a place they belonged. He moved quickly to ensure Fuechi didn't try.

Ling was the first to see him. The pale boy glared and hissed. As his eyes turned bright red, Dylan arched a brow. The Thing inside of him had suspected as much: Ling wasn't human, so the boys shouldn't have been friends. But as he watched how Ling protected Fuechi, he knew they shared an unusual bond.

"Hey, bud. Do you remember me?" Dylan cast his friendliest smile as he approached.

Fuechi studied him with the familiar intelligence from the movie theater and nodded.

"What are you doing out here?" Dylan wasn't referring to the maze.

"The Bad Man was scary." Fuechi glanced around as though the demon might jump out at any time.

"He won't hurt you. I won't let him," Dylan promised. "You want to go home?"

Fuechi nodded but didn't move.

"Your mom is waiting for us. She sent all of us to come get you." It wasn't a lie, even if it wasn't the complete truth. The goal was the same: get Fuechi home.

His eyes filled with tears. He missed his mama. But he remained seated, and Ling stayed protective, snarling as Dylan came closer.

"Listen, Fuechi. Dangerous things are coming. We need to go." Dylan tried to remain calm as the wall of hay bales shook from the zombies thrashing against them.

"Fuechi can't leave yet." He looked at Ling, who seemed to agree despite glaring at the newcomer.

"Why not?" Dylan was growing impatient, but Fuechi's following words surprised him.

"Fuechi's waiting for daddy."

Funderland was their special place. Kai used to hold onto him during every ride, but once he grew tall enough, his father let him sit alone. Last year was the first time he wandered the maze without help.

His father said he was a big boy now.

"I'll be waiting at the center of it. If you can find me—without crying, you can have whatever you want," said his dad with a wink.

Fuechi loved challenges and especially rewards. But he loved his father the most. He surprised Kai by how quickly he solved the maze, reaching him within minutes. The bond between father and son was just that strong.

Dylan frowned, wondering whether the ghost had led him to believe Kai was alive. But Ling didn't speak to him, and Fuechi wouldn't budge from his seat. The zombie children were much closer, and Dylan felt the spirits stirring again.

"He's not coming, buddy. We need to leave. Your Mama's waiting. It's too dangerous here," Dylan insisted.

Fuechi took him by surprise when he threw his arms around his neck. He clung to Dylan as he'd done at the movie theater, but this time, there was something else. His chest burned even more intensely as his head flooded with strange memories.

The Thing inside him curled into a fetal position. *Why did it hurt?*

The Thing was always angry and sad for no reason. It couldn't remember who it was or who it had been. It only knew that it yearned for something it didn't understand. Now, it was all coming back. The Thing saw itself enter this world as a baby. Soon, a familiar woman beamed and embraced him.

"Look at his hair! It's like the sun!" his mother exclaimed.

Fast forward, he now had a brother with hair as dark as coal. As the baby boy wrapped his tiny fingers around his thumb, he promised to always protect him. His mind flooded with many more images of the two brothers laughing and sometimes crying together. This bond was only second to one other—the bond The Thing would have with his own son.

Fuechi.

A single tear fell as Kai Khang remembered why he was angry and sad. He also remembered his spirit guides, who now celebrated gleefully. Kai tightened his arms around his son.

"Daddy!"

"How did you know?" All fathers thought their children were special, but Kai always knew Fuechi was a different breed. He was quicker and more intelligent than most adults, let alone children.

"Fuechi can always find Daddy!" He giggled but soon frowned. "Why do you look like this, Daddy? Are you hiding?"

Kai smiled. "I'll tell you later, bud. We've got company."

The man-eating children had arrived. Kai gathered Fuechi into his arms and glanced around for the nearest exit. But there was only the mysterious black door—and something terrible was behind it. There had to be another way. As Kai prepared to shatter the hay structure, his son whispered, "There's a girl in there."

Kai froze, even as the zombies closed in. "What did you say?"

"There are lots of girls in there, Daddy," Fuechi repeated. "I heard them."

Dylan Reed resurfaced to hear a familiar voice crying from the other side. *Mossy!*

"Dylan, don't—" Kai protested.

He didn't listen. Holding Fuechi tight, Dylan thrust open the door and leaped inside. The last thing they heard was the zombie children snarling after them.

Awakening

Alcatraz was a small island off the shore of San Francisco. For a long time, it was home to one of the country's most notorious federal prisons. Now, it was her prison. As she opened her eyes, she recognized the smell of the sea.

It was so cold, and the scent of mildew made it more miserable. The light in the room was minimal, illuminated only by a single bulb at each end. Whimpering and weeping voices from the other cells revealed she wasn't alone.

Her hands and feet were bound by rope. The heavy chain remained around her neck, locked to her chest like it was holding something in. She rolled to her side and shifted against the metal bars until she could sit up and scan the rest of the room. She gasped at seeing many faces staring back at her across the aisle.

The women looked like war prisoners with gaunt expressions and frail forms. It was hard to tell how old they were in the dark, but they all wore the same chains around their necks.

"You're awake." One smiled despite the situation they were in. Long dark hair framed a pretty face. She looked familiar, but Mossy couldn't remember where she'd seen her. "We were starting to wonder if the *phim nyu vais*, the beast, already ate your soul."

"My grandmother always described them as monkeys," Mossy replied with a frown.

"Our monsters always look different from those our parents grew up with." This time, it was a stocky girl with golden hair. Her eyes looked sorrowful as she met Mossy's gaze. "Mine was a cat. I hate cats!"

"Mine was a rat!" The other girl twisted her face in distaste.

"Is this what I think it is?" Mossy glanced around the cold room.

"You smell it, too, huh," said the girl with the dark hair. "It's funny. The old people never described Alcatraz when discussing getting kidnapped by evil spirits."

"The old people were wrong about many things," the second one said resentfully. When Mossy looked at her again, she noticed how hollow her cheeks were. She must have been one of the first to arrive.

"What's your name?" asked the slender one.

"Mossy."

She giggled. "You sound like a valley girl, Mossy! I'm Emma from Fresno, and this salty one over here is Lisa from Saint Paul."

Mossy's eyes widened in surprise. They were all Hmong girls from different cities across the United States. She glanced at the other faces watching her.

Lisa smiled and said, "Don't mind them. Most of them are too scared to talk. They're afraid he might hear. Emma and I have been here too long to care." There was a hint of rebelliousness in her voice, and Mossy decided she liked them both.

"Him? The beast?"

Lisa made a sound between a laugh and a snort. "No! If only! I think we could eventually outsmart that one. But this other one—he's different. We don't know his name. He looks like one of us—human. But he isn't. Sometimes, he visits, and sometimes, he takes one of us away. He's collecting us, I think."

Mossy thought of the Bad Man and shuddered. She looked at the other girls. "How long have you been here?"

"Too long!" Emma groaned.

"Time works differently here. It feels like forever, but we must still be alive. Souls with dead bodies have a different feel," Lisa clarified.

"How do you know?" Mossy tilted her head.

"My shaman mentor said the dead aren't interested in the dead," Lisa replied with a shrug.

That was why Lisa knew so much. Unlike Mossy and Emma, she had a teacher.

"Nothing is more special and powerful than the energy of life." As Lisa spoke, she offered her bound wrists for them to see. Slowly, a small light began to simmer and form. But she was too weak, and the orb was soon extinguished. "We won't last much longer if we stay."

Mossy felt her own powers flicker at her fingertips. The chains around their necks held back their spirit guides and dampened any powers they possessed. The chain had to be broken if there was going to be any chance of escape.

The large door at the end of the hall opened. Despite any show of bravado, all the girls shrunk away. The beings wore thick hooded cloaks and slithered across the cold pavement like serpents. They peered silently into each cell until they arrived between Mossy and the two other girls. There was a jingle of keys followed by Lisa's screams.

"No! No! Leave me alone!" Her fight was useless as two creatures pulled her from the cell.

"Lisa!" Emma cried, throwing herself against the bars.

One tossed Lisa over its shoulder like a sack of rice. She thrashed and kicked as they turned away. Whatever they were, they felt nothing and cared for even less. As they closed the door, all the girls grieved. They listened to her scream until it ceased.

For a long time, no one spoke. Emma, who had bonded with Lisa, had the most difficult time. She wailed and kicked at the cell walls, angry at their plight. Lisa had been the strongest and most intelligent among them. She should have been the one to survive. Without her, the other girls felt hopeless.

"What will they do to her?" Mossy asked.

Emma sniffled bitterly. "What else? They're going to eat her soul."

For a long time after that, nobody spoke. When the door opened again, it struck fear in every cell. But there were no hooded creatures this time. It was just a man—a man with beautiful dark hair and an elegant suit.

It was Du Yong. His presence made the already cold room feel like ice. He walked past all the other cells until he arrived before Mossy. His grin reminded her of the monster from her nightmares.

"You called him, and now he sees you!" said Aunt Padee.

"Well, well, well. Look whom the beasts dragged in." He was a hunter assessing his latest catch. "You look uncomfortable." He glanced around at the other girls, and laughter boomed across the room. "You all do!"

"This necklace doesn't suit me," Mossy offered between clenched teeth. "Kindly remove it, please?"

The hidden threat in her tone was clear, and Du Yong lifted a brow.

"I remember when you were little and afraid. You were cuter back then."

"And you're still a monster."

Du Yong's eyes flashed red. "It's too early for compliments. You're a slippery one, Mossy Cha. When you called me all those years ago, I thought you'd be the first one."

"First one?" Mossy was confused.

"But the gods are just as slippery as you are. You might have been mine that day without that pesky shaman."

Touso!

"Just like his ancestor, he's always taking what is rightfully mine. Every creature has its place, and I was collecting my fair share. Who is he to interfere?" Mossy wasn't sure whether Du Yong was still talking about Shee Yee or Touso. "He's taking from me just the way he's taking from you. Doesn't it feel unfair, Mossy?"

Du Yong slid into the room. He maintained his human form at the upper half but lifted her with the end of a serpent tail so that she was now facing him.

"Do you like being told what to do?" The question took her by surprise. "You were chosen to protect him. Chosen to prioritize his life. Chosen to sacrifice all your desires. Sounds more like servitude to me. Is that what you young folks call 'romantic' today? Does he even care at all what you want in life?"

Mossy remembered what Thai had said: "He knows all my greatest fears and uses them against me!"

"Your dirty games won't work on me," she hissed.

"It seems unfair," he continued, sounding sympathetic. "But to each their own. If you want something, you must fight for it. What do you want, Mossy?"

She thought about poor Lisa and how they had simply taken her away without a word. Why was Du Yong asking her so many questions? What was his game?

"Are you ready to give up your freedom?" He was close enough that Mossy smelled the sulfur of his breath.

"What is it to you?" she countered, daring to meet his gaze.

Even with the chain, her energy simmered like it was barely contained. He watched the purple flames ignite in her eyes and wondered how good it would feel to break her. Then, he shoved her against the wall with a force that knocked the breath from her body. As Mossy struggled to breathe, he tightened his tail around her and ran a long finger down her face.

"I told you once that you have two destinies. Choose him and suffer his fate or..." He leaned in so that their eyes were barely an inch apart. "Choose me and experience the freedom you've always dreamed of."

"Is this the deal you've made with all the girls in this cell?" Mossy asked, despite her own growing trepidation.

"Not at all," Du Yong answered. "I'm just eating them."

Mossy froze.

"In this world, you are either master or servant—predator or prey! Which would you choose, little girl?" He held her face so she couldn't look away. Mossy saw lust, greed, and destruction in those blood-red eyes. This creature tortured her cousin and Touso, and he treated it all as a game. Du Yong was the epitome of evil.

"Bite me." When Mossy spat into his face, the demon snarled and tossed her onto the ground.

"Fool!" Du Yong hissed.

Mossy laughed this time, which only aggravated the demon's fury.

"Touso will find me." Mossy rolled onto her back and stared up at him. "And I'll stand by his side. We'll find a way to end your existence together!"

Mossy thought Du Yong meant to strike her with his tail when he moved. Instead, the tail curled around her leg.

"The funny thing about humans is that they constantly change their minds. One just has to find the right button."

Mossy heard the bones snap before she felt the pain. Then, as she screamed in agony, Du Yong turned and slithered away. He only faced her after locking the door, and the bastard was smiling.

"Don't worry, my sweet. If I'm right, you'll be fine in no time." Then Du Yong was gone.

Mossy felt more confused than ever. The demon had said a lot without answering a single question. What exactly did he want from her? But these thoughts vanished as she was consumed by pain. While her cries echoed throughout the room, all the girls in the cells shrank away, hoping he wouldn't return for one of them next.

Chapter 6

"I don't know whether you're brave or stupid, girl." Emma's laugh was weak, a mixture of bitterness and gloom. "But I admire you for not cowering to that monster. He's taken so many of us already."

Mossy, lying motionlessly for what felt like an eternity, turned to look at her. Emma's cell wasn't far away, but it was hard to see in the dark. She asked, "What does he want with all of us?"

"At first, I wondered the same thing, but it's becoming clear that he wants what we have," Emma answered. "He's a demon that eats souls. Human souls sustain him, but he's the most powerful because of whom he chooses to eat. From what I've seen, he's taken us all for what we can do."

Mossy didn't have to read minds to know Emma was thinking about Lisa, who could conjure fire in her hands.

"And what can you do?" she asked.

Emma chuckled. "I can make things grow. That's probably why I'm still alive. Who wants the ability to grow leafy greens and carrots when you can eat souls that let you breathe fire?"

"My Aunt May would adore you," Mossy joked. "She owns a vegetable farm."

"That's nice! My family doesn't care too much for my endless salads." It was nice to laugh with someone, if only for a moment. Emma asked, "What can you do, Mossy?"

Mossy said, "I don't know. I can see things. I have spirit guides that try to help me sometimes."

"Me, too!" Emma sounded excited and irritated at once. "Sometimes, they're so demanding. All I want to do is sleep, but they always wake me early to check on the garden. If I ignore them, I have migraines all day, so it's easier to comply."

Mossy frowned. She had spent the majority of her life ignoring her spirit guides. As she thought about it, she remembered the expressions of yearning in their eyes every time she quickly turned away. Perhaps she was fortunate that her own had not retaliated like Emma's.

"I've never really believed in this stuff," Mossy admitted.

Emma considered her from across the way. "You must have been in so much pain."

"What do you mean?" Mossy frowned in confusion.

"Our spirit guides are a part of us. They're our thoughts and our conscience, the essence of our being! When we deny them, we deny ourselves. It's like refusing to do something you know you're supposed to do. For people like you and me, we can become really sick or mentally unstable."

"People like us?" Mossy repeated.

"Shamans," Emma patiently clarified.

Mossy remembered the vision of Gowli, Pao, Chee, and Kalia. Gowli had urged her to accept them before it was too late. They always knew Du Yong was coming and patiently waited for her to awaken. She had been too stubborn to feel the pain, but she was sure it was because they had eaten the pain for her. They had protected her as they protected her now.

"We're all shamans." Mossy glanced at the other cells in the room, where most girls listened silently. They wore the same amulet: a small ruby jewel that clung to the chest like a magnet. "Is that why they put these things on us?"

Emma nodded. "Can't have spirit guides just setting girls free!"

All conversation ended when the door to the cell block swung open. A few seconds later, the hooded figures returned to the room. This time, there were three of them: one tall and two peculiarly short. Unlike the others, they moved quickly from cell to cell.

The girls whimpered and begged to be left alone, and the creatures moved on without a word. By the time they stopped at her door, Mossy was prepared to fight. She was still sprawled on the floor where Du Yong had left her broken. But she would dig her nails into their faces should they decide to pick her up like a sack of rice.

"Mossy!" The familiar voice took her by surprise.

She strained to look at the face hidden beneath the shadows. As the hood fell back, she could hardly believe her eyes. Dylan Reed stood just beyond the metal bars. The two short ones appeared beside him and waited patiently.

"Dylan? Is that really you?" Relief was met with a wave of emotions. If this were a trick, it would shatter her last bit of hope.

Mossy heard the keys rattling against the metal door. Then she smelled Dylan's musky cologne as he gathered her into his arms. She could hardly contain the tears as she buried her face against his chest. She'd never been so happy to see him!

"What happened? Did they hurt you?" Dylan studied her carefully, eyes surveying the trusses that kept her still.

"I'm okay, I think." She hadn't moved for hours and wasn't sure how to begin.

"Who did this to you?" His voice was seething as he went to work on the bindings at her wrists and ankles.

She inhaled sharply, waiting to feel pain when he reached her feet. Du Yong had snapped her leg like a twig, and it was a pain she'd never forget. To her surprise, Dylan untied the restraints without causing any discomfort. She was also able to stand without pain. Mossy tested the leg, lifting the knee and stomping a few times before lifting her eyes to face him.

"What's wrong? Are you okay?" he asked.

"Never better," she said in awe. She was healed! Quickly, she pulled off the chain and flung it across the room. There was a pop at her chest where the ruby amulet had sealed her spirit guides away. She knew they were okay when they stirred and bubbled within her chest. Mossy turned to study the two figures beside Dylan. "Who are these little ones?"

He grinned and pulled back the hood of the one closest to him. "Look who I found joy riding in the spirit world!"

It was Fuechi, peering shyly back at her.

When she glanced at the other one, Dylan shook his head. "Trust me. That one can keep his hood on."

Ling looked up at Dylan in disdain, but there was no time to argue as commotion stirred down the hallway. Someone was coming.

"We gotta go!" Dylan said, turning to hustle everyone out of the cell.

"Dylan, wait!" Mossy glanced anxiously at the other girls who'd watched everything unfold without a word. "We can't leave them!"

"We don't have time!" Dylan said with regret. The voices—the growling was getting close.

"We need to make time!" Mossy cried. The girls started to moan and plead, and she couldn't bear to leave them.

"He's right, girl," said Emma, offering her a weak smile. "There's no time. We'll be okay. Just don't forget us."

Her permission only made Mossy feel worse. She didn't know Emma well, but they would have been good friends. Tears flowed down her face as Dylan started to pull her away.

"Mossy, we need to go!" he said as the footsteps came closer.

"If you see my family, please tell them I'm here!" Emma pleaded. "Tell them Sheng is waiting for them to bring her home."

Sheng! She was Thai's chosen bride. In horror, Mossy realized why Sheng's eyes had seemed so dark and empty. There was something else in her body!

"Emma Sheng Moua," repeated the girl behind the cell. "Don't forget!"

"I won't!" Mossy reached for her hands, but Dylan was already carrying her away. "I won't forget!" She would never forget how the girls cried as they were left behind.

A group of hooded figures appeared at the entrance of the cell block. Mossy glanced back just in time to see the beasts doff their cloaks. She recognized the cat and the rat beasts her friends had mentioned. They stood on two legs like men but snarled like the monsters they were. Among them was the pit bull that had taken her away. It locked its eyes on her and charged.

Dylan released Mossy and picked up Fuechi, who was too small to outrun the beasts.

"This way!" He headed toward the other end of the unit.

Fuechi's mysterious friend swiftly scaled the walls. When the hood fell, she recognized the pale little boy from the abandoned city! The familiar black eyes met her own.

Run!

Mossy did precisely that, following Dylan and Fuechi down the dark corridor. The beasts behind them shrieked as they gave chase. As Ling leaped from one place to the next, he knocked down tables and chairs. The obstacles were just enough to buy them time. But the pit bull wouldn't let Mossy go without a fight. It dropped to all fours and sprinted along the cell walls and table surfaces, sinking its sharp claws into everything it touched. Its vicious bark promised a cruel end, and they ran for their lives.

Mossy remembered that the central jail connected directly to the dining hall. But if that door were locked, there would be nowhere else to run.

She sighed with relief when Dylan opened it easily with one hand and shouted, "Hurry!"

Mossy didn't have to be told twice. She and Ling flew inside, and not a moment too soon. As Dylan secured the door with a rusty lock, the beasts threw their snouts and arms through the bars. Dylan and Mossy clung to Fuechi as they stumbled away from the snarling creatures. Ling hung from the ceiling, hissing in distaste.

"What do we do now?" Mossy asked, glancing at Dylan, who was already looking for their next exit.

"Why are there so many damn bars in this place?" He cursed in frustration.

Alcatraz was a maximum-security prison. The dining hall was open-concept, so the guards could see everything from any point in the room. There was nowhere to hide. Large windows ran all along the dense walls of the space, each one reinforced by metal bars.

They could expect nothing less from a place designed to keep criminals locked in. Nevertheless, Dylan was irritated by the hopelessness of their situation.

As the creatures clamored to get through the door, Mossy looked down at the little boy holding her hand. He was remarkably composed for a child and kept his attention on Dylan the entire time. It was sad that such an innocent soul could fall victim to such an ugly world.

When Fuechi smiled, her heart leaped with joy. The sparkle of his golden-brown eyes reminded her of Touso.

"How did you find me?" She turned to meet Dylan as he ceased pacing the room.

"You can thank Fuechi for that." His eyes had a peculiar pride as he glanced down at the boy. "He said he heard girls crying on the other side of the door."

"The door?" Mossy looked between Dylan and Fuechi.

"It was a black door just floating in the air," Dylan explained with a shrug. "As soon as we leaped through, finding you didn't take long. We just followed the hooded assholes."

"Dylan, watch your language!" Mossy covered Fuechi's ears protectively.

Awakening

As Dylan grimaced apologetically, Mossy thought about this floating door. Her grandmother used to speak of doors in the spirit world. They could lead one anywhere, and it was easy to get lost. Worst, some doors led to places so deep that they blocked out the sound of the gong, which kept the living anchored to their world. She hadn't heard the gong since the beast took her away from Touso.

"Where are we?" She was fearful again.

"Somewhere further than we should be." Unknown to Mossy, Kai spoke from the young man's body.

The spirit world was a place with many realms. Most shamans were only skilled enough to tread the first level. Leaping through doors was a risk many of them were unwilling to take because they could lead anywhere. Anywhere where the gong couldn't be heard was too far. While the spirit guides were supposed to protect their shaman, they were also known for abandoning them just as quickly if their warnings were ignored.

Kai persistently ignored and angered his spirit guides in pursuit of knowledge. Eventually, they gave up trying to quell his curiosity. He went where he pleased, with or without them. But the door was a tricky entity that moved all the time. They needed to find it again if they were going to leave the island.

Ling leaped erratically between the ceiling and the floor. The metal bars bent and screamed in a way that hurt her ears. As the bolts shifted, Mossy and Fuechi backed away. A moment later, the room shook when the giant door crashed onto the ground.

"Ling!" Dylan shouted at the ghost on the ceiling. "Take Fuechi around the back! Check for a door!"

Ling grabbed Fuechi, instantly transporting them both to the distant end of the room. Now, it was just Mossy and Dylan left to face the beasts. They glanced at each other. Both had grown up in Sacramento, where school field trips to Alcatraz were common. If memory served them well, there was a kitchen where staff prepared lunch for hungry children between activities. Wherever food was prepared, there was a way to throw away garbage. They both prayed for it as they turned to face the snarling beasts.

We are you, and you are us, Gowli had said.

This was especially true in the spirit world. Their knowledge, strength, and powers were her own. For every thought, there was an answer. For every event, there was a reaction. Her spirit guides were ready to serve and, if she allowed it, to take over.

At that moment, all fear disappeared as Chee took charge. His power filled every fiber of her body until it poured from her eyes like a dangerous light. Soon, a long staff formed in her hand. When she lifted the spear, its blade gleamed brightly against the gray pallor of the spirit world.

At least a dozen animal monsters were flying across the room now. She briefly marveled at the sight. Even something typically adorable, like a cat, looked terrifying on two legs. The razor-sharp claws and fangs only added to this effect. As the first beast leaped at her, Mossy met it with a quick thrust of the spear. Chee's impressive strength made each strike especially brutal.

The blade sliced through the creature's chest, sending it to the ground like a broken object. The next monster came from behind, and Mossy quickly sank the end of the spear into its neck. She held on to the staff, using the momentum of the falling beast to flip into the air and kick off several more. As she landed on her feet, Mossy ripped the spear from the monster's neck, sending its head across the room. She gasped when a powerful arm hurled her to the ground. It was while flying through the air that she caught sight of Dylan. His eyes glowed like bright yellow flares as he took out beasts with a majestic golden bow.

What in the world was going on?

All thoughts flew from her mind as the pit bull monster roared. She moved just in time to avoid the foot coming down on her chest. As the dog monster reached for her, she thrust the spear into its body. But the beast grabbed the staff and pulled her forward, catching her by the throat. The staff fell to the ground as she kicked and struggled. Its grip only tightened as it stared into her eyes. Du Yong laughed from its malicious gaze.

He was watching her!

Which side will you choose, Mossy Cha?

As she struggled to breathe, her entire body went numb. Then the pit bull roared and dropped her onto the ground. Mossy lifted her eyes to see Dylan release several more arrows into the beast's chest. As it collapsed beside her, she grimaced at the stench of rot. Du Yong's hideous face wavered and disappeared.

Then Dylan hovered over her. "Mossy! Are you okay?"

She barely had time to nod as Dylan took her hands and ran. Howling and snarling from outside the door indicated more beasts were coming. As they raced to meet the boys in the kitchen, Mossy saw the room was littered with broken monsters—many of them struck down by golden arrows. She glanced at Dylan, who focused on the destination ahead.

"There's something wrong with Dylan Reed, and I want to see what happens when he's around the gong and the rattle." Touso had said when she questioned his choice to use Dylan in the ritual.

Mossy had initially thought it silly, but now, there was only one explanation for his ability to draw magical weapons in the spirit world. He had spirit guides.

Relief was met with excitement as they found Fuechi and Ling waiting by a small door around the corner. Fuechi instantly ran into Dylan's arms, who embraced him with a peculiar level of affection in return. But Mossy didn't have time to deliberate on these details as the horde closed in on them. Dylan kicked the door open and let Mossy and Ling pass before jumping out with Fuechi.

Outside was little better than the dangers within the building. It was dark and heavy with gloom. Escaping along a small gravel path, they passed a recreation yard teeming with demons. The creatures leaped at the tall chain-link fence, causing the structure to wobble. It wouldn't be long before they broke free. Meanwhile, the beasts from the jail were close behind, breaking the kitchen door as they poured outside.

Mossy looked around desperately for the safest escape route. How would they get across the water if they got to the dock? What monsters awaited them in the sea or the city of San Francisco? They had to find a way out of the spirit world!

Mossy's heart was pounding as a solid structure became visible ahead. She remembered this place with the rusty gray door. It was the jail's morgue, where bodies were usually stored before a boat arrived to take them to the mainland.

"Dylan!"

Awakening

He was already headed toward the staircase leading them to the rest of the island. When he glanced back at her, she saw his thoughts were similar. There were too many monsters, and all of them too fast. The journey to freedom was risky, even if they got past the stairs.

"The morgue!" Mossy panted as she stopped before the door. We need to get inside the morgue!"

Dylan looked skeptical as he turned to the small structure at the bottom of the hill.

"I remember the tour guide said it has a secret tunnel that leads to the end of the island," Mossy explained once she caught her breath. "The tunnel has to be safer than being out in the open for these things to grab us!"

Dylan nodded quickly in agreement as the beasts arrived. At the same time, they heard the fence break, and the crowd of hungry demons poured out from every direction. Mossy and Dylan rushed toward the rusty door. But when Dylan paused a moment too long at the entrance, Mossy knew something was wrong.

"It's locked!" Dylan's eyes flashed anxiously. The boy in his arms looked ready to cry.

Mossy, the last to arrive, pushed at it in disbelief. The metal door squeaked, but the latch refused to budge. She growled in frustration. As she did so, a purple light flared, and the energy of Pao consumed Mossy. When she grabbed the door again, it cracked loudly before breaking away.

She seemed disoriented as the glow left her eyes but quickly recovered when the noise grew louder. Then, without looking back, she pushed the boys inside and bolted the door.

The morgue, built into a hill, was essentially a root cellar for dead bodies. It was small and cold, with a questionable examination table. The ruins of a desk and shelves lined the old brick walls. A grated skylight in the ceiling was the only barrier against monsters.

Mossy covered Fuechi's eyes so he wouldn't see the arms reaching for them. Dylan scoured the back for an exit.

"Daddy, Fuechi wanna go home," the little boy whined.

Mossy frowned and grew even more confused when Dylan answered, "Don't worry. We'll be out of here soon. You're being so brave, and I'm proud of you." A clicking sound got their attention. "I found it!"

A slender door fell open at the back of the room, and they were greeted by a cold draft that smelled like the salt of the sea. It couldn't have come at a better time as the horde behind them thrust ferociously against the door.

"Hurry!" Dylan didn't have to repeat it.

Mossy and the boys ran into the tunnel just as the front door crashed to the floor. Dylan slammed the door shut behind them.

The tunnel was narrow and only traveled in one direction. They had to follow the wall to get to the end, and Mossy could hear the ocean with each step.

"Fuechi scared!" He sniffled as he clung to Dylan.

"It's okay, bud." Dylan caressed his back to comfort him. "We're almost there. We'll be home soon."

Ling crawled silently above them, glancing back in the direction of the morgue once in a while. He was faster than all of them and could easily escape, but he wouldn't leave his humans behind—he wouldn't leave Fuechi.

The darkness around them started receding as a peculiar light overtook the small space. Dylan was startled to find it was Mossy. She was glowing.

"My spirit guide, Gowli, is the wise one. She's patient, kind, and responsible for helping me make wise decisions," Mossy explained. She had a strange look in her eyes as she continued. "She figuratively and literally lights the way when it's dark." This light grew even brighter the further they walked into the tunnel.

"Thank you, Spirit Gowli, for lighting the way." Dylan smiled but was cautious of the speculative looks Mossy kept tossing him.

"So, you're not freaked out?" Mossy's tone was thoughtful and suspicious.

"I'm hanging out in the spirit world, Moss." Dylan shrugged without looking at her. "I would say it's a little late to be surprised about magical spirit guides now. I'm more concerned about the ones trying to eat me."

Dylan hoped Mossy would leave it alone after that, but she remained persistent.

"You handled yourself pretty well, I would say. Do they sell magical bows and arrows at Costco now?"

Dylan stopped and put Fuechi on the ground. When they faced each other, Mossy could only see Dylan without the yellow flares in his eyes.

"What are you trying to ask me, Moss?" he demanded.

"How are you here, Dylan?"

He stared at her in disbelief. Then he laughed, a sound mixed between anger and amusement. "Are you serious right now? Excuse me for wanting to save the woman I love!"

Mossy wasn't convinced. He should have been terrified. Instead, Dylan Reed was battling monsters like a veteran demon slayer. She said, "There's more to it than that. You're too comfortable here."

Dylan shook his head. "Comfortable? That's a stretch. I'm here because of you. Don't you know by now what I'm willing to do for you, Moss?"

He stood so close she felt the heat of his body—the only warmth in this cold world.

"How did you pull out that bow and arrow?" she asked and grew alarmed as flames arose within his familiar blue-green eyes.

Dylan seemed tired as he said, "I think we need to focus on getting out of here, Moss. The longer we spend talking, the more danger we'll be in. Fuechi has already been out of his body for too long. You know what's at risk if we don't get him back soon."

"That's exactly what I mean!" Mossy exclaimed, looking at him in bewilderment. "How do you know that?"

"It's your fault."

The answer was so unexpected that she was momentarily speechless. As they faced each other, Fuechi moved to hold his hand. The argument was making him anxious.

"What do you mean it's my fault?" she asked.

In the physical world, Dylan Reed and Kai Khang were one. In the spirit world, they remained tethered. The nature of the magic kept them together, but now, the spirit of Kai Khang stepped back as Dylan confronted the girl he loved.

It's because I love you so much that I'm still here. He had given his body to the lost spirit to protect her. Otherwise...

They heard the snarling at the same time.

"We need to move!" Dylan picked up Fuechi with one arm and grabbed Mossy with the other. "Run!"

Mossy complied without question. As they sprinted down the remainder of the tunnel, some stomped along the gravel while others scaled the walls with their claws. Even as her spirit guides buzzed at her chest and prepared to fight, she knew there were too many.

A light at the end of the tunnel filled her with relief, but it was short-lived when they arrived at a cliff.

"No!" Mossy screamed. She glanced between the monsters and the crashing waves below. "This isn't right! The soldiers used this tunnel to get to the other side of the island. There shouldn't be a cliff here!"

As the wind thrashed at their bodies, a sinister laugh echoed. Du Yong was enjoying every minute of this perverse game. The monsters were just a few yards away now, and the sight of their prey hastened their chase.

"Moss."

She turned to see Dylan's pained expression and didn't like his thoughts.

He said, "We don't have a choice. We have to jump."

Even as she shook her head, Mossy knew he was right. Fuechi was curled completely around Dylan's chest, and Ling had settled on the cliff's edge. He, too, was sure this was the only option left.

This was the end of the tunnel. The spirit world was tricky, and things weren't always what they seemed. As Mossy stared at the angry waves below, she hoped this was another test. If they stopped at the cliff, the battle would be lost, but if they jumped... they might get to the other side.

Dylan whispered something into Fuechi's ear. Then, grabbing Mossy's hand, they leaped off the cliff just as the monsters arrived. The air filled with their furious cries.

Dylan would have laughed if it wasn't for the cold air blasting against his face. When they hit the icy water, he hoped it wouldn't hurt.

Du Yong appeared all around them as they fell.

You're very fast. Too fast for a girl who should have a broken leg!

The same leg tingled as he spoke.

You can run as fast as possible, but I'll eventually catch you.

Mossy shook her head fiercely. *Never!*

We'll play your game, Mossy Cha. Let's see how long you last trying to protect the Khang shaman. And when you tire, I'll be here waiting for you.

As Du Yong disappeared, Mossy heard a gong followed by the sharp cry of a horse. She looked up just as Neng dived from the heavens.

Touso clung to his mane, urging the horse to go faster. She was so happy she nearly cried. When he held out his hand—she caught it! But Dylan and Fuechi's added weight proved difficult for the magnificent horse.

Touso tightened his grip and tried desperately to lift her. The bottom was near, and time was short. He glanced past Mossy and Dylan to see his nephew. Fuechi clung fearfully to the man holding him and never noticed Touso's pained expression. Between Mossy and Fuechi, he could only choose one.

"Mossy!" The wind took her name as soon as it left his lips. He tried lifting them all again to no avail.

Her heart skipped when Dylan's hand began to slip. She looked down to see him staring at her. *Why did he look so calm?*

He said, "It's okay. Let go."

"No!" Mossy squeezed his hand.

"Let go, Moss!" She was incredibly strong and refused to release him. But if she didn't, they would all soon crash into the sea.

"I won't let go," Mossy cried.

Dylan Reed was supposed to be home. He never should have come to this place to rescue her. This wasn't how things were supposed to end.

"Let go, Moss. We'll be fine. Trust me," he insisted. There was a strange yellow flash in his eyes as Dylan pulled his hands away.

It was the most horrible few seconds of her life when Dylan and Fuechi disappeared into the mist below. She was still crying when Touso pulled her onto Neng's back.

As the flying horse returned them to the sky, Touso held her close. He said, "It's okay. I've got you."

Mossy sank into his chest. "They're gone!"

"No. They're not."

Mossy lifted her eyes just in time to see a dark body soar past them. It was another horse with a mane as black as the coat that glistened like ink. As it flew in a circle around them, Mossy saw Dylan, Fuechi, and Ling on its back. Fuechi and Ling giggled as the black horse danced across the sky.

Dylan met Mossy's gaze and smiled. When his mouth moved, she knew he was telling her, "I told you we'd be okay!"

Mossy laughed. Dylan had jumped into the spirit world and harnessed a magical bow to fight monsters. Of course, he had a flying horse, too!

Paj Vang

As the horses soared toward the gong sound, a massive black door appeared on the horizon. Mossy closed her eyes and took comfort in Touso's embrace. They were finally going home.

Chapter 7

First, there was only darkness, and then there was light. She opened her eyes to find Pahoua and Bao hovering over her. "She's awake!" Bao's eyes lit up with excitement. "Oh, we were so worried about you!"

Pahoua gently lifted Mossy's shoulders to help her to a seated position. "Don't move too fast. Take it slowly. You've been through too much."

Mossy quickly discovered Pahoua's words to be true. She was lying on the couch when she awoke and felt a wave of dizziness as she came to sit at the edge of the seat.

"How long were we gone?" Mossy strained her eyes to see the bright lights streaming through the window.

"About an hour." Bao was offering her something to drink and paused when she saw the expression on her face. "What's wrong?"

"An hour? It felt like forever!" Mossy thought of how long she lay there on the floor of that cold cell, thinking she'd never return home.

But the light was as bright as when they left that morning. It was even brighter, which meant much of the day remained.

"Time in the spirit world works differently," Pahoua explained. "You could be there for years and come back to find only a few days have passed."

Mossy glanced around the room and was relieved to find Fuechi and Nia embracing happily around the corner. Lihue sat with them, gently patting his grandson's head with affection. Dylan stood nearby, watching contentedly. Ling was absent and had remained where he belonged.

"He's okay?" Mossy's eyes brightened. "The little boy's okay?"

"He's perfect!" Pahoua smiled graciously as she wiped tears from her face. "He awoke in his mother's arms just moments before you."

"How did you guys find him?" Bao sat down and carefully placed a cup of tea in her hands.

It felt nice to clasp something warm, and for a long time, Mossy held it. The heat reminded her she was safely back in her own world.

Mossy said, "It was Dylan. He found Fuechi, and then they found me. Fuechi said he heard girls crying through a black door, and the door led them straight to me."

Pahoua and Bao exchanged glances.

"A black door?" Pahoua repeated with a frown. "Our little Fuechi must be very gifted. The black door doesn't come to anyone. It has to be summoned, and even when it comes, one should be careful about stepping through."

"Thank God it came to him!" Mossy stifled a soft cry as she recalled the dark cells and all the girls being held there. "It was a horrible place!"

Pahoua hugged her and said, "Thank you for bringing my grandson back safely!"

Her embrace had a calming effect, and Mossy smiled. She looked around and asked, "Where's Touso?"

Touso instantly leaped to his feet when he awoke in another part of the home. He marched fiercely into the room, heading straight toward Dylan Reed. He shouted, "Get away from my family!"

Touso shoved Dylan hard enough that he nearly fell to the ground. But Dylan recovered quickly and surprised everyone by smiling.

"Someone's a little grumpy when they wake up, huh." His teasing tone only intensified the situation.

"Who are you?" Touso's eyes burned bright with blue lights, and the chandelier in the room flickered.

There was always something peculiar about Dylan Reed. No ordinary human handled demons and spirits the way he did. Shadows surrounded him like armor. Everything about Dylan was hidden, and he didn't understand why.

Touso's own spirit guides remained confused, and they were rarely so. Chosen shamans danced when they heard the gong while evil spirits ran. Dylan couldn't be evil if he had a flying horse. These sacred beasts of the gods were only assigned to shamans.

"Is this how you thank someone who saved your nephew?" Dylan demanded. "You've got some serious issues, bro."

"Touso, what is the meaning of this?" Lihue came to stand between them. He was also worried about the strange shadows around Dylan, but this was not the time. His biggest concern was for his grandson.

"Touso, this isn't the time," Pahoua voiced her husband's thoughts. Souls needed to feel safe when they returned home.

"He's dangerous!" Touso stood between Dylan and Kai's family. "He fell into the spirit world and did things he shouldn't have been able to do."

"He saved Fuechi," Mossy said, stopping in front of Touso. "He saved me, too. I know you don't like Dylan. I understand why you don't, but don't you think this is too much? He saved us! All I can think of is lying broken on that cold ground and never coming home. It was Dylan who got me out of there!"

Touso's expression softened for the first time. Mossy didn't resist as he pulled her into his arms. He whispered, "There's something very wrong with him, Mossy."

She nodded. Touso was right about one thing: there was something strange going on with Dylan Reed. But he wasn't evil.

He couldn't be.

She said, "He saved us. And I'm thankful. I'll take him home now."

"You're not going anywhere with him," Touso retorted.

Mossy froze as Touso grabbed her wrist and heard Du Yong's taunting voice.

Do you like being told what to do?

Chosen to sacrifice all your desires.

Sounds more like servitude to me...

"You do not tell me what to do." Mossy's voice trembled fiercely when she met his gaze. "I am not your slave or your servant!"

Touso released her in astonishment. "Mossy—"

"I'm taking Dylan home so Nia and Fuechi can have some peace. If you don't like it, you can go—" Mossy finished the sentence in her head because Fuechi was listening.

Dylan whispered something into Fuechi's ear, and the little boy grinned. He was definitely up to no good, but Touso didn't understand why Dylan had chosen Fuechi as a pawn.

As Mossy's car disappeared down the road, Touso felt helpless. He was angry and afraid, but mostly, he was confused.

I am not your slave or your servant!

He wondered why Mossy would ever think he saw her this way, and he missed her terribly when she was gone.

Chapter 8

It was a quiet drive out of Folsom. The further she drove, the more aggravated she became. Soon, she was speeding down the highway like a mad woman, and Dylan secured the seat belt over his hip.

"Stop looking at me like that," she said.

"I can't help it. You're incredibly sexy when you're about to get pulled over by the cops." Dylan shrugged casually and shifted the seat to get more comfortable.

Mossy glowered as she adjusted the speed to comply with the law. She was already walking a fine line with her parents that weekend and a speeding ticket would not serve her well.

"You're doing it again." Mossy glanced at Dylan, who seemed to be falling asleep.

"I'm tired."

"No, I mean, you're being an asshole again. Why do you always have to provoke him that way?" Mossy was frowning as she spoke.

Dylan opened one incredulous eye. "Are you serious? I believe your boyfriend got all big bad wolf and tried to knock me down."

"He's not like that!" Mossy flushed. "Not normally."

"Whatever he is, he needs to check that attitude." Dylan now opened both eyes to watch her skeptically. "You need to rethink what you're doing here."

Mossy inhaled, recalling how Touso had grabbed her wrist.

You aren't going anywhere with him.

It had been a command, and she couldn't shake how it made her feel. Mossy had spent her entire life following rules. Was she marrying Touso only to inherit more?

"You don't know him, Moss. Why are you doing this? Is it because you're still mad at me?" Dylan frowned.

"I'm not mad at you anymore," Mossy said, keeping her eyes on the road." You don't understand. Things are happening."

"Even so, nobody should be tied to anyone because of fear," he retorted.

The shaman community was not without its ranks, and Kai Khang was among the highest. He had ignored rules and etiquette to travel to the most dangerous realms. He met and collected many spirit guides there, who gave him their skills and knowledge. For these reasons, he was one of the strongest shamans. Even the power he passed on to Touso was insufficient to extinguish this prestige. No one could see, read, or use him unless he permitted it—except for Du Yong.

Demons could only sustain themselves with souls from fresh bodies. With Kai's death, his soul was obsolete as sustenance. But Du Yong was ever cunning and found use for him in other ways. As punishment for taking his own life, the gods sentenced him to an infinite time as a lost soul. He had no memories of his previous life. He was just sad and angry for no reason. But Du Yong could use him against his own brother, and Touso would never see what was happening until it was too late. Now that Kai was awake, things were about to become more complicated. He locked his gaze on his brother's chosen bride.

"I'm not afraid of him," Mossy said.

"Then why did you run?"

People ran all the time from fear. Or they tied themselves to people they didn't love because of it. Kai hadn't given up his own life so that his brother could become a prisoner. Even now, Mossy Cha was driving away with another man. It wasn't promising.

"Because of Fuechi."

Kai narrowed his gaze. "What about him?"

"He's already been through so much. Didn't you see his face? He was getting scared of all the yelling. I think he was afraid for you! I don't know what you did to that kid, but he seems to like you." When Mossy frowned in distaste, he almost laughed. She reminded him of his mother, chiding them for misbehaving. "And you don't belong there."

"You don't belong there either."

If he meant to hurt her, he'd succeeded. The worst part was that she wasn't sure he was wrong. She ached for that regular and predictable life where her only goal was to find a way to attend the college of her dreams and be with the boy she loved. It seemed so simple compared to fighting a vengeful demon to protect the man she... cared about.

Mossy gripped the wheel tightly. Life was more complicated than it used to be. For a long time, they drove in silence. Dylan was frustrated, and she couldn't blame him. She wasn't the same person he knew. As she glanced at him, watching the peculiar expression on his face, she knew that he wasn't the same either.

"What happened to you?" she asked.

Kai Khang returned to the shadows as Dylan Reed emerged.

"For the last time, I didn't know you would be there. I was trying to help Fuechi."

"That's not what I'm talking about," Mossy said, growing impatient. "I'm different now, but so are you. I see things. I can see spirits, and I can travel to the spirit world. But I know why I'm able to do these things. I want to know why you can suddenly do it, too."

"What? White boys can't jump into the spirit world?" Dylan grinned, but Mossy wasn't amused.

"If you're going to keep evading the truth, then we are done." Mossy sighed sadly.

"It happened on prom night."

The admission was so unexpected that Mossy nearly hit the brakes in the middle of the freeway. Instead, she looked at Dylan with growing anxiety.

"I was coming to find you after that jackass took you away. I was afraid he was going to hurt you." Dylan's tone was solemn as he spoke.

"Touso would never hurt me," Mossy said quietly.

"I didn't know that! I still don't know that," Dylan growled in frustration.

Mossy was startled by a flash of yellow light in his eyes but kept her tone even. "Keep going. Tell me the rest."

"I was headed to your house when I noticed this thing sitting in the back. It had eyes like fire. Before I knew what was happening, it attacked me. Then my car rolled over, and I was dying." Dylan was emotional, and Mossy wanted to comfort him across the center console. But she remained silent as he finished speaking. "I was dying, Moss! And the only person I could think of was you. I thought if I died, no one would protect you. So, I did it. I let it happen."

"What did you do?" Mossy's heart raced as she waited for the answer.

Dylan's voice was strangely calm. "You want to know why I'm different, Moss? Look at me. I'm not alone."

His eyes ignited a bright yellow light that grew into a fire pit. The entire car filled with the heat of rage. Instantly, Mossy swerved into the next lane, nearly clipping another car. She struggled to regain control of the vehicle among a chorus of screeching and honking. When Mossy finally pulled onto the shoulder of the highway, it took a long time to catch her breath. Then she turned to face the one beside her.

"Touso's dangerous, Moss." The certainty of his voice was as clear as the thing seething from his eyes. "And I'm not going to let him hurt you."

Mossy's spirit guides started jumping and soaring.

Look! Look! Look closer! They urged. But all she saw was someone she no longer knew.

Chapter 9

It was early evening when Mossy returned to the Khang residence. The house was quiet as she entered, but the abundance of energy present suggested she wasn't alone. Mossy heard laughter from the kitchen. She found Pahoua making dinner as Bao and Nia busied themselves baking. An opened bottle of wine explained all the giggles.

"What's going on?" Mossy smiled as she studied each of their tasks.

Nia was decorating a chocolate cake with white frosting and glanced up with a sparkle in her eyes. As she licked her fingers, she said, "Oh! You're back just in time."

Bao pulled out several cake toppers in the shape of small cars. "Today's Fuechi's birthday! I had it planned so differently, but a quiet dinner seems just as good with everything that's happened."

Nia agreed. "You got that right, sis. This girl just wants to chill out after all that drama, and my little boy is starving! What you got cooking there, Mama Kai?"

"*Kapoon*—Curry noodles and egg rolls." Pahoua threw a smile over her shoulder.

"How did you do that so fast?" Nia stared at the food on the stove with fascination.

As a pot of red curry broth simmered in one corner, Pahoua finished frying a large batch of egg rolls. "A good Hmong mama always has frozen egg rolls stashed away. You'll learn why as Fuechi gets older!"

Nia nodded knowingly. "That boy definitely eats like his daddy."

"Then he'll love the egg rolls. It was Kai's favorite appetizer," Pahoua replied wistfully as she tossed a look at Mossy. "How was the drive? Were you able to get Dylan back without much trouble?"

Mossy caught the wisdom in her eyes and grimaced. "It was okay. He's home, and I'm back. That's all that matters."

"You should have let him stay a little longer. He's not bad to look at!" Bao grinned over her glass of wine.

Nia snorted in amusement. "You got that right!"

Mossy flushed bright red as Pahoua chided Bao and Nia. "Less talking, more working, girls! Dinner's almost ready. I want to get everything outside as soon as Touso's finished."

"Where is he?" Mossy glanced around. She wondered if he was still angry.

"He's outside decorating the table and veranda," Pahoua replied.

"Mossy, please! Go help him. Touso's good at many things, but being extra fancy is not one of them," Bao pleaded dramatically.

"Tell him we're almost done." Pahoua smiled gratefully as Mossy turned to walk out the door.

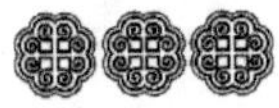

Evenings were her favorite in Spring and summer when the sun was the most excruciating. During this time, the sky was still bright enough to enjoy some time outdoors without any of the seething heat when the sun was up high. It made walks and naps so much more pleasant. After such a day, a nap sounded perfect. Mossy yawned as she stepped onto the porch. She nearly fell over as Fuechi threw himself at her.

"Miss Mossy!" His golden-brown eyes were bright with glee. "Where did you go? Did you bring back Mr. Dylan?"

Mossy blanked twice. She had only ever interacted with Fuechi in the spirit world. This was the first time they were meeting in real life. It felt strange, yet Fuechi seemed familiar—much like the rest of the Khang family. They were all connected.

"Hi, sweetie. No, I'm sorry. Mr. Dylan had to go home." She smiled ruefully, if only because the boy seemed to miss him. Fuechi had even called him "Daddy." He missed his father and was looking to fill that hole. She just didn't understand why he chose Dylan.

"Mossy, welcome back." Her future father-in-law arrived behind his grandson.

While Fuechi was lost, Lihue was pale with grief. But the color had returned to his cheeks, and a warm smile turned on his face. Lihue always seemed to waver between life and death. The head of the Khang household was too fragile during those uncertain times. But at the moment, he was energized by the return of his grandson.

"Yes. It seems there's reason for celebration." She smiled at Fuechi.

"Many reasons," Lihue agreed with a sparkle in his eyes. "You came back just in time. I invited your family over tonight. I hope that's okay."

Mossy parted her lips in surprise, and her heart lit up happily. She didn't realize how much she had missed them. "That's wonderful. Thank you!"

He was momentarily stunned when she hugged him. Then he smiled and patted her back affectionately. "Touso's waiting for you. He's a little cranky."

When she grimaced, he smiled with amusement. "My youngest son has never been good with social etiquette. With elders, he speaks when he is spoken to. With everyone else, he only speaks when he absolutely has to. In every case, you can trust his sincerity, but you may not always like what he has to say or how he says it. It's never mattered much until now."

Mossy blushed as she said, "We have much to learn about each other."

Lihue nodded in agreement. "Touso excels in everything but relationships. You'll have to be patient with him."

Mossy nodded as Lihue returned his attention to Fuechi. "Ready to get back to fishing?"

Fuechi beamed brightly and took his grandpa's hand. Soon, he was fishing from a rotating toy pond. His laugh was infectious as he caught one of the snapping fish, and Lihue applauded him proudly. It was heart-warming to see their bond.

Touso was wrapping presents when she found him. Her mouth dropped in surprise when she saw what he'd done to the veranda. Bao was wrong. Touso was a perfectionist even when he didn't enjoy the work.

Each column was swathed in cheerful yellow tulle and adorned with colorful balloons. It reminded her of a magical candy shop surrounded by floating lollipops. But in this decadent world of sweets, the shopkeeper refused to offer her any treats—not even a hello.

"Wow, this looks wonderful." Mossy smiled to hide her nervousness, but he never looked in her direction.

Touso continued wrapping the box as though she wasn't there. With the same precision used for folding ghost money, he carefully molded each corner with perfect creases. Then he topped it with a pretty bow and placed it along with the others.

She was excited, sure that he would face her now. But Mossy was annoyed when he turned his attention to a long strand of ribbon instead.

She said, "It's great that Fuechi gets to spend his birthday with his entire family. He called me Miss Mossy. That's so cute."

Silence.

Mossy furrowed her brows in growing exasperation. "He's a sweet kid. He asked if Mr. Dylan returned with me, but I told him he had to go home. Fuechi really likes him, so maybe I should go back and—"

Mossy felt a tug at her hand, and suddenly, she was sitting across his lap. The heat of his body melted away the last of her words. She froze as Touso lifted his eyes to meet her.

"Strings are important in our culture." She blushed as his gaze moved from her face to the rest of her body. "They lock away the things that mean to harm us. They protect us from falling into dangerous places. Strings connect things."

She watched as he began wrapping the ribbon around her wrist. "What are you doing?"

Before long, it was winding up past her elbow, and she resisted when the ribbon pushed against the back of her neck.

Slowly, Touso drew her in, much the same way Fuechi pulled the little fish from the pond. Only this time, Mossy was the fish, and Touso wouldn't be releasing her.

His eyes fell on the ribbon that crossed from his wrist to her own. "Strings bind souls together."

He drew her closer until there was no more than an inch between her mouth and his own. When the heat of his breath brushed her lips, Mossy swallowed with anticipation.

"This string represents our bond, Mo Cha. It can be short, or it can be long. It'll grow as long as necessary to keep us together. Nothing in this world can break it."

When Touso peered into her eyes, her spirit guides soared and danced. Gowli showed her a quick flash of their many lifetimes together, and Mossy gasped. When she tried to pull away, Touso tugged on the string once more. This time, their lips met, and Mossy lost herself instantly in his embrace.

Your soul has been chosen over and over... we have been with you in each new life, Gowli once said. This was also true of Touso.

As he kissed her, wrapping her in his blue energy, she saw glimpses of their past—laughing, dancing, singing... their children running across the grasslands. There was an abundance of joy followed by inevitable death. But they had promised always to find each other, and so they had. . .

"What am I seeing?" The flitter of images made her pull away in pain.

"It's us. It's our past," Touso replied quietly. "Sometimes, they even show me our future."

"They?"

He gently caressed her hair. "The spirit guides. Don't you understand, Mossy? Our union isn't random. We've always been together."

Mossy closed her eyes like it all hurt too much to bear.

"Mossy." He stared at her in confusion. When she still refused to look at him, he caught her by the chin and searched her pretty brown eyes. "Am I really so terrible?"

She met his gaze. "You don't understand, Touso. I've always had to do what I was told. Girls, especially, must never see the light of day without proper supervision. I thought I was finally going to be able to get away from that. Now, you're here, and as much as I want to protect you and keep you safe... we were chosen to be together. No matter how I see it, my life just doesn't feel like mine."

"You're neither my slave nor my servant. You'll be my wife. If I was too harsh, I'm sorry. If something ever happened to you—"

"Who would protect you?" Her tone was more bitter than she intended.

He studied her carefully. "That's what this is about. You think you're only here because I need you."

"Does it matter what I think? As long as I do my duty, everything will be okay." *It doesn't matter how I feel as long as I do what I'm supposed to do.* She smiled sadly.

The red ribbon between them sizzled as Touso peered into her eyes. "It matters to me. No matter how I found you, I accepted you. The question is, will you accept me the same way? Because that's all that matters. Not my life. Not destiny. Do you want to be here with me, Mossy?"

His passion stirred another vision from their past. Once upon a time, he had loved her and died for her. The gods had chosen her to protect him because it was her demand. She would protect him the way he had protected her!

Mossy nodded fiercely, and Touso smiled. Their hands tied by the ribbon were now curled together. She reached behind his head and drew him close. "I'm sorry. I just don't like being told what to do."

"Bossy Mossy doesn't like to be bossed around?" Touso teased.

She pulled back abruptly. "Who have you been talking to? The deceptively cute one or the annoying Irish twins?"

"I hate to break it to you, but they all threw you under the bus." Touso loosened the ribbon and looked at her more seriously. "With or without me, you are your own master. I'm just some guy who needs your help. But your life will always be your own, Mossy."

She grinned. "You're just some guy, huh? You're not exactly powerless, Touso."

"Even so, I'm better with someone watching out for me." He wrapped his arms around her shoulders. "But I would never want you to risk your life. Not even for me." Touso's heart still hurt whenever he remembered how she fell from the bridge.

Mossy sighed and rested against the warmth of his chest. "You know I can't promise you that. Just like I can't promise I'll listen to you."

Touso surprised her by laughing. "I can handle that. We'll work out our differences even if I have to toss you over my shoulder. Together."

"But what if I don't want to?" Mossy asked.

"Then I'll wait."

It was a simple answer that touched her heart, and Mossy turned to look into his eyes. *When did this stranger become so precious?*

She said, "You don't have to worry about Dylan."

When Touso's back stiffened, Mossy caressed the nape of his neck like taming an angry beast.

"I know there's something different about him, but he would never hurt me. Even still, he helped Nia and Fuechi. This day might have been much different without him."

For a long time, he didn't answer. There was no denying Dylan's role in Fuechi's rescue. But Touso didn't like surprises, and the mystery behind Dylan Reed's newfound powers was more disturbing than his relationship with Mossy. No matter how she felt, Touso and Dylan would never be friends.

"Touso?" As Mossy waited for an answer, there was a wave of new voices from a distance. She gasped in surprise as family members poured out of the house.

"Mossy!" Shengmii ran excitedly across the yard toward her big sister. Allen and Cheng followed with big grins while their parents stayed behind, chatting with Pahoua and Lihue.

"Yo, look at these two lovers!"

Mossy was surprised to see Thai waving at them from the patio. Sheng, his chosen bride, followed him quietly and closely.

Mossy and Touso turned to look at each other.

"Looks like it's time to start the party." Touso smiled and brushed his lips across her forehead.

"Promise me one thing."

"Anything."

"It'll be time for bed as soon as the party's over." She was incredibly exhausted and yawned as her body slumped against his chest.

"I couldn't think of anything better." He grinned mischievously.

Before Mossy could respond, Shengmii was already on top of them, pulling both into a tight embrace.

Chapter 10

Fuechi's eyes widened with excitement when he saw the white cake adorned with toy cars. Soon, a chorus of *"Happy Birthday"* rang from a much larger family than he had ever known.

Among all the smiling faces, there was one he wanted to see the most, but his daddy was nowhere to be found. As he blew out the candles marking his fifth birthday, Fuechi made a wish: he wished his daddy would come home.

When he blew with all his might and one candle remained burning, Nia became worried. After all, she was the one who had taught Fuechi that he had to blow out all his candles to make a wish come true.

Suddenly, a gust of wind took out the last flame, and everyone cheered. Fuechi squealed happily, and Nia sighed with relief.

Mossy and Touso smiled as Bao and Pahoua hovered over Fuechi. When they asked which piece he wanted, he only wanted the toy cars. It made everyone laugh—even Lihue.

Awakening

Something Kai always thought was impossible was unfolding: Nia and Fuechi were part of the Khang family. For the first time since his death, everyone was happy.

Dylan Reed was spread across the lawn chair, staring at the night sky. Even though the sun was still visible across the horizon, the full moon was already sitting high in the sky. The orange and yellow of the sun blended beautifully with the purple and blue of the night. As Dylan stared up at the moon, the spirit of Kai Khang emerged to ponder life with him.

"I don't think it's going to happen, bro." Kai smirked as he glanced at the other poor soul.

"What kind of shit are you talking about this time?" Dylan's tone was bored as he kept his eyes focused on the skies above.

"Mossy, of course. I'm still a little skeptical about her intentions, but after the way she dropped us off... that was cold."

Some things were too much, and Mossy stopped talking after Dylan revealed the secret of the thing inside of him. But now he wondered if she was afraid of his possession, or did she fear the warnings about Touso? Either way, she had turned away and refused to speak again. Mossy had much to think about, and Dylan didn't blame her.

"Mossy's always been smart," he insisted. "She's practical. What kind of life can she expect with a guy who chases evil spirits for a living?"

"Whoa, whoa, whoa! A little judgmental, aren't we?" Kai frowned. "We don't chase evil spirits. We banish them. You think people are just sane and healthy on their own accord? Evil doesn't fear humans because they're usually weak. Think of it like taking candy from a child. One must be especially strong to avoid evil and its influence and face it—humans fall too easily into temptation. Your soul remains fragile and distractable even when you're not cheating, lying, stealing, or killing. Shamans like Touso and I help get you back to ground zero so you can do better."

"Says the thing currently possessing my body," retorted Dylan with a scowl.

Kai Khang shrugged. Soon, his own tone became more wistful. "My time here is limited. I can already feel it."

Dylan's expression was hopeful for the first time. "Really? When?"

Kai snorted with amusement. "As soon as I take care of my family. It's the only reason I'm here." He stared at the moon, where he summoned images of his son and wife. They were still with his family, and they were happy.

"Taking over my body and distracting Mossy wasn't enough for you, huh?" Dylan arched his brows in disbelief.

"You ain't all that, Dylan Reed." Kai laughed. "Du Yong put me here because he wanted to use my powers against my brother. But I always knew this would happen. I just couldn't remember."

"How do you mean?" Dylan watched him.

"You have no idea who you're talking to, bro. As far as shamans go, you're staring at the crème de la crème. I was at the top of my game, man!"

"I thought we were done with bullshit." Dylan sighed and returned his gaze to the heavens.

"Anyway, our practice has rules and structure, just like anything else. Powerful shamans can see more than others, and vice versa—lesser shamans don't see as much. At the level I was able to reach before my death, no one can see what I'm about. That's why—boom! I can take out any demon and spirit before they even know I'm there. Same thing with other shamans. They might know of me, but they can't see what I can do—or what I am, for that matter. That's why Du Yong used me against Touso. I'm powerful, and I'm an asshole. That can do much damage if used the right way."

Dylan chuckled bitterly. "Then why didn't you just take out this monster yourself?"

"You don't get it, man." Kai shook his head. "Some things just aren't meant to be, no matter how much we want them. Most of us are just pawns, and I am most definitely that in this life. My destiny was to learn and build power to give it away to Touso. He's the only one who can save us all."

"You mean Fuechi." Dylan frowned.

"Yeah." Kai smiled sadly. "My kid. He's our future."

"And you saw this happen?" Dylan was skeptical, and Kai shrugged in response.

"My spirit guides show me things. I wasn't meant to be the hero. I was only meant to help the hero. Evil can only reap the souls of the living. This mother fucker Du Yong is ancient and powerful. He's picky about whom he eats, and it's made him strong. Too strong even for me. But he can't eat my soul if I'm dead, and I can only pass on my energy if I'm no longer alive."

"Energy is neither created—" Dylan began.

"—or destroyed. It's only passed on," Kai finished the law of energy, the only thing science and shamanism agreed upon. "And I gave it to Touso. Most of it, anyway."

Several spirit guides hovered over him, watching and waiting for his command. The wisest and strongest among them had always known he would return. They would serve him until those last moments came. Then they would all belong to Touso.

"So, you're saying he can kick my ass." Dylan's tone was rueful.

"Pretty much."

"But as long as you're here, you're technically me, right?" His blue-green eyes lit up.

"You're smarter than you look." Kai's spirit guides would protect Dylan Reed's body as long as he was there. But he wasn't sure how long he could stay since humans and spirits didn't belong together—unless they were spirit guides. Eventually, Dylan's body would reject him. There was no time to waste. "Listen, Dylan. I know you want Mossy Cha. In a better world, you could have her. You might still have a chance. But for now, she's keeping my brother and Fuechi safe. I can't let you mess with that."

Every hair on Dylan's body bristled as he remembered the events of the spirit world. He would never forget how broken she looked as he found her in the dark cell.

"Her life is in danger as long as she's tied to him!" Dylan growled.

"I know, bro. I get it." Kai relented. "We'll find another way. The spirits chose the brides to protect us, but it's a curse as much as a gift. I don't want my brother bonded to someone he doesn't love. There might be a way to do this so that you both get what you want."

Dylan nodded, and they returned their attention to the light of the moon. Fuechi closed his eyes to make a wish. When he blew out the candles, and one remained, Kai raised a finger to command the spirits of the wind. A moment later, the last flame was gone, and Fuechi was elated.

Dylan said, "He's a great kid. Nia's pretty cute, too."

Kai threw a dangerous glance at him, and Dylan laughed. "I'm just kidding, dude. Relax."

The souls of Kai Khang and Dylan Reed settled down to watch the rest of the images unfold across the moon. Kai kept his eyes on Fuechi as he unwrapped presents with glee. Meanwhile, Dylan's attention remained on Mossy Cha. Her eyes were as bright as the stars as she smiled at the little boy at the table, and he missed her very much. When Touso's face appeared next to her, Dylan's gaze hardened. He would get his girlfriend back, one way or another.

Fuechi Khang's last present was from his Uncle Touso. It was the large square box he was wrapping when Mossy first arrived. Regardless of the care it took to wrap it perfectly, his nephew only took a few seconds to tear up all the hard work. A moment later, he pulled out a large panda bear wearing a bucket hat.

Mossy gasped at the same time that Fuechi squealed with excitement.

He's coming, Mossy! He's coming! Aunt Padee's echoed. Mossy shuddered. What was inside that bear, and why was Touso giving it to him?

"It's a fishing bear!" Fuechi hugged it close to his chest. "He wears a hat like Daddy, too!"

"I love you!" The bear spoke cheerfully. "Let's go catch some fish!"

Everyone laughed as Fuechi squealed happily.

"Looks like your Uncle Touso knows you well." Pahoua snapped some more photos of Fuechi with his bear.

"Oh, Lord, I hope Uncle Touso likes to fish, too, because Mama sure doesn't." Nia looked worried. Kai was the outdoorsy one, while she much preferred indoor adventures. Their relationship thrived when neither forced the other to endure what the other couldn't.

"I got you, bud!" Touso grinned. "We can go any time."

"Yay!" Fuechi threw his arms around his hips and danced.

As this merriment continued, Mossy noticed Sheng sitting silently beside Thai. Like herself, the other young woman was now staying with her shaman to protect him. But something about Sheng's energy wasn't right. While everyone else chattered and laughed, Sheng stared menacingly at Fuechi and Nia.

A frown spread across her face. Sheng watched Nia the way Amy looked at Mossy—with jealousy. She glanced between Nia and the strange bride, wondering if they knew each other.

It was unlikely.

Suddenly, she and Mossy were staring at each other. She fell right into those bizarre black eyes that were as cold as the darkest well. Mossy remembered Emma from the spirit world.

Awakening

My name is Emma Sheng! Don't forget!

"Are you okay?" Touso's breath brushed against her ear, and Mossy was back in the present.

"Yeah."

He always knew when she was lying. "Tell me."

The moment was interrupted as Nia excused herself from the table. "I need to go grab something. I'll be back."

Fear gripped her heart when Sheng stood and followed her. Thai never noticed because he was busy laughing with Allen and Cheng over mouthfuls of cake.

Mossy pulled away from Touso.

"Where are you going?" His brows furrowed in concern.

"I'm just going to check on Nia." She tried to keep her voice calm. "It's been a big day for her, too."

Touso wasn't convinced but relented. "Come back soon. I'll miss you."

Her heart fluttered when he smiled. Then, she turned and hurried away.

Chapter 11

As Mossy entered the home, she kept thinking about Emma and the other girls on the cell block. They were all shamans with a special amulet that kept their powers restrained. If Emma and Sheng were the same people, what was in her body in the physical world?

Nia and Sheng were nowhere in sight. Her ears perked as someone cried in the other room.

"Nia!" Mossy found Nia weeping. "Are you okay?"

Nia turned in surprise. "Mossy! I'm sorry. I didn't know anyone else was here."

Mossy grabbed a box of tissue from one of the wooden tables and offered it to the other woman. She asked, "What's wrong?"

Nia accepted the tissue gratefully and wiped her eyes. When she looked at Mossy again, she said, "I just—I'm just so happy." Nia must have found her confusion comical because she laughed. "It was always just the three of us. I don't have much in the way of family, and Kai always said his family would disapprove. When we lost him—"

When Nia started crying again, Mossy hugged her. "I can't imagine how you must feel losing someone you love."

"I have my baby left, and that's all I need to keep going." Nia took a deep breath. "At least that's what I thought! But watching him tonight with the rest of Kai's family—he's so happy, and I'm so grateful! Fuechi won't have to grow up alone—like I did."

Mossy watched her sympathetically. Nia was a tall woman with a slim and athletic build. The butterfly tattoos along her arms made her seem especially tough and resilient. Butterflies symbolized hope, faith, and rebirth. She carried herself with grace and confidence, but she was also fragile because of what she'd lost.

Nothing could heal the wounds of losing someone you loved. Not even time.

"You're Hmong now, Nia Johnson," Mossy said and squeezed her hand. "You and Fuechi get a family and a clan. You'll never be alone again. I'm sorry."

Nia laughed at the woeful way in which Mossy spoke. "I think I can work with that. How are you doing? You've gone through many changes of your own."

Mossy glanced briefly between the bracelets on her wrist and the house around them. She said, "Life works in mysterious ways. We're still trying to figure it out."

"It certainly does. If you were twenty-one, we'd be having drinks." Nia nodded with empathy.

"You have to be twenty-one to drink?" Mossy asked, and they burst into laughter.

Nia grinned and gave her another hug. "I like you already, Mossy. Thanks for checking on me. I just needed a minute to get myself together, but I better get back before Fuechi wonders where I'm at. You ready to head back?"

"You go." Mossy waved at her. "I need to use the bathroom. I'll catch up."

Nia smiled at her one last time and then disappeared.

As Mossy went to the closest bathroom, she looked for Sheng. Even if the girl was shy, she should have seen them nearby. But there was no trace of the other chosen bride anywhere.

Had she already returned to the party? Mossy wondered as she walked into the dark bathroom and closed the door.

Almost instantly, the hairs on her body bristled. When Mossy lifted her eyes to the mirror, the sight she saw nearly stopped her heart. A girl with long dark hair stood facing the wall. As she slowly turned, Mossy inhaled sharply. The pretty face and the cold black eyes were just as they always were, except this time, Sheng was smiling.

"Sheng. What were you doing in here in the dark?" Her voice trembled as the other girl approached. But Sheng never answered. Instead, she lifted a pale hand and pointed a long finger.

Mossy noted the dullness of her skin and the strange ornaments that clung to the wrist. They looked like blessing strings but were black and carried the ominous energy of something much more sinister— like her eyes. Sheng's eyes resembled death! Mossy backed up against the door as the other girl reached for her.

"You're not really Sheng, are you?" Mossy whispered in horror. She thought of Emma stuck in that cell and stared at the thing standing before her now. Who or what was here in her place?

The creepy chosen bride sneered, showing yellow teeth against pale flesh.

Mossy's head throbbed, and her chest burned. Sheng wrapped her fingers around Mossy's throat. Little black veins grew from the neck and spread across Sheng's face.

"Who are you?" Mossy managed to choke out. "What do you want with Thai?"

Whomever this creature was, she was powerful. Even as Mossy's guides threatened to burst from her body, Sheng's dark energy locked them in. Long hair floated, darting at Mossy's face like serpents.

"Death." Sheng's voice was dry and brittle. "Death to them all!"

There was a knock at the door. The lights flickered and died.

"Sheng? Mossy? Who's in there?" Her cousin, Thai, was on the other side.

A second later, the lights returned, and Mossy was aghast to find herself alone. She quickly looked into the mirror. Her throat still ached from Sheng's death grip. But there was not a bruise or nail mark to prove it ever happened.

"Anyone in there?" Thai's voice pulled her back to reality

When Mossy opened the door, her cousin stared back in confusion.

"Are you okay?" Thai studied her strange expression and the room. "I thought I heard another voice in here. Have you seen Sheng?"

"I'm here." The soft voice came from down the hallway.

Relief flooded his face as he rushed to her side. "Where did you go?"

"I'm sorry. I got lost. It's a big house." Even as she spoke, her gaze remained on Mossy.

Thai laughed. "You're silly, Sheng. Next time, don't leave without telling me, okay? I was worried when I couldn't find you."

When Sheng nodded, he smiled. "It's late, and it's time to go home."

"Thai—wait!" Mossy surprised them both with the urgency of her tone.

He turned to look at her. "Mossy? What is it?"

All breath left her body. Mossy couldn't form words because Sheng was choking her again with her eyes. Mossy's face turned red as her throat closed.

"What's wrong?" Thai frowned in concern.

Mossy shuddered against the clammy hand that touched her forehead. Sheng frowned and said, "She doesn't look well. She feels warm! Oh, Babe, I think you're right. We should leave so Mossy can rest."

Thai nodded in agreement with his bride but couldn't resist a grin. "Poor cuzzo! Becoming a married woman is tough work, isn't it? I'll get your parents. It's time for all of us to go home. We'll let you rest."

It wasn't until the rest of Mossy's family started pouring into the room that Sheng released her. She gasped at the first full breath that filled her lungs and was startled when a pair of hands touched her hips.

It was Touso. "Mossy. Are you okay?

Mossy grabbed his shirt and pointed at Sheng, who smiled and laughed at something Thai said. It was the most normal she'd ever seen her behave. "Do you see anything wrong with her?"

Touso looked confused as he glanced between Sheng and Mossy. "You mean she's too young? I agree they're both too young, but it's unusual circumstances."

"No!" Mossy shook her head anxiously. "She's not normal, Touso."

"She looks fine to me."

Mossy stared at him incredulously. Touso Khang saw everything! So, why couldn't he see Sheng for who she was? Then Mossy remembered the red amulet that had locked away her spirit guides. Her eyes darted toward the black strings across Sheng's wrists, and she realized what those strings meant. Someone with very powerful magic was protecting her, and she could imagine only one group: the necromancers!

"Mo, why do you look like that? Are you not feeling well?" Blia Cha touched her forehead just as Sheng had done, except her hands were warm with the energy of life. She frowned and turned to look at Touso. "Would you go get her some water?"

He nodded and quickly complied with his future mother-in-law's request.

"Tell me what's wrong." Blia guided her daughter to sit.

When Mossy didn't speak and looked anxiously in the other direction, her mother sighed. "I know you're mad at us."

Mossy turned with a look of confusion.

"I'm sorry we didn't tell you about Touso and the curse," Blia explained, shaking her head. "We know how you are—m in the old traditions. How could you process becoming the bride of a cursed shaman?"

I would have run even faster, Mossy thought. Blia understood this just by the bewildered expression on her face.

"So, we didn't tell you. We just hoped you'd like him enough to change your stubborn ways!" Even as her mother admonished her, she smiled. "You do like him now, don't you? You both seem to be getting along much better than before."

Mossy nodded slowly.

"Your father and I are so relieved!" Blia choked up, and Mossy frowned as she wiped tears from her eyes. "We've always been so scared for you—ever since Touso's Aunt Padee told us about the evil spirit looking for you!"

Now, Mossy was anxious. She asked, "What did Aunt Padee tell you?"

"She said you called something that should never find you. You were so small, but I remembered how scared you were. Touso was the only one who could calm you down," her mother replied. When she saw the expression on Mossy's face, her eyes sparkled with amusement. "I've told you before that you've known each other longer than you think."

"Why couldn't I remember any of this until now?" Mossy grasped her temples as though she were in pain. She didn't understand.

Blia reached for her hand. "Sometimes the only way to deal with trauma is by forgetting, Mo. You were young, and you were scared. Aunt Padee said you kept crying about a monster. I thought you were just being naughty, but she believed you. She insisted on performing a ritual that would lock your soul to your body and hide you from spirits. And when she was done, it was as though nothing ever happened. You stopped crying about the monster."

Mossy stared in disbelief. "She made me forget."

"She protected you, and you forgot about it until now." Her mother shook her head remorsefully. "She didn't say much then—just that you were special and needed to be careful. Then when Touso's family arrived that night and explained what you did for him in the spirit world—what that meant—we knew it was all connected. We also knew what had happened to his brother and his chosen bride!"

Kai Khang and his bride died because they had broken protocol and failed to protect each other. "Mossy, you have no idea how worried your father and I have been. You'll be safe now!"

As her mother expressed this relief, Mossy glanced at Thai and Sheng. They were laughing and chatting with family across the room. When Sheng smiled and playfully hit Thai, she almost looked normal. Then she caught Mossy staring, and her black eyes emanated an energy that made Mossy's stomach curl.

She quickly looked away. Her mother was wrong. She was anything but safe.

"Mossy?" Blia studied her daughter carefully. "Why do you look so scared?"

She woefully shook her head. "I'm so confused, Mom! I don't know what to do!"

A long silence passed between them before Blia said, "It's my fault."

Mossy blinked in surprise. "What do you mean?"

"This all happened so quickly. I didn't prepare you well enough to know what to expect." Blia looked excited, even as she lowered her voice. "I'm so happy that you came to your senses and accepted your role by Touso's side. It's best this way. But I know this also comes with unfamiliar responsibilities."

Mossy realized what her mother was referring to and flushed with embarrassment. "Mom—"

"This is a new chapter in your life, Mo. Every girl must become a woman. When it happens—"

Mossy raised a hand in protest. "Mom!"

Blia laughed. "Fine. Maybe I don't need to say it after all." Her mother's eyes glistened brightly as she touched her face. "When did you grow up? We miss you. Your siblings still think you're coming home."

A pout touched her lips as she realized her home was no longer hers.

"Why don't you two spend the night before graduation?" Blia offered when she noticed her daughter's dismay. "It'll be closer and easier than coming from Folsom."

Despite herself, Mossy nodded excitedly. She had forgotten that high school graduation was on the horizon. As she thought about school, Mossy frowned.

"Mom, have you heard from Cindy?" Her young friend had been oddly quiet since she left their home.

"No, but I'm not surprised. That family's difficult." Blia shook her head. "But now's not the time to worry about Cindy. She'll be fine. For now, just worry about your wedding with Touso."

My wedding with Touso... just those words alone made her forget all her previous worries.

"That's in a few days, too," Mossy said breathlessly.

"Even so, you're here." Blia grinned at her daughter's innocence. "That means your new life has already started."

As Touso returned with a glass of water, Mossy thought only of her "responsibilities." He seemed confused as she grabbed the water and chugged it down too quickly. Blia chuckled and nodded at Touso.

"Take care of my daughter, son-in-law."

"Of course."

The moment was lost to another series of formalities and small talk as Keng, Lihue, and Pahoua joined them. Keng gave Touso another pep talk about his daughter's stubbornness. Pahoua promised that her son would refrain from being too bossy so that Mossy could tolerate him more. Lihue expected that they would both get along well with time. Blia reminded Mossy to behave like a "good" Hmong girl and listen to her husband. Before too long, everyone was saying their goodbyes.

Mossy embraced her siblings long and hard before they disappeared into the car. She missed their ruckus already. The only ones she didn't see again were Thai and Sheng. They were the first to get into the car, waving quickly as though they had somewhere to go. But since Thai couldn't drive, he and Sheng had to wait as the rest of the family finished their goodbyes.

When Blia saw the scowl on her face, she asked, "What's wrong, Mossy?"

"Mom, please watch Thai," she pleaded. "Just pay attention. I don't trust his bride."

Blia looked surprised and said, "You're always worried about others before you worry about yourself. Your cousin will be fine. But I promise I'll watch him."

Mossy hugged her parents one last time, and then they were gone. The pains of abandonment washed over her like a wave, and she desperately wanted to go home. But Mossy smiled as she turned and saw Touso waiting by the door. He was her home.

Chapter 12

Nia was admittedly glad when the Khangs insisted they stay with them until the danger passed. While Fuechi snuggled beside his grandpa, listening to a tale about their great ancestor, Shee Yee, it was as though they'd never been strangers.

For the first time, Nia didn't feel alone.

As Mossy chatted with her new sisters, she noticed Touso's absence. She finally bid everyone goodnight to find him.

"Your new life has already started," her mother had said.

Living with Touso meant she was his wife, and he was her husband. Her heart swelled with nervous anticipation as she entered their room.

"Touso?" She followed the sound of running water and found him kneeling by the tub. "What are you doing?

"I thought you'd like a bath." He pulled his fingers from the warm water and took her hands. "Come on. The water's perfect."

The room smelled of lavender and mint. Even though it was warm, she could feel the heat rise in her cheeks. She was grateful when he drew her into his arms, if only so she could hide her embarrassment.

"How are you feeling?" he asked.

"I'm tired." After a while, she added, "And I'm scared."

Touso stepped back to look into her eyes. "Why are you scared?"

"I'm seeing things I don't understand. I don't even know if it's real."

She had watched her family drive away with Sheng. But what could she do? No one had seen what she saw. Nobody could see Sheng for what she was. If someone like Touso couldn't see her, then it couldn't be real.

Could it?

"If you feel that it's real, then it's real," Touso said as if he'd read her mind.

"Even if I'm the only one that can see it?" Society called that "crazy."

"That happens very often with people like us."

People like us.

"What do you know about the necromancers?" Mossy asked.

"What do you want to know?" Touso frowned.

"How powerful are Alang and his father?" She felt shivers just saying their names. "Can they really control the dead? Can they control evil spirits, too?"

"They make deals to control things that shouldn't happen. Mossy, why are you asking this?"

"Something's wrong with Sheng. Something's wrong about all the chosen brides the necromancers are finding!" she exclaimed, unable to forget Lisa's screams as the hooded creatures took her away. "Touso, you don't know the kind of things I saw in the spirit world!"

He drew her into his arms when she couldn't stop trembling.

"These girls were locked up, and I think I know who they are," said Mossy.

Touso cocked his head. "What are you saying?"

"I think they're the souls of these supposed 'chosen' brides!" Fear spread across her face. "Emma and Lisa said they're all shamans. We wore these amulets that kept us from using our powers. The necromancers must be working with Du Yong to trick the other Khang shamans because that *thing*—" Mossy shook her head. "That thing is not Sheng!"

Touso considered all this information carefully. "The necromancers have always been shady, but I never thought they would go to this length for power. And if you're right, these fake brides are dangerous to all the Khang shamans. But we'll have to find all the souls Du Yong has stolen, and that won't be easy."

"The Black Door?" Mossy's eyes were hopeful. It had brought Dylan and Fuechi directly to her.

"The Black Door is an entity of its own. It is difficult to find and even more difficult to summon. As it is, my father has already promised many pigs and steers to the spirits who helped hunt the door so I could find you."

Mossy thought of all the pigs' jaws on the altar. It was usually a soul for a soul, and Touso was telling her the Black Door's price was much more expensive.

"What do we do?" Mossy searched his eyes.

"I'll summon the council tomorrow. We'll start there," Touso promised. "As for now, I want you to relax."

"How do I relax at a time like this?" Anxiety exuded from her pores.

Touso raised his palm. "You see this hand? It's calm. Shaky hands don't do well with hard work. But when the hands are calm, they work more diligently. Your soul is the same way, Mossy. It's frazzled by all these new things you're discovering. You must learn to stay in control, even when the world is falling apart."

Mossy sagged against his body and moaned like a child. "I don't want to."

Touso chuckled. "Come on. I'll help you."

Mossy froze as Touso's fingers slid beneath her shirt. A strange energy buzzed from his flesh and washed over her body in teasing waves of blue.

"It's time for our bath." He gently lifted the shirt over her head.

"Our bath?"

Touso grinned at the confusion on her face. "You like baths, don't you?"

Mossy nodded breathlessly as he tugged on the waist of her pants. After it fell, he walked around and lifted her hair. His lips brushed the side of her neck and lingered on her shoulder. Then her bra tumbled to the ground.

"Are you relaxing?" His breath teased her ear.

"No!" Mossy gasped.

He was in front of her again. Touso placed her hands on his firm belly and caught her when she tried to pull away. "Don't be afraid of me, Mossy. You're in control."

Tentatively, she explored the warm skin beneath his shirt and lifted it over his head. His eyes remained on her as her fingers curled into the top of his pants. As the last piece of clothes fell to the floor, Touso smiled. Meanwhile, Mossy was transfixed by the curve of muscles along his chest. He was beautiful.

"All that I am is here in front of you." He tipped her chin with a finger. "With everything I have, I'll take care of you."

The next thing she knew, he was scooping her into his arms. Mossy inhaled sharply as he stepped into the tub, sinking them into the warm, bubbling waters. Her senses filled instantly with the aromas of lavender and mint. As Touso leaned against the tub, he coaxed her head to his chest.

"Of everything in this world, I'm the last thing you'll ever have to fear, Mossy." He gently brushed the side of her hips. "Now relax. I'll be here if you need me."

The beating of his heart was like a lullaby. It didn't take long for the rest of her body to let go. She closed her eyes and curled her fingers over Touso's hand. He never moved any more than necessary to make sure she was safe. As Mossy drifted off to sleep, she knew that Dylan was wrong. Touso wasn't dangerous. It was everything else.

Chapter 13

She didn't remember much after the bath. There were clipped images of Touso lifting a sleepy Mossy out of the tub. Then he was gently drying her from head to toe. When she awoke the following day, Mossy was tucked comfortably in bed, wearing one of his shirts. But Touso wasn't there with her.

As she sat up, searching the room, her ears perked at a soft snore. She crept out of bed and found Touso sprawled along the couch. His arms were crossed over his chest like he was cold.

Mossy smiled helplessly. He had put her to bed and fell asleep like a gentleman on the couch. Now, she hovered over his face, studying the gentle turn of his cheeks and nose. Slowly, she traced the curve of his mouth with a finger before lowering her lips to kiss them. Instantly, his chest filled with life, and she giggled as he wrestled her onto the rug below.

"Good morning," she murmured between his lips.

"Perfect morning." He continued trailing kisses along her neck.

"Why are you here?" Mossy sighed as his mouth teased her ear.

"I was practicing control." His voice was thick with sleep and desire.

"Your... self... discipline..." Mossy nearly lost her train of thought as his hands disappeared underneath her shirt. "Is very admirable!"

"I'm glad you think so. It actually feels quite painful."

Mossy blushed as he lifted his eyes to meet her.

"How are you feeling?" She had been a ball of anxiety, and he was glad to see she was in better spirits that morning.

"Much better. You're a good bathing partner." She ran a finger along his jawline. "And how did you sleep?"

"Let's just say it was a different kind of struggle." His expression was thoughtful as he spoke, and soon, his fingers were toying with the bare flesh of her hips again.

"I never pictured you like this."

"How do you mean?" Touso looked at her.

"You're usually so serious. But you're kind of a flirt, Touso Khang." She shot him an accusatory look that made him laugh.

"I'm never like this." Touso sounded surprised himself. As they sat looking at one another, he said, "I've never felt this way about anyone. You're an extraordinary gift, Mossy Cha."

"Maybe those spirits know what they're doing after all, huh?" As she spoke, a colorful swirl of mystical beings danced around them.

Someone knocked at the door. Mossy and Touso groaned at once.

"We'll be right out," Touso shouted.

"Don't be late!" Bao seemed particularly amused as she sauntered off.

As Touso pulled Mossy from the floor, she asked, "What's the plan today?"

"It's Memorial Day. We always attend a celebration to remember the veterans from the secret war," he explained.

"Will there be any animal sacrifices involved?" she asked nervously. The last thing she wanted was to attend another large gathering with lots of chores and cooking!

Touso chuckled. "No, just a lot of already cooked food. But I have no doubt you could handle any chore tossed your way. The chosen bride I saw was plucking chickens very impressively the first time I glimpsed her."

Mossy gasped, "Were you checking me out?"

"Maybe." He looked coy. "You were cute."

Mossy frowned. "Cute, huh? I'm probably not as polished as the women you're used to!"

Touso, handsome and intelligent, was a few years older than her. It wouldn't surprise her if there were a string of women in his past.

"No." His expression was thoughtful as he drew her near. "I'm not used to anything of a sort. But I like cute."

Mossy's knees melted as he nuzzled her ear. Then he said, "I was just hoping we could hang out today?"

Mossy grinned. "Touso Khang, are you asking me out on a date?"

"Yes. After we've gotten engaged. That's how cool kids do it these days, right?" His face was so serious that Mossy couldn't resist a laugh.

"You are a funny guy, you know that?" She touched his face affectionately.

"Don't tell anyone. You'll ruin my reputation," he said woefully.

Mossy kissed him, lingering on the softness of his bottom lip. "I would love to just hang out with you, Touso. We don't know each other very well, do we?"

"No. But that doesn't change anything." When she looked curious, he explained, "We belong to each other."

As they kissed again, there was another knock at the door.

"We're coming!" They both shouted at the same time.

Touso always checked in with his father first thing in the morning. As he did so, Mossy found Pahoua in the living room. She was sorting supplies near a small wooden table and didn't notice as Mossy walked in.

"Good morning, Mom."

Pahoua was pleasantly surprised when Mossy greeted her formally for the first time. Because the wife of a son was a new daughter, the wife was expected to treat his mother as her own. As Pahoua smiled and beckoned her to come, Mossy felt extremely lucky. The Khang family already felt like her own.

"Welcome to your first lesson!" Pahoua's eyes were bright with excitement. She opened packs of joss paper next to a box of various items. She lifted her gaze as she burned several pieces of paper in gold-tone bowls. "We're building your altar!" `

Mossy gasped. "My what?"

"Your spirit guides need a place to rest. You also need somewhere to channel and filter your energy. The altar is important for every shaman and their spirit guides, my daughter! With that said, a shaman must build her own altar. It makes it more special!" She handed Mossy a clean towel and spray. "But first, we must clean everything. Even spirits like a tidy home! You clean the table while I finish burning bad energy off these plates and cups."

Mossy watched in awe as Pahoua continued lighting pieces of joss paper on fire within the bowls and plates. She waved smaller glass cups over a burning candle. When Pahoua frowned, Mossy quickly sprayed the table.

Her new altar was a rectangular coffee table made of solid wood. After wiping it down, Pahoua had her cover it entirely with white Joss paper. Then she sent Mossy to clean the bowls and glass cups again with warm water.

"Everything must be new and untainted," Pahoua explained as she handed Mossy an unopened water bottle.

After Mossy filled four cups, Pahoua handed her a small container of uncooked rice and an egg.

"The bowls represent their homes, the rice is the foundation, and the incense sticks are the pillars that keep them safe. You must be careful you don't disturb their homes when you clean. Just in case, the egg represents the parrot that will warn them if anything is amiss!" Pahoua warned.

Next, she had Mossy fill two plates with toasted rice. "Keep them well fed with fresh food, always."

After Mossy completed these tasks, Pahoua handed her a vase and a small bouquet, which was also waved over the candle to rid bad energy. Pahoua said, "White flowers represent purity, and help keep away negativity."

The table was complete with four finger bells and two candles. As Mossy lit the candles and incense from right to left, Pahoua passed her a gong. "Now, it's time to show them what you've made for them."

Mossy's mouth dropped.

"It's not hard." Pahoua's eyes bubbled with amusement. "You just call them like you call your siblings to come eat."

"Do I have to do it in Hmong?" Mossy asked bashfully. Unlike the rest of them, she didn't speak it fluently.

Pahoua shrugged. "Start however you like. They'll let you know if they want you to speak in Hmong or any other language."

Mossy narrowed her gaze and hoped her spirit guides wouldn't be difficult.

"Now hit the gong twice. As you turn to your right, do it again, and repeat until you complete a full circle. Once you're facing the alter again, start calling the names of each of your guides. Tell them to come home and rest. Today, you have built them a home," Pahoua said with a happy grin.

At first, Mossy felt awkward. She was so engrossed in this discomfort that she never noticed Touso watching from the hallway. He smiled as she stepped clumsily and nearly tripped over her own two feet. She even forgot to hit the gong. Feeling sorry for his bride, Touso sent a string of energy in her direction. Mossy was still frowning when the blue light formed a familiar figure before her eyes. Touso's ghostly face grinned back as his hands came to her hips.

It's just like dancing.

Mossy stared at him.

Hit the gong.

She did it twice.

Now step.

She followed.

Awakening

As Mossy completed the circle, hitting the gong perfectly now at every turn, she stared into Touso's sparkling eyes. The warmth of his energy playfully nudged at her hips until soon, Mossy faced the altar. Then the blue lights tightened around her shoulders like a pair of loving hands.

Now sing. Call them home.

"I call to Gowli, Chee, Pao, and Kalia... I have built you a home and now call you to eat. Come eat and rest. Come eat and gather your strength in this place I have built to keep you safe. Gowli, Chee, Pao, and Kalia, come home!" Mossy called them repeatedly and spoke in the language they wanted to hear: Hmong.

As Touso's blue figure disappeared, a swirl of colorful lights took his place. They danced around Mossy, chuckling and giggling excitedly. Mossy was surprised at her own happiness. But she rolled her eyes as Chee started to complain.

I'll get you your wine next time! Mossy promised. She couldn't help laughing as Chee huffed away.

A soft light rose beside her, and Mossy leaned into its warmth. *I'm proud of you, Mo. This is just the beginning.*

Mossy smiled as Gowli briefly appeared and disappeared. Soon, all of her spirit guides were feasting and forgot about the young shaman watching over them.

"This is now their place of peace. This is your haven as well." Pahoua stood next to Mossy, staring at the altar. "You'll come here daily and light the incense. It will rejuvenate both you and your guides to see that light and smell the sandalwood in the air. Anything you ask, any instructions you give, will happen here. This is your safe place, Mo. Even if it's only to cry, this altar will serve you."

Mossy studied the pretty altar that looked quaint next to the massive ones that belonged to the other shamans in the house. She used to think it was one large altar, but now she recognized each as a standalone unit. The Khang family members had been doing this for a long time.

"One day, your altar will rise to that level," Pahoua said with a knowing smile. "Until then, there is much to learn."

As Mossy kept her eyes steadily on the altar, she thought, "That's what I'm afraid of."

Chapter 14

The Memorial Day event at Discovery Park was large and festive, with dance and singing performances from local artists. The organizers chose that location so attendees could dip in the water when it got too hot. There was something for everyone to enjoy, between the food, games, performances, and water activities.

Mossy was especially enamored with food, dragging Touso between each table. As she scarfed down spicy pork sausages with sticky red rice, Touso remembered her appetite at the Shamans' Club. She ate the way bears did before hibernation. But as long as she was happy, he'd keep feeding her. When surviving guerilla warfighters took the stage to speak, a respectful hush came over the crowd.

Ger Yang was only a teenager when he worked as a scout for the CIA. His nickname was "Bird" because of how quickly he flew through the jungle to report news of enemy soldiers. Between these missions, he learned how to treat wounded casualties. These experiences led him to become a doctor later in life. But Ger had lost a young family.

"In those days, you became a man much earlier. I lost my wife and our son when the Lao soldiers came. But it was in their honor that I continued to fight." Now, Ger was seventy years old and stood at the podium with a walking cane that looked like a royal scepter in his hand. His mission was to make sure that no Hmong child forgot about their warrior spirit.

"The Hmong have fought for freedom since the beginning of time. With communism looming over us—trying to take away our livelihood, those days were no different. Seeing all these bright faces today, I know our mission was not fought in vain. Continue making us proud."

Mossy wiped away tears as Mr. Yang was led off the stage.

"Are you okay?" Touso held her hand and frowned.

Mossy smiled sheepishly. "I always cry when I hear these stories. It reminds me of my *Pog*, grandmother. When the enemy soldiers attacked their village, she had to leave behind her beloved dog and its puppies. Can you imagine abandoning the things you love just to survive?"

"It wasn't just to survive. It was to save her family," Touso said.

Mossy frowned. "She was just a little girl, Touso!"

He shrugged. "At some level, we understand our roles, even before we're old enough for anything to happen. Your grandmother made those tough sacrifices because her soul knew she would eventually give birth to my bride's father."

"That sounds like a lot of trouble for little ol' me. I'm just a girl trying to graduate high school!" Mossy made a face.

Now, it was Touso's turn to frown. "I don't think you know how important you are. You're more than just a girl. You've always been a warrior."

Mossy inhaled sharply. His amber eyes were like crystal balls that reminded her of a different time and place. But there was much hidden behind a dark cloud.

She smiled. "Today, I just feel like a girl trying to get to know her future husband. What's your favorite color?"

"Blue."

"Favorite food?"

"Hot sauce."

Mossy frowned. "That's a condiment."

"Hot sauce makes everything better." Touso shrugged. "Especially if it's military food."

"Fine. What about your favorite song?" she asked.

"I don't really have one," he replied.

Mossy's face turned with shock. "What? Everyone has a favorite song!"

"I don't. I like quiet." He didn't look regretful, at the least. After a thoughtful moment, he said, "My brother used to sing 'Don't Worry, Be Happy' all the time, and I kind of picked it up as a coping mechanism. I guess if what I like is what I sing the most, it would be that song."

Don't worry, be happy... Mossy wondered again why it seemed so familiar.

"What's yours?" Touso asked, interrupting her thoughts.

He wasn't prepared for what happened next. Mossy leaped to her feet and started singing—in Korean! Eventually, he worked out the English words "save me," but they were few and far between. She sang into an imaginary mic and danced gleefully, only slowing when she noticed his strange expression.

"What—you don't like BTS?" she demanded.

"I don't know what that is," he admitted.

Mossy's eyes grew incredibly wide as she fell beside him and grasped his face between her hands. "Touso…"

"What?"

"I knew you were older than me, but I didn't think you were that old." She shook her head remorsefully.

Touso watched his bride as she went on to list several other songs he'd never heard of. Every time he shook his head, her face scrunched together adorably. Eventually, he stopped listening and kept saying "no" because her reactions were entertaining. Finally, Mossy sighed and said, "I'll talk to my dad about your dowry. Don't worry. You've only lost a smidgen of your value."

"Is that right?" he asked, arching a brow.

She nodded. "You can cook, at least?"

"Yes, ma'am."

Her heart always raced a little faster when he saluted her. She grinned and crawled around his back. "Forget songs. Want to know what my mother taught me about caring for a husband?"

Touso blinked in surprise. They were sitting on a blanket under a tree that protected them from the full blast of the day's heat. His parents were visiting with other families while Bao flirted with a young man who had successfully intrigued her with papaya salad.

Alone, Mossy started massaging his muscular shoulders. "My mother says a good woman takes care of her man."

"Your mother is very wise," Touso said. "What does that entail?"

"Well, it depends on your love language," Mossy replied as Touso's muscles flexed and softened underneath her fingers. "I think your love language is touch."

He chuckled. "I don't think so. I've always avoided touching people."

When Mossy dropped her hands, he frowned. "Why did you stop?"

"You just said you didn't like touch!" Mossy grinned knowingly.

Touso growled and placed her hands back on his shoulder. "You may proceed with your wifely duties."

Mossy rolled her eyes but smiled as she continued softening the knots at the base of his neck. "Why do you avoid touch?"

"Do you really have to ask?" When Mossy shrugged, he continued, "Every life has energy, and every touch is a gateway. I feel too much when people touch me. It's not so bad when they're happy. But when it's pain, sorrow, regret, or anger... it hurts my soul."

Mossy rested her hands on his hips. "And what do you feel now?"

When Touso turned to look at her, his nose brushed gently against her own. He studied the dark almond-shaped eyes that glistened like jewels underneath the shade. He savored the warm energy that flowed from her body. The loose strands from a messy bun only made her prettier. Touso said, "I don't know if I can say those things out loud."

As Mossy blushed, he brushed his lips against her mouth. "What else?"

"What else?" she repeated in a daze.

"What else did your mom teach you about caring for a man?" he teased.

She straightened. "Oh! I don't know if you'll like this one."

"Try me." Touso arched his brow.

"She said... 'Always keep them chasing you!'" Mossy leaped to her feet. "Let's see how fast you are!"

Before Touso could react, Mossy was gone. As he climbed to his feet, he saw the puzzled expression on his parents' faces. Mossy had dashed right by them like a thief. Meanwhile, Bao laughed so hard she almost dropped her food.

She shouted, "You better hurry up, Touso—before someone else catches her!"

Mossy was fast and already on the other side of the park. He knew she was headed toward the river. With a growl, Touso took off after her.

Mossy always enjoyed running. It was the only time she felt truly free. As she ran down the path toward the beach, feeling the air hit her face and the blood rush through her veins, she realized how much she missed it.

She glanced over her shoulder, wondering how long it would take Touso to catch up. She giggled when he was still nowhere in sight. They were supposed to get to know each other better. Today, he'd learn to keep up.

Mossy only slowed her pace after arriving at the river. Feeling sticky from the heat, she strolled toward the water. That was when she noticed a young girl with blue pigtails.

Kalia! Mossy leaped joyfully to meet her elusive dragon friend.

Kalia's eyes lit up when she saw Mossy.

"That's why you're never home. You're always playing!" Mossy wagged her finger with mock annoyance.

Kalia grinned. "Shhhhh. My parents are always watching! But today, I got my brother to come out with me!"

Mossy frowned. *Brother?*

She turned to look at the figure sitting lazily on a tree trunk that had fallen into the water. At first, Mossy thought it was a young woman because of the long, sweeping hair down the back. But a closer look revealed it was very much a man—a very handsome one at that. He looked like Kalia with the same blue-black hair and eyes as black as night. When he looked at her, his expression was bored. But for a few seconds, Mossy fell into the depths of those eyes. Something was hiding there.

"Kalia, must we really stay here all day?" The sharp tone of his silky voice pulled Mossy back to reality.

Kalia pouted. "Argh! Work is boring. The spirit world is boring! I just want to play! Stop being boring, Kaw."

Kaw. It meant "fang" in Hmong. The ominous meaning made Mossy shudder. "This world is boring."

Mossy realized he was looking directly at her, and she frowned. But before she could say anything, Kalia grabbed her hands.

"Ignore my brother, Mossy. He's grumpy, but he means well! Will you play with me before we go?" Kalia implored desperately.

Mossy forgot about Kaw and laughed. "Yes! But just for a little bit. Touso's looking for me."

Kaw rolled his eyes. "Great. Someone else I can't stand."

Now, Mossy turned to glare at him. "Do I know you?"

It was such a familiar scene that she nearly expected him to reply, "Everyone knows me, Mossy!"

Instead, Kaw said, "No."

"Let's play!" Kalia begged again.

Mossy threw Kaw another seething look as Kalia tugged her into open water.

When the dragon girl said she wanted to play, Mossy thought she meant making sand castles, throwing rocks, or even just swimming. But she should have known better. Kalia, the dragon guide and protector of the realms, was anything but boring.

"You ready?" Kalia grinned mischievously.

"For?" Mossy's eyes grew wide with suspicion.

A moment later, she found out. Kalia changed from girl to dragon in an instant. A tail with glittering pink-blue scales curled around Mossy's body, and soon, she was straddling the back of Kalia's neck. She held on tight as the dragon dove underneath the water and tried not to scream when she spun like a torpedo. On the surface, the water rose into giant waves that hit the beach with a loud crash.

Mossy came up from the water just in time to see other beach patrons run excitedly toward the new waves. On a hot day, no one questioned mysterious water activity. Instead, they were thrilled. The next time Mossy disappeared into the water, she was much more relaxed, and when Kalia blasted through the length of the American River, Mossy remembered how it felt to run.

She felt free.

Awakening

Touso Khang stared at the beautiful girl lying across the sandy beach. She looked peaceful and happy, with a smile plastered across a glistening face. She must have just come from the water because she was utterly soaked from head to toe. His eyes lingered on a wet shirt that clung to her body like a second skin.

"Mossy, are you awake?"

She nodded without opening her eyes.

"Did you go swimming?" he asked.

She shook her head.

"So, what happened?" Touso lay down beside her.

Mossy turned to look at him with a sparkle in her eyes. "Kalia took me for a ride."

Touso nodded but didn't seem surprised. "It's nice to see you bonding with your guides."

Mossy rolled on top of him. "Touso! It was so exciting! She took me underwater and spun around in the craziest way! I didn't even have to breathe! I also met her brother. Did you know dragons had siblings?"

"Believe it or not, gods and spirits all have families of their own, in one way or another," Touso explained.

She didn't realize she was wiggling on top of him until she saw the strained look on his face.

"Touso? What's wrong?" When he didn't say anything, she turned remorseful. "You were looking for me, weren't you? I'm sorry if I made you worry."

"No." Touso shook his head and tenderly touched her face. "I wasn't worried. I knew you were safe."

Mossy frowned and looked at him sideways. "Then why do you look like that?"

Touso grinned. He was tuned in to her feelings, but Mossy was still learning this skill. As realization dawned on her, Mossy leaped and almost fell back into the water. Touso moved quickly and caught her, drawing her into the safety of his arms.

Mossy stared at him breathlessly.

"Is this fast enough for you?" He looked first into her eyes and then at her lips. They always looked so soft and sweet. He wanted to taste them constantly.

Mossy nodded. "You'll do!"

Touso drew her deeper into the water. The further they went, the more her shirt floated to the surface. When Touso lifted it above her head, she didn't resist, so mesmerized by the intensity of his gaze.

"You look hot," he said quietly.

"I feel hot," she whispered.

He toyed with the strings of her bikini top and hovered his lips over the side of her neck. "How else would you like to know me today, Mo?"

"What would you like to tell me?" Her eyes fluttered shyly as he studied every part of her body.

"Not tell. Show."

The kiss started with a gentle tug of her lips, and then it became more urgent. When Mossy straddled his hips with her legs, he released a moan much more like a growl. Then Touso wrapped his arms around her and sank them underneath the water.

There, they gazed at each other without batting their eyes. Colorful swirls of energy glided around their floating figures. Mossy had challenged him to a race, and now he tested her endurance. How long could she hold her breath as he explored every inch of her body?

Touso kept their legs interlocked as they reached the bottom. The flowing water pushed them together, bouncing her hips against him. Touso smiled, enjoying the way her expression changed from coy to excitement.

Finally, they shot up for air.

"Wow! That was crazy!" Mossy gasped as they broke the surface with a splash. When Touso just smiled in a strangely hypnotic way, she said, "What?"

"You're beautiful." He wrapped his hands around the small of her back.

Mossy inhaled sharply as he pulled her close.

"Did you ever imagine it would be this way?" he asked.

The energy radiating between them was palpable. Feeling shy, she tried pulling away, but Touso held tight.

"How come you won't answer me?" He lifted her chin so she could see his eyes.

Before she could speak, he kissed her. His fingers curled into the soft flesh of her backside just as she wrapped her legs around him. They stayed this way for a long time, kissing and touching... getting to know each other in ways they never expected.

Then Mossy broke away and grinned. "My mom taught me something else."

"What's that?" His gaze turned suspicious.

"Don't put out on the first date!" She turned and swam back to shore like a shark was after her.

His chosen bride was still running away from him, and he wondered if that would ever change. Too bad for her, he was stubborn. Touso smiled and went after her.

Again.

A few yards away, someone watched the couple with a melancholy gaze. The dragon Kaw had pretended to be bored, even irritated with Mossy Cha when they met. But as he watched her and Touso Khang, his heart filled with old sorrows.

"Do I know you?" Mossy had demanded.

"No," Kaw had answered. What he should have said was: "No. Not for a very long time now.

Chapter 15

The Cha family's visit came with two blessings. Mossy's mother brought her clothes, and her dad gifted her the car she stole to rescue Touso.

Keng thought it would make life easier if she could get around. It would certainly make going to school more convenient. As Tuesday morning arrived, she was excited to exercise her newfound independence.

Mossy was a budding shaman and a bride now, but it seemed unnoticed by the rest of the world. As Mossy pulled into Valley High School and walked to class, everything felt the same.

When she checked her text messages, there was one from Touso; he missed her already. Another was from Dylan; he wanted to see her today. The last message was one she had sent to Cindy. It remained unread. Mossy tried one more time to call without success.

Where was she? It was unlike her to be silent for so long.

Mossy jumped when somebody smacked her bottom. She whirled around to find Eva glaring at her.

"You little bee!" Her best friend fumed with a scowl. "I was so worried about you! What the hell happened? Where were you?"

Mossy surprised her onery best friend with a long embrace. "I'm so sorry. I missed you so much and wanted to call you, but there was no time."

The hug was working. Eva already looked less angry as they parted. "Did you talk to Dylan? He's been looking for you."

Mossy grimaced and shook her head. "I'll see him later. Hey, you haven't heard from Cindy at all, have you?"

Eva shook her head. "I haven't seen her since Friday night. You mean she's not with you anymore?"

"Her mom asked her to go back home Saturday. I haven't heard from her since." Mossy's expression was pensive.

"Is there reason to worry?" Eva frowned.

With Cindy's family, there was always a reason to worry. Mossy said, "I think I'll stop by her house later."

"Hold on, you slippery little ninja. Don't try to distract me. Where have you been all weekend?"

Mossy pouted. "It's a long story. But I promise it's a good one!"

"It'd better be!"

The first-period bell rang, and Mossy grabbed her hand. "I'll tell you later! Let's go before we're late."

As she hustled her friend toward class, Mossy saw something from the corner of her eye. She thought it was a black hoodie and a blur of bleached blond hair.

Cindy?

Faint laughter disappeared in the wind.

Mossy frowned. *It couldn't be...*

For the rest of that morning, Mossy's spirits felt troubled, but she didn't know why.

They sat together at lunch, fingering their overcooked pizzas and cold fries more than eating. Finally, Eva sighed and threw a fry at Mossy.

"At least he's cute," she relented. "What I can't get over is how Dylan got there. Talk about awkwardness. How does he even know Nia and Fuechi?"

"They met at the movie theater that night when Dylan came to look for me. Fuechi really likes him. The blond hair must remind him of his dad," said Mossy. It was the only answer that made sense.

"How's Dylan taking all of this?" Eva asked, nibbling on a cold fry.

Mossy said, "He's pissed."

She conveniently left out the part that he was also possessed.

"It figures. The quiet Mossy Cha has two hot guys fighting over her." Eva put on her best anchorwoman routine and asked, "How does it feel, and what advice do you have for the rest of us commoners?"

Mossy made a face. "It's not funny. I've never seen Dylan so worked up before. Part of me wishes he was as into Amy as I thought."

"But now you know." The familiar voice nearly stopped her heart. Mossy turned to find Dylan standing behind her. He said, "It was never about Amy, and you know it."

Eva stood and picked up her tray. "And that's my cue to leave! I need to catch up with Jeremy anyway. You two play nicely."

"Eva, wait!" She felt betrayed as her best friend hurried away. Mossy didn't want to be alone with Dylan.

"See you, Ev," Dylan said, but his eyes remained on Mossy as she gathered her things. "So, you're just going to walk away from me?"

"There's nothing to say, Dylan!" Mossy turned to face him. "I don't know what you expect me to do."

"I just want you to be who you used to be." The sadness in his tone made her regretful.

She sighed. "Things are different now. I've made my decision."

"He's dangerous, Mossy!" Dylan exclaimed.

"Stop saying that!" The ire in her voice surprised them both. More quietly, she said, "Touso's not the danger here. I've been telling him the same about you, but now I don't know anymore."

Her spirit guides were stirring again, and Mossy began to wonder if it was Dylan they were concerned about.

"I just feel like there's some discrimination going on here. Touso can chase all the spirits he wants because he's Hmong, but because I'm White, I can't be possessed by something possibly sinister without judgment." Dylan frowned, but his eyes glistened with mischief.

Mossy scowled at him. "Even possessed, you can't be serious."

"Just making the best of a strange situation."

"Well, your best looks like you're sick," Mossy said as she studied him.

Despite any show of bravado, Dylan was pale with shadows beneath his eyes. She surprised him by touching his face. "Dylan, are you okay?

He chuckled bitterly. "I've been possessed. I think we've established 'okay' is far from it."

"I'm serious. You should ask your dad to check you out," Mossy insisted.

Dylan cast her a sardonic expression. "How does that work, Moss? 'Hey, Dad, there's a ghost inside me. Can you check my vitals?'"

"I don't know, but you can't just stay possessed!" Mossy glared at him with exasperation.

"Right now, I don't have a choice," Dylan said and looked away.

Mossy hesitated and asked, "Did you really let it in because of me?

He was serious for the first time as he turned to face her. "I would do anything to keep you safe, Moss. All I could hear was you crying as I died."

Mossy shook her head. "Dylan! We need to find some help. This can't be safe. Whatever's inside you—it's already draining your energy. Maybe Touso can—

"I'm fine!" Dylan's eyes flashed yellow, and Mossy staggered back. He was remorseful when she looked afraid. "Mossy—wait!"

She was already running away. As Dylan watched her disappear around the corner, Kai Khang appeared beside him.

"Way to go, bro. You're a real ladies' man." The spirit of Kai Khang emerged beside him.

"What's happening to me?" Dylan's voice trembled with anxiety. Mossy wasn't imagining it. There was something wrong. He could feel it.

"Your body's breaking down," said Kai without his usual humor. "Normal human bodies can only host an entity for so long. Everyone's different. A few hours to a few days. You're a stubborn mother fucker, so you've been doing good, but we're running out of time."

"What will happen?" Dylan asked.

"You'll die."

Dylan cursed loudly. "Why won't you just go?"

"I can't. We're stuck together until I complete my mission or someone more powerful pulls me out of you."

"Then what do I do?" Dylan closed his eyes, feeling the energy of his life waver.

"We do whatever we can to help the people we love."

As the two souls wondered about the future, they noticed something strange brewing in the air. Their spirit guides whispered about danger. Dylan frowned and immediately went searching for Mossy.

As Mossy hurried down the hallway, her phone kept buzzing. One was a message from Touso, wanting to know if she was okay. The other was from Dylan, asking where she was. Mossy wished both would leave her alone.

The only person I could think of was you.

I thought if I died, no one would protect you.

So, I did it—I let it happen!

She'd almost killed Touso, and now Dylan was possessed. If she was destined to heal and protect, she was doing a horrible job. Mossy was hurting everyone she cared about.

Her chest tightened with a sharp buzz. A black hoodie and blond hair turned the corner ahead.

Cindy? Mossy went after her. "Cindy—wait!"

As she arrived at the end of the hallway, Cindy glanced back with a wry smile. Then she turned and sprinted toward the track.

What was she doing at school? Mossy worried that something terrible had happened at home.

Mossy...

Cindy's voice rang in her ears.

No fair, Mossy. She sucker-punched you. Let's get even!

Mossy's steps slowed as the voice grew louder.

Get her! Get her! Make her pay!

Mossy gripped her ears. Why was Cindy screaming inside her head? No. It was more like the snarl of an enraged animal.

Don't let her hurt you again!

"Cindy—stop!" Mossy's head throbbed, and her body ached from the dark energy swarming her.

"Mossy?" The familiar voice brought everything to a standstill.

Amy Edwards and Ashley Brandt were smoking by the bleachers. Suspended, the prom queen wasn't supposed to be on campus either. She wasn't even allowed to attend graduation anymore after she assaulted Mossy.

Amy threw her cigarette on the ground and hopped off the bleacher to face Mossy. "Speak of the Devil. I was hoping to see you."

"I hope you're here to apologize," Mossy said as the other girl approached. Something strange was happening. The world seemed to be getting darker, but she tried to keep her composure.

Amy laughed. "Apologize? To you? Who are you? I should have kicked your ass a long time ago, Mossy Cha. You're not good enough for Dylan!"

"Seems like you're not either," Mossy said with a sneer.

Amy's eyes narrowed. "No one's going to save you today, you little bitch. There's no Dylan and no graduation. There's nothing to lose. But I'll take a little payback for my troubles."

"Let's make this live so everyone else can see!" Ashlie laughed and appeared beside her with a phone.

As the girls mocked her, something dark floated around Mossy Cha. At first, it hovered and crawled along her body, then melted into her pores. Mossy felt the thing that possessed her and didn't resist. If anything, she welcomed it.

Rage filled her heart, and her eyes glowed red.

Amy and Ashlie barely had time to react as Mossy's crazed eyes locked onto them. With a feral growl, she lunged at Amy, her nails digging into her scalp and yanking her hair with brutal force. The impact of Mossy's fist against Amy's face was like a sledgehammer, leaving behind a trail of fiery pain and a burst of blood from her nose. Before Ashlie could even fully process what was happening, Mossy turned on her, unleashing a flurry of blows that felt like shards of glass piercing her skin. As the two girls crumpled to the ground, Mossy snarled with satisfaction.

Amy fell back in horror as Mossy turned to look at her. She wore the same crazy expression she had that day when she discovered Dylan sitting with them at the mall. The snarl from her lips sounded more animal than human. When Mossy leaped at her, Amy screamed.

Somebody grabbed Mossy by the waist before she could reach her. Amy continued screaming as Dylan hauled Mossy away. Mossy snarled and snapped at him like a rabid beast. Finally, Dylan tossed her onto the ground. As Mossy prepared to attack, she heard the sound.

Awakening

It was a gong. More accurately, it was two aluminum trash lids hitting each other, and it was excruciating. Mossy screamed and fell back onto the grass, writhing in pain. Soon, a dark energy leaped from her body, and Mossy stopped screaming.

"Mossy?" He rushed to help her up.

She grabbed onto his shirt.

"What happened? What's wrong?" Dylan held on to her as she sobbed.

She said, "Dylan, we have to go to Cindy's house. Now!"

He didn't argue. As he helped Mossy toward the car, he paused by a still hysterical Amy.

"Dylan!" Amy flung herself at his feet. "She's crazy. She's crazy!"

When his eyes flashed yellow, Amy fell back and began screaming again. Smirking, Dylan crushed the phone that was still recording on the ground and continued walking away with Mossy.

Chapter 16

The Thao house looked like usual: disheveled and surrounded by gloom. While the rest of the neighborhood bathed in sunlight, a persistent cloud hung above this home. Only Mossy and Dylan knew its true darkness.

They knocked on the door and waited for someone to answer. When no one came, they knocked again and refused to leave. Someone was home. Finally, the door cracked open.

It was Mrs. Thao.

"Oh, Mossy! It's just you!" Cindy's mother pretended to be pleasant but was clearly annoyed.

"Hello, Mrs. Thao," Mossy said with a polite smile. "Is Cindy home? I have something to give her."

Mrs. Thao shook her head. "She's not home right now, but I could give it to her."

Mossy glanced at Dylan, who shook his head. Like Mossy, he didn't trust Mrs. Thao, who was surrounded by a thick haze of darkness. Something was amiss.

"That would be great. I really miss her!" Mossy made a show of lifting a gift bag for her to see.

"I'll tell her you came by," Mrs. Thao said, moving to unlock the deadbolt on the heavy door.

"I've been calling her, but she's not picking up her phone," Mossy continued with a pout.

Mrs. Thao laughed. "You know how she is. She's irresponsible—always has been! You're the only one who can tolerate her."

It was such a mean-spirited thing to say that Mossy couldn't believe this was someone's mother.

Mrs. Thao stuck her hand out. "Give me the bag. I'll make sure she gets it."

Mossy asked, "Do you think I could say hello to the boys? I have some candy for them, too. They always loved getting candy."

"No!" Mrs. Thao snatched the bag from Mossy. "Cindy isn't home, and the boys don't need your candy!"

Dylan grabbed the door as Mrs. Thao tried to close it. She looked baffled when he yanked it back.

She sputtered, "What are you doing? You can't do that—you're trespassing! Get off my property!"

Dylan nodded at Mossy. "Go find Cindy. I'll deal with her mother."

Mrs. Thao tried to stop her, but Dylan pushed her against the door. "Touch her again, and you'll be very sorry."

Mrs. Thao stopped resisting and swallowed the rest of her words.

Mossy hurried down the dark hallway to Cindy's room. Today, the air was heavy with something much more toxic than dust and grime, and her heart ached for the children who had to live in this dark hole.

As Mossy thrust open the door, she was disappointed to find only an empty bed and room.

Nobody was there, but there was a strange smell. Her chest tightened and burned. Something was very wrong.

"Cindy?" Mossy started shouting. "Cindy! Are you home? It's Mossy!"

Mossy ran to the next room and found David and Billy huddling in a corner. They looked dirty and skinny, like they hadn't bathed or eaten in a long time.

"Boys!" Mossy rushed over to them. "Are you okay? Where's your sister?"

When Billy, the youngest, started to cry, David put a hand over his mouth. They were terrified of something, but she didn't know what. Mossy whirled around as Mr. Thao walked into the room, looking more like a corpse than a man.

"Please help us." He staggered toward her. "Help us!"

Mossy pulled away as he reached for her. "What do you mean? Who's trying to hurt you? Is Chewy here?"

Chewy was supposed to be in jail for assaulting Mossy and Cindy. *Was he back?*

Something crashed in the room next door—in Chewy's room. Cindy always said nobody was allowed in there. Now, Mossy quickly moved in that direction.

"Cindy!" she shouted but stopped as someone grabbed her wrist. "David, let go."

"Don't go in there, Mossy!" His whispering voice trembled.

"Why?" Her heart raced with terrible anticipation.

"She's in there!"

The words instantly relieved her, but why did David look so horrified? Any relief quickly turned to dread as she imagined what Chewy was doing to her friend.

Mossy glared at Mr. Thao. "What kind of father are you? Why don't you do something? Why are you always letting him hurt her?"

Unable to handle it anymore, Mossy broke away from David. She nearly knocked over Mr. Thao as she raced toward the room with all the noise. It sounded like someone was throwing things against the wall.

All of Mossy's spirit guides whispered:

Don't go.

Terrible.

Go back!

When Mossy wouldn't listen, a peculiar wind gathered and pushed her back. Finally, Mossy grabbed the knob to Chewy's door and growled in frustration when it wouldn't budge. It was locked from the inside. She slammed her shoulder into the hollow door without success.

"Pao, help me open the door. Open the goddamn door!" Mossy cried in desperation, but the giant spirit guide behind her strength refused. She didn't look up when someone touched her shoulder. "They won't help me open the door."

Dylan gently pushed her aside and put a hand against the door. It cracked and then crashed onto the floor. But any relief was instantly replaced with dread when she saw the expression on Dylan's face. He tried to block her view, but she struggled against him until finally...her soul released a scream.

Chewy Thao was indeed home, strapped to a chair at the far corner of the room. His beady eyes bulged in terror as something clung to his bald head. It was Cindy, but she wasn't the same.

She sat on Chewy's shoulders with her arms wrapped menacingly around her brother, locking his mouth with her pale hands. She glared at them through bloody eyes and grinned.

"Cindy!" Mossy gasped.

Mossy... The voice in her head was dry and brittle. *I don't have to be scared anymore.*

As Mossy wept, Dylan drew her away. "Let me take care of this."

She stared at this thing that was, at one moment, her friend and then a hissing creature. It clung to Chewy's body possessively. He had hurt so many people, and it would make him pay.

Mossy pleaded, "Don't hurt her.

Dylan nodded and stepped into the room, and Kai Khang emerged. As a skilled spiritualist, he knew exactly what to do.

Ghosts used to be people. People had souls, and souls had paths to follow. All one had to do was convince them to follow it. But Cindy was difficult because she was angry.

She also didn't want to leave Mossy.

At first, she fought him and refused to listen to reason. She even threatened to come after him next. Ghost Cindy was very much like Human Cindy—stubborn as hell. Eventually, Kai came to Dylan with her terms.

He turned to look for Mossy, but she was gone. His brows furrowed as he followed a weeping sound to Cindy's old room. His nostrils flared at the strange scent that grew stronger with each step.

Finally, he found her sitting on the floor by the closet, and his gaze fell on the lifeless hand in her lap.

Mossy studied the dull blond hair peeking across the closet floor. Cindy still wore the same clothes the day she left Mossy's house.

She wants me to come home... She wants a fresh start!

Cindy must have died that night. As Mossy held her hand, everything around her began trembling.

A powerful energy burst from her pores as her hair waved wildly above her head. Inanimate objects soon quivered and moved away. Before Dylan could react, Mossy threw back her head and cried. The sheer force of the energy sent him flying from the room. The walls of the house shook, while every window shattered. People on the streets gasped as glass shards scattered along the pavement.

Dylan hurried back to see Mossy cradle the lifeless hand at her chest. Her spirit guides were with her, and Kalia's blue tail wrapped them all in a protected circle. As Mossy Cha mourned the loss of her friend, all her guides dropped their chins and wept with her. But to Dylan's dismay, no one could convince Mossy to say goodbye.

Chapter 17

Touso Khang and Dylan Reed stood outside the door, scowling with their arms crossed over their chests. However, neither of them paid attention to the other as he thought of what to do. Dylan had brought Mossy home, but she wasn't alone.

"Cindy said she'll only go if Mossy tells her to," Dylan repeated the words the ghost had told Kai.

"She isn't ready," Touso said, pacing the hallway.

"A troubled soul attached to a human will only cause trouble," said Dylan.

"Don't you think I know that?" Touso snapped and stopped to face him. "Better yet, how do you know that?"

"I watch a lot of movies." Dylan shrugged, but his eyes darkened as his thoughts returned to the alarming situation behind the door.

He had tried without success to convince Mossy to send her friend away. Instead, she protected the snarling ghost like it was a precious child. Dylan had no choice but to bring Mossy home with the ghost of Cindy Thao.

"What's your plan?" Dylan asked, arching a brow at the shaman pacing the hallway.

"What choice do I have? I'll have to send it by force."

Touso curled his fingers into a fist. Cindy was feisty but innocent and had been one of Mossy's closest friends. He felt the pain of her loss like his own and knew banishing her wouldn't be easy.

"Okay, ghostbuster. Do you need me to do anything?" Dylan's offer surprised Touso, who cast him a curious expression. "I'm not doing it for you. I don't want Mossy to get hurt," he quickly added.

"Just don't get in the way." Touso frowned and thrust open the door.

Mossy sat in a recliner with Cindy Thao at her feet. The ghost snarled a warning when it noticed Touso and Dylan and leaped behind the chair. Its blood-red eyes glared from over Mossy's head.

"Stop it—you're scaring her!" Mossy sounded irritated as she turned to face them.

"Mossy, she's a ghost. More appropriately, she's scaring me," said Dylan. The entity behind the recliner hissed. "You're breaking my heart, Cindy. Don't you remember stealing my food?" Dylan ducked when the ghost threw something at him. "I guess not."

"Mossy, she can't stay," Touso said calmly. When she refused to look at him, he continued, "She doesn't belong in this world anymore. She needs to move on."

"She didn't deserve this!" Mossy was tearful again as she faced him. "I should have protected her better."

"This isn't your fault." As Touso approached, Cindy jumped in between them.

My friend! A low possessive growl warned him to stay away.

Awakening

Immediately, Touso reached for the red beans in his pocket. Red beans burn ghosts the way tasers fry criminals. He only stopped because of Mossy's expression.

"Don't you dare hurt her!" she snapped.

"Mossy, don't you see what she's doing? She's keeping you away from me. That's how it starts."

Mossy frowned in confusion. "She's protecting me. People have been hurting her all her life, and she wants to protect me from the same fate."

"But why would she need to protect you from the ones who love you the most?"

Love... Mossy's brows furrowed in question.

"It's not healthy, Mossy. She'll drain your energy." Touso glanced at the angry ghost prowling at Mossy's feet. "Even if she doesn't want to, she will. That's what ghosts do when they don't move on. They feed from the life they can no longer have."

The grotesque thing turned into a much more pleasant-looking Cindy and held Mossy's hand. *I would never hurt you, Mossy. You're my sister!*

Mossy's eyes filled with tears. She'd suspected trouble when Cindy's mom asked her to return home. She should have never let her go. A strong gust of wind tossed books and papers onto the ground, and she was surprised to see Gowli, Pao, and Chee.

"What's happening?" Mossy shouted, throwing her arms around Cindy when they seemed determined to take her. "What are you doing?"

Touso said, "Your spirit guides are angry. They want you to listen. If you don't send her away, they will."

"No! It's not fair! She's not dangerous," Mossy insisted.

Gowli touched her shoulder. "Mossy, you're a rising shaman. You must know right from wrong and always pursue the most righteous path. Every soul must complete the life cycle, or there will be severe consequences to pay. This one has not had an easy life. She will not have peace unless you send her to the Lake of Life."

The Lake of Life was where all souls traveled to shed their memories and sorrows. One had to go there before going anywhere else. But Cindy was young and should have had a long life ahead of her. She wasn't supposed to know about the Lake of Life for a long time!

"Mossy. It's the way it has to be." Touso spoke carefully from across the room. "She doesn't belong here anymore."

"The longer she stays, the more disruptive she'll become," Dylan agreed quietly. His eyes remained on the ghost that hid behind her. "She's only strong when she absorbs human energy. What do you think will happen to you? To anyone else around you?"

Mossy shook her head in disbelief. When Pao and Chee moved toward Cindy, she spread her arms wide.

"Stay back! Don't you touch her!"

Cindy curled up anxiously behind her leg. *Don't send me away, please!* The way she looked like a scared little girl only made Mossy more determined to protect her.

"You must send her away, Mo," Gowli pleaded.

"Ghosts don't belong with people." Chee lifted his spear and pointed at Cindy. "We will not accept this."

"This is the only way." Pao's slender eyes were both sad and determined.

"Stop telling me what to do." She glared at her guides and the two men in the room. *You're my guides, not my masters. You didn't help* me earlier when I needed you. You'll listen to me now. Leave my friend alone!"

"Mossy, please." Touso's eyes implored her to see reason before it was too late. When shamans and their spirit guides disagreed, there could only be pain. Soon, Mossy would feel their wrath, and Touso wanted more than anything to protect her. As he moved to do so, Dylan put out his hand.

"Don't." His eyes fixed on the unstable light around her body. Dylan had seen this happen before.

"What are you talking about?" Touso scowled with impatience until he noticed the change.

As the spirits surrounded their shaman, a strange wind picked up again. But this time, it was because of Mossy. Her eyes were glowing dangerously. It was already happening. Mossy wasn't just protective of her friend. She was projecting the anger and sadness of the entity that clung to her. Meanwhile, her tolerance was feeding it, and the ghost of Cindy was getting stronger. As Mossy stood against them, the ghost rose above her and snarled viciously.

Without further hesitation, the spirit guides moved in. Touso tried to get Mossy out of the way. No one was prepared for the blast that followed. The explosion threw Touso across the room and instantly scattered the energy of the spirit guides. The blinding light seemed to last an eternity. As Touso landed against the wall and crumpled onto the ground, he struggled to overcome the ringing in his ears.

Dylan Reed stepped out from the safety of the hallway and shrugged. "I told you."

Mossy and Cindy were gone when they returned to the room.

Fuechi Khang was building a race track with his Legos when he saw the clouds gathering outside. His mama was preparing a snack in the kitchen and expected him to behave until she returned. But he became distracted when he heard the noise. As he moved to peer out the window, whispers urged him to wait for his mama. But something strange was happening, and he wanted to see what it was.

Fuechi frowned at the shadows in the sky. When he walked with Grandpa that morning, the sun was bright with blue skies. It was suddenly very dark for an afternoon. As Fuechi pondered on these details, something sprinted across the lawn.

Aunt Mossy? The thing hovering over her reminded him of Ling.

A moment later, his Uncle Touso and Mr. Dylan were running after them. If they were playing hide-and-seek, he wanted to play, too!

Fuechi leaped off the couch and ran toward the door. He was tired of playing Legos, anyway.

The Ghost of Cindy Thao watched as Mossy slumped against a large oak tree. Her pretty face was swollen from crying, but she smiled at Cindy. She said, "It's okay. I won't let them hurt you."

The ghost stared at Mossy without smiling back. She didn't know happiness or relief, only sadness, anger, and despair—such were her feelings before her last breath. But she remembered Mossy Cha and wanted to stay with her.

She felt safe.

So, when Mossy held out her hand, she followed.

"They don't know you like I do, Cindy," said Mossy, sniffling as the entity glided to her side. "You're a good person. You're a good soul!"

Cindy had returned to a more pleasant version of herself, but her blond hair looked grey, and her skin was so pale it was nearly blue. She was a very sorrowful ghost.

Cindy rose and hovered closer to her body. She was fascinated by the energy exuding from Mossy's pores—the energy of life. The sad and angry entity wanted to touch and consume it.

She couldn't.

Mossy Cha was a precious gem—she was her friend! But that energy of life smelled so good. Finally, she wrapped her arms around Mossy and rested her pale head on her shoulder. A stream of energy floated from the human girl to the ghost attached to her.

Mossy yawned and smiled at Cindy, who seemed a little brighter now. The blond was returning to her hair. "I'm sorry I couldn't protect you, Cindy."

The ghost girl ceased sucking the energy from Mossy Cha and wondered why she was so sad. Then Cindy remembered how Mossy used to protect her against bad people.

Can't take too much... Mossy is special friend!

Mossy straightened and shouted, "Cindy!"

It was too late. Pao appeared out of nowhere and thrust the creature onto the ground. Chee caught her ankle with a golden lasso and reeled her in. Gowli hovered nearby, conjuring a portal against the forest landscape.

As Mossy attempted to free her friend, a sharp pain struck her head. She fell to the ground, grasping at her temples. It felt like millions of needles were sinking into her brain. Mossy knew at that moment that her spirit guides were punishing her.

Stay down! Chee's voice was fierce.

Mossy cried and rolled in agony as Cindy became a snarling ghost. She snapped her teeth at Chee when he trapped her with the lasso. With the energy she took from Mossy, Cindy broke free and leaped into the dense forest.

A moment later, Mossy was being whipped on all sides by the wind of furious spirits.

Stubborn!

Insolent!

Careless!

Mossy covered her ears, but it was useless. The screaming continued inside her head. Never have her spirit guides been so angry. They were a part of her, and she was a part of them. As such, they understood her every happiness, pain, and grief. But Mossy had broken the rules this time, and they wouldn't accept this. As another searing pain struck her head, Mossy stumbled onto the ground.

"Stop! Please stop!" She rolled into a fetal position.

"You are a shaman. There are rules you must obey." Gowli stood over her one moment and disappeared the next.

"She's not dangerous," Mossy cried again. It was a mistake that brought more pain throughout her body.

"It's not human!" When Chee thrust his spear into the ground beside her head, Mossy shuddered. "She fed from you. Did we raise you all this time to become ghost food?"

"Bad Mossy." Pao looked disappointed as he stood over her. "Ghosts are no good!"

"She didn't hurt me." Mossy shook her head adamantly, and this stubbornness baffled the spirit guides. How much pain was she willing to bear for the gruesome creature?

"Not yet." Gowli's dark eyes flashed. "Let this be your first lesson. Things must go where they belong or else."

"Or else what?" Mossy was sure that they would strike her again for her insolence. But Gowli leaned down and cradled her chin between elegant fingers.

"Or you'll watch the darkness you protect eat all the ones you love." Gowli's voice was ominous and followed by a blinding light.

Mossy was transported into another part of the vast forest. It was darker there because of a thick mass of clouds in the sky. She heard the soft humming before she saw the little boy standing a few yards away.

Fuechi! What was he doing out there? She frowned when he stopped walking to study something in the trees.

"Are you Fuechi's friend, too?" Mossy wondered who he was talking to.

A dark figure leaped down from the shadows. It was Cindy, and she did not look friendly. Fear gripped Mossy's heart as the ghost girl studied Fuechi how a dog might look at a tender piece of meat.

"No..." Mossy refused to believe it. "She wouldn't hurt him. He's just a baby."

Chee smirked as he flooded her mind with images of children lost to hungry ghosts throughout history. They were small and slow but so full of life. Children were easy prey with ample reward. The crying of all the lost children was so devastating that a sob broke from her lips. It was at that moment when Cindy attacked Fuechi.

"No!" Mossy rushed to intervene. To her surprise, a powerful weight forced her onto the ground. Mossy lifted her gaze to the spirit guides who surrounded her. "What—what are you doing?"

"Ghosts do not belong with people, Mossy. Remember this day. Remember the role you play in protecting life." Gowli's expression was unmoving as she spoke. Now, you must watch and learn."

"But he's in danger!" Mossy couldn't believe what was happening. She twisted and struggled to escape but failed.

"You let it happen." There was no compassion in Chee's voice.

"Bad choices, bad consequences." Pao was already crying as he waited for the scene to unfold.

Mossy shook her head. This was not what she wanted. Tears filled her eyes, and she lifted her fingers desperately toward the little boy. Fuechi was terrified as he parted his mouth to scream.

Fuechi hummed a tune as he strolled the woods. The happy song made him feel less lonely, especially since he couldn't find his Uncle Touso or Aunt Mossy.

Mr. Dylan was the one he really wanted to see. He wanted his daddy.

Awakening

Fuechi jumped as the trees trembled from one place to another. His heart began to race the way it did whenever something scary was about to happen. He heard the vague whispering before his eyes fell to the dark space between branches. It was the thing that looked like Ling, except that it was an older girl. It was also very creepy, with pale eyes and a mouth curled into a sneer.

"Ling is Fuechi's friend," he whispered to the thing watching him intently. "Are you Fuechi's friend, too?"

The creature answered with a low growl. The ghost of Cindy Thao had escaped the spirit guides but knew they would soon catch up. The energy it took from Mossy was already weakening, and it needed to find a way to replenish its strength. That was when it heard the little boy singing in the woods. As it watched him, the ghost tilted its head in fascination. He had the same bright energy as Mossy, warm and robust with life. If the ghost could have his power, it wouldn't have to touch Mossy again for a long time.

Mossy... My friend! It didn't want to take from her any more than necessary.

It leaped from the trees and landed at Fuechi's feet. The little boy stumbled as the awful thing grinned and wiggled long fingers at him. When it snarled and charged, Fuechi opened his mouth to scream. But the only sound heard was the piercing cries of a rattle. The metal discs clashed repeatedly, and soon, Fuechi saw another figure emerge from the darkness. It was his grandpa!

"Shee Yee has blessed this land. You are not welcome here, ghost!" he roared in a voice Fuechi didn't recognize.

His grandpa was frail and quiet. Now, he looked especially fierce as lightning flashed across a grim expression. He swung the metal rattle, chanting words that brought the wind and shook the trees. But the ghost girl wasn't to be deterred. It needed energy—it needed the boy!

As it whirled on Fuechi, a new shadow flew across the clearing. It turned into a blaze of yellow light that hit the creature's shoulder. As it staggered, the light hit it again on the other side, sending it to the ground. Fuechi yelped in surprise when someone scooped him off his feet. His eyes lit up as he met the familiar face.

"Daddy!"

"Are you okay?" Kai felt joy and agony as he embraced his son. He was almost too late!

The ghost girl shrieked with rage. Father and son looked up just in time to see Touso and Lihue trap Cindy on either side. The Khang patriarch was slower recently, but he was still powerful. A ghost threatening his children would never pass. As Lihue chanted, the sky thundered, and a portal to the spirit world opened.

Touso stepped toward the seething ghost girl. "Cindy Thao, you are no longer welcome in this world. It is time for you to move on to your next destination."

Human Cindy would have laughed at his authority. Now, Ghost Cindy crouched and growled. This one was like her brother—always telling her what to do! When she responded by suddenly attacking, Touso cast a spray of red beans. The pellets grazed her ghostly flesh, breaking a trail of hot lava across her face. The pain triggered a series of traumatic memories. Chewy always enjoyed burning her with the butt of his cigarettes.

"Cindy." This time, Touso's voice was pleading. "Release your attachment to Mossy Cha. She is no longer your concern."

Awakening

Mossy... The ghost of Cindy recognized Touso. A vague memory of an angry Mossy from the movie theater resurfaced. *Pain. Heartbreak. Sorrow.* He had hurt her friend! Chewy and this shaman—they were all the same!

"Please. Don't make me hurt you." Even as he implored her, Touso knew all the pleading in the world would result in nothing. Ghosts only understood the most basic of instincts. At the moment, this was survival, and Cindy leaped at him with open claws.

Touso Khang never moved. As she came flying toward him, he cast another bean. It sailed sharply past her toward a mysterious destination. A moment later, the sharp sound of a gong came. Another toss triggered a spray of specially marked ghost paper. Cindy howled in pain when the pieces fell on her like paper rain. This was the land of a shaman family. Every crevice and tree was rigged against evil spirits.

While Cindy staggered, Touso cast more red pellets in numerous directions. A chorus of screaming metal followed it. He watched without emotion as the ghost girl wailed. To his dismay, Cindy continued to charge at him. She snapped her teeth, determined to sink them into his flesh.

She never got the chance.

Lihue thrust the hoop at the furious host, and it struck with an impact that sent her crashing against a tree.

A stream of lights swarmed Cindy as she struggled to regain her footing. She fought furiously to escape, and this determination shook the surrounding leaves. With her remaining energy, Cindy charged Touso once again.

The air was churning in a clockwise circle, and soon a portal opened. It revealed a world where thunder and lightning raged. Touso waited for Cindy with a small dagger. In a weakened state, the spirit guides could finally take her away. As the ghost reached him, he plunged the knife into her chest.

The flesh of a ghost was immaterial and light as air. A powerful one could form into something much more solid, but any pretense of flesh remained thin without blood to support life. As the dagger came down, the blade sunk into something solid... and warm.

Touso gasped as Mossy staggered. She had leaped between him and Cindy, and now the dagger's hilt stuck out in the soft area between her shoulder blade and spine.

Cindy stopped screaming as Mossy embraced her. She flinched from all the pain she felt. The ghost was nothing more than a bundle of agony, and because of it, Mossy held tighter. She needed Cindy to know she was loved, and as she relaxed, Mossy knew she did.

Both girls recalled shared moments of joy: eating dinner at the Cha house, watching movies with Eva, baking with her brothers, and taking them trick-or-treating... Cindy would have given her life for any one of them and, in a way, she had. With her death, Chewy would be locked away forever and never hurt anyone again.

"Mossy? Why are you so sad?" The ghost lost her grotesque visage and frowned from a familiar freckled face.

Mossy stifled a sob. Cindy always preferred her hair pulled out of her face, but it had fallen loose during the struggle before her death. Now, Mossy took the band from her own hair and went to work. The motion provoked sharp pains across her back, but she continued until a neat, blond bun sat at the top of Cindy's head.

Mossy said, "You're about to take a trip, and I can't go with you. You know how much I love you, don't you? You are the bravest and most selfless person I've ever known. You've always protected me, and now I must protect you."

Mossy took a deep breath to prepare for what she had to do next. She grimaced as breathing became difficult. With great effort, she chanted, "Cindy Thao, it's time to go where you belong. You must leave this place now and move on to the next. May your ancestors embrace you and shower you with the love you never knew in this life. May your next life be full of the joy you deserve!"

"I'm scared, Mossy." Cindy sounded so incredibly sad, and Mossy fought another round of tears.

"Don't be afraid. You won't ever have to be scared again!" said Mossy, hugging her friend one last time.

Keeping portals open took a lot of energy, and Lihue chanted like he was running a marathon. The door to the spirit world wavered erratically as it took shape. When Mossy felt Touso's hands on her shoulders, she knew it was time for Cindy to go.

She said, "I'll miss you so much. I love you, Cindy!"

When the spirits arrived to take her away, she didn't fight. Instead, Cindy whispered, "I love you, too."

She had promised to leave when Mossy asked her to go, so she did. As Cindy disappeared into the portal, Mossy Cha collapsed into Touso's arms. She faintly heard him shouting her name, asking if she was in pain.

Yes, she thought. *So much pain ...*

She was thinking about Cindy, not the dagger still stuck in her back.

Blood soaked Touso's chest as he gathered her into his arms and carried her home.

Chapter 18

Pain. He was in pain. Touso felt Mossy's wound as though it were his own flesh, except he wasn't the one bleeding to death. He wasn't the one struggling to breathe—she was!

Pahoua was a nurse practitioner who was used to treating severe injuries. Bao's spirit guides helped her heal most pains. When they both gazed at Mossy, shaking their heads, he knew it was. Even worse, he couldn't stay with her.

"I won't leave her alone!" Touso Khang never cried, but he sobbed now as he held his bride. He tucked her head against his chest as though his heartbeat alone would wake her.

"You can't go!" Pahoua's voice was firm despite the anguish on his face. "You can barely control your emotions right now. What will you say when they ask what happened? Can you influence them without frying their brains? Or will you tell them the truth and get arrested instead?"

Awakening

Touso buried his face in her neck, begging her to stir at least once. Mossy had used the last of her energy to send Cindy away. Now, she was deathly pale.

"Touso—please! We're running out of time," Bao implored her brother. She had pulled the car up to the front, but Touso refused to let Mossy go without him.

"I'll take her." When Touso glared over Mossy's face, Dylan added, "I'll tell them we got attacked while out together. Everyone knows me at the hospital, so they won't ask as many questions."

As he hesitated, Touso felt a firm grip on his shoulder. His father said, "I know your pain. I know you're afraid. But if you don't let her go, she'll die."

When Dylan reached for Mossy again, he didn't resist. He frowned when her arms fell limply during the transfer, but Dylan quickly cradled her and left.

A shaman walked a lonely path—seeing and battling monsters no one knew existed. Usually, he bore those burdens alone. Touso didn't realize how much his life had changed since Mossy came. He wasn't just safer from the curse—he was happy. She was the light and the keeper he never knew he needed.

As she disappeared down the driveway with Bao and Dylan, Touso felt that light recede. Finally, there was only the darkness he used to know, and a taunting laugh came from those shadows.

Oh, Touso... it's been such a long time...

Dylan was calm when he took Mossy from Touso, but as he held her limp body, he lost all control, shouting, "Mossy! Hold on. We're almost there!"

She was so pale and barely breathing. When she opened her eyes, he asked, "Mossy! Are you okay?"

"Dylan..." Her voice was weak and disoriented. "Where's Touso?"

"He's home. He couldn't come," Dylan answered with a grim expression.

As her eyes closed again, he became angry. This was precisely what he feared would happen. Her life with Touso Khang was dangerous. Ordinary people didn't get attacked by ghosts!

Kai said, "Au contraire, bro. Normal people get attacked all the time by ghosts. It's only because they fear something punishing them that they don't do it more often."

"She doesn't deserve this life," Dylan retorted.

Bao, who couldn't hear or see her dead brother, glanced at Dylan through the rear-view mirror. "We're almost there. Don't worry—she's going to be okay!"

As Dylan held Mossy's hand, his fingers stretched to feel her pulse. It was slow, like her breathing.

"Pull it," Kai said.

"What?" Dylan gasped.

"Pull the dagger," Kai repeated more slowly.

"But she'll bleed out!" Dylan looked horrified. She had already lost so much blood.

"We're almost at the hospital. Pull the blade. It's a very unique blade with Touso's prints all over it. It'll lead the authorities back to him!" Kai said.

Dylan scowled. "Sounds like a great idea to me!"

"Listen, asshole. I know you love this girl, but this is not the time. Her body's weak, and her soul is lifting. If we don't do something now, things will worsen for them both! Pull the dagger!" As Kai's order echoed throughout his mind, Dylan inhaled sharply.

Finally, he curled his fingers around the hilt. "Fine!"

Mossy was so weak that she never stirred when he pulled the blade. He quickly dropped it to keep her head tucked safely against his chest.

"Dylan!" Bao cried in horror. She had just arrived at the hospital when he pulled the dagger. "Why did you do that?"

Breathing heavily, he answered, "We're here now. They'll take care of the wound. But if they get that knife, your brother will have more to worry about than me taking his girl."

Bao didn't have time to respond as a team arrived to take Mossy away. Then she glared at him and said, "If she dies..."

Dylan met her gaze. "She won't."

Finally, Bao turned to follow the medical team inside the hospital.

"Way to go, bro," Kai said as Dylan glowered at the dagger. The one thing you learn about love is that it's all about sacrifice."

Chapter 19

Touso Khang saw it repeatedly: the moment the blade plunged into her flesh. It wasn't just that it happened. He had seen it happen *before*. Since Kai's death, his seeing powers had a way of creeping into Touso's dreams. He saw things before they occurred— mostly short glimpses, and stabbing his bride was among them. Only, in those visions, it happened somewhere else.

He was destined to stab her again.

How could I stab her twice? He couldn't imagine stabbing her at all!

Pacing in the living room, Touso waited impatiently to hear how Mossy was doing. But he knew she would survive because of the same ominous vision.

He was furious. *Why is she always risking her life?*

That's her nature! Kong had a habit of joining his internal debates, and tonight was no different. *Chosen brides act first and think later. That's what makes her special!*

Touso didn't want to hear from Kong, who enjoyed fighting and appreciated any acts that gave him such opportunities. He was undoubtedly a fan of Mossy's.

Instead, Touso waited for the opinion of Blong, a peaceful spirit whose wisdom was much more appreciated.

Cindy was her friend. A chosen bride who does not care for the people she loves is not worthy. Blong's answer was not received well.

"She broke the rules!" Touso shook his head. "How do I keep her safe if she doesn't follow the rules."

Does a king protect his knight? Kong asked.

"Does a King marry his knight?" he countered with a frown.

Blong laughed. *It's irrelevant. Kong is trying to say that you're letting your emotions blind you. Mossy is not just your chosen bride. She is your guardian. You'll get in the way of her training if you try to protect her too much. She must stumble to learn, and sometimes it will be very tough to endure—very tough to watch. But you must not get in the way.*

Touso stood abruptly to pace the room. The new ghost of Cindy Thao should not have been that strong. But her anger had drawn her back home, where she fed first on the fear of her family before settling on her dear friend Mossy. It was especially Mossy's shaman energy that gave her the most power. Without his interference, Cindy would have drained her completely.

You stabbed her, Blong pointed out.

Because you didn't trust her, added Kong.

Touso froze in dismay.

The next time you doubt your chosen bride, remember you didn't send the ghost of Cindy Thao away. Mossy did. Blong chided gently.

With that, she'd passed her first test, Kong concluded with satisfaction. Again, he was Mossy's biggest fan.

"I see what this is. You're calling me a control freak again." Touso shot them a scowl so furious that his spirit guides quickly departed, chuckling back from which they came.

Touso straightened. Something was different. The sore spot near his shoulder blade receded, and the tightness in his chest relaxed. He inhaled deeply, feeling like he could breathe freely for the first time. Immediately, Touso dialed Bao's number.

"Is she okay?" he demanded as soon as his sister picked up.

When Bao cried, it was out of sheer relief. "You won't believe it! She's perfectly okay!"

Touso fell against the couch in shock. It was the best news he could have hoped for, but he didn't understand. "What happened?"

"I don't understand it either. Dylan pulled the dagger out as we got to the hospital—I thought he was nuts for doing that!" Bao started to explain.

"What?" Touso was furious.

"No—there's more," Bao said quickly. "I was so worried when they rolled her inside, Touso. There was so much blood! Then the doctor came out with this strange look on his face. He asked us what happened. Dylan and I kept trying to explain that she got stabbed, but he looked at us like we were crazy."

"What are you trying to say, Bao?" Touso raked his hair impatiently.

"The doctor said it was just a scratch!" Bao was nearly shouting with happiness.

"What's she saying? How's Mossy?" Pahoua asked as she and her husband arrived.

Touso pushed a button, switching the call to video. Soon, Bao was on the screen smiling tearfully. Behind her, Dylan stood next to a sleeping Mossy. She had left the Khang house looking as pale as a ghost, but the color had returned to her pretty face. She looked peaceful.

"She's okay?" Pahoua glanced between Bao and Touso.

Bao nodded. "Yes! He didn't understand why her clothes were soaked when there was only a small cut next to her shoulder blade. He called it a 'scratch.'" Bao giggled again as though it were such a ridiculous notion. "She's dehydrated, but she's stable!"

Pahoua and Lihue cried with relief.

Touso remained quiet as he watched Mossy over Bao's shoulder. Dylan Reed was holding her hand. "How long will she stay?"

"Just overnight. They want to get her more hydrated and monitor her vitals tonight. But our girl's looking good, Touso! I don't know how to explain it, but she will be okay!" Bao's excitement shook the entire screen.

Touso nodded. "I'll be right there."

"We—I can stay with her tonight," Bao offered, quickly amending her first mistake.

Touso said, "No. You've done enough, Bao. Thank you. Please just watch her until I get there. Then come home and rest."

Bao knew it was pointless to argue when Touso made up his mind. After a few more words about Mossy's condition, she disconnected before she said anything she might regret.

Lihue noticed his son's agitation and asked, "What's wrong?"

"I don't understand." Touso shook his head in disbelief. "I stabbed her. Badly! How is there only a scratch now?"

Lihue and Pahoua looked at each other.

"Every bride has her unique strengths, Touso. I can read dreams. Your grandmother before me had the strength of a thousand men. Mossy, it seems, can heal herself faster than normal. It makes sense now when I think about it. Her ribs healed very quickly, didn't they?" Pahoua said thoughtfully.

She'd hurt her leg at the shamans' club, too, and was fine the next day. She always bounced back much too soon. Now, they knew why.

"Your chosen bride continues to surprise us at every turn," Lihue said, shaking his head.

"I know this should be a blessing, but why do I feel so afraid?" Touso asked.

Pahoua smiled. "Because you care about her."

Lihue rested a hand on Touso's shoulder and glanced affectionately at his wife. "Our chosen brides are blessings from our ancestors, my son. It is only right to fear losing what we should treasure the most. Go to her. Take care of her. It sounds like she'll be fine."

As Touso turned to leave, he prayed it was the truth. But as he drove toward his bride, he saw himself stabbing her over and over again.

"Mossy, you're going to be okay." She stirred at Bao's husky voice.

"Moss, can you hear me?" She was vaguely comforted by the warmth of Dylan's strong hands.

"Hmmm?" She would never know how happy Dylan was to hear this brief response. She hadn't answered any of their questions before now.

Mossy was healed, but she was still weak. This had little to do with the injury and everything to do with Cindy's ghost.

"That ghost took her strength," Bao sniffled now as she watched over Mossy.

"It didn't help to get stabbed either." Dylan scowled.

Bao looked up sharply. "It wasn't his fault. He was trying to help her."

"He could help her best by leaving her alone!" Dylan snapped.

Mossy's moan admonished them both to silence.

"I'm sorry," Dylan said after a while. "It's just hard to watch her like this."

Bao nodded. "I understand. You care for her. But I think you and Mossy need to talk seriously about your future. Things are different now."

Dylan snickered. "So, I keep hearing."

"Touso..." Mossy reached out, but her eyes remained closed.

Bao squeezed her hand. "Touso's coming."

When Mossy's eyes fluttered, she briefly saw Bao's lovely smile and tried to smile back. But she was weak and soon closed her eyes again.

"Whether or not you like it, Dylan, they have a bond. No one can break it." The remark was not as unkind as it was simply a fact.

"She almost died, Bao, and it's all connected to your brother. I can't just stand by and watch," Dylan replied.

"What will you do? Force her to leave?" Bao's tone seemed to pity Dylan more than anything, making him angry.

"I'll find a way to make her remember our life together," Dylan replied.

Bao shook her head sadly. "You can't change fate, Dylan. Touso is her destiny."

"The hell he is!" As Dylan snarled, he felt the ire of the thing inside of him.

"She almost killed my son today." Once again, when Kai Khang spoke, it was only for Dylan to hear. This spirit was usually smirking and poking fun at them, but for the first time, he wasn't joking.

"She didn't know he was there," Dylan said, defending Mossy.

Kai sneered. "She was being stupid. You don't defend a ghost."

"Says the ghost! Cindy was her friend. What is wrong with you people? You don't just forget the people you love!" Dylan's sudden outcry had both Bao and Kai staring at him.

Sighing in exasperation, he turned to leave.

"Where are you going?" Bao asked.

"I'm going home," Dylan answered without turning around. He needed to figure out his next move.

In the hall, he noticed a bored security guard standing outside a room. Dylan stopped a passing nurse and asked, "Hey, Jess. What's going on there?"

Jess, a pretty new grad, frowned. "Trying to get me in trouble already, Dylan? You know I'm not supposed to say!"

He gave her his most charming smile. "Oh, come on. I'm bored. Make it exciting for me."

Jess grinned and leaned in. "Just a catatonic convict. They're trying to figure out where to put him, but his brain seems toasted."

"What do you mean?" Dylan frowned.

"They brought him in after an incident earlier. He just stares without much response to stimuli. Anyway, we're monitoring until they figure out whether it's off to the jailhouse or the looney bin," Jess explained. "You didn't hear it from me!"

"Hear what?" Dylan looked confused.

Jess laughed. "I gotta go. See you later!"

After she was gone, Dylan continued staring into the room. All he could see was a monitor from inside the door, but the upper half of the patient was hidden around a corner. His vitals looked normal as the man rested utterly still.

Dylan glanced back at the officer, engrossed in a game, and shook his head. Whoever it was, at least he wasn't dangerous.

As Dylan Reed disappeared in the elevator, the police officer continued to play on his phone. But the mysterious patient was no longer in bed. Instead, he stood behind the door, staring off into the distance. Smoky worms clung to a bald head.

Yesssss... yessssss... we seeeeee you, Mossy Cha!

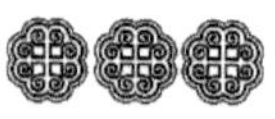

Get up. Get up!

Mossy furrowed her brows as a cool breeze blew at her face. A monitor with her vitals kept beeping until she opened her eyes. She didn't remember getting to the hospital but remembered Bao and

Dylan's voices speaking to her. Glancing around the empty room, she wondered where they were. *Where was Touso?*

Get up. Get up! Her spirit guides were anxious.

As she sat up at the edge of the bed, there was a terrible pounding in her head. Her chest tightened, and soon, there was a familiar burn. This only ever happened for one reason. *Danger.*

At the same time, Mossy noticed something glimmering from underneath her pillow. A moment later, she stared at a small dagger with a unique symbol of an elephant's foot. It meant "family."

As Bao left, she whispered, "I gotta go for a while, sis! This dagger will keep away the scary dreams while I'm gone!"

Mossy smiled. Knives were weapons against evil spirits and bad dreams. It was very Hmong of her sister-in-law to sneak it into her hospital room.

Listen!

Mossy straightened as her spirit guides yelled at her again. She heard the footsteps before she saw the shadow at her door. Without further hesitation, she grabbed the dagger and moved.

Chapter 20

Chewy Thao was a lifelong criminal whose demons had led him to do many terrible things. It should have been a done deal when he was arrested for attacking his sister and her friend. But as always, his mother protected him. After he was released on bail, Chewy convinced her to do another thing: get his sister to come home.

As Cindy returned, excited to make amends with her family, she never suspected that Chewy and his demons waited for her. But she fought hard. In the end, she just wasn't strong enough. She was powerless against the beefy hands around her throat. As the light faded from her eyes, Chewy laughed.

It was this sound that kept Cindy's ghost from floating toward the light of the spirit world. He was too lazy to bury her, tossing the body in the closet like a bag of clothes. Ghost Cindy was understandably pissed. In life, she was powerless, but in death, she would make him suffer.

She didn't waste time either. He took her life before lunch, and she was trolling his every move by dinner. People left living Cindy alone because of her surly attitude. Ghost Cindy proved so hostile that even his demons soon abandoned him.

He became worried when he saw her ghastly reflection in every mirror and window. When she crawled over his body to drain his energy, Chewy was afraid for the first time. The ghost of his sister dug its claws into his flesh, clinging on like a leech... and fed.

By the time Mossy Cha and Dylan Reed found him, he was catatonic. Cindy had nearly drained him completely. He arrived at the hospital in the same state and never responded to questions or tests. But when Mossy Cha was checked in, her energy awakened the demons within.

The opportunity to seize a chosen bride's soul was too tempting to pass! Chewy only needed to wait for the right opportunity.

The guard at his door was a rookie who should have kept his job at the mall. When he wasn't scrolling through social media, he played word puzzle games on his phone. When he noticed his patient was missing, he became frantic and ran impulsively into the room.

"Hey."

The guard's face turned with surprise as Chewy emerged from the shadows.

"You want to trade?" he asked.

Before the guard could react, Chewy whipped him over the head with a landline phone. As he crumpled onto the ground, Chewy picked up the smartphone.

'Thanks, man!" Chewy smirked as he turned and walked out.

Finding Mossy's room was easy. He imagined the shock on Mossy's face when she saw him, making him deliriously excited. That's why he wanted the phone—to record every second of what he was about to do. After locking the door behind him, he tapped the "record" button.

"Hey, girl, it's time to wake up." Chewy held the phone forward as he walked toward the bed. "Daddy wants to play."

He had watched the woman and man leave. It would be too late if anyone got back to Mossy's room. But the maniac was disappointed when he arrived only to find an empty bed. He glanced around furiously. *Where had she gone?*

He was annoyed when the demons alerted him about Touso's arrival.

"She's exhausted, but she'll be fine," Bao said as she met her brother in the hospital lobby. Mossy was sleeping when she left, and she was sure it would remain that way for the rest of the night. "The doctor has her on fluids. Unless something changes, they'll let her go home tomorrow."

Touso glanced around. "Where's Dylan?"

"You still worried about that guy?" Bao made a face.

"I'm not worried. I just don't like him."

"He went home a while ago." When her brother continued to scowl, she said, "They have a history together, Touso. He's not a bad guy. Can you imagine someone just showing up and taking the person you love? They both need time to process these changes."

"I'm not concerned about his feelings, Bao," Touso replied.

"Then you should think about Mossy," she admonished. "She's going through a lot of changes. Try not to lecture her when she wakes up."

Touso looked agitated. "Am I really so coldhearted?"

"I just know how you feel about rules." Bao smiled sympathetically. "She's waiting for you upstairs. If she woke up at all, she asked for you. Stop worrying about the other guy. She's your chosen bride and has already chosen you."

Touso looked away. Mossy was to become his wife. Was it abnormal to want his bride entirely to himself? It was a question Kai could have helped him with—if he were there.

He asked, "What happened to the dagger?"

Bao grinned sheepishly. "Uh, don't be mad."

"What did you do?"

"I stuck it underneath her pillow," Bao explained quickly.

"You what?" Touso leaned close and whispered, "I just stabbed her with that thing!"

Bao grimaced. "Family secret. You didn't mean to do it, and it's a protection tool, okay?"

Touso rolled his eyes and said, "Go home."

Anxious to see Mossy, Touso ran toward the elevator, but he became more apprehensive as he got closer. Something wasn't right. Touso's body tingled with sensations he had come to associate with one thing: fear.

Mossy's fear.

He almost knocked over a nurse as he ran out of the elevator and searched for her room. His heart raced erratically when the door was locked, and a stocky shadow hovered over her bed.

Awakening

Touso summoned his spirit guides to help him bust open the door but nearly fell when it swung open. The shadow was gone, and the only noise was the soft humming of the machines in the room.

"Mossy?" When Touso pulled the curtain aside, he was relieved to find her in bed. She must have been cold because she was curled under the covers and never stirred as he approached. "Mossy? It's just me. I'm here."

Touso frowned when his fingers sunk into something soft. He pulled the blankets back to find only pillows underneath. He was so distracted that he didn't notice his spirit guides warning him—he didn't hear the footsteps until it was too late.

Touso's fingers flew up just as a thin cord closed around his throat. He heard a crazy chuckle and turned enough to see Chewy Thao's wild eyes.

"Looking for your girlfriend?" Chewy was incredibly strong as he cinched the cord tighter, cutting off Touso's air. "Me, too!"

As he twisted the cord around his throat, Chewy imagined what he should do: kill the man now or make him watch while Chewy played with his girlfriend. It would be fun to see his expression when she died! But Touso wasn't making it easy with this endless struggle.

Chewy threw him against the wall and said, "I'll deal with you first. Then I'll play with Mossy. It's going to be so much fun!"

Furious, Touso's eyes burst into blue flames. But something strange happened before he could tear at the cords and limbs clinging to his throat.

Chewy released him unexpectedly and began a struggle of his own. Touso spun around, gasping for air. The crazy man stood frozen as a purple glow surrounded him.

Mossy floated behind him, dressed only in a hospital gown. Her face showed no expression, but her eyes blazed with a strange light.

"Mossy!" he gasped.

Whether or not she heard him, she didn't respond. Instead, Mossy curled an arm around Chewy's throat and tightened the grasp until the creatures inside him slithered and screamed for mercy.

Demons!

Furiously, she thrust a glowing purple hand into the man's head. Chewy's blink expression turned to agony. But Mossy was hunting and wouldn't stop until she found it. Finally, Chewy crumpled onto the ground. In her hand was a creature with three cobra heads.

They snapped their fangs and curled a lengthy tail around her body, but Mossy's expression never changed. Instead, her light grew even brighter until it burned the thing that clung to her.

As the demon howled, Mossy lifted a familiar dagger and executed three quick jabs into each of its heads. Soon after, it exploded into a spray of ash.

Touso caught Mossy just as she collapsed from this deadly trance. In his arms, she finally released the dagger. He was relieved when the lashes fluttered to reveal beautiful brown eyes.

"Touso..." she whispered, sounding much weaker than he liked.

He leaned close and asked, "Yes, Mossy?"

"I'm tired."

As Touso cradled her, his eyes fell on the weapon. She had saved him with the same blade that nearly took her life.

Touso wept silently. "It's okay. Go to sleep. I'm here. I'll keep you safe."

Chapter 21

Mossy should have been preparing for her wedding with Touso. Instead, she made funeral arrangements for her friend. Without parents or close relatives, the responsibility of putting Cindy to rest fell to Mossy and her family.

While she worked with the funeral home, her parents focused on the traditional parts of the service that she didn't understand. Any free time was spent walking the school halls like a ghost, wondering if life would ever be the same again.

Since her parents were a vital part of the process, Mossy returned home. Her in-laws were helpful, stopping by to assist wherever they could. While Lihue and Touso helped Keng procure the right people and animals for the service, Pahoua and Bao prepared food and entertained the children.

Blia was grateful for the company, but Mossy was especially reserved. It was difficult to face her in-laws with all the questions in their eyes.

Touso remained with Mossy during this stay, but they slept apart. They rarely spoke except in passing, and she avoided running into him alone. Her parents thought they were being modest, but Touso knew why Mossy wouldn't look at him.

Mossy was upset with him. She was angry at all of them. So, she stayed away from everyone, even refusing to eat with the family. If she smiled, it was for Billy and David, the people Cindy had loved the most.

They were good boys, even though their world had turned upside down overnight. Until other arrangements were made, they were staying with the Chas. Allen, Cheng, and Shengmii proved to be good distractions with games and food. Blia thought keeping them connected with Cindy was important, so she and Pahoua taught them how to fold paper blessings.

"Why is the paper so shiny?" David asked, staring at the thin joss paper between his fingers.

Pahoua answered, "Gold represents wealth. You want to send your sister away with riches, don't you?"

"Why does it have to be a boat?" Billy wondered.

"To make sure she travels safely," Pahoua explained.

"Why does she have to go anywhere at all?" David demanded.

Blia looked at him with sympathy. "It doesn't seem fair, but your sister was in much pain. She's going somewhere much better."

Pahoua added, "Remember that she's not gone. She's just moving on, and her journey will be much more comfortable if we send her away with nice things."

"I'm going to make her lots of boats!" Billy proclaimed with admirable determination.

"I wish she'd take us with her." As the older of the two, David was the most affected by Cindy's death. He was often somber and quiet unless spoken to.

Blia shook her head. "Everyone has their time, child. This trip is not yours to take just yet, but she'll be waiting for you. She hopes you'll live a long and wonderful life for now."

"How do you know?" David frowned in disbelief.

"Because she loved you." Blia gave him her most reassuring smile. "Now, what else do you think your sister might enjoy seeing? Does she have a favorite animal?"

"She loved snakes!" Billy's eyes were bright with excitement.

"And pit bulls." David laughed, which was a welcome change. "She loved how mean they are!"

"Well, I don't know how to fold snakes or pit bulls, but we can try." Blia's expression was thoughtful as they continued folding.

Mossy listened from the living room with a sad smile. Cindy enjoyed all the mean animals because she liked the idea of biting people who irritated her. She would be thrilled to receive a team of snakes and pit bulls to escort her to the afterlife. As the chatter continued in the other room, Mossy gently folded the hemp clothes prepared for Cindy's journey.

She thought Cindy should wear something soft and silky, so she asked her mother, "Why hemp?"

"Don't you know how rough this journey will be?" Blia gasped.

No. Mossy's eyes grew wide with confusion. She didn't know. How would she?

In a hushed voice, Blia continued, "If she's not facing lions and tigers, she'll climb mountains and walk through wind and rain. So, she'll need to wear something much sturdier than silk!"

Mossy studied the woven hemp jacket and shoes. They didn't look especially tough. So, she went shopping and bought a pair of shiny black combat boots and a thick leather jacket. It even had a hoodie to protect her head. Now, Mossy was certain her friend would prevail in any storm.

She was scrolling through photos for Cindy's memorial slide when Pahoua sat beside her. "How are you feeling, daughter-in-law?"

Mossy blushed. She hadn't been a good daughter-in-law lately and was surprised Pahoua wasn't upset. "I'm okay. I wish I had more pictures of her smiling."

Cindy hated taking photos and always frowned or made faces when Mossy and Eva forced her into them. They recovered a few more from family albums, but Mossy eventually wondered if it was worth it. Her friend had lived such a sad life.

Pahoua smiled. "They say a picture is worth a thousand words, but they don't convey everything. That's where loved ones come in. You knew her best. You can always create one if you can't find the photos you want."

Mossy contemplated these words.

"Now tell me the truth. How are you really doing?" Pahoua studied her.

Mossy grimaced and admitted, "I feel resentful."

Pahoua said, "Of everyone?"

Mossy nodded. "No one understands. She was my friend and deserved better."

Pahoua didn't say anything for a long time, and Mossy wondered if she would say anything at all. Finally, she said, "Be that as it may, there is something else we must discuss."

Mossy asked, "What do you mean?"

"Your powers are growing."

Mossy looked away. She didn't understand what was happening and was afraid.

"Not once, but twice, your energy exploded," Pahoua continued. "As chosen brides, we share certain powers, but some strengths are uniquely our own. You've been especially blessed. I see it. But your strength will destroy you if you don't learn to control it."

"I was upset!" Emotion spread across her face.

Pahoua remained firm. "Even so, you could have hurt someone. Whether sad, broken, or pissed, you must protect yourself and the ones you love."

"That's what I was doing!" Mossy sobbed.

"What about Fuechi? Touso? Dylan? And my husband? What of their lives? You were so focused on one person that you put others in danger. You must always remember the bigger picture, Mossy," Pahoua chided.

Suddenly, Mossy was glowing again, and the photo frames on the wall rattled.

Pahoua said, "Control yourself, Mossy Cha. Imagine yourself back at home, in front of your altar. Think of the soft white paper. The incense is simmering. The flames are burning gently. Everything is calm. This is your place of peace."

When Mossy closed her eyes, she saw the altar in flames. "Everything is burning!" she cried.

"Our energy can feel like a separate entity, but it's us. This is the difference between feeling and knowing. Knowing what will happen if you don't make the right decisions is the beginning of strength. The fire you see is the one raging inside of you now. What good will come if you let it burn?" Pahoua asked.

In her mind, the fire spread to a wall that held photos of familiar faces: her parents, siblings, the Khangs... But the wedding photo of Touso and Mossy was the most disturbing. Her lack of control could destroy something that was yet to happen!

"Take a deep breath. When something is hot, what does it need? When you're sad, what makes you feel better?" Pahoua's voice seemed very far away.

Raindrops.

When her soul was lost in the jungle, it was hot. It was only when the rain washed over her body that she felt better. It was in Touso's arms that she was safe. As she thought of this, a gentle shower fell over the fire raging in her soul. Eventually, the flames slowed to a simmer, and the altar in her mind returned to a peaceful place. The walls in the Cha home became still.

Mossy opened her eyes. "I didn't mean to hurt them."

"But in your pain, you forgot them. You lost control and could have lost more than just a friend that night." Pahoua reached for her hand. "Cindy deserved better in this life, but her needs changed when she died. Your responsibilities as an aunt, wife, friend, and daughter didn't. Your destiny as a shaman means you'll always have to think about the greater good. If you don't learn this, you'll become dangerous to everyone you love."

If Pahoua meant to shame her, she had done well. So, Mossy was surprised by her next words. "I'm proud of you."

She blinked in confusion.

"You made the right decision, even if it took time," Pahoua said, touching Mossy's cheek. "You saved Touso at the hospital. Even in your weakest state, you woke up to protect him. That is who you are. That is what we do. But if we're not careful, these gifts can become destructive."

Mossy burned with shame, knowing she could have hurt them all.

Pahoua hugged her and said, "Chosen bride, your life will not be easy, but you're not alone. Remember that!"

As Pahoua rejoined the others, Mossy stared after her. This chosen bride had already protected her shaman for decades and now relied on another to protect her remaining son. If anyone had a hard life, it was Pahoua.

Something shiny caught her eye. The dagger from that horrible night rested next to the photo album. Pahoua must have left it behind. Mossy turned the small metal hand until her eyes found the small elephant's foot engraving that meant "family."

For the first time, Mossy understood. The chosen bride didn't just protect her shaman—she protected the family.

Cindy looked like she was sleeping when the coroner rolled her into the room. With her makeup done, including the cattails at her eyes, she looked like she was sleeping. Because only loved ones dressed the dead, this responsibility belonged to Mossy and her mother.

They cried the entire time, making sure not to mess up her makeup. In the end, Cindy looked lovely in a white hemp outfit, complete with a robe, apron, and skirt. A black leather jacket and combat boots finished it off.

Cindy Thao was ready to travel to her afterlife in style.

Taking Pahoua's advice, Mossy worked with Jeremy to design something unique to honor Cindy's memory. It was important that whatever it was represented her true character. The result was a projected image of a warrior-like Cindy, garbed in a leather jacket and combat boots. Like the last movie they saw, she held a golden lasso, and an army of pit bulls stood behind her, ready to battle anyone for the people she loved.

It was perfect.

Hmong funerals were usually three days, but the Chas kept it short and intimate. They didn't expect many people to attend, and Cindy would have only wanted her closest family and friends present, anyway. Ultimately, it was just Cindy's brothers, David and Billy, Mossy's family, and the Khangs. Cindy's older sisters couldn't attend the funeral but offered to pick up Billy and David afterward.

Dylan and Eva came to pay their last respects. But Dylan kept his distance. Like her spirit guides, he was angry with her, but she didn't know why.

Nia and Fuechi returned home when she discovered what happened in the woods. She felt Fuechi was in more danger with the Khangs and wasn't entirely wrong. A war was brewing, and the Khangs were at the center of it.

Awakening

A soul guide arrived at the funeral to ensure Cindy completed her journey safely. He gave her directions and taught her to collect the tools she needed for safe travels. David and Billy's contribution of several oddly shaped animals would make the trip especially interesting.

If the soul guide's job was to instruct the soul on how to reach the afterlife, the lusheng player's job was to keep the soul on that path. It was an arduous journey that followed every place the soul ever lived until finally, it reached the Lake of Life. The music was so powerful the soul had no choice but to follow, and this kept it from getting lost on the way.

The musician was the Pied Piper, leading souls away to the afterlife. He wasn't much older than Mossy, but he played with the experience of men twice his age. The music of the lusheng was particularly haunting, and Mossy was soon spellbound. He danced and played the bamboo instrument with his eyes closed, twirling and leaping gracefully every time the path changed. These spontaneous movements made it easy to believe he was walking this journey with the soul.

Mossy wished more than anything that she could walk alongside her friend. Once Cindy arrived at the Lake of Life, she would be free, and Mossy prayed that the Gods had good things waiting for her.

When the soul guide announced that she had completed her journey, it was time to take her body to its final resting place. As her pallbearers—Touso, Keng, Dylan, Lihue, Allen, and Cheng—escorted her to the burial ground, everyone else followed in tears.

Then it was time to say goodbye.

Mossy handed the brothers each a white rose to toss into the bed. They were so quiet until that point. So, when the boys began wailing, Mossy's heart shattered again. It was hard not to join them.

"Don't leave me!" David screamed.

"Come back, Cindy. Come back!" Billy cried.

It was heartbreaking. Blia gathered them into her arms. "It's okay to cry for her. Cry as much as you need to, sweet boys. Today is the day to remind her she is loved."

After letting them weep for some time, Blia finally led them away so everyone else could bid farewell.

"I'll miss you, you sassy bee." Eva chuckled in a broken voice. "It won't be the same without your dirty looks and wicked smile."

Dylan tossed down several chocolate bars. "Cindy, I know these were your favorite. Here's some for the road, kid. Travel safely, and don't beat up too many people on the other side."

Her parents and the Khangs were the last to toss their roses. While everyone turned to leave, Mossy stayed behind. She stared at the cherrywood casket holding her precious friend's body, once again hoping to wake up from this nightmare. Tomorrow, she'd pick up Cindy from her house, and just like usual, they'd walk to school together.

"Are you okay?" Touso curled a hand around her fingers.

"No," Mossy whispered as the world became a blur. "I don't know if I'll ever be okay again."

She had lost her grandparents, but it felt different when it was murder. It was wrong. Her heart was heavy with that injustice.

"Death is never easy." Touso understood her pain. It wasn't long ago since his own loss.

"How did you do it?" She wiped her eyes and looked at him. "How did you get over Kai's death?"

A shadow came over his golden eyes. "I didn't. Life just keeps you busy, and sometimes you forget."

"Will you help me to forget?" Mossy asked.

Touso furrowed his brows. It wasn't a "figurative" request. She wanted him to make her feelings disappear. "Even if I could, it's against the rules."

"Why?" She sounded irritated.

"We have rules, Mossy."

Rules. It was back to the rules. She frowned in distaste. Like Dylan, her spirit guides had ceased talking to her, too. They were all especially quiet since Mossy sent Cindy away.

"How many rules are there?" she demanded.

"Many." Touso gave a small smile. "But I'll give you the top two. First, you can't take a life, and second, we don't use our powers against our own family."

"Well, I didn't break any of those rules, but they're still pissed at me." Mossy's voice dropped as she thought of her spirit guides.

Gowli, Pao, and Chee were always with her, whispering and protecting her at every turn. But they had grown quiet since she refused to banish Cindy's ghost. Gowli said Mossy needed to learn to follow the rules or suffer the consequences. She never imagined one of those consequences might be Fuechi's life. She had only wanted to protect her friend. She didn't mean to...

"Is Nia mad at me, too?"

Touso shook his head. "She's scared. Nia wants to protect him, but she doesn't understand our life. Whether or not Fuechi's with us, our blood runs through his veins. Our ancestors will eventually call him to honor our traditions, and his spirit guides will expect him to fight.

It'll be easier if he learns from his own people, but she'll have to come to that on her own."

"Or there'll be consequences." She wasn't able to hide the bitterness in her voice.

"Mossy, you were wrong." Touso took her by the chin so she would look at him. "You chose the wrong side."

"What side? She was my friend!" Mossy pulled away angrily.

Touso's expression was solemn. "You still don't understand, and that's why they won't speak to you. "Shamans exist to maintain a balance. We protect life. Ghosts, spirits, and demons exist but don't belong with us. You saw what Cindy was doing to you. If Dylan didn't get to Fuechi when he did, that ghost would have—"

"Stop!" Mossy threw her hands to her ears. "I get it! I was stupid, okay? But that ghost was my friend, Touso. I was supposed to protect her, and I didn't, and she died because of me!"

"She died because of something evil!" Touso corrected her with a fierceness that surprised her. "Something took that boy's soul long ago, and the Thaos lost a daughter by protecting him. The only way to honor someone we've lost is by helping them to move on to a better place."

"And if it was me?" Mossy demanded. "If I was on the wrong side, would you just send me away?"

Touso stiffened.

"Answer me."

"Yes." Touso met her gaze without faltering. "I would send you somewhere—anywhere as long as it meant your soul would be safe. That's what we do for the people we love."

Mossy stared at him, at a loss for words. Cindy's ghost had been sad, angry, and vengeful. It only knew pain, and it had made her hideous—and dangerous. It was far from the peace her friend deserved. With a loud sob, Mossy finally accepted that Touso was right. And when Touso reached for her again, she didn't resist. Mossy crumbled and wept.

"I hate that you're so smart." She sniffled.

Touso chuckled. "Some say I have a heart of stone."

"I don't believe it." Mossy shook her head. "I'm sorry for putting everyone's life in danger. I know she's better off where she is now. I just wasn't ready to say goodbye."

"You can do it now," Touso spoke softly against her ear.

Mossy gazed down at the casket in the ground. She said, "Cindy, I hope your soul has found peace. I know part of the reason you wouldn't leave is because you were worried about us. I'll keep in touch with your brothers and watch out for them. Don't worry about me anymore, okay? I'll be strong, just like you always wanted. I'll see you again someday, my friend."

As Mossy tossed her rose, Touso pulled out one of his own. "Cindy Thao, I promise I will protect Mossy in your place. Don't worry. Be happy, friend. Find peace."

Don't worry, be happy... Where did she know those words?

"Are you ready to go?" Touso asked.

As Mossy met his gaze, something stirred deep within her chest. A moment later, her spirit guides leaped and soared around them. They had missed her just as much as she'd missed them. Even Kalia, ever busy with her royal duties, took a moment to sail the skies.

There were rules in their world, and Mossy Cha had just learned the most important one: things must go where they belong.

"Yes." Mossy smiled as Touso held out his hand. "I'm ready now."

Rest in Peace
Cindy Thao

Chapter 22

Nia Johnson was glad to be home, but something didn't feel right. The ominous feeling had started nearly as soon as they returned. No matter how bright or warm outside, their tiny home felt dark and cold. Shadowy figures seemed to follow them everywhere, and Fuechi refused to be left alone. Now, they sat together on the couch, where he watched an episode of "Paw Patrol" while she folded the laundry.

"Mama, I miss Grandpa," Fuechi whined without looking away from the television.

"I know, baby. But isn't it nice to be back home?" Nia mustered her most cheerful expression, but Fuechi wasn't convinced.

"No. I miss Grandpa."

Nia sighed as she returned to folding the laundry that had been left out since Fuechi went to the hospital. At first, she was grateful to have the Khang family. Fuechi already adored them. They had saved him and quickly embraced both of them as part of their family. But Nia couldn't shake the feeling that it was dangerous to be around them.

One moment, she was making cookies for her son in the kitchen; the next, he was gone. Then Touso returned with an injured Mossy and wouldn't answer any questions. Nia was beyond hysterics by the time Dylan returned with Fuechi.

"What happened?" Nia demanded as Dylan handed him over.

"Mama, ghost girl wasn't nice," Fuechi answered before Dylan could explain.

Nia glanced between the both of them in bewilderment. "Ghost girl?"

"She went home," Fuechi answered again, strangely unbothered by the paranormal event. "Uncle Touso and Aunt Mossy sent her home."

"Dylan, what the hell is going on?" She turned to the young man who was always conveniently around when her son needed help.

"Ghost girl—"

"Fuechi, I'm talking to the adults!" Nia finally snapped.

"Nia, something terrible happened." Dylan tried to stay calm, but the bloody scene before them didn't help.

Nia inhaled sharply. Something *terrible* was always happening.

"Mossy lost a friend, and this friend needed help moving on," Dylan continued.

"Friend was mean," Fuechi added with a pout.

"What do you mean 'moving on?' Why does Fuechi keep talking about a ghost girl?"

"Mossy's friend died!" Touso finally tore his gaze away from his bride's pale face. His eyes were raw with emotion. "She didn't want to leave Mossy—and I stabbed her while trying to send Cindy away. Oh, God—Mossy, wake up. I'm so sorry!"

Awakening

Blood was pooling on the ground where he held her. Mossy, who was always so bright, was very pale... Nia couldn't handle it anymore. She had lost her husband, her son was seeing ghosts, and now this poor girl was dying! It was too much. Nia grabbed Fuechi and hurried toward the door.

"Nia, wait. Where are you going?" Dylan followed her with a worried expression. "You shouldn't be alone right now."

"I can't do this." As Nia shook her head, she turned to look at Touso. "Kai always said this family lived very differently. I'm finally starting to understand why he didn't want us—why he didn't want Fuechi to be a part of it. No child should have to live this way!"

Touso couldn't look away from his bride, who moaned and shuddered in pain. He didn't try to stop Nia when she left with Fuechi.

Now, mother and son were back home. She should have been happy, but Nia felt empty. She liked the Khang family. But Nia was sure that Fuechi was in as much danger with the Khangs as he was without them.

Kai. I wish you were here. He always knew what to do.

Suddenly, the power went out. An eerie silence followed as the animated noise of the television died.

"Mama! The lights are out again!" Fuechi wailed.

Nia set the laundry down on the coffee table. Outages were happening more often, and strangely, it only affected their apartment. She'd have to call management again.

"I know, baby. I'll go check it out. You stay here, okay?"

"Mama, Fuechi is scared," he moaned.

Nia put on her best smile and tucked the panda bear into her son's arms. "Mr. Foo will protect you."

Fuechi had named it himself. When she asked where he got the idea, Fuechi shrugged and said, "That's what he told me."

"I'll be back soon," Nia promised as Fuechi hugged Mr. Foo and slipped underneath the covers.

All the apartments on the third floor shared a breaker panel at the end of the hallway. When the lights started going out, Nia thought one of the neighbors was pranking her. But as the outages continued, she was sure something was wrong with the wiring. Still, management insisted there was nothing wrong. Now, even the lights in the hallway flickered as she made her way to the other end.

Nia never noticed the shadow following her. Daisy Vang's haunted soul scaled the ceiling, pausing every time Nia stopped and proceeding every time Nia moved. Once, the length of her coarse hair fell and brushed the young woman's ear. Nia flicked back her hand, assuming it was a fly. Flies were notorious during the warmer months!

Finally, Nia entered the small maintenance room no bigger than her closet. There was only one incandescent bulb to light up the entire space. She squinted her eyes and followed all the switches until she arrived at the number 307. There were three switches for each apartment, and Nia usually restarted all three to avoid the back and forth. As she leaned to begin the process, she felt the tickle at her ear and behind her neck. Again, she swiped with her hand. But when the tickling continued, Nia paused and frowned. Her heart raced.

Thoom-thoomp! Thoom-thoomp! Thoom-thoomp!

When something cold and stiff brushed the flesh of her neck, Nia gasped and whirled around. A grotesque creature hung from the ceiling. Its coarse black hair fell like a curtain of death as one bloody red eye peered back. Then it leaped and landed in front of Nia. As the creature moved closer, the contorted features of a woman became more visible. The stabbing pressure of the panel switches against her spine reminded Nia that this wasn't a nightmare.

It was real!

"Mama!"

Fuechi?

When Nia turned to look down the hall, her cheeks brushed the clammy skin of the thing next to her. It laughed and instantly grabbed her throat with a length of sticky black hair. As Nia dangled in the air, the creature flashed a row of yellow teeth.

"You!" The dreadful voice rang in her ears. "Your fault... your fault!"

One of the bodies that Daisy haunted belonged to Emma Sheng Moua. While she slowly drained Thai Khang's soul for her master, she never expected to meet Kai's family. Daisy could think only of her own loss as she watched Fuechi blow out his birthday candles. Kai Khang had rejected her for this woman and child, and because of that, Daisy lost everything.

"You took what was mine!" The entity snarled and tossed Nia onto the ground. "Now, I will take it all from you."

Nia landed several feet into the hallway, where the lights flickered erratically. Quickly, she scrambled to her feet and began sprinting for the door. But Daisy was faster, wrapping her hair around the woman's ankles again. When she yanked, Nia fell to her knees. She cackled as the woman kicked and screamed, then tossed Nia against the wall.

The wicked spirit of Daisy Vang stood over her. "You will all pay!"

As Daisy shrieked, Nia found her strength—and punched her. The impact was just hard enough to knock the creature off its feet. Then

Nia made a quick dash for her apartment. Her only thoughts were for her son as the creature behind her gave chase.

She was caught off guard when the entrance to her home opened, and a man and child stumbled out. For a second, the blond hair made her think of her husband. But when the man turned to look at her, she gasped.

"Dylan!" She arrived just in time to take Fuechi from his arms.

"Run!" Dylan pushed them toward the exit just as a team of shadows spilled from the apartment.

The shadows turned into several gaunt and pale women with long, coarse hair. As they shuffled forward, the one stalking Nia leaped out from behind. It stood at the front of the ghastly horde with all the fury of a woman scorned.

"You!" Daisy glared at the soul of Kai Khang. She could see him. That was how strong their bond remained.

Kai froze when he saw the creature that used to be his chosen bride. Daisy Vang was a beautiful woman full of sass and light. This thing that she had become... it was a terrible shame, and his heart fluttered between sorrow and regret.

"Dylan?" All the color was gone from his face, and Nia didn't understand why he wasn't moving. As Daisy and the phantoms charged forward, she finally grabbed his hand. "Move, asshole!"

She pulled him out the door just in time. A moment later, they were back in Nia's car. The tires burned against the pavement as she hit the gas and sped away. But it was a long time before Kai stopped hearing Daisy scream.

Sarah Khang returned home much earlier than expected and was ready for war. No matter what their parents believed, she wouldn't let them force her brother to marry. He was too young, and the idea behind it was ridiculous. Thai was sick—not cursed! Sarah was determined to do whatever she needed to keep her brother safe.

"Mom, for the last time—there's got to be another way!" Sarah crossed her arms with determination.

"Don't you think your father and I have tried?" May shook her head. "The doctors haven't been able to do anything—but Sheng has kept your brother safe! Don't you see how healthy he's become?"

Sarah sighed. Fifteen-year-olds weren't supposed to be getting married to be safe from demons and other evil things. They were supposed to be kids!

"Sarah, just calm down. Tomorrow is the wedding ceremony, and your brother needs you to be the bridesmaid. You can't go to her family's house, causing drama." Yer tried to reason with their daughter, but he knew it would be fruitless. She was a modern young woman who never connected with the traditions of her culture.

"That is the only thing I will do if you insist on this wedding!" Sarah promised.

"Listen," May said finally. "It's useless for you to argue with us. Why don't you go upstairs and talk to your brother? Sheng's upstairs, too. Maybe if you meet her and talk to them both, you'll understand. This must happen, Sarah, or—"

Awakening

Sarah frowned when her mother stifled a sob. She couldn't believe it. She was always thankful that May wasn't old-fashioned like Mossy's mom, and now Sarah felt betrayed. Her mother really believed there was a curse.

She glared at both her parents. "Fine. I'm going upstairs right now to talk some sense into the both of them—since you two won't!"

As Sarah disappeared up the stairs, May and Yer looked at each other in dismay. It was going to be a long night.

Sarah hadn't been home long. As soon as she walked through the door, she immediately looked for their parents. They'd been sitting together in the kitchen discussing plans for the wedding. Since she couldn't convince them, Sarah was determined to get Thai to see reason. Even if she had to take him back to Los Angeles to help him figure things out, she would gladly do it. Anything was better than getting married! Again, Sarah shook her head in disgust. Everyone had gone crazy in her absence.

Sarah slowed as she approached Thai's room. The door was ajar, and the room itself was dark. Only the light from the hallway showed his feet resting on top of the bed. He was asleep.

"Thai?" Sarah gently pushed open the door.

At first, there was no response. Then she heard the slightest moan from the shadows. When Sarah pushed the door the rest of the way, she gasped. A young woman was sitting on top of her brother! Immediately, Sarah felt the heat rush to her face.

"Oh! I'm sorry!" She turned away with embarrassment but soon felt a wave of irritation. "Argh, why don't you two lock the door?"

When neither responded, Sarah paused and returned her eyes to the situation in the room. She assumed the young woman was her brother's intended bride. She remained sitting on top of Thai with her back leaned forward like they were in a passionate embrace. But her brother's arms rested strangely beside his body. His legs twitched underneath Sheng's weight like he was struggling.

"Thai?" Sarah stepped into the room and narrowed her gaze.

The girl ceased what she was doing and straightened. Despite the awkward embrace, Sheng was completely dressed.

"Sheng?" Sarah took another careful step. "What's going on?"

Sarah was now close enough to see her brother's face. Thai was in a daze, his mouth gaping wide. Then suddenly, Sheng turned around. Sarah nearly fell as she met the hollow black eyes of a grotesque face. When a long tongue slid from a horrid grin, Sarah screamed.

Chapter 23

Mossy's mood after the funeral remained somber and took a turn for the worse after David and Billy left with their estranged sisters. Without them, she lost her last ties to Cindy. Mossy cried the entire way home, and there was nothing Touso could do to ease her pain.

She was grateful when he finally left her alone to wallow in her sorrows. Mossy just wanted to hide under the blanket for the rest of her life. But even sleep offered little peace because she kept hearing the sound of weeping chosen brides.

Whenever Mossy closed her eyes, her soul would leap into the underworld. She'd see the Black Door hovering at the end of the horizon or just beyond a tree. But every time Mossy got close enough, it would disappear.

Touso said the Black Door was its own entity. Sometimes, it took people to the places they wanted to go the most. Other times, it took them where they needed to be. But most of the time, these places were too dangerous because there was no guarantee of return. Mossy Cha only wanted to go back to one place. She wanted to find all the girls she'd left behind.

"Mossy! Don't forget us!" Emma Sheng would weep from behind the door.

Mossy cried every time the Black Door vanished into thin air. It was a cruel joke, and she knew Du Yong was behind all of it. She heard his mocking voice everywhere.

"Why don't you just come back to us? I would gladly open the door for you, my sweet." His mocking laughter made it all the worse.

But these moments with Du Yong were always brief as her spirit guides pulled her back to safety. As much as they could, they protected her. Talking to demons was always dangerous, especially when it was Du Yong.

The last time she saw the Black Door was in her room. It floated just behind the foot of the bed. She was mesmerized by its glow. It was a door that shined like a powerful gem—like rubies. This time, when Mossy moved, the door stayed still. It waited until she was close enough to touch it, and it remained as she pressed an ear against the smooth glass. It pulsed against her flesh like a heartbeat. Then Mossy heard the sounds: Voices. Crying. Emma!

"Let us out!"

"Take us home!"

"Don't eat us!"

"Mossy, don't forget!"

As soon as Mossy lifted her fists to bang on the door, she heard knocking. But it came from somewhere else.

Awakening

Mossy blinked as she awoke in bed. At first, she wondered where all her BTS posters were and why her walls were grey. Then she remembered this was Touso's room—her new room in a new home.

"Come in." Mossy touched her face. Her eyes and cheeks were swollen from sleep and crying. She'd probably find a mess if she dared look into a mirror now.

Someone pushed the door open, and she was surprised to see Bao. The pretty woman beamed and skipped excitedly inside.

"Good! You're up!" Bao grabbed the covers and pulled them away. Before Mossy could say a word, she'd already grabbed her hand. "Come on. I need your help!"

A moment later, Mossy was in Bao's room. All her anxiety waned as she watched Touso's beautiful sister model a sexy red cocktail dress in front of the mirror. The plunging neckline around her ample breasts was most impressive.

Bao asked, "What do you think? Too much?"

"It's perfect for a party, but maybe too much for all those old cats at the Shamans' Club," Mossy replied.

Bao grinned mischievously. "If someone's not having a heart attack, I'm not doing enough!"

Mossy chuckled at her sister-in-law and realized how much Bao reminded her of Cindy; she was a free spirit. As Mossy lost herself in these thoughts, Bao disappeared into the closet. Then she returned with a sleeveless coral dress that shimmered beautifully in the light. There must have been hundreds of tiny crystals sewn into the feathered chiffon skirt.

"What about this one?"

"I love it!" Mossy's face lit up excitedly.

"Good! Because it's yours." Bao winked at her.

Mossy's mouth dropped in surprise. "What? Why?"

"Come on. I have to go to the club tonight. Why don't you go with me? It's a good excuse to dress up and drink!" Bao's enthusiasm was catching as she grabbed Mossy's hands.

"You do know I'm underage, right?" Mossy reminded her.

"You know we're going to a secret Hmong club, right?" Bao made a face before laughing at her expression.

Mossy recalled all the activities she'd witnessed: smoking, drinking, gambling... the only vice missing was an orgy, and she was afraid to ask. But Bao was right: drinking was the least of her worries.

"I don't know." Mossy hesitated. She thought about how she had brushed off Touso all day and wondered how he would feel if she ran off with Bao in a cocktail dress. "Does Touso know about this?"

"Don't worry about him! He's out with my dad. They'll be gone all night!" Bao began dancing around the room with the coral gown as her partner. "Come on—please! I've never had a sister before. This will be so much fun!"

Bao was also too much like Eva. It was hard to resist her charm. As Mossy finally nodded, the other girl yelped excitedly. Before Mossy knew what was happening, Bao shoved her off to shower. She needed a clean slate for the magic she was about to perform.

Touso Khang and Alang Vang were not friends. Everyone was reminded of this as the two faced off in front of all the other shamans in the room. They were both the youngest of their clans. They were also very dangerous in their own right. Touso had an army of spirit guides behind him. Alang was incredibly clever with his own bag of tricks. Kou and Ying glanced nervously at each other; if this escalated any further, there would be no "club" to tend to that weekend.

"I'm going to ask you one more time." Touso's eyes flickered between gold and blue. "What are you doing with the chosen brides?"

Alang grinned. "I'm going to tell you one more time. We have simply united them with their shamans. You're welcome!"

"This is preposterous!" Seng shouted from his table. "How dare you stand here and accuse us of such a crime?"

'It is a crime!" Touso rarely raised his voice, but it now thundered across the room. "Something isn't right with those brides. Have you seen their eyes? They're empty!"

"The results speak for themselves. How many shamans have been better since we found their brides?" Alang asked.

Chatter erupted in the room. The only ones still affected were the ones who were alone.

"See?" Alang smiled triumphantly. "You're alone in your presumptions, Touso. But then again, your family has a history of rejecting chosen brides."

Everyone gasped. It was the first time the Vangs had spoken of the matter since her death. People continued to whisper about the arrogant Khang shaman who turned away from his chosen bride, but none were ever so bold to speak of it. Now, everyone watched anxiously as Touso and Alang confronted the matter.

"This has nothing to do with Kai and Daisy." The tension in Touso's voice could have sliced through metal.

"Doesn't it? They'd both be alive today had he not been so stubborn. How many more people must die so the Khangs can rest on their morals?" Alang demanded.

"Shamans are still dying, Alang. Just more slowly."

The amusement in Alang's eyes disappeared. But soon, a smirk spread across his handsome face. "I have no idea what you're talking about. As usual, the Khangs have trouble reconciling any solutions that aren't their own. If anyone has any complaints about our services, let them speak."

When the room was silent, Alang threw up his hands in victory. "Anything else? Any more accusations you'd like to get off your chest before the rest of us get on with our day?"

"No." Touso's gaze didn't falter. "But if you're hiding anything, it'll come to light. Our people are actively looking into all these chosen brides. Remember that what's not seen in this world can be seen in the next."

When Alang narrowed his gaze, Touso grinned. He hadn't revealed what Mossy had seen in the spirit world, and Wang Meng was tracking all the chosen brides. If something was wrong, they would soon find out.

The moment was saved when Ying interrupted in his usual boisterous tone. "All right, if that settles tonight's agenda for the honorable shamans, let's conclude. The club will be opening up shortly."

Only when Lihue nodded did everyone stand to leave. But those who enjoyed the club's festivities didn't go far. Many retired to the bar to begin their evening as others set off to different parts of the room. Touso watched intently as Alang and his people headed to their usual table. Seng and his son were engrossed in a long conversation. The older Vang looked angry, while the younger appeared pensive. Then Seng took off, and Alang followed. They were most definitely up to no good.

"What do you think?" Touso turned to his father.

"Something isn't right. Tomorrow, let's visit Thai and his family." As Lihue prepared to leave, he paused to look at his son. "You and your brother are not the same. He had a different destiny, and I now understand why he made certain decisions. The most important thing we can do is to do what's best for everyone from here on out, including Fuechi."

"How do you handle it?" Touso frowned as he met his father's eyes. "How do you handle watching your wife suffer because of you?"

For a long time, Lihue didn't respond. Finally, he answered, "It isn't my job to change her fate. I can only love her. That is also what you must learn to accept."

Touso continued thinking of his bride long after his father left. Cindy's death had taken a toll on her mentally and physically. Touso understood that the young girl's fate was always tied to Mossy's training as a shaman. There were things she was chosen to protect and things she needed to accept. Death would frequently be a part of that.

Seng Vang was furious. As he stalked off into the club's shadows, his son followed. He had taught Alang repeatedly not to let his emotions get in the way of his actions. Emotions and attachments were for the weak. If they expected to overcome the Khangs to become the most powerful shamans, discipline and sacrifice were essential.

"Why did you have to bring up your sister?" he demanded.

"I don't see the problem." Alang's expression was bored and passive.

"It's motive, you idiot!" Seng snapped. "While we remain calm, we look neutral. But now that you've brought up Daisy, it'll look like we're seeking vengeance."

"Forgive me, Father. Isn't that exactly what we're doing?" Alang arched a brow.

"Fool!" Seng exploded. "You've never been able to see the bigger picture. This is about power."

Alang stared at his father until the other man shook his head.

"He must never discover what is happening with the chosen brides," Seng growled.

"He won't." Alang's certainty only rattled him.

"How do you know this?" Seng demanded.

"The purpose of the succubus is to drain them slowly. Du Yong gets what he wants without rousing suspicion, and we get what we want in return. Isn't everyone perfectly happy?" Alang's voice held an edge of sarcasm.

The succubus were servants of Du Yong. As they fed from human souls, they also fed their lord. It was the worst kind of evil hive activity. Seng had summoned the Succubus Queen just for this reason. As long as Du Yong was happy, he was content to reward the necromancer's efforts.

"That last Khang son is a thorn in my side. I thought Du Yong was dealing with him!" Seng cursed quietly.

"Be careful, Father. He hears all," Alang chided with amusement.

"As long as he's alive, he'll hinder everything. Just my luck, he actually found his chosen bride. We should have taken her soul when we had the chance!" Seng continued with his frustration.

"You know why we couldn't," said Alang.

Mossy Cha was unusual. When the necromancers summoned the spirits to find all the chosen brides, they couldn't locate the most essential one. Mossy had been hidden from their eyes. She had eluded them, whether it was due to her spirit guides or her own strength. Now, her bond with Touso kept him alive.

"Deal with it." Seng's gaze locked on Alang. "As long as she's alive, the Master won't be able to have him, and you know what will happen next."

Du Yong fed from all his servants, especially the human ones. Like the succubus, his human minions would serve him one way or another. If Du Yong became unhappy with their services, Seng and his kind were at the top of that list.

"As you wish, Father." Alang's reply was casual, but his gaze hardened.

His father would stop at nothing for power. As his son, it was Alang's job to make it happen. He hid his relief when Seng finally turned to leave. His demands were constantly draining on Alang's soul.

As his father exited, Alang noticed the entrance of two lovely women. One wore a beautiful red dress that hugged her every curve. The other glowed in a coral gown, making her look more ethereal than human. While Bao Khang and Mossy Cha giggled their way across the room, Alang sighed. It was time to return to his father's dirty work.

Chapter 24

As Mossy and Bao arrived at the Shamans' Club, the peculiar doorman stood and bowed dramatically.

"I didn't know royalty was coming!" he said with a wink.

"Oh, Uncle Vue, you're too kind. Keep going!" When Bao batted her lashes, the doorman laughed.

"You came just in time. The big meeting just ended. Aunt Kou will need some help getting everything back in order." Vue gestured with his little opium pipe before turning to look at Mossy. "Oh, good—you didn't run away from him after all!"

Mossy blushed. *Were there no secrets?*

Bao saved the moment by pushing Mossy through the entrance. "We'll get going! See you, Uncle Vue! Watch out for the vagrants and evil spirits!"

Vue chuckled as he returned to smoking his pipe. "Always do."

"Don't mind Uncle Vue. He's kind of the community gossip—he knows everything, but it's what also makes him so useful. As long as you stay on his good side, you'll be fine." She grabbed Mossy's hand and led her the rest of the way.

As Bao and Mossy entered the club, she accidentally bumped into someone passing by. It was a tall man in a suit. The distaste in his eyes was evident as he met her gaze.

Seng Vang! Mossy recognized him from Thai's house. But Seng wasn't interested in exchanging words and quickly left. As Bao pulled her into the club's energy, Mossy soon forgot about the necromancer.

They were greeted by music and cheers in every direction. Customers ordered drinks, shouted at dealers, and happily lounged in their designated spots. The air itself smelled of fried beef and garlic. Mossy's spirits stirred excitedly. They loved music and food.

While Bao went to look for Auntie Kou and Uncle Ying, Mossy sat at the bar alone. She recognized many of the shamans in the room this second time. They were elders who often looked very solemn as they completed their duties. But with bright eyes and wide grins across their faces, they looked like different people.

"Why do you look like you're staring at exotic animals in the zoo?"

Mossy jumped at the familiar voice and was displeased when she saw Alang Vang by her side.

"Just looking out for the deadly ones," Mossy replied.

Alang smiled. "Touché."

"What do you want, Alang?"

"Oh, just checking on chosen brides. It seems to be my job lately."

Mossy was furious. "How can you sleep at night knowing what you're doing?"

"I don't know what you're talking about." When Alang feigned ignorance, it only enraged her more.

"You're playing with innocent lives! What if one of those girls were your own sister?"

Alang stiffened, seemingly more affected than Mossy anticipated. "If it were my sister, whoever is responsible would be very sorry."

Mossy stared at him in disbelief. "Then why are you doing this?"

Alang locked onto her gaze. "I asked you once, Mossy Cha. What do you think is the intended purpose of being a chosen bride? Is it just to sit there and be pretty? How is it that you're expected to protect the shaman? What are you willing to sacrifice? In ancient times, our people used to gift maidens to the dragons. Do you think there was a romantic wedding? No, I think they just killed her—all to protect everyone else."

"What are you saying?" Mossy's heart was racing.

"I'm trying to tell you that being a chosen bride is the equivalent of death." Alang smiled with a shrug. "Didn't Touso tell you about my sister?"

Mossy blinked at the unexpected question. *Sister?*

"Daisy was supposed to marry his brother, Kai. Long story short—she's dead."

"Daisy?" A beautiful face resurfaced in her mind. "Daisy Vang? The one who owns the boutique downtown?"

Now Alang was the surprised one. "Owned. I told you she's dead now."

"I'm sorry." Mossy's expression turned with sympathy. "I bought my prom dress from her store. She was so beautiful and so sweet. She knew I couldn't afford such a gorgeous dress, so she gave me a discount. She didn't have to, but she insisted it was a gift from a sister to another sister."

The Alang she was used to was taunting and dangerous. This new Alang looked like a sad little boy.

Mossy felt sorry for him. "She was very kind, and I'm sorry for your loss. But whatever you're doing now with the chosen brides, it's not right."

Alang sneered bitterly. "What exactly do you think I've done with them?"

"I saw them."

The smile on his face disappeared.

"I know they're being collected and locked away. Du Yong is eating the brides and the shamans. You, of all people, should know that's wrong!"

"The Khangs killed my sister!" Alang furiously downed a shot of whiskey before returning his gaze to her. "You're a clever girl, Mossy Cha. Don't let this little life of yours slip away by attaching yourself to that family. This is your last warning."

Before Mossy could reply, Alang was already gone. The rest of the world chattered and laughed as though nothing ever happened. Then, as Mossy blinked in her confusion, Bao returned.

"What's up, sis?" Bao noticed her expression and frowned.

"I just saw Alang." Mossy started to explain.

Bao rolled her eyes. "Oh, that asshole! Here—have a drink. You'll forget all about him!"

Bao shoved a glass of gold fluid into her hand and matched it with her own. "Bottoms up!"

Hesitantly, Mossy followed the command. Soon, Mossy forgot this confrontation with Alang just as she'd forgotten his father. With a few shots of whiskey and lots of food, Mossy felt alive again for the first time since Cindy's death. Soon, she laughed out loud and teased uncles and aunties she didn't know. She even won twenty dollars rolling dice! But nothing was more invigorating than dancing. As Mossy leaped and threw her arms into the air, she felt her spirits soaring and lifting her throughout the room. Now, she understood why shamans needed a place of their own. Outside of the club, there were stringent rules that controlled every move and decision. In the club, they were finally free to do whatever they liked. It was a much-needed reprieve from the demanding life they led.

Finally, the music slowed, and Bao excused herself. "It's my turn to sing!" She blew a quick kiss as she disappeared into the crowd.

Mossy clapped excitedly and stood on her toes to watch the other girl climb the stage. With all the hooting and hollering, it was evident that everyone enjoyed hearing Bao's lovely voice. Soon, the music slowed to a soft tune, and Bao started to sway. When she opened her mouth a moment later, a sweet tenor swept through the room. As her sister-in-law sang about eternal love, Mossy leaned into the warmth of the body behind her.

"Where have you been?" She looked up at Touso.

"I've just been watching my bride." His eyes glowed with amusement. "You and Bao could be twins the way you hustle the crowd. I thought you wanted to stay home and rot away there?"

Mossy smiled. "Not if your sister has her way. She's pretty persistent. I would say, as a healer, she's number one."

He drew her into his arms and whispered, "You look beautiful."

Mossy blushed as his eyes grazed the soft flesh peeking over the bodice. The coral gown was strapless with a corset, making her slender figure especially alluring.

"Remember our first dance?" She laughed when he frowned.

"Yes. You didn't want to dance with me." Touso placed his hands on her hips, and soon, they swayed with the romantic melody.

"I didn't know you." Mossy made a face.

"And what do you think of me now, Mo Cha?" Touso's expression was curious.

Mossy stared into the warmth of those beautiful golden eyes. Touso had held her hand when she was a scared little girl. He had rescued her numerous times from dangerous entities since then. She was his chosen bride, destined to protect him. But he was always protecting her instead.

"I think I love you now," she whispered.

Touso froze, and a series of emotions flickered across his handsome features.

"Is that okay?" His reaction made her feel like she'd broken another rule.

He grabbed her hand and rushed her out of the club. Touso walked so fast that Mossy found herself running to keep up. Even Uncle Vue was surprised as Touso passed without a word. By the time they stopped, she was breathless.

They stood at the center of the Tower Bridge, lit up by lights across the river. The water gleamed like stars against the backdrop of city lights.

Mossy searched his face anxiously. "Touso? Are you mad at me? I know I'm not easy. All my life, I thought I knew what I wanted. I used to want to fly like a bird—I just wanted to be free to do whatever my heart desired. But now, I think my heart desires you. I love you, and I'm sorry if this scares—"

She lost track of everything when Touso kissed her. Wrapped in the intensity of his embrace, she heard his heart, felt his heat, and would have been happy to melt right into his flesh. He was her home. When they finally parted, there was a glisten of tears in his eyes.

"Kai used to see glimpses of the future." Touso finally broke his silence. "It's part of what made him such an asshole. He knew it all but wouldn't tell anyone a damn thing. Hell, he's probably someone's spirit guide right now, being vague."

Mossy laughed. Spirit guides were infamous for being like elders; they only revealed what one absolutely needed to know.

"Anyway, he gave me some of those powers when he passed away. Now and then, I see bits and pieces of the future and always see this bridge. I don't know what it means yet. I just know there's me, you, and this bridge. It's important somehow." Touso's heart was pounding as he gazed at his chosen bride. "At least tonight, I'll know one of those reasons."

"How do you mean?" Mossy held her breath.

Touso touched his head to hers. "Along with some of his powers, my brother taught me about love. He fell in love with Nia and rejected his chosen bride. I was angry at him for not following the rules for a long time, but now I understand. Had it been me, I would have done the same. Even if you weren't my chosen bride, I would have chosen you, Mossy Cha. I know that a life with me will not be easy, but there's no one else I would rather have by my side. I love you more than my own soul. More than anything."

Touso surprised her by dropping to one knee. Passing cars were already honking excitedly as he slid a ring onto her finger. She gasped at the sight of a small diamond gleaming against the moonlight. "Will you marry me?"

"Isn't it a little too late for this?"

Touso laughed before resuming more seriously. "You've always struggled with being told what to do. This is your life. You deserve to choose."

Tears flooded her eyes, and Mossy threw her arms around him so suddenly she nearly knocked him over.

"Is that a 'yes?'" Touso's mouth tickled her ears.

"Yes. In this lifetime and every lifetime!" Mossy held him tight.

Touso lifted her and twirled her around, and in a tone she'd never heard, he shouted, "You make me so happy, Mossy Cha!"

Her world was spinning with the tower bridge lights and the stars above. When he finally put her down, her legs felt like jelly. But Touso was happy to hold her.

Mossy gazed into his eyes. "Let's go home."

She was still giddy and felt lightheaded as they pulled into the driveway.

"Touso," she giggled as she stumbled out of the car. "I think I'm drunk..."

He caught her around the hips. "I don't think it's the alcohol," he whispered.

Confused, Mossy looked up at him. "Oh? Then what is it?"

Touso lowered his head and playfully nipped at her lips with his teeth. "Can I show you?" he growled.

Mossy grinned mischievously. "Only if you can catch me!"

With newfound strength in her legs, she leaped across the driveway and flew into Touso's home with a burst of purple light trailing behind her.

She'd made it all the way upstairs and was just about to shut the door when Touso effortlessly lifted her into his arms.

"How did you get here so fast?" she panted.

"Drunk people are never as fast as they think," he chuckled.

"I'm not drunk," Mossy said breathlessly, her heart racing as Touso's soft lips trailed down her neck.

"Perfect," he murmured, setting her down gently on her feet.

Her dress suddenly became too constricting under his intense gaze, and Mossy shivered as Touso unzipped it for her. She moaned as his heated touch sent shocks of pleasure through her body.

"You're not trying to run away again, are you?" Touso asked with a hint of playfulness.

It seemed like he was always chasing her, and Mossy couldn't help but wonder if she would run again if he continued with the fire burning across her flesh.

His intense gaze fell on her now exposed skin, sending shivers down her spine.

But when she tried to pull away, he gently caught her hand.

"Are you afraid of me, Mossy?" he asked softly.

"No," she answered without hesitation.

"Good," Touso said, his blue energy glowing more intensely as he drew her hand beneath his shirt. "Remember, you're in control."

Mossy wasn't sure what to do, but as she explored the firm muscles of his chest, she found herself becoming bolder. She turned away for a moment but then surprised Touso by suddenly turning back with a determined look in her eyes. With one hand tangled in his hair and the other on his chest, she pulled him into an electrifying kiss.

Lost in their passion, Touso lifted Mossy off her feet and carried her to the bed, where they continued to learn more about each other for the rest of the night.

Chapter 25

She used to be afraid of him. Whether it was his sharp gaze or his confident demeanor, he seemed like a threat to everything she held dear.

In many ways, she'd been right.

Marriage meant giving up on her dream college and being unable to live with her best friend. It meant forfeiting all the adventures she had planned with Sarah. But she was willing to make those sacrifices for a lifetime with her soulmate.

As a shaman, Touso Khang wielded immense power. However, as her future husband, he was gentle beyond belief. He patiently waited for her hesitation, stood strong when she felt weak and happily taught her when she knew nothing at all.

With one leg intertwined with his own, lying in his arms, Mossy couldn't imagine being anywhere else. But there was always a hint of bitterness mixed with every sweet moment. As soon as she closed her eyes, she could hear the girls crying out from the other world.

They were trapped in their cells, reaching through the metal bars with desperation. The fiery jewels on their chests glowed with malice. Without their spirit guides, they were powerless.

"Mossy…Mossy! Please hurry!" It was Emma's voice. But it was the next one that confused her the most.

"Mossy! Help us!"

Sarah?

Someone banged on the door. *Thump! Thump! Thump!*

Mossy sat up abruptly and squinted against the morning light. The remaining shadows indicated it was still dawn. As the banging continued, she wondered who it could be at such an early hour.

Touso found his father standing outside. "Dad, what's wrong?"

Lihue's face was serious. "Come downstairs. Something has happened. Bring Mossy with you."

As her soon-to-be father-in-law walked away, Mossy felt dread. She had been in this situation before, and her heart raced as Touso climbed back into bed. His solemn expression confirmed her worst fears.

"It's Fuechi. I can feel him." Touso said, sensing his nephew's energy downstairs.

Familial shamans did not always have such a strong connection, but there was something special between Touso and Fuechi now. He had inherited more than just powers from his brother—he was responsible for Kai's son.

Mossy became increasingly anxious as her phone rang.

"Who is it?" Touso asked, peering over her shoulder.

"It's my mom," Mossy replied as she answered the call. "Hey, Mom. Is everything okay?"

"Mo! Thank goodness. Where are you?" Blia asked, wasting no time with small talk.

"I'm at Touso's house—our house," she said, frowning as her mother continued speaking. "Wait. Slow down. What's wrong?"

Blia took a deep breath. The next time she spoke, it was practically a whisperer. "You asked me to keep an eye on Thai and his bride. Well, there is definitely something wrong! It's terrible, Mossy. Your aunt and uncle are beside themselves!"

"Can you please just tell me what is going on?" Mossy pushed away from Touso and sat at the edge of the bed.

"Thai! He's very sick, and his bride—she's acting like a *poj dab*, some kind of crazy witch! And worst of all, Sarah—"

"Sarah?" Mossy was instantly on her feet. "What happened to Sarah?"

Blia sniffled loudly. "No one knows. She returned from college and passed out while visiting her brother and Sheng. She's been in the hospital since last night, and this morning, when I checked on your aunt, she said Thai's gotten worse."

"How is Sheng?" Mossy asked, although she already knew the answer.

"She's crazy! She won't speak to anyone or let them near your cousin. You were right about her, Mo. What did you see?"

"Something I hoped to be wrong about. Mom, I have to go. We'll come over soon."

Mossy rushed to her closet, frantically searching for something to wear. She had managed to stay composed while talking to her mother, but now she was falling apart. A minute later, she was throwing clothes and hangers onto the floor in frustration. When Touso pulled her into a hug, she couldn't hold back her tears any longer.

"It's okay. Let it out. It's not healthy to keep everything bottled up," he said soothingly.

Mossy cried, "Why does everything have to be so difficult? Life was supposed to be simple. Study hard, attend college, get a job, and live happily ever after! That's what they teach us in school, right? But because I'm Hmong and have these crazy spirit guides, that can't happen! I'm apparently meant to become some powerful shaman and protect everyone instead."

Mossy cried even harder when those words came out, sounding harsh and bitter. Touso would have laughed at the irony of it all if she didn't look so miserable. Instead, he gently rubbed her back and let her cry it out.

"My friend just died, and I don't even have time to mourn her before more chaos breaks loose. I don't know what I'm supposed to do—how am I supposed to handle all of this? Can't I at least graduate first? Can't the world give me a break?"

Mossy knew she must seem hysterical now, but she didn't care. Every part of her felt like it was in pain—her head, her chest, her entire body ached.

Finally, Touso lifted her chin and looked into her eyes. "I understand this is all overwhelming. This life is new to you, but just take things one step at a time. I was even younger than you when my spirit guides first started pushing me to embrace my destiny. Unlike you, I always knew it would happen. But I still fought against it. I was already an awkward kid and the last thing I wanted was to stand out even more. Kai tried to push me out of my shell, but the more he pushed, the more I resisted. Until one night, my Aunt Padee came to me in a dream."

Mossy's breath caught. Aunt Padee had a habit of invading dreams. "What happened?"

Touso's smile was bittersweet. "She said: 'You think this is about you because you feel the pain, but this pain is a reminder that you must become stronger to protect those you love.' I know it's difficult to hear, but all the struggles and suffering we face happen for a reason. You lost a friend, and I'm truly sorry. But if Cindy's death taught us anything, it's that bad things happen when evil is allowed to prevail."

"I don't feel strong. What am I supposed to do?" She looked as lost as she felt.

"You keep moving forward, taking whatever blows come your way, and learn from them," Touso replied. "I used to worry about living a normal life until a dead woman reminded me that a normal life isn't worth anything if you can't protect the people who give it meaning. My brother sacrificed his own life to protect me. I'll do everything in my power to protect his son."

"And you. I don't even have to think about it. I just stab things for you," Mossy said in awe.

Touso chuckled. "And I'm grateful for every moment of it. But don't you understand? Life can be hard and demanding, but what other choice do we have? You and I know we could never stand by and watch someone suffer without trying to help."

Mossy sniffled. "We didn't even get a chance to enjoy last night."

Touso raised an eyebrow. "We didn't? I think there may be some difference of opinion there."

Mossy playfully smacked him on the shoulder. "You know what I mean. Sometimes I wish we could just have a normal day, to experience life without any worries."

"Let's take things one step at a time. Let's get dressed and see what's happening downstairs, then we'll go visit Thai and Sarah," Touso suggested.

"And then?" Mossy asked with a mischievous glint in her eye.

Touso wrapped his arms around her. "And then I promise you, my love, I will fight the gods themselves if it means we can have a few days of peace and normalcy."

Mossy laughed and wiped away her tears. "You would do that for me?"

"I would do anything for you, my chosen bride." Touso gently caressed her cheek and felt her tension slip away.

"I knew it was worth stabbing things for you," Mossy joked, but there was no doubt she would face any challenge to keep him safe. She surprised Touso by pulling him into a passionate kiss.

"Where are you going?" he asked when she pulled away.

Mossy looked back over her shoulder with determination. "I'm getting ready for a fight!"

Touso watched his strong and determined bride disappear into the bathroom. One moment, she was innocent and vulnerable, the next, fierce and fearless. Part of him wanted to protect her from all harm, but he knew deep down that she was destined to face even greater challenges.

"Fuechi Khang, who taught you how to eat like that?" Aunt Bao exclaimed as Fuechi shoved sausages into his mouth with one hand and used the other to scoop up pancakes.

"Don't look at me. Kai called them Hmong chopsticks!" Nia warned her son with a smile. "Remember what I told you about using your fingers to eat?"

"Sorry, Mama!" Fuechi said sheepishly.

Lihue chuckled and patted his grandson's head. "It's alright. Let him use his 'Hmong chopsticks.' It'll make his fingers strong, right, Fuechi?"

The boy nodded happily.

Bao turned to look at her father. "Where's mom?"

"She's not feeling well," he answered with a somber expression.

Bao sighed and shook her head. "I keep telling her she needs to cut back on her hours at the hospital. Healing is draining, whether it's modern medicine or shamanism."

Lihue remained quiet as Bao continued her rant, but Nia noticed his peculiar expression. It was the same one Kai wore when he was keeping secrets. Despite her anxiousness about returning to the Khang house, they had no other place to go. Ironically, it was Dylan who insisted that only the Khangs could protect them.

They arrived late at night, finding only Lihue and Pahoua at home. But the trouble began when Touso and Mossy returned. The happy couple triggered something dark within Dylan, her new friend.

Nia felt increasingly uneasy around him, sensing that something was wrong. He no longer looked like the star-quality, charming boy she first met.

Now, he just looked sick.

"What?" He finally snapped at her from across the table.

Nia shrugged and said, "Have you looked at yourself lately?"

"I haven't been sleeping well," Dylan grumbled.

"I may not have any special abilities like the Khangs, but I can tell it's more than just lack of sleep," Nia said cheerfully.

"Alright, Boss-lady, tell me what it is then," Dylan replied sarcastically, but Nia could see glimpses of Kai in his golden eyes. When he was annoyed with her for nagging him too much, he would call her "Boss-lady."

"What did you call me?" She asked, her brow ring glinting as she furrowed her brows.

Something shifted in Dylan's eyes, and he looked uncomfortable. "Sorry, Nia. I'm just grumpy. I should have gone home last night. Next time we run away from soul-sucking ghosts, remind me to take my own car."

Nia observed him closely. "I could have given you a ride."

"I know, but that would've meant you driving back alone. It's not safe for you right now," Dylan replied.

His words touched Nia's heart unexpectedly. Dylan always spoke like someone much older and seemed to genuinely care about her and Fuechi, having rescued them both more than once.

"Don't your parents worry about you being out all night?" Nia asked.

"I haven't had a curfew since I started sneaking out," Dylan answered with a smirk. "Just kidding. I'm eighteen, Nia. My dad's always at the hospital, and my step-mom has her Pomeranians. I'm my own man."

Nia pursed her lips. "Clearly. But don't you find it strange being your own man at your ex-girlfriend's future husband's house?"

Dylan's expression turned sour. "That's a mouthful of words I never want to hear again." He then refocused his attention on Fuechi, who was happily munching on sausage and coloring without a care in the world.

Dylan was at the Khang house because of Kai, just as he had checked on Nia and Fuechi at Kai's request. Kai's purpose was to help his brother, but he missed his family.

At the Khang house, they were safe and protected. But when Nia ran away with Fuechi because of Cindy, Kai was furious. It was the first time in his undead existence that he felt such intense anger toward someone for not following the rules. Mossy Cha should have known better. Humans and ghosts weren't meant to be together!

With their return, Kai spent the night guarding his wife and son. As Nia and Fuechi slept, he held onto his son's hand and gazed at the wife he missed.

She'd lost weight. Her cheeks were more angular, and her curvy figure seemed frail. The sadness in her eyes broke his heart. She was always his light in the darkness and the reason he stayed alive as long as he had. It just wasn't his destiny to grow old.

It was to protect Touso and Fuechi.

Awakening

In all possible futures he was shown, Fuechi only remained alive if Touso was alive. It would only stay that way if Kai died. He was a rebel for a reason.

He had to break the rules.

Shamans protected life, but Kai had taken his own. As punishment, he lost his memories. Without them, he wouldn't find the Lake of Life. He wouldn't know he was supposed to go there. A lost soul was destined to become lonely, angry, and sad forever.

Du Yong believed he was clever by placing the lost soul inside Dylan Reed's body, but Kai had foreseen this future as well. In life, he had acquired power and knowledge, and in death, he would ensure that Touso used these gifts to help their family. It was the only way he could fight without worrying about the fate of his soul.

The one future he never saw coming was his chosen bride going after his wife.

Daisy Vang was one of the few surprises in Kai's life. As the daughter of necromancers, Kai had anticipated despising his chosen bride. However, Daisy was as kind as she was beautiful.

She donated clothes, mentored at-risk kids, and used her social media platform to teach girls how to manage money. As the only daughter in her family, Daisy had a strong sense of responsibility for the sisters she never had. Anyone mistreating his wife or employees might get a flat tire or broken bones.

In some ways, she inherited her father's fierceness. But she had trusted Kai to save them both, and he had failed her. Now, she was coming after everything he loved.

He was sure that Du Yong was behind all of it.

Thinking about evil was the same as calling it. As soon as Du Yong crossed his mind, Kai felt an intense wave of pain.

Nia noticed his distress and asked if he was okay, but her face changed into Du Yong's smirking expression.

"You're awake," the demon said with disappointment. "I had such high hopes for you as a homewrecker."

Kai's gaze turned fierce as he retorted, "Destroying things is still my game."

Du Yong chuckled. "Those are bold words, Kai. Don't you think they're a bit pointless now that you're dead?"

"Your words don't intimidate me," Kai replied with determination.

"Impressive," Du Yong remarked mockingly. "But you look absolutely terrible."

Kai clutched his chest.

"What's wrong? Is your human body finally giving out on you?" Du Yong sneered knowingly. Human bodies were not designed to host spirits for long periods of time. Initially, the spirit's energy invigorated the body, but over time it became draining. Eventually, the spirit had to depart or risk killing the host.

"You should have stuck with our plan!" Du Yong taunted.

"I'll never comply with you," Kai spat.

Du Yong shook his head. "Well, it would have made things easier, but what are a few more tears when achieving one's dreams? Sure, they won't be my tears, but still."

Kai glared at the demon with satisfaction. "I have seen the future. Your plans will fail."

Du Yong grabbed Kai by the throat. Lifting him up so they were eye-to-eye, he said, "Feasting on souls is child's play. Living...now that could be fun."

For the first time, Kai felt fear. Seeing glimpses of the future was like putting together a puzzle with missing pieces. What was he missing? He demanded, "What do you plan to do?"

"Curious, aren't we?" Du Yong taunted as he threw Kai to the ground. "Your time has come and gone, Kai Khang. If you want to protect those you love, stay out of my way."

Kai shouted, "You won't get to him! He's strong, and he has his chosen bride. You're too late!"

"At first, that angered me too," Du Yong remarked casually. "But even an old demon can learn new tricks." He shrugged as he turned away from Kai. "I'm starting to like her just as much as your brother. Which one should I choose?"

The question caught Kai off guard. *Choose?*

Du Yong laughed, feeling silly. "What am I saying? I can have them both!"

Kai stumbled toward the retreating demon. "Stay away from my brother!"

"Save that energy for Fuechi, my dear old friend." Du Yong smirked at him over his shoulder. "You won't have much left." Then he disappeared, and the dark world crumbled.

"Dylan!" Mossy Cha's voice brought him back to reality.

He saw her frowning down at him and asked, "What happened?"

"You passed out," Nia said, taking his face in her hands. "Are you okay?"

Kai almost hugged Nia when Fuechi jumped into his arms. He said, "Hey there, buddy. I'm fine, don't worry."

"Then you should go home." Touso Khang scowled from across the room. He didn't like Dylan around his family.

Mossy asked, "Dylan, what are you doing here?"

"Nice to see you too, Moss," he replied as she inspected the discoloration on his face. He had dark circles under his beautiful eyes.

Mossy said, "You don't look well. Why aren't you resting at home?"

Bao furrowed her brows and asked, "How long have you been sick?"

"I'm fine!" Dylan insisted with frustration. "Just tired."

"I don't think so." Everyone turned as Lihue approached. "You were in the spirit world. That wasn't supposed to happen."

Touso always suspected something was wrong with Dylan's soul, but the gong had revealed something unexpected: Dylan had spirit guides.

"It's because I'm White again, isn't it?" He pulled himself up and stood. "I may not look like it, but I am part Patwin native. We have our own ties to the spirit world, too!"

"Young man, this is not a laughing matter. What you did is unheard of. There are only two ways to enter the spirit world—by getting lost or being guided, and you were definitely guided." The head of the Khang family faced him with a pensive expression. "There's a barrier around you, Dylan Reed. What are you hiding?"

Kai Khang gazed into his father's eyes, feeling the weight of his power. But no one could see him unless he wanted them to.

"I just wanted to help Nia and Fuechi," said Dylan. Then he surprised everyone by taking Mossy's hand. "And I came to get my girl."

It was exactly the distraction that Kai needed. Before Mossy could pull away, Touso landed a sharp punch on Dylan's face.

He touched his jaw, tasting blood on his lips. "See what I mean, Moss? This guy has a short fuse."

Mossy lunged at Touso as he reached for Dylan again. "Stop! Both of you!"

Nia pulled Dylan away and said, "Boy, you need to quiet down!"

"No." Dylan shrugged her off and locked eyes with Touso. "I'm tired of this guy acting like he's in charge of everything. Do you think we owe you something just because you're cursed? No one owes you anything, Touso Khang. Not me, not Mossy. We have our own lives to live. Look at Nia and Fuechi! Do you know what was chasing them when I found them?"

Nia shifted uncomfortably as all eyes turned to her and Fuechi.

"Fuechi was surrounded by freaking ghosts! Nia was running for her life. Kai knew the risks when he brought them into this world. You know what Mossy is risking by being with you. How much more fucking selfish can you be?"

"Dylan!" Mossy gasped.

"No, Moss. It's the truth. You still have a choice—you can choose a different life. We can still go to the Bay and do everything we planned." He held her shoulders and looked intently into her eyes. "You don't have to be with this guy and fight his demons."

"But I want to," she said, removing Dylan's hand. As she did so, he couldn't help noticing the diamond ring on her finger. "I know you don't understand, but this is where I belong."

"Moss—" Dylan started.

Touso pulled Mossy back and faced Dylan. "You heard her. It's time for you to leave."

"No," said Lihue, surprising everyone. "Whatever happened during the ritual, Dylan Reed is our responsibility now."

When Touso started to argue, his father cut him off, saying, "You know the rules, Touso. If anyone becomes a shaman in our presence, they become one of ours. It's our duty to keep him safe until we understand what's happening."

"Hold on." Dylan held up his hands and took a step back. "I don't need to be cared for like a child!"

He felt someone touch his arm and turned to see it was Bao.

"My father's right. You're not well. Whatever has happened to you, we are responsible for you now. Sit down and let me make you a drink. You'll feel better," Bao promised as she guided Dylan toward a chair. It took effort to keep her composure because he smelled of sulfur and death.

"If you kids are finished, let's get on with why we're here." Lihue was tired and took a sip of coffee to clear his thoughts. "Nia and Fuechi were attacked yesterday, and I received some disturbing news this morning. It seems all of the chosen brides from the necromancers are acting strangely. My spirit guides tell me it's all connected."

Mossy's heart raced with fear. "My mom just called! Sarah is in the hospital, and Thai is very sick. She says Sheng is acting insane!"

Despite feeling lightheaded, Dylan added, "The thing that attacked Nia—it had a personal vendetta against her."

Mossy furrowed her brow in confusion. "What do you mean?"

"The creature that came after her used to be a chosen bride," Kai explained in Dylan's place.

Touso and Lihue exchanged sharp glances, but when Kai didn't elaborate, Lihue said, "Touso, visit Thai and see what's happening there. I'll gather the other Khangs. We must find a way to stop this before we lose any more lives."

"Seng is behind all of this," said Touso.

"Perhaps, but for now, our priority is to take care of our brothers," Lihue replied as he stood. "Bao, keep an eye on Nia, Fuechi, and Dylan."

"I don't need someone watching me like a child." He attempted to stand but was hit with a wave of nausea.

"No, you're not fine," Bao retorted, shaking her head. "If you keep pushing yourself, you'll only make things worse. Drink your tea and rest."

Dylan seethed in his seat as everyone dispersed. When Mossy chased after Touso, he wished he could stop her. Why couldn't she see that she was at risk?

Kai answered the question for him: "She's his chosen bride. Whether we like it or not, they are bonded."

"We were too!" Dylan shouted. And he would find a way to remind her.

"Thanks for throwing me under the bus," Kai said, forcing Dylan to drink the bitter concoction that smelled of rotting wood.

Dylan swallowed and coughed. He said, "You know I'm right. Nia, Fuechi, and Mossy wouldn't be in danger if it weren't for you two idiots."

Kai shook his head. "That's where you're mistaken, bro. Everyone comes into this life with their own destiny predetermined. We're all just following a script. What matters is how well we play our roles."

As Dylan wondered how to make Mossy to leave Touso Khang, Kai turned to look at his wife and son. Nia cradled Fuechi in her arms, humming, "Don't Worry, Be Happy."

Don't worry, Nia baby. I'll protect both of you with my soul.

Touso paced back and forth, his usually calm demeanor replaced with erratic energy. He hastily changed his clothes and packed his shaman bag without saying a word. When he finally turned to face her, she was alarmed at the storm in his eyes.

She reached to touch his face and felt the tension in his muscles.

"He's right," he said, his voice tight with emotion. "Your life will always be in danger because of me."

He pulled away and continued pacing the room.

"A man is supposed to protect his wife," he muttered, "not the other way around."

He kept his distance from her, afraid that his mere presence could put her in harm's way. Mossy was confused and hurt by this sudden change in behavior.

She said, "Touso, it doesn't matter. I choose you. For better or for worse, I will stay with you."

Touso refused to meet her gaze. "Maybe you shouldn't."

Frustrated and angry, she yanked off the ring from her finger and threw it at him. "You want to see? Let's find out! I'll go get Dylan, move to the Bay Area, go to school, maybe get married, and have a bunch of kids. I'll forget all about what happened here. I'll forget about the idiot who made me believe I was smart enough to choose what I want."

Mossy turned to leave, but Touso pulled her into a tight embrace. "I'm sorry."

She stood stiffly in his arms as he turned her to face him. He said, "I don't want you to get hurt because of me, but the thought of you leaving is killing my soul already. Please, don't go."

His golden eyes glistened with desperation as he held onto her.

Mossy sank into his arms. "How can you be so smart and yet so clueless at the same time? I couldn't leave you now even if I tried!"

As they embraced, a bright string of colors appeared above them. Touso took the ring from the spirit, and slipped it back onto Mossy's finger.

"I know spirits and demons. You'll have to teach me about women," he conceded with a smile.

Mossy playfully caressed his nose with her finger and said, "I'll teach you the two most important rules."

Touso pulled her closer, a hint of amusement in his eyes. "Oh yeah? And what are they?"

With a mischievous smirk, Mossy replied, "First rule: never make a woman ask for something."

Touso raised an eyebrow and waited for her to continue.

"And never make her tell you twice," Mossy finished.

Touso chuckled, feeling a weight lift off his shoulders. He asked, "Who taught you these rules?"

"My mom!" she answered.

"Remind me to buy your father a drink," Touso joked, earning a laugh from Mossy.

After a while, Mossy asked, "Should we go now?"

Touso's expression sobered as the gravity of their situation returned. "Are you sure you want to go?"

Mossy nodded. "It's my family. I need to be there."

Touso looked at her with a mix of pride and apprehension. "Just promise me one thing."

Mossy furrowed her brow in question.

"Try not to be too brave," he pleaded.

Mossy laughed and kissed him, but she didn't make any promises, and Touso noticed.

Chapter 26

Sheng Moua didn't move when the men entered the room. She sat quietly beside Thai on the bed and stared listlessly out the window. The morning sun shined against her pale face, but even the light couldn't bring life to those empty eyes.

"That's all she's been doing. She just sits there silently until someone tries to approach her. And then—" May gasped as Sheng hissed at her. She jumped behind Seng and Alang in fear. "What's wrong with her?"

Seng was surprisingly calm as he turned and smiled. "We'll talk to her. It's normal for brides to get cold feet."

May peered over his shoulder. Her son frowned like he was trying to wake up from a dream. "This is normal? She's snarling like an animal and holding my son hostage!"

"Mrs. Khang, maybe you should wait for us downstairs," Alang suggested. "We'll find out what's going on."

May hesitated as she glanced between her son and the necromancers. He was fine when they took Sarah to the hospital. Sheng was even decent enough to help Sarah downstairs. Now, she was acting crazy, and Thai seemed as sick as ever.

May was at a loss. His chosen bride should have ended all these worries. Finally, she nodded. "We'll be waiting."

Seng waited for May to leave before the smile disappeared. Then he marched over to Sheng and slapped her across the face, but the girl never flinched. Instead, she returned to staring listlessly out the window.

"Dad!" Alang stared at his father in shock.

Seng ignored him as he glared at Sheng. "What the hell do you think you're doing? All the brides are acting crazy because of you!"

Daisy Vang didn't answer, but a small smile turned at her lips. She was the Succubus Queen. She saw everything the others saw. She controlled everything they did. Relatively, they felt whatever she felt. She was angry, and now so were they. The calls from all the shaman families had been nonstop.

"She's attacking everyone!"

"She's acting like an animal!"

"She won't let him go—she's hurting him!"

The chosen brides who were supposed to protect their Khang shamans were suddenly feral, and the families were furious. Since the necromancers found the brides, they were responsible. Everyone expected Seng to fix this before their sons were lost. But they weren't the ones he was concerned about. Du Yong would be visiting him soon if the problems weren't resolved.

Seng faced the sullen girl staring out the window. "You know what's at stake here. Du Yong promised us absolute power in exchange for our services. With the succubus controlling the brides, he can drink from the shamans without anyone suspecting or resisting. But you're ruining everything with your emotions!"

"Dad—" Alang tried again to interfere, but Seng silenced him with a blow to the face.

"You stay out of this!" Seng hissed. "You and your sister will be the death of me. You never learn!"

Alang tasted blood but smiled bitterly. He was used to this kind of rage.

"What lesson did you want us to learn, Father?" Daisy's succubus voice was high, vibrating throughout the room. It could be incredibly hypnotic or excruciating, depending on her mood. At the moment, it was undecided. Daisy turned away from the window and faced him. "That one should forsake the bonds of blood and family to achieve great power?"

Alang stared at Daisy before turning to his father. "What's she talking about?"

Seng shook his head in frustration. "You don't understand. Not just any power! Absolute power. Everyone will fear us the way they fear gods and demons. We'll be unstoppable!"

Alang grabbed his father by the collar. "What did you do?"

When Seng didn't respond, Daisy's laugh radiated throughout the room. "You've always been so naïve, brother! Don't you know that our father made a deal with Du Yong?"

Alang froze.

"A *poj ntxoog*—a succubus is born from the rage of a broken heart. When our father knew I was Kai's chosen bride, he saw an opportunity. A chosen bride isn't just connected to her shaman. She has a connection with her sisters." Daisy locked her cold eyes onto her brother. "He knew I could find them all and that Du Yong would reward him for it!"

Alang stared at his father incredulously. "Tell me that's not true. You didn't sacrifice your own daughter!"

"It was the only way!" Seng's voice struggled over his son's fingers, pressed against his throat.

Alang Vang had never acted against his father. Through all the shaming and cruelty, he always remained a devoted son. But this was a blasphemy he couldn't forgive. He cursed and threw Seng onto the ground. "You killed my sister!"

"No! She's alive. She's just different." Seng's voice faltered for the first time. He needed his son to understand. "Look at her. She's more powerful than she's ever been. She was destined to serve that scoundrel Kai, but now she's a queen! Don't you see? She'll serve us instead of those damn Khangs!"

"She'll serve the demon until her soul rots away."

Alang and Seng turned at the new voice in the room. Touso and Mossy had arrived unnoticed and heard everything.

"She'll never know peace. She'll never be reborn. She'll never rise to be with the gods in the higher planes because you sold her soul and made her a monster!" Touso also had a sister and shared Alang's rage. "Seng Vang, what have you done to your own child?"

Seng leaped from the floor and glared at all of them. "Don't you dare judge me, you filthy Khang! You're no better. You sit on your high horse and think you control all of us. Just you wait—you're all doomed!"

Seng moved to strike Touso, but the younger shaman tossed him easily against the wall. Alang never moved.

Awakening

As Daisy cackled, objects flew and crashed throughout the room. Her head dropped back, and her mouth fell open. A moment later, Daisy Vang's spirit crawled out with a devilish grin. Long hair slithered around Thai's throat and squeezed. Then, he was dangling from the ceiling, and no amount of kicking or squirming could help him escape.

"No! Stop it!" Mossy ran forward, but Touso held her back.

"Mossy." There was a strange expression on his face. "What's going on? What do you see?"

She blinked. "You don't see her?"

"He can't." Alang's eyes remained on his sister's dark spirit. "We blessed each of the brides with protection strings against the shaman's eyes."

Mossy's gaze fell onto the black strings on Sheng's wrists. She looked up at Touso and Alang. "But I can see her!"

"Because you're connected as chosen brides." Alang looked at Mossy. "That's why you can still see Daisy, and that's why you saw the brides in the spirit world. You're all connected."

They were distracted when Thai cried out again. These screams brought his parents running into the room.

"Thai!" May shrieked in horror. His chosen bride remained frozen in a stupor on the bed, but her son was hovering at the ceiling. "Oh, my god! What's happening?"

"Aunt May, this chosen bride is not right. Emma Sheng's soul has been stolen! A *poj ntxoog*, a succubus, is now controlling her body!" Mossy held on to her aunt to keep her from falling.

"No. How could this be?" May gasped.

"Please—help him!" Yer shouted.

"Daisy," Alang spoke quietly, emotion finally returning to his voice. "I know you've suffered. Let him go. We'll find a way—"

"No!" Daisy demonstrated this fervor by shaking the boy in the air. Then she turned her eyes to the only two people who saw her: Mossy and Alang. "Bring me Kai Khang. Or I will drain every single one of them tonight!"

"What's going on?" Touso demanded when he saw the shared expression between Mossy and Alang.

"She wants your brother!" said Mossy.

Touso frowned. "But he's dead."

Alang was thoughtful as he faced him. "My sister is pissed for a reason. Your brother must be closer than you think."

Mossy's heart raced as she remembered Dylan Reed's recent oddities. He was incredibly strong, lifting Chewy and breaking locked doors without effort. He jumped into the spirit world and fought evil like a master shaman. He was never as scared as he should have been. He even had a flying horse!

Fuechi had called him "Daddy."

Mossy grabbed Touso.

"What is it, Mossy?" He searched her face.

"Dylan," she whispered.

"What about him?"

"Kai is Dylan!"

Touso staggered, and when his spirit guides cried, he knew it was true.

Daisy Vang laughed hysterically.

Chapter 27

Bao's mysterious potion of bitter tree bark and herbs was working. Dylan started to feel better within an hour of drinking the nasty mixture, and soon, he could stand without feeling nauseous. Now, Dylan playfully boxed with Fuechi in the family room.

"Block your face." Dylan waited until the little boy lifted a hand over his cheek before throwing a light hook. "There you go. You always gotta protect your face. Now, do it again!"

Fuechi blocked and ducked low as Dylan threw a hook-jab combo and giggled when he was hoisted into the air. He said, "You're a natural, kid!"

Nia's expression was thoughtful when she heard the question.

"Are you okay?"

She looked up in surprise when Pahoua sat down next to her. The older woman had been missing all morning and continued to look fatigued as she smiled at Nia.

"Yes. Just watching these two mess around," Nia replied.

Pahoua glanced at Fuechi and Dylan. "They have a special bond, don't they?"

Nia nodded. "Fuechi likes him a lot."

"He must miss his father." Pahoua was sympathetic.

"He still thinks Kai is coming back." Nia grimaced.

"Maybe he sees him."

The strange comment caught her attention. "Sorry?"

"Has Fuechi lost any of his teeth yet?" Pahoua asked.

"No." Nia's brows furrowed. "Why?"

"Have you ever heard that young children are likelier to see spirits?" When Nia shook her head, she continued. "The Hmong believe that before children lose their first tooth, they are more susceptible to seeing spirits. Maybe Fuechi doesn't believe his father's gone because he sees him."

"Do you see him?" Nia studied her with a mixture of hope and fear.

Pahoua shook her head. "Not him."

It was another strange comment. Nia returned her gaze to Dylan, who was still boxing with Fuechi. "I think Dylan reminds him of his dad."

"It's probably the blond hair," Pahoua said with a smile. She sipped from a teacup Bao had prepared. "But I must admit, Dylan sometimes reminds me of Kai, too."

"He's kind of an asshole, huh?" Nia offered.

Pahoua almost choked on her tea. "Oh, Nia. I can see why my son loved you so much. You just say it the way it is."

Nia smiled. "Most of the time, it needed to be said."

Pahoua nodded. "My son wasn't easy, but he loved very passionately. He wanted to protect all of us so much."

"I wish he would have prepared me more." Tears glistened in Nia's eyes. "Fuechi is so much like him. I know he has these special gifts. I just don't know what to do about them. How do I help a child who sees things I can't?"

Pahoua squeezed her hand. "You raise him as best as you know how, and we'll help with the rest."

Nia made a sound that was somewhere between a laugh and a cry. "I'm sorry. I shouldn't have left with Fuechi like that. You all must have been so worried!"

"We were," Pahoua admitted. "But what matters is that you're here now. I won't lie to you. These are dangerous times for our family. But we'll get through it if we all stick together."

"How are you feeling?" Nia frowned. Pahoua had shadows under her eyes.

She glanced at Fuechi. "I'm fine! I missed my grandson and hoped to take him for a walk. We could both use the fresh air, I think!"

Pahoua abruptly stood and walked over to the family room. "Fuechi, dear. Do you want to go feed the chickens with grandma?"

"Yes!" Fuechi threw his arms around her hips. "Fuechi love chickens!"

Dylan frowned. "Bro, I thought we were bonding here. Are you choosing chickens over me?"

Fuechi nodded and pumped his fists into the sky. "Chickens! Chickens!"

A moment later, Fuechi and Pahoua were gone. Surrounded by silence, Dylan sunk onto the ground. He was deep in thought when the footsteps approached.

"Don't take it personally. Fuechi loves animals," said Nia.

"I know." Dylan shifted to let her sit beside him.

"How do you know?" she asked.

Dylan hesitated. "Most kids like animals, don't they?"

Nia considered him before asking, "How long have you been boxing?"

Dylan snorted. "Not long. I mostly play around. You know—video games."

"You move like my husband." Kai was an exceptional fighter, and Dylan moved just like him. He even made the same goofy faces when Fuechi hit him. She wondered if he was just as fast.

Dylan froze as Nia's shoulder brushed his arm. He was aware of the warmth radiating from her body. He chuckled nervously, "Oh, yeah? Did he play games, too?"

"No. He boxed for real." Nia was so close now that he felt her breath against his face. She looked like she was trying to figure out a complex puzzle.

"Nia?" He cocked his head to the side. "What's wrong?"

It happened very quickly. Nia threw a sharp right hook. Dylan skillfully ducked to the side. As he grabbed her wrist, Nia toppled forward. But instead of letting her fall, he tucked her into his arms and rolled. A moment later, she was on top of him.

Nia gazed into his eyes. "This is crazy."

"What is?" Dylan asked.

"I see him, too." She surprised them both when she kissed him.

Kai Khang didn't hesitate. He eagerly wrapped his arms around Nia's waist and pulled her close. She tasted just as sweet as he remembered. As his hands traveled the curve of her hips and slid beneath her shirt, she released a moan that drove him wild. But Nia abruptly ceased it all too soon.

She pulled away, whispering, "I'm sorry!"

Kai wanted to draw her back against his chest, but she was too distraught. There were tears in her eyes.

"This is so embarrassing. I'm sorry, Dylan. I just—you just reminded me so much of Kai. I miss him so much!" She dropped her face and wept into her hands. "I miss him every day. I don't know what I'm going to do without him."

Kai wished that he could look into her eyes and reveal the truth. *I'm here. I'm right here with you!* Instead, he said, "He was lucky to have known you. You're the mother of his child, and in a way, a part of him will always be with you."

Nia smiled. "I know. It's just that I still feel him every day. Especially when I'm with you. Fuechi feels it, too. Isn't that strange?"

Kai met her gaze. She was his wife. Of course, she would notice.

"When you lose someone you love, you'll always see things that remind you of them." After some hesitation, he took her hand. "He chose you, Nia. He loved you with all his soul. I'm sure if he could come back to say anything, it would be to tell you how much he misses you, too."

Nia sniffled. "It's not fair."

"No, it's not. But everything is going to be okay." Kai gazed into a future that she couldn't see. "You and Fuechi will be safe, and that's all that matters."

Nia pulled back and stared at him with the same strange expression from before. "Dylan. How are you so sure?"

Because I gave up my life to make it happen!

They stared at each other for a long time. With each passing second, their faces drew closer... until eventually, their mouths hovered just inches apart.

"Nia..." Kai's fingers curled tightly around her hands.

"Dylan? Nia?" It was Mossy who spoke, but both she and Touso stood over them with peculiar expressions.

Nia scrambled to her feet and pulled at her braids self-consciously. "You guys are back already? How is your family?

"They're okay," Mossy replied.

Touso's gaze remained on Dylan. Color had returned to his cheeks, and his energy seemed restored. But there was still something odd about him, and a powerful wall protected it. Touso stared deep into those blue-green eyes. He dug and broke through every barrier until he found the yellow spark of his brother's soul. *There you are, asshole!*

Dylan was taken aback and stood. "Okay. This is getting weird. I'll leave."

Touso crossed his arms and stood in his way. "No. I don't think so."

Dylan frowned. "Oh, yeah? Who's going to stop me?"

"Don't you want to find out what happened when we visited Thai?" Touso's tone was casual as he paced the room.

"What does that have to do with me?"

"Well, it's just that you seem to care about Nia and Fuechi so much," Touso replied.

"What about them?" Dylan asked.

Touso made a show of looking for Fuechi. "Where is my nephew, by the way?"

"He's outside with grandma," Nia answered.

Touso's expression perked up. "Oh, that's perfect. Let's get everyone together. This really should be a family discussion."

"Then I should leave." Dylan started to exit, but Touso got in his way.

"Oh, no. Remember what my father said. We're responsible for you now. You really must stay. I think you'll find this interesting." Touso locked his gaze on him and smiled. "I promise."

Touso Khang didn't like Dylan. He wanted the man as far away from Mossy as possible. This sudden change of heart was disturbing, and now Dylan scowled. "Get out of my way!"

Touso surprised him by stepping aside. "Fine. I guess we don't need you. This thing that's gotten a hold of Thai and his bride... it'll be just as happy if we just bring Nia."

Dylan whirled around. "What did you say?"

"Well, that's what I was going to tell you. This thing—it's a succubus. It's taken over all the chosen brides and fed on our shamans. It's angry for some reason, but it promised to let go of them all if we give up Nia. Now, what I can't figure out is why that is?" Touso cast a quizzical look at his sister-in-law. "What do you think, Nia? Didn't that attack seem somewhat... personal?"

Nia's eyes grew with surprise. "She said I took something from her. I've never seen her before in my life."

Touso's brows furrowed. "Well, it must be something big, Nia. Angry spirits—they don't give up easily. The easiest way to get rid of them sometimes is to give them what they want."

Nia parted her mouth in confusion. "What do you mean?"

"We'll have to take you to her," Touso answered.

When Nia gasped, Mossy curled her fingers around her hand. "Touso, stop. You're scaring her!"

Touso's eyes hardened. "Mossy, we've talked about this. There are rules. This creature has been offended and wants compensation. If we bring it Nia, it'll let everyone go."

Mossy and Nia gasped when Dylan turned and punched Touso in the face. The impact sent the other staggering. Touso straightened and touched his jaw. A trail of blood started from the corner of his mouth, but he only grinned.

"Look who's got anger issues now. Did I say something to offend you, Dylan?"

"You asshole. This is your brother's wife you're talking about! Nia and Fuechi are family!" Dylan grabbed Touso by the shirt and thrust him against the wall.

"A soul for a soul. That's always been the rule," Touso replied. "And this succubus only wants one in return for many. I can't refuse."

Dylan hit him hard enough this time that he fell to his knees. "If you touch her—"

Touso laughed and looked Dylan straight in the eyes. "What will you do? Do you think you can stop me?"

Dylan moved to strike Touso again, but the other ducked and followed with a fist into his ribs. The hit momentarily took the breath from his body, and Dylan stumbled.

"What's the matter? You don't like getting hit?" Touso asked.

Dylan growled and returned with a string of cross-hooks and knee kicks. But Touso was ready and swiftly blocked each move with a step, a block, or simply by leaping out of the way.

"Dylan—stop!" Nia screamed.

When Dylan glanced at the crying woman, Touso punched him in the chest and thrust an elbow across his face. But Dylan was surprisingly agile and retaliated with a combination of jabs, knee kicks, and punches. At first, Touso blocked them, then curled forward and rammed Dylan against the wall. A loud crash followed with dozens of photo frames tumbling to the ground. As the two men fell together, a strange light lifted them back onto their feet.

Nia and Mossy stared in shock. Something strange was happening. The light that saved them from falling now wrapped them entirely in its energy. As Dylan glowed in yellow, he grabbed Touso by the neck and slammed him onto the ground. But the other was also glowing in shades of gold and blue. As soon as Touso hit the floor, he was already being lifted back onto his feet. Then he smashed Dylan with a blow that sent him flying across the room.

"Someone once told me that you can't protect anyone if you can't protect yourself." Touso advanced on the fallen man.

"Stop! You're hurting him!" Nia threw herself at Touso, but the light around him tossed her back.

Mossy caught Nia but kept her eyes on Touso. She had seen him angry before, but this was different. He looked the way one might when they felt betrayed. These emotions now summoned a storm that was tearing apart the room. A moment later, Touso's spirit guides stood beside him, glaring at the man on the ground.

"Stop hiding. Let me see you!"

Awakening

Dylan groaned as he turned to face Touso, his eyes lit in flames. Kai Khang smiled and said, "You still punch like a girl, Tou-Tou, but at least you're paying attention."

Chapter 28

Bao was in the middle of processing sales on her laptop when she heard the storm in the living room. Lihue quickly blew out the incense on the altar and hurried to the back of the house. Pahoua picked up her grandson and ran home. Now, everyone was gathered in a room that looked like it had suffered a tornado.

Pahoua and Lihue studied the fallen photo frames, the damaged drywall, and what remained of the furniture. Then they turned their eyes to the two men at the center of it all. Touso stood over a fallen Dylan, and no one knew why.

"What the hell is going on here?" Pahoua demanded.

Lihue narrowed his gaze. "What is the meaning of this, Touso?"

Their son didn't respond for a long time. Then he said to Dylan, "Show them."

Mossy held on to Nia, who continued to watch Dylan pensively. In a short period, they had developed a bond. They were strangely comfortable with each other, and now it all made sense. But Nia still didn't know, and Mossy feared what would happen when it was finally revealed.

Touso knew his brother would make it difficult. Kai was notorious for working alone. He would save them all and didn't need anyone's help—even if he was dead. In the end, Touso played the only card he had: Nia.

"Show them!" The strength of Touso's voice shook the room.

Dylan stood and tossed an irritated glance at Touso. Finally, he faced Pahoua, Lihue, and Bao. They watched as Dylan chanted words he shouldn't have known. Soon, an invisible wall shimmered and wavered around him until it revealed the being behind it.

Pahoua grabbed her husband, who gawked incredulously.

Bao shouted, "You fucking asshole!"

"Hey, sis. Nice to see you, too." Kai grinned.

"How is this..." Lihue looked between Touso and Kai. "What have you done?"

Kai met his father's gaze. "Some things don't change, do they, Dad? Even in death, I'm still responsible for any funny business."

Lihue's face twisted in a rage. "How dare you? I thought you died. I thought that monster took you!"

When he wavered and gripped his heart, the sneer disappeared from Kai's expression. Instantly, he was at his father's side and was alarmed by how light he felt.

"I'm here, Dad," Kai said more gently. "I'm home."

Lihue stared at him in disbelief. Then a sob escaped, and he embraced his son. "You're here. You're really here! But how?"

Amber eyes shined from within their blue-green shell. "It's a long story."

Nia glanced at Mossy. She was the only one who couldn't see. "What's going on?"

Fuechi answered this question when he leaped at him. "Daddy!"

Kai held him tight. "Hey, bud! Looks like the secret's out."

Nia reeled with confusion. "What the hell is going on?"

"Hey, Boss-lady. Don't be mad." Kai smiled at his wife.

Nia staggered and abruptly pulled away.

As gently as she could, Mossy said, "You're not going crazy. It's Kai. He's been with Dylan this entire time."

"No!" When Nia cried, everyone felt her pain. She was still learning how to cope with his death. She didn't know how she was supposed to handle his return. "This isn't happening. This isn't real!"

Kai put Fuechi down and carefully approached his wife. "Nia baby, It's me. I'm here."

Nia baby. Kai called her "Nia baby" whenever she was upset. She straightened as he moved toward her. With each step, a shimmer revealed bits of her husband. Blue-green eyes became as gold as honey.

"Get away from me!" She struggled as Kai took her hand.

He held on even as she beat him across the chest. He said, "Nia, I'm here. I'm sorry I left you. I'm sorry I lied. I'm sorry for everything!"

Nia finally crumbled in his arms. "Why are you doing this to me? Why are you torturing me? You left me! The dead don't come back!"

Kai buried his face into her hair. "I'm sorry, Nia baby. Please don't cry anymore. I love you so much. You and Fuechi—I had to protect you no matter what. Don't you understand? It was either die or be eaten... and I wouldn't be able to protect you the other way."

Nia pulled away to stare at him. "What are you saying?"

"If the demon ate his soul, he would be lost to us forever." It was Pahoua who finally spoke as Kai clung to his wife. "Kai wouldn't take his chosen bride. He chose you instead. In doing so, he had to make another difficult choice so that he could keep protecting everyone he loved."

Lihue's expression turned with realization. "You knew!"

Pahoua was immediately regretful as she faced him. "I didn't know it would be like this! We were only trying to protect his soul!"

"It's against the rules!" Lihue admonished in a tone no one had ever heard him use with his wife.

Nia gasped, "You left us on purpose?"

"I left to protect you." Kai implored her to understand. "I was already dying. Didn't you see how sick I was getting? It was the only way for me to stay alive for you somehow."

When Nia's knees buckled, Kai fell with her. He gathered her into his arms as they both wept.

"You idiot," Nia whispered.

Kai rocked her sorrowfully. "I know."

They were both startled when Fuechi crawled in between them. "Mama. Don't cry anymore. I told you Daddy would be back!"

Nia laughed. "He never believed you were gone."

"Didn't you know? This kid can find me anywhere." Kai glanced proudly at his son.

As the little family finally embraced each other, everyone else watched in awe. Pahoua and Bao smiled tearfully at their reunion, but Lihue's expression remained grave.

When Touso pulled Mossy into his arms, she asked, "What happens now?"

"I don't know." But the apprehension in his voice said otherwise. Touso agreed with his father: Kai and Pahoua had broken the rules, and now the soul of Kai Khang was somewhere it didn't belong. They could only expect trouble to follow.

Lihue always retreated to the altar when he was especially happy or incredibly distressed. Lately, it was the latter. He often sat there, thinking and asking for strength. He prayed as he lit the joss sticks, refilled the cups, and placed several eggs into bowls with new rice. He prayed for forgiveness most of all. He heard Pahoua arrive long before she spoke but kept his golden-brown eyes firmly placed on the candles of the altar.

Finally, his wife said, "It was the only way."

When he didn't respond, Pahoua hurried to his side and implored him to understand. "You saw how weak he was those last few days. Du Yong was draining him slowly. If he had died that way—he'd be gone forever! Choosing death was the only way to protect himself and his family."

When Lihue remained painfully quiet, she became angry. "Why are you always this way? You're so hard on all of us. Everything must be your way or nothing at all. Why do you think he didn't come to you?"

"Because he knew it was wrong. It is wrong, Pahoua!" He spoke passionately, but his eyes were anxious when he turned to face her. "Don't you understand what you've done? It all makes sense now."

Awakening

At first, Pahoua was confused. Her husband's complexion was pale, and the cheeks hollow. When her eyes met the mirror on the wall, there was no denying the truth. They were *both* sick.

She shook her head. "I'm just tired!"

Lihue surprised her with a bitter chuckle. "You've always been so wise, my love. You're my chosen bride. My ancestors chose you for me because of your unique strength and wisdom. Has motherhood blinded you so much?"

When Pahoua struggled for words, her husband smiled. "You've always thought I was too hard on Kai. You thought I didn't love him as much as I love Touso. But everything I did was to protect him. If he had listened, he'd still be alive!"

Pahoua froze as he touched her face. She closed her eyes and savored the warmth of his hands. Even after all these years, she loved him so much. A chosen bride cherished her shaman more than herself. Had she truly committed a wrong?

Finally, he said, "If he had listened, you wouldn't have done what you've done. And now the gods are punishing both of us."

"It's not true!"

Lihue drew her into his arms. She was as beautiful as the day they met. He only wished he was strong enough to protect her from what was coming. He pulled back to look into her eyes. "How long has he been coming to you?"

The softest quiver of her mouth confirmed his worst fears.

"There are rules for a reason. Everyone pays a different price when they break one of those rules. It is forbidden to take a life, whether someone else's or your own. When Kai took his own life, the gods took his memories, making him a lost soul. When you helped him, the gods stopped protecting you."

Pahoua cried. "I'm so sorry. I've failed you!"

"You've always protected this entire family," Lihue spoke softly as he held her close. "A mother must protect her children, and a husband must protect his wife. I should have known better and stopped you and Kai from performing that ritual. It is I who have failed you, Pahoua!"

"No! I was wrong. I was wrong," Pahoua wept.

"Don't cry, my love." Lihue caressed the soft hair of her head. "You've always carried the burden of protecting this family. Now it's my turn."

Pahoua's expression turned with alarm. "What are you going to do?"

Lihue's eyes glistened. "What I must do."

The shocking revelation took a toll on the Khang family, and everyone soon dispersed to sort out their emotions. Lihue was upset with Pahoua for keeping this secret. Still in shock over Kai's return, Nia retreated with Fuechi to their room. Even Touso disappeared. Bao, forever the caretaker, prepared lunch while everyone sorted their pains.

As Dylan Reed stood on the porch and stared into the distance, he heard the door open from behind. He didn't have to turn to know it was Mossy. She had been the quietest during the entire revelation. Now, she approached carefully and wondered who she was going to meet.

"Hey, Moss."

Mossy frowned as she glanced at him sideways. "Is that really you, Dylan?"

"You don't recognize your old boyfriend anymore?" Dylan smirked as he looked at her.

Mossy stared and relaxed only when his blue-green eyes remained clear. Then she asked, "Will you walk with me?"

The request surprised him, and it was another moment before he finally nodded.

It was their first time back in the woods since Cindy was sent away, and now Mossy marveled at what she saw. Every tree on the Khang property was decorated with bells and tiny copper discs. While some tree trunks were wrapped in braided joss paper, spirit money, and protection spells hung from the branches above. It was so well placed that passing strangers could easily mistake it for décor. But trained eyes knew better. Everything on the trees protected against evil spirits. Instead of Christmas trees, these were spirit trees.

"This is creepy." Dylan studied the strange ornaments with a frown.

"It's protected here. Everything here warns evil spirits to stay away," Mossy explained.

"Is that why you brought me here? To tell me to go away?" Dylan asked.

Mossy said, "That's not fair."

"Then what are you doing, Moss?" There was an edge to his voice. "Why are we out here like you suddenly care?"

Mossy looked as though he'd slapped her across the face. But instead of showing anger, she dropped her chin and cried.

Dylan quickly took her hand. "I'm sorry—that was out of line."

She sniffled. "No. I'm the one who should be sorry. I've been so selfish that I haven't even thought about what you're going through! You're right. This is my fault. If it weren't for me, this never would have happened to you."

"You're probably right." When she whimpered at this answer, he smiled. *God, he loved her!* "I just hope you understand now how I feel about you."

She tossed him a strange expression. "Don't you think letting my fiancé's dead brother possess you is taking it too far?"

Dylan shrugged. "Some call it petty. I prefer the word progressive."

Now, she scowled. "You never take anything seriously!"

"Actually, I don't think I've ever been more serious." Confusion spread across Mossy's face as Dylan dug into his pocket. She was confused when he pulled out a shriveled rose with dry leaves and slid it over her wrist.

She stared at the corsage above her engagement ring. "Is that...?"

Dylan nodded. "I was going to give it to you that night before I got stupid. It was the last thing I grabbed just before the car exploded."

She touched the dried petals in awe. They were pink and would have looked lovely against her purple gown.

"I still wonder if things would be different had I put this on you first," he said.

Mossy glanced between the corsage and ring, each representing a different life. "It seems like such a long time ago."

Dylan grasped her by the shoulders. "No, Moss! That's exactly it. It wasn't that long ago. Feelings don't just change. You and I are supposed to be together. I love you, and you love me. Don't you remember all the promises we made to each other? What did he do to you to make you forget?"

For a long time, Mossy was lost in his blue-green eyes. She remembered the first time she saw Dylan on campus. He was the cool guy surrounded by friends and adored by all the girls. But he would abruptly stop everything to open doors for teachers or sit and chat with a lone kid in the lunchroom. Once, he caught Mossy watching him. He didn't just smile. He had tried to talk to her then, but she had run away, just as she always did. He always came to the track more often after that. Eventually, his persistence won her over, and Dylan Reed became the first boy she ever loved. Unfortunately, he was also the first ever to break her heart.

Mossy abruptly pulled away. "He didn't do anything. You're the one who went to prom without me. I'd been waiting all year for that night, and you took Amy instead—because what? She fits your lifestyle better than I do. Don't try to make this about Touso, Dylan. He just took your place when you left me in the wind!"

Now, Dylan was the one who looked like he'd been hit. A storm stirred in the summer sky, and she knew Touso was looking for her.

Finally, Mossy said, "This isn't why I brought you here. I don't want to fight with you, Dylan. I just wanted you to know that I'm sorry. Your life is in danger because of me, and I want to help you. Can't we at least be friends?"

"But I don't want to be your friend, Moss!" Dylan simmered.

"Then our story will have to end here." Mossy looked into his eyes. "I love him, Dylan. This is where I belong."

He surprised her by laughing too loudly. Only when she saw the yellow glow did she understand it wasn't Dylan anymore.

"I'm impressed, Mossy Cha! I thought you were just watching out for your own tail." Kai Khang crossed his arms.

"My own tail?"

"Get married or die, right? Isn't that the deal the spirits have made for us?" Kai paced around the clearing. "Old people, man. They never stop telling us what to do! I had hoped that with my death, Touso wouldn't have to make that deal."

When Mossy looked confused, Kai said, "What if they hate each other? What if you love someone else? Wasn't it just yesterday you were swearing your undying love to Dylan Reed?"

As Mossy burned with embarrassment, Kai grinned. "I'm just saying—we shouldn't be stuck to anyone just to survive. I didn't want it for myself; I didn't want it for my brother. We can fight our own battles."

"But you died," Mossy reminded him.

"Yes, but on my terms," Kai pointed out. "I died so I could give Touso my strength. Haven't you wondered why he's been able to hold on so long before you came?"

"You can give your powers away?" Mossy's expression turned with shock.

Kai's eyes glistened. "You can give anything away— just like Dylan gave his body to me, and just like how you gave your body to Cindy."

Mossy inhaled sharply.

"Come on. That's the only way humans can get possessed. They have to let us in! Don't you know anything?" Kai gave her a strange expression.

"But I didn't—"

Kai smiled. "Oh, but you did. You know you've wanted to beat that chick for a long time. You didn't resist, that's for sure."

She shook her head. "That's not what I wanted."

"Listen, Mossy. I'm not here to judge. Kicking ass is what I do! And trust me—she deserved it." He winked at her. "What I want to know is: can you really protect my brother, Mossy Cha? Do you really want to?"

As Mossy considered these questions, Kai abruptly grabbed her wrist. A string of electric shocks struck her as he dug deep into her soul, searching for all her secrets.

This blatant invasion infuriated her so much that when Chee's energy crawled across her flesh, she didn't resist. Without warning, Mossy shot a fist at his face. Kai ducked to the side and pulled her forward. But she fell and hooked her legs across his own to flip him onto the ground. Instead of falling, a string of golden light kept him on his feet. Mossy's own spirits quickly pulled her up to face him. Kai Khang studied her with interest.

Finally, he let her go. "You're learning. You never used to listen to them. Most people second-guess what they should do. That's why you got beat up by Amy the first time. That's why you got hurt by Cindy. You listened to your feelings instead of your guides."

"How do you tell which is which?" Mossy was curious. All of it was emotional.

"One's more useful than the other," said Kai with a shrug.

Mossy rolled her eyes. "I don't know how Touso puts up with you. You don't give any straight answers."

"My responsibility is to teach, not to give answers." When she glared at him, he said, "Consider this. Is it right or wrong to kill?"

"Wrong," Mossy answered.

"Why?"

"Because killing is wrong," she replied impatiently.

"Right! You didn't have to think about that, did you? You just know what is right. Just like you should know that someone who hits you gets hit back. When a person dies, their soul goes somewhere else. When you know the answers, why hesitate?" Kai explained.

"It's not as simple as that," Mossy protested.

"For some things, it is."

"Then why are you here?" she asked.

The shadows returned to his eyes, and he smiled secretly. "Better leave that one alone, my dear sister-in-law. You won't like the answer."

"Things must go where they belong. That's what I keep hearing. You don't belong here anymore, Kai. You're hurting him."

"You're talking about Dylan now. That's cute that you're worried about your boyfriend even as you protect your future husband." Kai's eyes glistened with amusement.

"Don't make it sound like that! He's my friend, and I care about him. If I've learned anything, it's that spirits drain energy. You're killing him while you're in there!" Mossy's eyes flashed fiercely.

Kai lost his arrogance for the first time. "I won't stay that long. I just need a little more time."

After a long silence, Mossy knew he wouldn't reveal those plans. Finally, she said, "Touso says you see the future. You saw something just now, didn't you?"

His swift answer surprised her this time. "You have two very different futures. I approve of one but not the other."

You've been chosen with two destinies... Mossy shrunk back as Du Yong's words returned to haunt her.

"What's wrong?" Concern flashed across his face.

Mossy shook her head. "Du Yong once told me the same thing! What does this mean, Kai?"

Dark shadows spread across his eyes. "It means you'll have to choose. One will pit you against the one you love, and one will cost your soul."

Mossy scowled. "Your brother also said you were a vague asshole. Now I believe it."

Kai laughed so hard she thought he might fall to the floor. Instead, he straightened and wiped tears from his eyes. "What's the point in revealing the future? You should understand that better than anyone, Mossy Cha. Neither of us likes being told what to do—not even when it's destiny."

Mossy contemplated this silently. Kai was obnoxious, but he was right. Whatever the future held, she wanted what she wanted.

"Listen." Kai was finally serious as he met her gaze. "No matter what the future holds, one thing remains true. You choose what you want to do and trust yourself. Trust your guides. I see what my brother sees now. You're strong. Much stronger than you know."

Mossy hadn't expected to hear any compliments from Kai Khang. "You asked me earlier if I wanted to protect Touso. The answer is 'yes.' More than anything. I'll protect him with my life if that's what it takes."

Kai looked at her with curiosity. "Do you really love my brother?"

"Yes!" Mossy answered without hesitation.

"Not just because you're chosen."

"Because I choose him!" Mossy spoke fiercely now, and her eyes glowed with this passion. "I love him!"

Kai nodded. "Then your union is truly blessed."

"Didn't you feel anything for your chosen bride?" Mossy asked. She knew the strength of that bond and found it difficult to see how he could so simply deny it.

Kai turned away and was silent for so long that she thought he would never answer. Then he said, "Of course, I felt something. I'll never forget the look in her eyes. She was so scared! This fear drove her to become something terrible. Yes, I blame myself for that! But he would have gone straight for my brother if I had married her. Touso's strong but not strong enough. Not yet. Giving him my life was the only way to buy him more time."

"I still don't understand. You have a family. Why would you give up your own life?"

Kai met her gaze. "We all have a role to play. Touso is special with a greater purpose. What's more, in the future that the spirits have allowed me to see, my son stays alive because of him. That's all I need to know."

He was about to say something else when a sound came from the trees. It was a miserable wail that sent shivers up her spine. Dylan returned to push her behind him.

"I thought you said evil things wouldn't come here." His blue-green eyes scanned the surrounding trees.

"They're not supposed to!" Mossy felt nervous as she studied the forest, which seemed darker by the second.

"Stay here. I'll go take a look." Dylan started walking away.

"I'll come with you—"

"No. I don't need your help." He never looked back as he disappeared into the forest.

Mossy stared after him. He was upset, and she couldn't blame him. In one breath, he lost his girlfriend and became possessed. Worst, the thing he shared his body with was Touso's brother. Dylan was losing in every way, and Mossy didn't know how to help him.

Something stirred in the bushes, and Mossy whirled in time to see a shadow leap away. "Who's there?"

When her question was only met with silence, she started backing away.

"Dylan? This isn't funny." Her heart raced as she glanced around the trees. "You can be mad at me all you want. But please—stop trying to scare me!"

Mossy jumped as a hand touched her shoulder. With relief, she turned around. "Dylan—"

The words trailed from her lips. It wasn't Dylan who had returned from the woods.

It was Alang Vang.

Like most people looking forward to a day at the lake, he wore a tank top and shorts. But he was too far from the beach for it to be convincing. His dark eyes glistened with amusement as he tilted his head sideways.

"Oh, dear Mossy Cha. Don't you know?" She held her breath as he leaned very close and whispered, "You should be scared."

Chapter 29

Dylan saw the rose corsage on the ground and frowned. When he glanced around and saw no trace of her, he knew she was done with him. She'd chosen Touso, but tossing away a token that had meant so much was heartless.

How could it end like this?

When the thing in his arms moaned, Dylan straightened. It wasn't especially large but grew heavier with each second. It was injured and needed help, and it was a good thing he knew where a bunch of healers lived.

As Dylan returned, Touso ran out and shoved him. The thing in his arms yelped as Dylan stumbled.

"What the hell, dude!" Dylan scowled.

"Where is she?" Touso demanded.

The door opened, and Nia and Bao hurried toward them.

"Where's who?" Dylan gawked between Touso and the women now studying him. His gaze rested a moment longer on Nia.

"Where's Mossy?" Touso reached for him again.

"Whoa! Chill out, Touso!" Bao threw herself between them. Then she studied the bundle in Dylan's arms. "What do you have there?"

Dylan looked down at the creature wrapped inside his shirt. When the animal wouldn't stop struggling, he used the only thing he had to keep it safe in his arms. Now, it was so weak that it hardly moved. "It's a dog. It looks like it was hit by a car."

Bao peaked under the cover. The miserable face of a young pit bull blinked back at her. "Oh, poor thing! It's too hot out here. Let's get it inside."

Dylan shifted back on his heels and gladly complied. It was only with hesitation that Touso let him pass. A moment later, the animal was laid out on a bed of blankets in the living room. As Nia heated some hot water, Bao assessed the wounds.

"Should we get your mom?" Dylan asked.

Bao shook her head. "No need. It's not as bad as it looks. She definitely got hit by a car and broke a leg. I can fix that. But that's not the only problem."

Nia arrived with a pot of hot water and now studied the animal anxiously. "Tell me right now I don't need to throw this at a demon dog!"

Bao chuckled. "No demon dogs today. But we might get puppies."

"Puppies!" Nia and Dylan exclaimed together.

"Yup. She's about to become a mama. That's half the reason she couldn't get up. The poor thing broke a leg at her heaviest!" Bao's mouth turned with sympathy.

"How did she get so far from the road?" Dylan stared at the animal, who was already more comfortable in the safety of its soft new bed.

"You'd be surprised at how far a mom will go to protect her babies," Bao replied as she sorted through an emergency medical box. As if agreeing, the dog whimpered and licked her fingers.

"Should we get her to the vet?" Nia asked.

She set the pot down and prepared warm rags to clean the wounds.

"It's better for her to stay here for now. Once we get her cleaned up and bandaged, she'll be better. Plus, it's too painful for her to move." Bao glanced at Dylan. "I'm surprised she didn't bite you, Dai!"

"Dai?" Dylan frowned.

Bao beamed innocently. "You're such a cute couple! Dylan. Kai. Dai. You're welcome!"

While Dylan and Kai glared at her with irritation, Bao ignored them and continued caring for the animal. The hairs on his neck bristled. Dylan turned to see Touso waiting impatiently.

"Where is Mossy?" he demanded again in a low growl.

Dylan glanced around. "Isn't she here? She was gone when I got back with the dog."

Touso straightened and took a step toward him. "She was afraid. I felt her!"

Dylan faced him with a scowl. "She was fine when I left. I figured she just went home. What—you think I took her there to bury her in the woods? You have a lot of nerve, Touso Khang. You're not the only one who cares about her."

"Oh, yeah?" Touso was in front of him with a smirk on his lips. "Tell me again how you've shown your care, Dylan? Did you know that the first time I ever had to help Mossy was after she found you having lunch with another girl?"

Dylan stiffened.

"That's right. You didn't even bother to check on her while she cried her heart out in the bathroom. Meanwhile, something was stalking her the entire time. You put her there for that creature to attack!"

Dylan clenched his fists.

"That's right. There are consequences for every action, Dylan. You hurt her. What did you think would happen? Actually, I should thank you."

When Dylan looked confused, Touso grinned. "Because of you, Mossy's learned which of us will always be there for her."

When Dylan punched him, Touso stumbled once before quickly returning with his fist. It hooked Dylan across the jaw. But instead of going down, Dylan turned and hurled himself at the other. As the two men wrestled each other onto the ground, Bao and Nia shouted for them to stop.

One moment, the men locked their arms around each other's necks. The next, they were being lifted off the floor. Touso and Dylan stared at a mysterious ball of light growing between them. Then it exploded, sending each in opposite directions.

As they groaned and lifted themselves from the ground, they saw Mossy standing across the room. She had entered from the patio door while they were fighting and now faced them, carrying a small bag over her shoulder. She looked furious.

"I'm so sick of you two fighting! Isn't there enough going on? When are you going to grow up?" As she glared at them both, Nia and Bao came to stand by her side.

"I'm glad you said it, sis." Nia shook her head in dismay.

"Just wait until I tell Mom and Dad!" Bao frowned with disapproval.

The dog, quiet the entire time, lifted her head and whimpered. *They were in trouble now.*

Touso and Dai stared at the women before turning to each other. Then they abruptly turned away, crossing their arms with a scowl. As they each simmered and marinated in stubbornness, their spirit guides arose to chastise them... and laugh.

The first time Mossy met Alang Vang, she knew he was bad news. He was cunning and manipulative, having helped his father build an empire based on dark promises. Indeed, anyone participating in the kidnapping of souls had to be particularly conniving.

Additionally, he enjoyed taunting her, sneering as though he knew she was about to walk into a giant mouse trap. But the necromancer was not who she thought he was. As Dylan disappeared into the woods, searching for the mysterious sound, and Alang cornered her, Mossy was prepared to fight.

"What do you want?" Mossy demanded as she leaped away to maintain a safe distance between them.

Alang looked less threatening than usual in the daylight, dressed casually in summer attire. The lean muscles of his arms glistened in the sun as he crossed them over his chest.

"I want to be friends."

"Friends?" Mossy repeated incredulously. "It's a little late for that. You and your father have gone too far!"

She was surprised when Alang looked remorseful.

'I know you have no reason to trust me, Mossy. But I'm not here to hurt you," he said finally.

"Then why are you here?"

"To help."

Mossy stared at him in disbelief. But when her spirit guides seemed willing to listen, so did she. "How?"

"Let's take a walk." Alang smiled and beckoned her to follow. When she remained suspicious, he became more serious. "Please, Mossy. I promise: no funny business."

She considered him for a long time before finally relenting.

As they followed one of the dirt trails that led into the woods, Mossy was again astounded by the peace. The peculiar ornaments on the many trees were both aesthetically pleasing and reassuring. Because evil avoided the protective aura of the land, the forest was abundant with life. It was this positive energy that finally helped her to relax in Alang's company.

"My father has always been a cruel person. I thought it was because of the way he grew up. He was penniless and was always determined to rise in this world. I'm his youngest son, so I knew early on he would rely on me the most, and he did," Alang explained as they continued to walk toward an unknown destination.

Mossy listened thoughtfully.

"I didn't agree with many of the things he did. I don't agree with much of it now. But I'm his son. My place is to honor him by following him. Additionally, I thought that if I could help him achieve his goals, he might stop being so hard on himself and everyone else."

When Alang laughed, there was a hint of sadness. "My sister Daisy—she was always his favorite. Or at least I thought she was. She was the only daughter, and she was smart and beautiful. He let her escape with things the rest of us would have died for. When our father wanted her to marry Kai Khang, I foolishly thought he just wanted to protect her. He hates the Khang family. There had to be a good reason for him to support this union. Who knew this reason would turn out to be so terrible? I know I didn't."

"What are you saying?" Mossy found her voice for the first time since the walk. Alang's tale was beyond anything she could have anticipated.

"You've met Daisy. That sweet and kind woman who helped you get your dress? That's who she was most of the time. She's always been kind but was also ruthless when it came to protecting people."

Mossy frowned. "I don't understand."

"The one characteristic chosen brides share is their desire to protect. Her most unique power is that she's invisible. When she's with her shaman, Du Yong can't see him either."

"Like the protection strings!" Mossy gasped.

Alang nodded. "You're Touso's protection string. You're also connected to your chosen bride sisters. You sense them like you and Touso sense each other because of your tied fates. At some point, Du Yong must have figured out someone else could find the brides for him. He could take out the shamans more easily if he took the brides out of the picture. I don't think I have to tell you that my father has always relied on darker forces to accomplish his goals."

Most shamans prayed to Shee Yee for guidance and protection. Rumor had it that the necromancers prayed to someone else...

"When he found out that his own daughter was a chosen bride, he made a deal with Du Yong," Alang revealed.

Mossy's eyes grew wide in shock. "He sold out his own daughter?"

Alang nodded. "If Daisy could help find all the chosen brides, then Du Yong would agree to bless him with unlimited power."

Mossy could hardly believe what she heard. "How could a father do that to his own daughter?"

"It wasn't just him. Daisy had to agree to make this work. For weeks, they tortured her mind, making her desperately afraid. It tore her apart when Kai Khang finally arrived just to reject her. She became more angry than afraid."

"So, she agreed!" Mossy's mouth parted in disbelief.

Alang smiled bitterly. "What do they say? Bad blood runs deep? My father knew exactly how to play her to get what he wanted. My sister, despite all her best qualities, had pride. It was what made her the most like our father. He knew he could use that to his advantage. I think he knew Kai would reject Daisy, which would piss her off enough to make her do something she normally wouldn't."

Mossy looked at him in an accusing way. "But you brought Sheng to Thai's house knowing she would hurt him!"

Alang became furious. "I was angry! When Daisy died, I blamed Kai Khang. When she became the Succubus Queen, I was foolish enough to see it as due justice! I told you—children all emulate their parents somehow. Daisy had her pride, and I'm no better. After she died, I was ready to feed all those Khangs to Du Yong!"

His voice dropped to a whisper. "But I didn't know what he'd done. I didn't know until that night that we were all there. She's a monster because of our own father!"

"She helped Du Yong find all those chosen brides.' Her voice trembled with the revelation. "What will happen to all of them?"

Alang's eyes darkened. "While the succubus resides in the bodies of the brides, they'll drain the shamans slowly for Du Yong. But once they become weak enough, he'll finish them both. He'll eat them all, and their shaman energies will increase his powers immensely. With that, his vengeance against Shee Yee will also be complete."

"What can we do? How do we save them all?" Mossy demanded anxiously.

Just then, they arrived at a remote dirt road where Alang had parked his car. As Mossy waited for his answer, he retrieved a small bag from inside. He returned to her with a firm expression. "As necromancers, we have learned to manipulate spirits through amulets."

Mossy remembered the red jewels and the black strings. The necromancers had created them to bind and protect. She stared in confusion as he handed her the small bag. It was heavy.

"I'll give you all the names of the chosen brides we've found. Get these on them. Once their souls have been released, the amulets will draw them immediately back to their bodies. Du Yong will no longer have any power over them," Alang explained.

"But how do I find the girls? The Black Door keeps eluding me!" She looked helpless as she studied the bag in her hand.

Alang smiled mysteriously. "I know a place where everything is sold for a price. Including the Black Door."

Mossy was stunned. Finally, she asked. "Why are you helping us if you hate the Khang family so much?"

Alang's smile disappeared. "I'm not doing this for them. I'm doing this for Daisy."

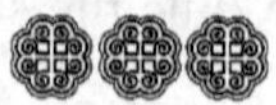

Mossy glared at Touso and Dylan. They were fighting again when there were many more important things to consider. Thai's life was in danger. There were chosen brides to rescue. Sarah was sick. Dylan was possessed, and Nia's dead husband possessed him! With all these problems to resolve, she didn't understand why they couldn't set their differences aside. Exasperated with them both, Mossy turned and ran upstairs.

"You really did it this time, bro."

Touso tossed him a glare. "Shut up, Kai."

His brother grinned ecstatically. "How did you know it was me?"

"You're a bigger pain in the ass," Touso quipped as he pulled himself up.

"She's right, guys." Bao glanced briefly at them as she returned to caring for the wounded dog. "There are more important things at hand. If you keep pissing her off, she might just break up with both of you— you know what I mean, Kai."

Touso and Dylan scowled at each other, but it was Kai who followed him to the kitchen.

"Bro, that chick's got some major anger issues! I think I'm starting to like her. Did you see what she just did? Can all chosen brides do that? You better let her have whatever she wants!" Kai hopped onto the countertop and took a bite out of an apple from the basket. He was hungry from all the events of that morning.

"Stop it!" Touso whirled to face him. "What is wrong with you? You killed yourself, Kai. You died. You left all of us here dealing with your secrets. You left me to clean up your mess. You left Nia and

Fuechi to fend for themselves. Your son can see things that neither he nor Nia understand. They didn't even know they had a family after you died. You made them think they were alone! Stop joking around like you haven't hurt us as much as you have!"

Touso curled and uncurled his hands as though he might hit him again. He was always the calm one—the pacifier. It was clear his little brother had changed much during his absence. Finally, Kai said, "I'm sorry. I know I was wrong."

Touso shook his head. "Some things you just can't take back."

"I told you why I did it!" Kai sounded frustrated.

"You think that justifies the pain you've caused? You should have come to me—you should have trusted me!" Touso looked at his brother with quiet rage. "You killed us all when you killed yourself."

"I was trying to save you!" Kai leaped off the counter and faced his little brother. "Do you think it was easy to do it? You don't know what I've seen, bro. The only way to protect all of us was for me to die—and give you everything I have—including my son!"

"You still don't understand." As Touso spoke, tears glistened in his eyes. "He needed his father—not me. We needed you alive. Not like this!"

A sad expression came over the oldest Khang son. The hardest thing about knowing the future was knowing no one would understand. If he couldn't have Nia or Fuechi, there was no other life for him. If he couldn't protect his brother, they were all doomed.

Finally, Kai said, "You've always been the one to follow the rules, bro. One day, you'll understand. We can't always choose what we want to do. We just pick the best of the options available."

"What are you hoping to do now in this body?" Touso demanded. "You couldn't have picked a less conflicting one? It had to be Mossy's ex-boyfriend?"

Kai laughed. "That's messed up, right? But that's on the ugly bastard who lost his horns. He wanted me to help Dylan break you two apart. We were so close!"

Touso scowled. "Nice to know what team you're playing for."

"Hey, that was before I remembered, okay," he said defensively. "Still, are you sure you want to do that, bro? Do you really want to marry her?"

Touso cast him a strange look. "Why wouldn't I?"

"Because she's your chosen bride?" Kai rolled his eyes.

Touso's gaze didn't falter as he answered, "No. Because I love her. I know you made a different decision for your own reasons. I understand it better now that I've met Nia and Fuechi. But I love Mossy, and keeping her safe is all that matters."

Kai whistled. "Bro, it's like you two rehearsed that shit. She pretty much said the same thing about you!"

Touso frowned. "You spoke with Mossy?"

"We had a little showdown in the woods." When Touso moved toward him, Kai threw up his hands. "Relax, man—nothing happened! Her spirit guides are ancient and powerful. Mossy can take care of herself."

As Touso relaxed, Kai studied him. Finally, he said, "Bro, you got laid, huh?"

When Touso glared at him, he laughed out loud. His little brother was all grown up! "You've changed a lot. You're kicking ass, getting laid, and getting married—all in that order! Soon, you'll be having kids. Man, I'm getting old!"

"No. You're dead."

Kai scowled. "Bro, that was harsh."

"Too soon?"

Kai threw the apple at Touso, who quickly caught it and grinned. He took a large bite and said, "Dead or alive, you're still an asshole."

"Just doing my job. You're welcome." As the tension between them finally eased, Kai looked at Touso more seriously. "Listen. I want you to know I never meant to hurt you. I would trust you with my life. But my life isn't important in the big picture. The big picture is all about you. And Fuechi."

Touso furrowed his brows in confusion. "What do you mean?"

"I can't tell you that, bro! You know the drill!" Kai smiled sadly. "When the time is right, you'll know and understand. Right now, no matter how wrong it is, I'm glad I can see you one last time."

Touso inhaled sharply. "How long do you have?"

"I don't know," Kai replied. "Not long. I foresaw that I'd get to come back somehow. I thought it was to help you, but after everything I've seen, the puzzle pieces are fitting differently."

"What do you mean?"

Kai's eyes flashed yellow. "You have your chosen bride, and she seems legit. You don't need me anymore. I think I'm here to take Daisy back with me."

"Your chosen bride." Touso's expression darkened.

"Women, man. Not even in death is there peace!"

"If you had just followed the rules," Touso scolded in a teasing way.

Kai straightened. "Rules are made to be broken, and you know me. I like a good fight."

"I hope you're ready." Touso sobered as he fixed his gaze on his brother. "Because she's pissed."

Kai's expression said he was more than ready. He would take his chosen bride back to hell, kicking and screaming.

It took the rest of the night to save the dog's life. While Bao brewed herbal medicine, Nia splinted her broken leg. By the time she was resting comfortably, they had named her Zena. It was a fitting name for such a strong pup. As their patient finally fell asleep, her caregivers departed for their own rest.

Nia was careful not to wake Fuechi when she slipped into the washroom. She pulled the blood-stained shirt over her head and set it in the warm water pooling in the sink. She rubbed a small bar of soap against the red stains. Soon, she was scrubbing with a fury. By the time the bar slipped from her hands and fell across the floor, Nia was crying. Her grief poured like the water from the faucet.

She hadn't spoken to Kai or Dylan since leaving to put Fuechi down for a nap. In truth, she had avoided them altogether—hiding in her room or running between rooms if she needed anything. She didn't know how to face him. It was hard enough to lose a loved one. They weren't supposed to come back from the dead.

Finally, she came outside when Touso started looking for Mossy. That was when Dylan returned with Zena in his arms. Even as she helped Bao tend to the wounded dog, she kept her eyes averted from Dylan. She moved every time he came too close. And when he and Touso began fighting over Mossy again, it was all she could do to check her emotions. The man fighting for Mossy was Dylan, but the eyes watching Nia belonged to her husband. She didn't know what to do.

Nia jumped when a pair of hands touched her hips.

"Don't cry. I hate it when you cry."

It was Dylan—Kai! He had used his shirt to wrap Zena and now stood behind Nia, half-naked. He gazed at her through the mirror. The heat of his flesh teased her backside. When he tried to make her look at him, she resisted.

"I can't!" She pulled away and refused to turn around.

"Do you hate me?" His fingers hung in the air where she had left them.

"No." Nia tried to keep her voice quiet so she wouldn't wake their son.

"Then what is it? Why won't you look at me?"

"Because this isn't you!" Her tortured expression was heartbreaking.

Kai reached for her hands and was relieved when she didn't fight. "Close your eyes."

"Why?"

"Because it's the only way you'll see me."

They stared at each other for a long time until she finally complied with a big sigh. Then he took her hand and rested the palm against his jawline. "I'm here. Don't you feel me?"

His breath caught when her fingers moved against his cheek. Slowly, they traveled down the side of his neck and lingered over the muscled curve of his chest. With her eyes closed, she saw him as clear as day. His copper blond hair was soft underneath her fingers. The blue koi glided up and down his muscled arms as they closed around her body.

Nia kissed him. It was carefully done, as one might taste a new flavor for the first time. Dylan Reed tasted different, but the moan from his lips sounded like Kai. He also moved like her husband, lifting her hips over his own and hungrily kissing her until she was breathless.

When they finally broke away, Nia didn't dare open her eyes, fearing it was all a dream. There was even a strange guilt for kissing another man even though the soul inside of said man was her husband.

"Nia?" Kai whispered, his breath fanning her lips, making her shiver. Hearing another man say her name with so much love was strange. But the tenderness and admiration there was her husband at the very core.

He gently brushed his thumb across her cheek, and she let out a small, breathy chuckle.

"I'm sorry. I just need a moment," she confessed, leaning in. "It's just…a bit overwhelming."

Kai smiled. "You know, there's one good thing about living in another person's body without any memory of who you were."

Kai always had a strange way of looking at life, and the benefits of possessing another man's body proved to be no different. If she had opened her eyes at that moment, she would have seen his brimming smile; he loved watching the ever-changing expressions on her face. Her brows bumped adorably together as she contemplated his words. "What? What would that be?"

Slowly, he placed his forehead onto hers.

"Getting to know and falling in love with you all over again," he confessed. "Even as Dylan, I was drawn to you. I saw you with my heart, not my eyes."

Her mouth parted speechlessly.

"You felt it, too, didn't you? From the moment you met Dylan, you knew there was something different." He took her hand with his free one and placed it across his exposed chest. "You heard my soul calling to you. No matter what's happened, our souls are intertwined. I love you, Nia."

Her eyes snapped open. She could suddenly see her husband, Kai. The love of her life.

Somewhere between forever and almost no time at all, he lifted her onto the countertop.

"Kai," she whispered in breathless anticipation.

From the moment he remembered who he was, he had wanted nothing more than to touch her. Now, as a soft whimper escaped her parted lips, he wanted more. He wanted to feel her in every way...

Nia surprised him by crying.

"What's wrong? Should I stop?"

"No!" She clung to him in desperation. "Don't stop. Keep going. I've just missed you so much! And I'm afraid... you'll disappear.'"

He tenderly touched her face. "Don't be afraid, Nia baby. I'm here. Right now, I'm here."

Nia nodded. "I love you!"

"I love you, too. Forever."

When he kissed her again, she let go of all her fears. She sank into his arms, savoring the heat of his mouth against her flesh. And as they lost themselves in this heated embrace, the tears of pain shed over the last few months finally became tears of joy.

Mossy didn't turn when Touso walked into the room. She stared out the window, her thoughts betrayed only by a scowl. She didn't turn even as he said her name. Finally, Touso touched her shoulder. She surprised him by throwing her arms around him and burying her face in his chest.

As Mossy cried, he asked, "What's wrong, Mo? Are you upset that I was fighting? I'm sorry. It was stupid!"

Mossy shook her head. Whenever she tried to speak, she choked on the words and returned to wailing. He held her, caressing her back until finally, she calmed down enough to form clear words.

"It's my fault!" she gasped.

He looked confused. "What are you talking about?"

"Alang said—"

Instantly, he grasped her shoulders. "When did you see Alang?"

She blinked and wiped the tears from her eyes. "In the woods. He came to see me in the woods."

Touso looked furious. "I'll kill him if he's hurt you!"

"No!" Mossy shook her head. "He didn't hurt me. He came to help."

"Help? Those necromancers never help anyone."

"No, Touso. This time, it was different. He was different. He came to give us this." She handed him the black drawstring bag that she'd brought back.

"What's in it?" he asked suspiciously.

"Soul-locking amulets," she replied, finally regaining control over her voice. "He says if we put the locks on the chosen brides in this world, it'll draw their souls back to their bodies and cut off the connection to the succubus spirits!"

Touso lifted the bag and stared at it as though it held venomous snakes. "How do we know we can trust him?"

Mossy frowned. "Touso, he lost his sister. He's in pain. He's trying to make things right."

Touso wasn't convinced as he placed the bag on the table and looked at her. "What else did he say?"

"He said Du Yong figured out somehow that he could use Daisy to track down other chosen brides since we're all connected. That's how the necromancers have been finding the chosen brides. Then they steal their souls and replace them with the succubus spirits!"

Mossy sobbed again as though she couldn't bear what she was about to say next. Finally, she said, "I think this is my fault."

"What's your fault?"

"Remember when I got in trouble for playing with the split horns?" Her eyes spread wide with anxiety.

Touso nodded.

"Aunt Padee said I called it, and now it sees me and is coming for me!" Mossy's face twisted in sorrow. "When I saw him in the spirit world again, he said he's been looking for me ever since. What if... I think it was because I called him that he realized there was a way to find the other brides. He's going to eat them all because of me!"

Mossy was hysterical now, and Touso held her as she trembled.

"Mossy, you were just a child. You couldn't have known. We still have a chance to find them and bring them home." He gently caressed her hair and waited for her to speak.

She gazed at him with a new determination. "We have to do it soon, Touso. They're running out of time!"

"What do you need me to do?"

Mossy glanced at the black bag on the table. "I need you to get all the chosen brides together and get these locks on them."

"And what are you going to do?" Even as he asked, Touso knew he wouldn't like the answer.

When she looked at him again, her eyes were glowing purple. "I'm going to find my sisters." She was going to bring their souls back.

Chapter 30

Alang Vang had done as he promised. He gave Mossy all the names of the chosen brides that Daisy had found. Most had arrived to stay with their local shamans. A few resided much further away. Touso and Kai would gather the ones nearby. Lihue sent Wang Meng and his vast network of associates to care for the rest. He handed Wang Meng the remaining amulets and said, "Be careful. The Queen sees and hears everything through their eyes."

Wang Meng understood. Use discretion when possible and force when only necessary. "I'll use every trick in the book, Boss!"

After the man was gone, Lihue turned to his sons. "Are you two sure you know what you're doing?"

"Are you kidding me?" Kai snickered as he leaned against the wall. "I can do this with my eyes closed."

"Except for the Queen, the other succubus are low-level spirits. They should be easy to catch and lockdown," Touso answered. As usual, one reserved more tact than the other regarding their abilities.

Awakening

They were gathered in the living room before the altar. Lihue poured fresh water and rice wine into shot glasses while his wife and daughter placed new rice and eggs onto the shelves. He implored Shee Yee and their ancestors to gather and bless their sons before their journey. He especially asked them to be patient with Kai. As a shaman, the spirits revered him. As a soul breaking the rules, they were tempted to drag him back to the ancestral home and whoop him. Lihue asked them to bless him with just a little more time.

Bao's medical elixir had helped Dylan rejuvenate his body's cells, but Kai's immense energy was draining. If Dylan Reed was to survive, the soul of Kai Khang needed to go where it belonged.

Lihue looked at his eldest son and ended the prayer by saying, "In life, you were reckless. May you practice more care in death."

"Great pep talk, Dad." Kai straightened and scowled. "Glad I could come back for this."

"May you talk less in your next life," Lihue continued, but there was a hint of a smile this time. Then he turned to his youngest son. "Touso Khang, as a son of Shee Yee, you are a hundred times blessed. May your spirit guides keep you safe on this dangerous journey. May you gain strength for each success and wisdom from any failures. May your battle be blessed with victory on this day."

Kai and Touso bowed to their father and their ancestors, and then they straightened. Both men frowned when they noticed the way their parents avoided each other. But their father carefully watched Pahoua as she left the room. Touso cast his brother a knowing look and excused himself to find Mossy.

Kai faced his father for the first time since returning. "Don't be too mad at her, Dad. It's my fault. It's always my fault."

Lihue remained quiet for so long that Kai wondered if he would speak at all. But his father surprised him when he replied, "No. It's mine."

Seeing the stir of emotions in his father's eyes was one of the few times Kai Khang felt uncomfortable.

Lihue shook his head sadly. "Your mother always protected you too much because I didn't protect you enough. I was too hard on you, Kai. I was so busy trying to get you to follow the rules that I never asked what you were seeing or going through. That was my failure as a father. You should have been able to come to me during your last days, and the fact that you didn't will always remain my biggest regret!"

When Lihue sobbed, Kai hurried to ensure he didn't fall. His father also looked too frail. Lihue and Pahoua appeared increasingly ill, but neither would admit to the truth. Kai was sure they were sick because of what he had done.

"Don't do that. I'm much more comfortable when you're angry with me, Dad. You've always been the strength we all needed. You taught us right from wrong. You and Mom taught us how to protect the people we love. Sometimes, that means sacrifice. I'm happy that Fuechi will get to learn from both of you when I'm no longer here." Kai's voice was sad but grateful all at once.

"That boy is extraordinary." Lihue chuckled through tears. "He's so much like you but smarter."

Kai laughed and wiped his eyes. "It's because of his mom. Nia has always been able to see right through my bullshit. Please. Take care of them both after I'm gone!"

Lihue's expression quickly grew somber. "Are you sure you're ready for this?"

Kai scowled with some frustration. "We don't have a choice. Daisy threatened to drain them all if I don't go to her. And then I'm pretty sure she'll come for Nia and Fuechi next. If she wants a battle, she's got it. I've already given up too much to let a succubus mess with my family over a little heartbreak."

"Kai, you still haven't learned anything after all that's happened." Lihue shook his head in disappointment. "Sometimes the way to victory is compassion. Daisy was your chosen bride. You must make this right."

"How am I supposed to do that?" Kai demanded. "She's dead. We both are!"

Lihue furrowed his brows. "How do you know Daisy will even be there?"

"She'll come because I'll be there. She thinks she has the numbers to defeat me, but she doesn't know what I've been doing all these years," Kai answered.

"What have you been doing, son?" Lihue demanded suspiciously now.

"Just a lot of fighting, Dad." Kai grinned secretly before turning serious. "Listen. If we make it back—when we come back, I would like you to do something for Nia."

Kai moved to whisper in his ears, and Lihue listened pensively. When his son finished speaking, he nodded with an expression that gave his son immense relief.

It was at this time that they heard the approach of new visitors. Nia walked into the living room with Fuechi.

"Kai? What's going on? Are you leaving us?" She studied both her husband and father-in-law anxiously.

"Daddy, don't go!" Fuechi ran and threw his arms around his hips.

The mighty Kai Khang fought the urge to cry as he held his son. "Hey, bud. I'm just going to work. I'll be back later to tuck you in, okay?"

Fuechi shook his head in disbelief. When Kai held out his hand, Nia took it breathlessly. She couldn't speak because she was choking back her own tears.

"Nia baby, I have to wrap up some unfinished business. I promise I'll be back." When Kai implored her with his eyes, she understood they both needed to remain strong for their son.

Finally, she said, "Don't be late, or else!"

"Yes, Boss-lady!" His eyes glistened as he kissed her.

As Lihue watched the young family embrace, he felt powerless. It didn't matter how strong one was in body or reputation when he couldn't give his own child life.

Mossy was staring anxiously out the bedroom window when someone knocked on the door. Pahoua Khang walked in with a tray of hot tea. Her own mother always served tea when someone was ill or anxious. She missed her very much and turned away to hide the tears. But Pahoua wasn't a fool. She set the tray down and beckoned Mossy to come.

She said, "I figured you'd need something to calm your nerves. Come sit with me."

As Mossy complied, Pahoua studied her. "You're scared."

Mossy inhaled sharply to keep from sobbing. She said, "I'm trying so hard to be brave, but I'm so afraid Touso will get hurt. I'm so afraid that I won't get their souls back. What if I let them all down? I don't know anything. I'm just a kid!"

"Your training began nearly as soon as you stepped into this house," Pahoua said as she filled a cup. "You learned to call Touso's soul and respond when your spirit guides want you to do something. You also learned what they can do to you when you refuse. But, most of all, you learned how powerful you can become when you embrace your purpose."

When Mossy continued to look fearful, she asked, "Would it make you feel better if I told you I saw the future and you'll be just fine?"

Mossy nodded.

"Well, I can't." Pahoua chuckled as Mossy's chest deflated. "Kai and I get warnings about the future, but not everything we see is helpful, and not everything is final. What matters most is your will. You know what will happen if you fail?"

"They'll all die!"

Pahoua smiled strangely. "That won't happen. Drink your tea. Before you leave, we'll go to your altar and commune with your spirit guides to prepare. Remember the perfection and peace of your altar no matter where you are. It will help you hone your powers and stay in control. Most of all, remember your purpose. As chosen brides, we are the protectors of the Khang shamans. Our pain is secondary to their lives. We'll protect them at any cost. Don't you agree?"

Mossy contemplated these ominous words with a frown. She studied Pahoua, who had become unusually quiet. Her mother-in-law was increasingly distracted, eyes darting about like she was expecting something to jump out of the shadows. The brightness of her energy was waning, and Mossy didn't know why.

"How are you doing?" she finally asked.

Her mother-in-law turned away to fill her own cup. "Some rules are never meant to be broken. I helped Kai end his life, and for whatever reason, he's back. But there's a price to pay, and I'm afraid we'll both pay it now."

"You and Kai?" Mossy gasped.

"My husband and I," Pahoua corrected.

Mossy put her cup down and faced her. "What are you saying? Are you both dying?"

Pahoua shook her head. "I don't know. I just know I'm much weaker than I used to be. He could never see me before, but now he sees me. The gods must have stopped protecting me when I broke the rules. And now he sees my husband, too!"

"That's why!" Mossy gasped. When Pahoua looked confused, she said, "I've wondered why you couldn't see what was inside of Sheng. You've been disconnected." The powers and blessings that made her a chosen bride were gone.

Pahoua staggered, and Mossy quickly took her hand. Finally, she said, "It is what I deserve for what I've done."

"What can I do? How can I help?" Mossy asked.

Pahoua shook her head. "There is nothing you can do for me, daughter. Save the souls of our sisters, Mo. Keep my son safe. As long as you do that, I'll have the strength to fight my own battle."

Mossy put her arms around Pahoua. "I'll bring them all home. I promise."

"Is everything okay here?" Touso watched them from the door with a pensive expression.

Pahoua quickly wiped her tears. "Just giving your bride some words of wisdom."

Touso didn't believe her but said, "Auntie Kou just called. All the brides and shamans are there."

"It seems risky to have so many together. Are you sure that's wise?" Pahoua's eyes were wide with concern. One succubus was a handful. They were endless pits that only existed to suck souls for Du Yong. A room full of them sounded horrifying.

Touso replied, "It won't be easier, but it'll be faster. As long as Mossy releases their souls, everything will return to normal."

Pahoua nodded, but she remained anxious as she turned to Mossy. "Remember what I said. Believe in your purpose, and you'll protect the ones you love. I'll leave you and Touso to talk, but don't forget to go straight to your altar after."

As Mossy nodded, Pahoua hugged her son and left the room.

"She's not well, is she?" Touso stared after his mother.

Mossy said, "No. She's struggling. Once we get the brides back, we must go after Du Yong and end this for good."

Touso's eyes darkened. Even just hearing Mossy say it out loud struck fear in his heart. Destroying Du Yong would be the most difficult task, and he feared what it would cost. There was a knock at the door, and they were both surprised when Fuechi walked in.

"Hey, kid," Touso said with a smile. "What are you doing here?"

"Mr. Foo wants to go with you." Fuechi walked straight to Mossy.

Mossy smiled excitedly as she knelt to face Fuechi. "That's so sweet! But it's going to be dangerous. I don't think Mr. Foo will be safe coming to work with me."

Fuechi shook his head and put the teddy bear in her arms. "Mr. Foo says he must go with Auntie Mossy."

She glanced up at Touso, who only shrugged. Finally, Mossy hugged Fuechi. "Thank you. I promise I'll keep him safe!"

Fuechi smiled as though she was being silly. "Mr. Foo will protect you!"

With those last words, he turned and ran out the door.

"That's strange." Touso's expression was thoughtful.

"Yeah. I don't want to take the creepy bear with me!" Mossy exclaimed.

"No. I mean the name."

Mossy looked at him. "How so?"

"Foo is the name of Shee Yee's son that Du Yong killed," said Touso.

Mossy frowned. "How does he know that?"

"His horns are in that body," Touso answered. "He probably told him."

Instantly, Mossy dropped Mr. Foo on the floor. "What? How?"

"I put it there," Touso said with a shrug. "It was the horns that defeated Du Yong the first time. They're still very powerful weapons of protection. That's why I put them in a toy for Fuechi to carry around. They belonged to his father."

"That bear connected me to Du Yong," Mossy gasped, remembering how its eyes glowed the first time. "Now I know why!"

Touso shook his head. "The horns have been blessed. They belong to us more than they belong to Du Yong now. Fuechi calls the bear Mr. Foo, the name of Shee Yee's son. This can't be a coincidence."

"What do you mean?"

"Maybe Foo was trying to warn you. You saw Aunt Padee, didn't you? She was trying to warn you about Du Yong," Touso explained.

Reluctantly, Mossy nodded. "You think Shee Yee's son is inside the horns?"

Touso's eyes darkened. "He eats our souls and takes our powers. Much of Du Yong's strength was in these horns. I'll bet Foo's energy remains a part of it."

"This is really too much!" Mossy sighed dramatically as she finally picked up the bear. She stared at it for a long time before saying, "All right, Mr. Foo. You can come, but no funny business!"

As Mossy stuffed Mr. Foo in a mini backpack and slung it over her shoulder, Touso stopped her.

Mossy looked up. "What is it?"

Touso studied her with fascination. She constantly wavered between fear and courage. Now, she was calm again—ready to face the monsters. Mossy was going on her own mission without him, and he didn't want her to go. But she was his chosen bride—a warrior chosen by their ancestors. He couldn't stop her. "Are you ready?"

She nodded. "Are you?"

He drew her into his arms. "As ready as I'll ever be. Promise me you won't be too brave."

She smiled regretfully. "I already told you I can't do that."

"And I'll never stop asking." He hugged her again so that she wouldn't see the painful expression in his eyes.

"Just get those locks on," Mossy said as she squeezed him tight. "Alang says that as soon as we break them out, the souls will come straight home toward the amulets."

Touso promised. "I'll be ready."

Pahoua Khang was waiting for Mossy at the altar when Kai appeared beside her. Her gaze remained forward as she began filling the cups with fresh water. Then she dusted the surface, doing anything and everything but looking at her son.

"Hi, Mom." Kai smiled the way he did when he might be in trouble. *Carefully.*

Pahoua lit the incense. "Hello, my son."

"We haven't had a chance to talk," he continued, studying her thinning hair and pale complexion.

"You have a family. They've missed you." She kept her eyes on the altar.

"You're my family, too. You're my mother!" Kai spoke with so much emotion that Pahoua finally turned to face him.

"I haven't been a good mother." She said it so quietly that he almost didn't hear. "I'll always regret that day."

Kai watched her incredulously. "It's I who haven't been a good son!"

Pahoua began weeping. "Why didn't you tell me this would happen?"

Awakening

For a long time, he didn't speak. Kai had known he would die in one way or another. He had chosen the path that would benefit them all the most. In a dream, he saw himself looking into a mirror where the man peering back was someone else. Behind him was Du Yong, laughing and watching him with evil delight.

Dylan smiled weakly. "What could I have said, Mom? I'll be back in another man's body. See you soon? I've already asked enough of you. I couldn't ask you to carry more secrets."

"But why? Why are you back?" Pahoua demanded. "You know what we must do now, don't you?"

"I didn't expect anything less." They would have to send him away. His soul was earthbound for a reason. No matter what he said, when the time came, he would resist. He would do anything to stay with his family, and this resistance would take a toll on both Kai and the shaman he faced.

"Your death was hard on all of us, my son. But it nearly destroyed your brother." Pahoua struggled to keep her voice under control. "He didn't eat or drink anything for days. I thought for sure you had it wrong—your power wasn't going to save him after all because he was only getting weaker. Du Yong was ready to snatch him up! Then, it was like he awoke from a spell."

"He found out about Fuechi," Kai said.

"It gave him a new purpose," Pahoua agreed and fixed him with a pensive expression. "What I mean to say is—your death was hard enough. Now, he'll have to send you away."

"He'll do it," Kai replied solemnly.

"But at what cost?" Pahoua was shouting and struggled to control herself. She stared at a candle flame, willing it to dull to a simmer. "Your brother isn't like you. He holds things in until they eat him away. Your second death will be another hit to his soul."

"This is the only way." Kai followed his mother's gaze to the candle. "He's stronger than he was. He doesn't question himself the way he used to. He's going to beat all of this, I know it!"

"Why did you come back, Kai?" Pahoua finally asked.

He furrowed his brows. "Du Yong brought me back. He hoped my desire to regain my memories would motivate me to help Dylan take Mossy from Touso."

Pahoua inhaled sharply. "He wanted to keep them separated."

Kai nodded. "They're more vulnerable apart, as we all know. But it doesn't look like that'll be an issue anymore."

"Mossy and Touso have grown close in a very short time," Pahoua said, relief softening her voice. "She's something else, isn't she? All brides are born with gifts that make them strong, but Mossy…" She shook her head faintly. "She's especially powerful. Almost like a ticking time bomb."

Her gaze drifted toward the house. "It's been good having her here to watch and learn. All that raw, unfiltered energy would've caused her pain eventually."

"It won't be easy for her or Touso." It was an ominous comment that made his mother frown.

Finally, she asked, "Why are you still here if you no longer plan to keep them apart?"

"I have to take home my chosen bride," Kai simply answered.

Pahoua looked like she might hit him, and he winced.

"Better late than never!" Kai held up his hands defensively.

Pahoua was furious. "Your father was right. I should have beaten you more often! What exactly is your plan?"

Kai only straightened after he was sure he was no longer in danger. "What else can I do? I'll go find out what she wants. It's my fault she's become what she is."

"No one can force you to become a monster!" Pahoua snapped.

Kai fixed his mother with a strange expression. "Fear as much as love can drive one to do crazy things."

They shared a long moment of silence. Kai thought of everything he'd lost, while Pahoua thought of everything she must do.

"I'm sorry."

Pahoua looked at him in confusion.

"I never followed the rules. You and Dad fought because of me, and then I still asked you to do something terrible." Kai's voice thickened with remorse as he looked at his mother. "I never even thanked you. Thank you for loving me. Thank you for breaking the rules for me."

His expression faltered. "Are you in pain?"

Pahoua shook her head. "I'm okay!"

"You're lying again." Kai chuckled sadly. "You're my mentor, Mom. You taught me to be brave and to be good. 'Shamans don't lie,' you've always said. You've been around me too much."

"The real pain is not being able to protect my family!" Pahoua said passionately. "My heart was broken when I lost you. Now, I might lose your father and brother. How can I think of my own pain?"

"How can you protect anyone if you can't protect yourself?"

Pahoua stared at him. "What?"

"That's what I always used to tell Touso when he was being a pussy."

When Pahoua glared at him, Kai grimaced. "Sorry, Mom. Language—I know! Anyway, I should have been listening to myself. I messed up. I left a lot for Bao and Touso to clean up, thinking I knew what I was doing."

"Your brother and sister love you. They'll always take care of your family," said Pahoua.

"I know. But they shouldn't have to. That was my job. Dad was right. What would have happened had I just gone to him—worked with the family instead of fighting alone?" Kai searched her gaze. "You know you don't have to do this alone, right, Mom?"

Pahoua looked away. "A mother protects her children. A chosen bride protects her family. That is the way it is."

Kai studied the tight line of his mother's mouth. If Bao was like their father, he knew from whom he inherited his own stubbornness. Pahoua Khang would do things her way, just as he had. Finally, he said, "I love you, Mom. Thank you for letting me be your son in this life. You broke the rules for me, and I hope one day, in another life, I'll be able to repay you!"

As Kai cried, Pahoua's strength crumbled, and she embraced her son. "You silly boy! You're my baby. There is no debt to pay. All I've ever wanted was for you to have a good life!"

"I gave the world a son. My job is done."

Pahoua smiled. "Even in death, you're still the same. Save the bad jokes for your next mother."

Kai grinned. "I'll wait for you."

Pahoua stared at her baby boy with the sun on his head. "You've always been your brother's keeper. But tonight, make sure you both come back safely."

Kai put his arms around his mother and held her tight. "I have seen the future. Everything will be okay."

As mother and son sat at the altar, Kai started to sing, "In every life, we have some trouble, but when you worry, you make it double… don't worry, be happy… don't worry, be happy, Mom."

Chapter 31

Touso knew Mossy would be tending to her own mission of helping the brides, but he didn't know whom she was going with. As Mossy headed north, there was a "ding" from her phone with a shared location. A quick tap set her GPS to lead her straight to Alang Vang.

It was late evening and still incredibly hot as Mossy arrived at a small, dilapidated store in South Sacramento. The young necromancer wore a stylish suit that hugged his broad shoulders and trim waistline. Alang seemed to have only two styles: completely casual or immaculately dressed. Mossy was wearing shorts and a tank top. It was much too hot for anything else!

"I know this was last minute, but could you at least dress like you care it's our first date?" Alang's expression was wry and amused as she exited the car.

Mossy glared. "What do you wear that says 'I'd rather be somewhere else?'"

"Nothing works for me." Alang grinned before turning around and leading her into the building.

Mossy studied the place he had brought them to. She recognized the little grocery store owned by a local Her family. It sat between two other shops, a clothing store and a beauty salon. Its large windows were plastered with outdated Hmong music concerts and festivals.

Her mother often sent Mossy to grab cooking ingredients, saying, "If you can't find something, Her's Market always has it." The small store also sold things like ghost paper and incense. There was a strange variety of products available within such a limited space.

Despite how much her mother praised its convenient supplies, Mossy quickly remembered why she hated Her's Market. The entire place was covered in dust, and the overhead lights flickered like they were always seconds from burning out. There was just enough light to make out the products lining the shelves, but every aisle seemed to disappear into shadow.

More than once, Mossy would enter an aisle crowded with customers, only to blink and find herself completely alone.

Her's Market gave her the creeps.

A young man with long, shaggy hair glanced up from the game on his phone before immediately looking back down. "Welcome. Let me know if I can assist."

Even saying that much seemed exhausting to him. He sighed, then checked the clock like he was counting down the minutes until he could crawl back to sleep.

"I thought we were looking for the Black Door?" Mossy asked, frowning at Alang.

"We are." Alang walked casually toward the store's only employee. "Haven't you heard? Her's Market has everything."

"Alang, we don't have time for games!" Even now, she felt Touso's growing apprehension. Soon, they would be surrounded by a room full of succubus spirits if Mossy didn't restore the rightful souls.

"I don't play games," Alang said as though he were telling her he didn't like vegetables. Then he fixed his eyes on the man behind the counter. "Jesse, where is it?"

Jesse shifted in his seat but kept scrolling on his phone. If Mossy had to guess, he was around Thai's age. He wore a dark shirt and a single gold chain, though his long hair made it difficult to get a clear look at his face.

"Where's what, bro?" Jesse asked.

Alang slammed a crisp hundred-dollar bill onto the dusty glass counter.

This time, Jesse looked up, grinning widely. "Oh, you must be talking about the Black Door."

Alang's expression didn't change. The necromancer scared almost everyone, but Jesse was indifferent. Mossy watched nervously as he glanced at his phone again. Just when she thought he'd return to scrolling the screen, Jesse slid something small and silver across the counter.

"Aisle eight. Last shelf on the right."

Mossy stared at the spoon before Alang snatched it away.

"Remember," Jesse called after him, leaning back in his chair, "the old lady doesn't like extra people on her back."

Mossy hurried to catch up to him. "What does he mean? Who's the old lady? What does she have to do with the Black Door?"

Alang didn't look at her as he studied the shelves. "One thing you must learn about the spirit world, Mossy Cha, is how much it runs like a business. Nothing is free. The Khangs would have to sacrifice at least one hundred steers to even remotely get the door even remotely interested in appearing."

Mossy remembered how many Lihue sacrificed to help Touso find the door. There was no time to do it again.

Alang said, "The Black Door is tricky and difficult to call. Only the Slave Spirit can take you to it without sacrificing lives. But she has one condition: you must pay her in silver, and you must go alone."

Alone?

"You can't take your spirit guides," he said.

"You're kidding!" Her spirit guides went with her everywhere.

"The old lady was once a cruel businesswoman. The gods have punished her with this fate of taking shamans where they want to go, but only on her back. She doesn't like it, but she has her rules. You must pay her in silver and go alone," Alang repeated.

Mossy's spirit guides stirred uncomfortably.

"You'll be disconnected from them all once you're in. Those are the rules. Are you ready to accept?" Alang said, turning to her for the first time.

No!

Don't do it!

It's too dangerous!

Mossy inhaled sharply. *Forgive me…*

"I accept her terms." There was no other choice.

Alang smiled. "Good!"

She watched as he searched for something on the bottom shelf.

"Ah, found it!" He returned with a red candle.

Mossy stared at the hardened drips alongside it. "Why does it look used?"

He shrugged. "Because it is. People always seek the Slave Spirit for one thing or another."

She followed him carefully down a hallway leading to the back supply room. What she thought was a small table at first turned out to be an altar with a bowl of rice, egg, and incense sticks.

"What are we doing?" she whispered, even though they were alone.

"What—you want me to hold on to the candle the entire time?" Alang asked.

"I don't know!" she said, shaking her head. He kept doing things without explanation. Mossy wondered if being Hmong meant one should be born knowing. Everyone expected her to know the path and the way—and she didn't.

When he finally lit the incense and the red candle, she marveled at how much it changed the lighting in the dark space. While the rest of the store was dusty and cluttered, the altar was surprisingly neat and dust-free.

Even spirits like a clean home… Pahoua explained.

With the altar prepared, Alang returned his attention to her. "This candle is connected to the Slave Spirit. Once the flame begins, she'll know we're calling. When I wave the spoon above the flame, she'll come."

Mossy shuddered. It sounded terrifying.

"Be ready because she has no patience. After giving her your answer, she'll invite you to sit in the basket."

"She's going to carry me?" Mossy gasped.

"Why else would she have a basket?" Alang shot back impatiently. "Once you arrive at your destination, she will let you out. But…"

"But?" Mossy's eyes narrowed suspiciously.

"She might leave," he admitted.

"What?" she shouted. "How will I get back?"

"Listen, don't let it hurt your feelings. She just doesn't care. But you've got some time as long as I'm holding silver," he said calmly. He lifted the spoon for her to see. "When it becomes too hot, I'll call you. Don't hesitate, or you'll be stuck there!"

This is too dangerous… Gowli insisted.

Mossy closed her eyes. "I have to go, Gowli. I need to rescue them. I'll be brave, and I'll be back. Please watch over my body, and I'll take care of my soul."

When Mossy opened her eyes again, Alang was watching her. She said, "Let's get started."

He gestured to a small bench beside the altar

"Make yourself comfortable, Chosen Bride."

As Mossy complied, he ran the silver spoon over the flame, chanting words she didn't understand. Pahoua explained that Touso had many spirit guides and spoke their preferred languages. Mossy understood all those words, but the ones Alang spoke were alien.

She wondered who his spirit guides were.

Finally, he said, "Slave Spirit, we offer you silver for your service. Come now and do our bidding!"

The flame on the candle vanished. Less than a second later, it reignited, revealing an old woman with long gray hair and tattered clothing. In a dry and brittle voice, she demanded, "Where must this slave take you today, girl?"

Mossy gasped when it spoke directly to her. But she answered, "Take me to the Black Door."

There was a moment of silence as the Slave Spirit stared at her. Finally, she knelt on the ground, offering a large woven basket with a deep hollow space.

"You have paid your silver. I will take you to the Black Door," the spirit replied without emotion.

Alang made an impatient gesture that said, "Get in!"

Quickly, Mossy climbed inside the basket, surprised at how spacious it was.

As the Slave Spirit stood, Alang said, "Remember, I'll be watching. Listen for my voice. I'll call you when you're running out of time."

Mossy nodded. Then the Slave Spirit started walking, and the room blurred until only darkness remained.

Alang Vang studied the young woman on the bench. The soul of Mossy Cha had left with the Slave Spirit, but her physical body remained. She quivered gently as she chanted the ancient language of her spirit guides.

Alang maintained the spoon over the flame but kept his eyes on Mossy. It was all very interesting. She didn't know anything about shamanism, but something inside her knew precisely what to do.

"Ancestors, gods, and goddesses, I must leave my spirit guides behind… I call on you to guard my soul as I enter your world; hide my path so that no evil will find me; clear the way so that the Slave Spirit will take me quickly to my destination; bless me with your strength so that I may find my sisters and bring them home safely…" This was the song Mossy chanted without his guidance.

Something—*someone* was listening and watching over her. Meanwhile, her spirit guides guarded her body, waiting anxiously for the return of her soul.

Who is this girl? Alang wondered.

Finally, he returned to the candle. The Slave Spirit was treacherous and would consider the job complete if the spoon stopped moving even for a few seconds. He was not a fan of the Khang family, but he had promised to keep Mossy safe, and he would.

Chapter 32

By the time Touso and Kai arrived at the Shamans' Club, a large crowd was gathered at the door. Touso felt the anxiety and fear. The only shaman missing was Seng Vang.

It was just as well because everyone wanted his head.

"How can this happen?" demanded one father.

"She's gone crazy!" cried another.

"You must save him!" They all implored with desperation.

Touso met them with a grim expression. Finally, he turned to Ying and Kou, who waited by the entrance to the hall. Touso had given them specific instructions to invite the brides for a special dinner they couldn't decline.

"They're all inside," Uncle Ying said with an anxious expression. He and his wife had led the brides and their shamans to their respective tables like honorable guests. But it was terrifying to watch the shamans trail behind their possessed brides like zombies. "Sheng wouldn't come at first, but when I mentioned Kai—she changed her mind. She was glad to have all the brides come, if only so they could all savor what's about to happen—but I don't understand. Kai's dead, isn't he?"

"No."

Uncle Ying and Auntie Kou turned to look at the White man beside Touso. Their expressions were confused.

"I'm not." Kai revealed himself through the wall around his soul.

The room exploded with shock.

"Oh, my gods and goddesses!" Auntie Kou exclaimed, grabbing her husband by the arm. "How can this be?"

"Kai—you sneaky bastard! We thought Du Yong took you!" Ying threw his arms around the young man. "Let me look at you. Why are you in this body?"

"It was the only way I could visit." Kai grinned.

"You terrible boy!" Auntie Kou smacked him across the shoulder. "Don't you know how much we've all mourned you, and you're still joking!"

Kai hugged her. "I'm Okay, Auntie Kou. I've missed you, too."

As she wept in his arms, he patted her quivering back. Unlike Touso, Kai was a regular at the Shamans' Club. When he wasn't indulging in club activities like his sister, he was helping with club operations. Ying and Kou didn't have children and had always treated Kai like their own. Seeing him again was like ripping open an old wound.

"If Du Yong didn't get you, what happened?" Ying asked.

"It's a long story," Kai replied, shaking his head. "But he didn't get me. I'm here and must make something right before I return."

Ying and Kou glanced at each other in confusion before returning their attention to him.

"The thing inside of Sheng... that's my chosen bride," Kai explained.

The couple dropped their mouths at the same time.

"That makes sense now!" Ying exclaimed.

Kou shook her head. "The rumors are true. She's angry at you, isn't she?"

Auntie Kou used to lecture him about the consequences of casually toying with the hearts of women. Kai grimaced regretfully. "I guess you were right. Women will be the death of me."

"That bastard Seng! He's gone too far this time!" Ying was furious as he yanked at his long goatee. "We can't let him get away with this."

Touso gave a short nod. "He won't. But for now, we must care for the brides and the shamans."

"We couldn't separate them," Auntie Kou said regretfully. "Those brides were fine as long as we didn't touch the men!"

"We don't need to separate them. But we need to get these on the brides." Everyone gawked as Kai pulled out a bundle of silver chains with rectangular padlocks.

"My chosen bride has gone to free their souls. But they'll only know the way home if we get these on their bodies," Touso explained.

Auntie Kou grinned. "I knew that girl was special!"

Touso turned to face the others. Among them were the fathers of the Khang shamans affected. The senior shamans from the other clans had also gathered but remained relatively silent as they watched everything unfold. "We must get these amulets on the brides to save your sons, but there are too many. Will you fight with us tonight?"

His request was met with silence. Everyone, even the fathers, turned away their eyes. It was one thing to call a soul back. It was something else to battle the Succubus Queen. Legend claimed that once she chose her soul, she never let go. While they wanted Touso to rescue their sons, they weren't willing to risk damnation themselves.

"Why not just give her what she wants?" The sea of shamans parted to reveal Lipao Xiong. The Xiong leader's expression was indifferent, as though he didn't know why he'd come. He was sure the Khang's demise was none of his business. Nevertheless, the answer appeared simple enough, and Lipao's gaze didn't falter as they fell on Kai Khang.

"My thoughts exactly!" Teng Lee, tired of the Khang arrogance, pointed his stocky finger at the blond man. "She's angry because you broke the rules, Kai Khang! Why must everyone suffer on your behalf?"

"He shouldn't even be here!" Another shouted.

"He's already dead. Give him to her!" cried someone else.

Touso Khang clenched his fists but felt a hand hold him back. He turned to see Kai shake his head. *There was no point.*

"Uncle Teng, I hear your daughter is single now. Should I visit her after this is all done?" Kai asked, feigning concern.

At first, the Lee shaman was too stunned to speak. But soon, he cursed out loud and moved as though he meant to attack the younger shaman. Kai was undisturbed by this attempt at bravado. Teng was always more bark than bite, and everyone knew the old man was grateful when the others held him back.

Touso and Kai shared a look of amusement as Ying barked at the crowd, "You cowards! You cry about saving lives but ultimately refuse to get your hands dirty. Shee Yee should rip back the blessing he bestowed you—you're not worthy!"

"Tsov Tom! Bastards! You're all kicked out—two weeks at least!" Kou huffed. But when she turned to face Touso and Kai, she smiled. "It's our club. Nobody gets to have fun without us. We'll fight with you, boys!"

Kai and Touso nodded gratefully. Neither feared losing to Daisy. They were anxious about time. There were over three dozen brides to wrestle. They had to move quickly, or the souls would have nowhere to return, and Touso shuddered at the risks Mossy would take if that happened.

"If you're that afraid, you might as well stay out here," Touso said with a grave expression. "There will be no room for mistakes once we go past those doors. I give you my word. We will save the brides and your sons. But I would be a fool to refuse your blessings. Please guard this door well. Make sure nothing escapes and gets in unless it's the souls of the brides."

These last words were met with another wave of silence. Then Touso turned to address Kai, Ying, and Kou. "It's time. We must do it now."

Kai's eyes flashed. "It's about damn time."

"We're with you!" Ying reaffirmed with his wife by his side.

"Remember, once you get the locks on, they won't be able to remove them," Touso reiterated as he handed them each their own collection. "But it doesn't mean they won't be able to hurt you. Watch them, but don't look into their eyes."

Everyone nodded. Those hollow black eyes would quickly disarm them of any will and strength, just as they had done to the young shamans they kept.

Touso glanced at the two men who gripped the double doors. One looked young enough to still be in high school, and sweat poured from his forehead like he was in the summer heat. But Touso knew he was afraid... as he should be. Nobody wanted to think about what would happen if the Khang brothers failed this mission. Finally, Touso said, "Open them."

The men quickly complied, thrusting the doors back with a loud metal thump. The clans watched as Touso, Kai, and the Club owners disappeared inside. There was just enough time to see all the brides quickly hop to their feet, followed by a chorus of snarls. Then, the scene was cut short as the men promptly swung the doors shut and locked them.

Chapter 33

The Slave Spirit traveled silently, never quickening or slowing her pace. Sometimes, it was unbearably cold. Other times, it was sweltering. But one detail remained constant: it was always quiet. No one seemed to talk in the spirit world.

The journey was so long that Mossy contemplated taking a nap. It was at this point that the constant movement of the spirit ceased. A moment later, the bottom of the basket hit the ground, and the Slave Spirit said, "You have arrived."

When Mossy hesitated for a moment too long, she thought she heard an impatient sigh. But the Slave Spirit never moved or said another word. Quickly, Mossy climbed out of the strange basket and expected to see the spirit leave as soon as her feet touched the ground. She was surprised when it remained kneeling.

"Will you wait for me?" Mossy asked.

"This Slave Spirit will wait for you as long as the silver burns," it replied without looking at her.

Awakening

The sullen spirit with tattered clothes remained terrifying, but Mossy felt instant relief. Without her spirit guides, it was her only way back to her world. As long as Alang kept his word, she'd be safe. Feeling more confident about her return, Mossy turned to see what awaited her.

It was another surprise. She now stood in a bright paradise instead of a dark and barren place. The land was covered in tall grass for miles, with the closest mountains peeking at the horizon's end. The sky was a brilliant blue with dozens of fluffy white clouds. At any moment, Mossy expected to see a herd of wild horses running through the land.

Is this heaven? she wondered. *Where was the Black Door?*

Mossy heard something like thunder and turned just in time to see a powerful black horse racing across the field. A beautiful girl clung to its back. At first, Mossy thought she was on the run, but a closer look revealed a smile. Suddenly, the girl drew a bow and aimed an arrow directly at Mossy.

It was at that moment that she heard the squeal. She whipped around just in time to see a boar. It ran toward her, snorting ferociously. Someone pulled her into the grass before Mossy could scream. A moment later, a sharp whistle across the air was followed by the sound of death. Her eyes bulged as the boar collapsed just a few feet from her face.

Mossy turned to look at the person holding onto her wrist. It was a familiar face with dark eyes and a beautiful mane of blue-black hair.

Kaw!

The dragon spirit scowled but remained silent as the girl leaped off the horse.

"I did it! I got it!" she cried excitedly. Mossy gasped as the girl ran right past them.

She was about Mossy's age, except she wore the clothes of someone who lived centuries ago. Her dark jacket was simple, wrapping across a small chest. A matching skirt was paired with black leggings that protected against harsh winds and prying eyes. Her hair was done in a unique style of intricately braided locs, pulled up into a clean bun at the top of her head. She was a beautiful girl with intelligent eyes that swept up toward the heavens. Now, those same eyes lit up like stars as someone else approached.

Unlike her, the man wore clothes of finer materials in light shades of blue and gold trimmings. The thick leather garb around his chest and shoulders indicated he was a soldier. The long broadsword across his back was nearly covered by long blue-black hair.

Mossy's eyes darted to Kaw, who remained silent. His fingers tightened around her wrist to prevent her from speaking.

"That's a clean shot to the heart," the soldier said admiringly. "Nice job, Maihua!"

"Nice?" Maihua scoffed. "That's perfection! None of my brothers can do that. I'm the best hunter and the fastest rider. I should be chosen. Not them."

The soldier frowned. "Is that really the life you want?"

"Who wouldn't want to protect the God of Thunder? It's better than staying in the village and being bossed around by a bunch of boys!"

"You handle those boys just fine." The soldier grinned, but his eyes softened as he looked at the girl. "The gods are a different matter.

They're temperamental and needy. Your own desires will always be second. Don't you want to have a family of your own someday?"

Maihua furrowed her brows. "You serve him. Do you have any regrets?

There was a long silence before he said, "Yes."

At first, she seemed surprised. Then she laughed. "Oh, Kaw! You're joking again. How can you regret a life of adventure with your best friend? You might hurt his feelings if he heard you."

"Maihua." The soldier, Kaw, reached for her hand.

Stunned, she gazed up at him. "Kaw? What's wrong?"

"What if I could offer you another life?"

She seemed confused as she said, "What do you mean? What's better than serving the gods?"

Kaw frowned with a hint of frustration. "Maihua. You're a smart girl. Do you really not know how I feel about you?"

Now, it was Maihua who frowned. "Stop playing around, Kaw. This isn't funny."

"I have never been more serious in my life!" Kaw retorted.

Maihua pulled away, studying him in disbelief. Finally, she drew a sharp knife from her belt and moved toward the boar. "It's late. I need to get this back to the village before dark."

"Maihua—"

"No!" She whirled around to face him. "You are a general in the heavenly army. What is more important than serving the gods, who protect all that is sacred to the ones we love?"

"You." She couldn't look away when Kaw held her face between his large palms. He was so tall that his beating heart felt like seductive taps against her cheek. "I would give up immortality for just one moment with you."

A small gasp escaped her rose-colored lips. "Kaw..."

Thunder roared across the sky, and Maihua abruptly broke away. Her eyes darted to clouds that were darker than before. Finally, she said, "Tomorrow, I will compete in the tournament and win the honor of serving the Thunder God."

Kaw's already black eyes grew darker. He shook his head in resignation. "Then we can never see each other again."

Maihua glared with confusion. "What are you saying? You're his best friend—his general. You can't just leave!"

"I'm his cousin. Not his slave. I can go anywhere I please. If you choose this path, Maihua, I can't be with you. I won't save you anymore." He implored her with his dark eyes. *Choose me. Choose anything else... a life with the Thunder God would only cause her pain.*

Maihua surprised him by throwing her arms around him. His fingers curled tentatively against the small of her back. In a quiet voice, she said, "You have always been my dear friend, Kaw. But in this life, I have already chosen. Take care of yourself, and don't worry about me. I'll be fine."

Mossy stared at the soldier Kaw and the girl Maihua. It was like watching a scene in a fantasy movie, but it was all real. As the sky darkened and the couple faded, Mossy finally returned to the man still holding her wrist to the ground.

"That's you!" Mossy glanced between Soldier Kaw and the one who seemed annoyed with her now. "What is this place?"

"You're in the realm of memories." Kaw's answer was curt as he scowled. "How did you get here?"

"It was supposed to take me to the Black Door!" Mossy replied. She paced around to peer at the spirit's haggard face. "Why did you bring me here instead to watch some lovers quarrel?"

To her dismay, the Slave Spirit remained silent.

"The Black Door?" Kaw repeated. "The door that takes you to which you seek can only be found in a moment of significance."

Mossy frowned. "I don't understand."

"The Black Door lives in memories that are important to you. Its power thrives on these important moments," Kaw explained.

Mossy met his gaze. "That wasn't any memory of mine."

Kaw's dark eyes glistened with distaste. But before he could speak, the ground beneath their feet trembled. Mossy's jaw fell as the sky turned, and the grass receded across the plains. The lush scenery was soon replaced by something familiar. *Aunt Gia's apartment!*

Mossy glanced around the small living room with the clean white walls. It was exactly as she remembered, with the large window and small altar. There was even the faint scent of the pine cleaning solution that Aunt Gia preferred. The only thing amiss was people. Where were her parents, the Grandma Shaman, and Touso?

She couldn't find any of them. But she did see the Black Door. It hovered where the normal door to Aunt Gia's apartment used to be, and someone was knocking!

"Why do you seek the Black Door, Mossy?" Kaw asked.

"I have to save them," Mossy answered.

"Why do you always have to save someone?" Kaw sounded irritated again.

Mossy frowned. "You wouldn't ask that if you were my spirit guide."

Kaw finally smiled. "The youngest always does the grunt work."

"I don't have time for this!" Mossy sighed with exasperation.

As if to agree, the knocking on the door grew more urgent.

"Well, are you going to open it?" Kaw arched a curious brow.

Mossy stared at the Black Door. In her memories, Du Yong had always tried to reach her from the entrance. She was sure the demon was standing behind the door now. Opening it to face this terror sent goosebumps across her flesh.

"I have to save them," she repeated.

Usually, when she was this anxious, her spirit guides gave her encouragement and strength. But she had come without them and only had the Slave Spirit that didn't care. It remained silently kneeling in the kitchen, waiting for Alang to make a mistake with the spoon.

Kaw's eyes flashed briefly with the vertical pupils of the dragon. "The Black Door only shows up in the most important memories. What does this place mean to you?"

Mossy turned to meet his gaze. "I lost myself here."

It was in that room that she first called Du Yong. It was the first time she had lost her soul. Mossy was sure this pivotal moment gave Du Yong the idea to search for all the brides. It was all her fault! And when Aunt Padee performed the ritual to protect her, she also lost all the memories that connected her to Touso and her spirit guides. Now, the only way to save them all was to face the terror in that room.

Come to me, Mo...

"Then you must answer the door." Kaw watched her with a grim expression. "Are you sure you want to?"

As the pounding on the Black Door grew louder and more violent, Mossy started pacing in a circle. He studied her when she seemed to talk to herself. Finally, he asked, "Are you repeating positive affirmations?"

She paused to scowl at him. "I don't have my spirit guides and need good vibes. Somehow, I don't think that's what you're here for."

Kaw shrugged. "You're the one who invaded my memories."

"Well, you're in mine now." Mossy returned her gaze to the Black Door—the incessant knocking was stirring a migraine! But she was so afraid...

Don't forget us, Mossy...

I thought if I died, no one would protect you!

I love you more than my own soul...

What was it that Aunt Padee had told Touso? "You think this is about you because you feel the pain, but this pain is a reminder that you must become stronger to protect those you love.

Mossy clenched her fists. This wasn't about her fears. It was about saving Touso, Dylan, and her sister brides. She had also promised Gowli she would be brave.

Thump! Thump! Thump!

Mossy and Kaw stared at the Black Door.

"If you go there, you might not return," Kaw warned.

Mossy tightened her lips. "Positive vibes only, Kaw."

Without further delay, Mossy reached for the knob and turned. A moment later, she was gone, sucked into the darkness on the other side.

Kaw watched it happen without moving, but the vertical pupils of his eyes flashed in dismay. Maihua had never been a proper girl. She always got into trouble for riding horses, shooting weapons, and jumping into perilous situations without considering her own safety. Several lifetimes hadn't changed her at all.

The darkness dissipated to reveal a cluster of short buildings with blue metal roofing.

Valley High School?

Why had the door brought her to school? But it wasn't the same one she knew. This was the spirit world, where death mimicked life. When the bell rang, only shadows and whispers ran through the halls.

Something brushed against her shoulder. But when she turned, there was nothing.

Another tap.

Mossy whirled, and this time, she faced a creepy version of Mr. Nguyen. Dark hair was plastered against dull and slimy skin. His eyes were as yellow as his toothy grin.

In a voice that reminded her of a screaming chalkboard, he said, "Miss Cha, you better run along to class. Everyone's waiting for you!"

Mossy inhaled sharply. "Which classroom?"

Creepy Mr. Nguyen laughed. "Where else does one learn about life? Biology, you silly girl!"

Biology. The science department was at the far end of campus. She suddenly knew that Du Yong had all the brides locked away there. Mossy turned and ran.

"You better hurry, Miss Cha. He's not very happy with you!" His taunting voice followed her across campus. Soon, he was singing one of Mossy's favorite BTS songs. "Please save me tonight…save me, save me…I think not!"

Mossy never looked back. The closer she got to the biology room, the hotter it became. She felt all the fear and anxiety just beyond that door. Most of all, she felt Du Yong's menacing eyes. He was expecting her.

Come to me, Mo... I've been waiting such a long time.

Mossy pulled open the heavy blue door, prepared to see him on the other side. But she only saw the brides. They sat at the lab tables, staring ahead. The girls were no longer bound, but the red amulets kept them in a trance. They neither blinked nor made a sound to indicate they saw her.

Emma sat front and center like a class leader. But Mossy's attention fell immediately on the girl beside her.

"Sarah!" Mossy gasped.

Like the others, her cousin stared at the front of the room. But she didn't have a red amulet. Her eyes glistened as though she'd been crying. Sarah was in shock.

Mossy grabbed her by the shoulders. "Sarah! Are you okay? Can you hear me?"

When she didn't respond, Mossy shook her. "Wake up, Sarah. It's me—it's Mossy! Wake up. I've come to take you home!"

Home... something about that word struck a chord, and Sarah stirred from her stupor. Finally, she said, "Mossy?"

Mossy threw her arms around her. "Yes! It's me!"

Sarah sobbed with relief. "Mossy! Oh, my God! How are you here?"

Mossy patted her back. "I'm here to take everyone home."

Sarah wiped at her eyes. "Where's Thai? Is he okay?"

"He's with Touso at the Shamans' Club," Mossy answered. When Sarah frowned in confusion, she added, "Never mind. He'll be safe as long as we get everyone out of here. Do you recognize that girl?"

Sarah turned to the pretty bride sitting beside her. "Is that…"

Mossy nodded. "It's Thai's bride—the real one! They've all been trapped here for too long while the succubus spirits have been draining the shamans. But why are you here?"

Sarah turned to look at her cousin. "I caught 'it' feeding on my brother. The next thing I knew—I was here. How long has it been? I thought I was never going to see anyone again!"

Mossy held her as she cried. "Things feel different here, but it hasn't been long. Come on, help me with the girls. We have to get out of here before Du Yong gets here."

"Du Yong?" Sarah repeated. "That monster with the horns?"

Mossy froze at the same time something buzzed from the small bag on her back. "He's a monster. But he didn't have horns before."

Sarah frowned. "Well, this one does. They seem longer every day."

Mossy scanned the room of women with trepidation, paying close attention to the empty seats. "Sarah, were there more girls?"

Her cousin nodded. "He's been taking one every day!"

Mossy's heart raced. How many shamans and brides had Du Yong eaten? If his horns were growing back, then he was already much stronger than before. It was no wonder the brides were left untied. He could control them in other ways now.

"We have to go!" Mossy's voice shook as she helped her cousin out of her chair.

The room became hot like a furnace had been switched on. Something tapped quickly at the front of the classroom. Mossy spun around to see a tall man in an elegant suit writing on the board. Long black hair wavered like snakes as he wrote in bold letters: "Mr. Du Yong."

"Leaving so soon?" Du Yong feigned a hurt expression as he turned to face them. "Things were just about to get interesting."

Mossy narrowed her gaze. She didn't remember Du Yong looking so young. In all her memories, he was a monster. Now, with a change of clothes, he could pass for a college boy. He glowed of all the souls he possessed!

"What have you done?" Mossy demanded.

Du Yong shrugged. "I've been eating well. Have you come to offer dessert?"

"I'm taking them home!" Mossy promised.

As her eyes burned with purple flames, Du Yong considered her. Mossy Cha was also stronger than he remembered. She was more confident. Finally, he gestured at the girls. "Are you sure they want to go back with you?"

There was a shuffle of feet as all the brides stood.

"Believe it or not, Mossy Cha." Du Yong paced the floor just ahead of them. "Most of these ladies are here of their own free will."

"You're lying!" Mossy's face turned with disbelief. Who would willingly walk with a demon?

Du Yong grinned. "Why would I lie? After all, there are rules: one must willingly offer their body for another to take over. Isn't that right?"

Mossy inhaled sharply.

"When I went to them, many were ready to escape a life they couldn't control. Don't you remember what that was like, Mossy?

Being told what to do—having no say in what became of your own life?"

She remembered. In some ways, she still felt this way.

His eyes flashed knowingly. "That's precisely why they were so eager to leave their meager lives behind. I offered them a chance to become part of something much bigger. I still do. What do they gain by staying in your world?"

"Life!" Mossy stepped away from Sarah and Emma to glare at him. "You lied to them. You misled them when they were most fragile— fearful of a future they didn't understand. Do you think they would still come with you, knowing they were walking away from their soulmates?"

Du Yong's eyes darkened. "Daisy most certainly did."

Daisy... Mossy gasped at the image of the angry Succubus Queen.

"Tonight, she'll get her vengeance. By the time she's finished with him, he'll regret not letting me carve up his soul like a steak!" The entire room trembled as Du Yong laughed.

"You corrupted her!" Angry energy flickered at her fingertips.

"I gave her control!" Du Yong hissed. Suddenly, he was in front of her, running a long claw down the side of her face. "What would you give for a little more control of your destiny, Chosen Bride?"

As Mossy met his gaze, she heard Touso's voice: *Remember, you're in control, Mossy...*

She thrust her fist forward, aiming for his heart, but Du Yong disappeared.

"Very well!" His voice boomed and bounced off the walls. "You have made your choice. Let's see what the other brides have to say."

"Mossy!" Sarah shrunk away as the brides turned on them. The daze was gone from their eyes, but now they glowed angrily in sheens of red. They snarled like rabid animals as they advanced.

"What's happening?" Sarah scrambled to her side. "What the fuck is going on?"

Mossy turned to face her. "Sarah, I don't think I have to tell you that all of this is real. Now, I need you to listen carefully. These girls don't know what they're doing. He's controlling them."

"But how do we stop them?" She looked terrified as the brides surrounded them with outstretched fingers.

Mossy squeezed Sarah's hand. "Remember when we were kids, and you used to take things from me?"

Sarah looked confused. "What does that have to do with anything?"

Mossy pointed at the red amulets. "We need to get those off them."

Sarah studied the strange chains around their necks. Despite her initial trepidation, she was a fighter and didn't like being bossed around by humans or spirits. The fear soon dissipated, replaced by new determination. "You want me to steal their jewelry? That's a bitchy move."

Sensing the change in attitude, Mossy grinned. "Precisely!"

Sarah's eyes sparkled. "If that means getting out of here, let's do it!"

The zombie brides were led by Emma, who had a strange sneer on her lovely face. Mossy walked forward to meet her.

"Emma, are you in there?" When the girl only snarled as an answer, Mossy said, "If you can hear me now—I'm sorry."

When Emma scowled, Mossy punched her in the face. As the bride crumbled, she stood over her body and snatched the amulet from her chest. It glowed with an angry heat in the palm of her hands, and for a moment, Mossy stared at it, transfixed. Then she threw it against the wall, where it shattered into pieces.

"Mossy?" Emma blinked up at her in confusion.

Mossy quickly helped her to her feet. "Emma! Are you okay?"

Emma touched her temple. "I think so. Just a little light-headed. What's going on?"

Mossy frowned. "You're still here. That means Touso and Kai haven't gotten the amulets on your bodies yet."

"Who? What?" As Emma continued to look more puzzled, Mossy grabbed her hand.

"Sorry, Emma. We don't have much time." They both turned at the sound of a woman huffing and shouting. Sarah had one girl in a chokehold as she kicked another to the floor.

"Mossy! I got one!" Sarah held up a chain in triumph as she let the girl in her arms fall to the ground.

Mossy returned her gaze to Emma. "We need to get all the necklaces off the girls. It's the only way we can all go home."

Emma nodded without question. She knew better than anyone what those chains were capable of doing. Without it clinging to her chest, her powers were already stirring, and Emma smiled when she heard her spirit guides. Her eyes lit up with a brilliant green light. "Home. I want to go home!"

Mossy watched as Emma turned away to join Sarah, who was already wrestling with another girl on the ground. She didn't add that they would only go home if Touso got the soul locks on the brides.

Awakening

"Touso," Mossy said aloud. "Please hurry."

With a sigh, Mossy returned to ripping at every necklace she could.

To her dismay, she couldn't do it without punching more brides.

Chapter 34

The shamans, young and old, sat at the tables, staring listlessly at nothing. Their brides were beside them, guarding each as a dog might protect its food. But the brides stood and snarled when Kai and Touso entered with the club owners close behind. Finally, they left their shamans and gathered at the center of the room to face the new visitors.

Daisy Vang emerged from the sea of possessed brides, dressed in a black gown that hugged every curve of her body. The smile on her lovely face was serene. Unfortunately, the evil in her glistening red eyes told another tale. She said, "Kai Khang, I didn't think you'd have the balls to show up."

"I didn't think you'd become a soul-sucking succubus, but here we are. What do you want, Daisy?" Kai replied.

Her eyes flashed. "I want you dead, but it's too late."

Kai smiled. "Problem solved. Did you hear I did it myself?"

"Even dead, you're still full of it." Daisy scowled.

"I hear that a lot," Kai replied.

Awakening

Daisy walked ahead of the chosen brides but stopped just a few feet before him. "You don't look good, Kai. This body doesn't suit you."

Kai's complexion was already paler, and his energy was waning. As talented as Bao was, no elixir would allow humans to suffer possession long-term. Now, he studied the body of Sheng Moua, whose flesh maintained a healthy complexion despite the evil possessing it. Finally, he asked, "How do you stay so pretty?"

Daisy smirked. "The almighty Kai Khang doesn't know that shaman bodies are hardier than normal humans? You should have taken your own brother's body if you were going to come back. Not this."

When Daisy gestured at Dylan's weakening body in distaste, Kai shrugged. "Nah. I'm just visiting."

She scowled. "I want to know. Was it worth it?"

"Dying?" Kai arched a brow.

"Defying destiny!" When Daisy hissed, the walls shook, and the brides behind her growled. "Your arrogance cost us both everything!"

"I didn't force you to sell your soul, Daisy."

For a long time, they held each other's gaze.

Finally, Daisy smiled. "And here we are. You're dead, dying, and I'm still pissed. I don't know what my father's told you about me, Kai, but I'm hard to please. How about I kill you again today and ensure your spawn doesn't survive to produce another generation of heartless assholes? We can call it even, then."

Kai furrowed his brows as if considering it. Then he said, "No."

Daisy's laughter boomed and rattled all the windows. "You must think you came here to negotiate! How funny. My brother was right. You Khangs think the world revolves around you."

"No, Daisy. The world doesn't revolve around us, but it depends on us," Kai said, meeting her gaze. "You need to stop this craziness now, Daisy. Let the brides and the shamans go."

She stared at him in disbelief. "You're unbelievable. Even after what you've done, you're still telling me what to do."

"No." When Touso came to stand beside his brother, her eyes darted to the hoop rattle in his hand. "Kai's asking. I'm telling you: leave the shamans and the chosen brides or else."

Daisy laughed as she scanned their small group. "Or else, what? You're outnumbered, Touso Khang. Even as you tackle one of us, another will come right behind you. Your strength will wane against our numbers. We'll drain you before you take your next breath. You don't stand a chance!"

When Touso only smiled, she became irritated. "Didn't you hear me? If you value your life, leave your brother behind. This is your last warning."

Touso's eyes flashed blue. "The sons of Shee Yee have not lived this long by bowing to *poj ntxoog*—succubus spirits! This is your last warning, Daisy Vang. Leave our shamans and their brides, or we'll make you."

Daisy's eyes burned so red that the immediate space around her became the tent of her rage. "Then do it!"

Touso Khang didn't waste time. The brides started howling the moment he swung the hoop rattle. The clashing metal discs sent shock waves that brought them to their knees. As the spirit brides wailed, Touso shouted to Kai, "What are you waiting for?"

"I just want her to look at me." Kai grinned triumphantly when Daisy glared in his direction. "There you go. Now we can party!"

He ripped open his shirt to reveal a small copper gong tied to his belly. As Kai drew two wands from his back, Daisy shrunk back in anticipation.

"Oh, don't worry, babe. You'll love this." Kai's eyes glistened with yellow light as he began drumming against the gong on his body. The banging was loud and rapid, growing stronger with each round.

Daisy shrieked and fell back against the other brides, already cowering on the ground.

"Louder!" Touso shouted above the noise. "They have to leave those bodies!"

Kai drummed faster. His expression turned with satisfaction when the spirits screamed even louder. Touso followed by increasingly quick shakes of the rattle. Finally, they heard it. When a spirit left a body, it was almost silent. But when it was a large group like the one they faced, it sounded like bones cracking. The suffering spirits climbed up the spines until they poured out the mouths of each chosen bride like a cloud of smoke. Touso and Kai didn't stop playing until the last of the spirits lifted.

As the bodies crumpled onto the ground, Kai turned to Ying and Kou. "Now!"

Everything was going according to plan. As Touso and Kai distracted the succubus spirits, Ying and Kou would secure the brides with their soul locks. Now, the couple leaped quickly to complete this final task. Touso and Kai didn't need to defeat Daisy and her minions.

They just needed to draw all the souls back. Everything else would fall into place after that.

"*Tsuag-tsuag*—hurry!" Kou said to her husband as she jumped from bride to bride, threading their lovely heads with each silver necklace. She apologized each time their heads slumped and hit the floor or each other. "Sorry, sweety!"

"I'm going as fast as I can!" Ying was a large man and wasn't nearly as graceful as his wife. He stepped carefully in between the bodies, trying not to break them.

"Better broken bones than possessed brides!" Kou shouted over her shoulder.

"Easy for you to say," Ying mumbled as he hung the last necklaces over a bride. "It's done!"

At the same time, Kou hollered, "I'm done, too!"

Kai threw his wands into the air, cheering. "Woohoo! Score for the shamans—"

This celebration was cut brief as a rope of hair wrapped the base of his throat and squeezed. As Kai clung to the strands at his neck, he caught the glimmer of one last chain dangling from his pocket. At least one bride was still missing a soul lock! Now, Kai was being lifted off the ground. A moment later, he stared into the eyes of the Succubus Queen, Daisy Vang. Her hollow black eyes tore into his soul, rendering him paralyzed.

"Your second death belongs to me, Kai Khang," Daisy hissed, running the tip of her shriveled gray nose against his face. "And when I'm done with you, I'll visit your little family. I wonder which one will scream louder... Nia or that cute little boy of yours?"

Kai kicked his legs, but the world around him was blurring

Awakening

"Don't... touch... my family..." Kai stammered as everything faded. The last thing he saw was Daisy's hideous smile.

Mossy, Sarah, and Emma fell against each other in exhaustion. Standing back-to-back, they stared breathlessly at the horde of brides closing in.

"This wouldn't be so bad if they stopped coming after us after we got the amulets off!" Sarah panted as she threw a whiteboard eraser at one of the zombie brides. "I'm training to be a nurse—not a demon slayer!"

"They're not demons." Emma's tone was defensive as she looked at the girls with glowing red eyes. "They're our sisters. He's making them do this!"

"Look!" Mossy gasped, pointing when several of the girls froze.

The red lights were dropping from their eyes as if a circuit had blown. Now, expressions of confusion crawled across each of their faces.

"What's happening?" Sarah asked.

"They've done it. Touso and Kai got the soul locks on their bodies!" Mossy straightened and walked forward.

"Mossy—are you crazy? What are you doing?" Sarah demanded, reaching to pull her back. They had managed to snatch all the amulets off the girls, but she ached from the battle.

"Don't you see? They've all stopped." Mossy glanced back at her cousin.

At first, it was just a few of the girls. Now, everyone was frozen in confusion. They stared first at each other and then at the three who stood opposite them. But before anyone could speak, something else happened. The girls were fading.

As they started to scream in apprehension, colorful lights rose to swirl around them. It was their spirit guides! The girls ceased everything to stare at something they hadn't seen in so long. It was like watching the return of family members, and many began to cry.

Mossy wanted to cry with them. Alang hadn't lied. The soul locks were pulling back the souls of the brides. The lights grew brighter, and soon, a mighty wind lifted all the transparent brides.

"Don't worry!" Mossy shouted. "You're going home! You're finally going home! Don't fight it, girls!"

A moment later, they were gone.

Mossy, Emma, and Sarah stared at the empty room and then turned to look at each other.

"What about me?" Emma asked with disappointment.

Mossy said, "You're the Succubus Queen. Maybe they haven't gotten to her yet."

"She's a bitch!" Sarah offered with a scowl. Daisy had dragged her soul to that hellhole when Sarah caught her draining Thai's energy.

"What am I supposed to do?" Emma looked anxious as she studied the vacant space her sister brides once occupied.

"Don't be afraid, Emma. Touso will figure something out." Mossy sounded confident as she wrapped the girl in a warm embrace. "He's not going to leave any of us down here."

"Touso?" Emma repeated. "Like the son of Thunder? That's his name?"

Mossy nodded.

"How strange." Emma frowned. "Lisa used to tell us stories to distract us from our fears. Once, she told us about the God of Thunder."

"God of Thunder?" Mossy immediately thought of the girl Maihua, who wanted to serve the same god.

"The story says that *Xob*, So, was the great enforcer of all the laws passed down by the gods. Any creature who broke these rules faced punishment," Emma explained.

Mossy chuckled. "Strangely, that is very fitting for Touso. He's always talking about rules!"

"Well, one day, he broke those rules," Emma said, catching Mossy's attention. "They say he fell in love with a human, and the gods punished him."

Mossy's eyes grew wide with fascination. "What would a god see in a human girl?"

Emma shrugged. "I dunno. But legend says he refused to give her up, so they stripped him of his position in Heaven."

Mossy and Sarah glanced at each other like little girls listening to a camp story.

"Well, go on. What happened next?" Sarah prodded.

"Yeah, what happened to the God of Thunder and the girl?" Mossy asked.

"They both died," Emma finished.

Mossy and Sarah scowled at the same time.

"What?" Emma blinked with confusion.

"No offense, Emma, but you suck at telling stories!" Sarah rolled her eyes.

Emma laughed. "Sorry. But I can grow a mean tomato!"

"My parents will love you, at least," Sarah teased.

Something pounded violently against the door, followed by a ferocious roar. The girls huddled together, with Mossy and Emma meeting each other's gazes.

"What is it?" Sarah demanded as she noticed their knowing expressions.

"It's the beasts!" Mossy answered. "Du Yong must have sent them after what happened."

"He must be furious," Emma gasped.

"He just lost all his energy bars. Of course, he's pissed." When Emma looked perplexed, Mossy lifted her hands. "Isn't that what we are to him? He eats us for our powers, right?"

"What do we do now?" Sarah looked impatient as the thrashing continued at the door.

"We run!" Mossy headed for the second exit at the back of the room. "And don't stop, no matter what!"

Mossy heard the door crash inside the classroom as they escaped through the other end. She didn't have to look back to know the pit bull beast was coming to get her.

Kai was on the brink of losing consciousness when he heard a familiar voice.

"Get your mother-fucking paws off my man!"

His eyes flew open just in time to see Nia hit Daisy over the head with a chair. Instantly, the creature dropped him and turned on the woman. Nia quickly snatched the drum wands from the floor and held them like daggers.

"When a man says he's not interested, don't make him tell you twice," Nia chided. She shrugged as she met her husband's questioning gaze. "I followed you. Call me impatient, but we want you home early for dinner."

"We'll talk later," Kai choked, still recovering from the death grip around his throat.

Daisy snarled and whipped Nia with a long rope of hair and became angrier when she missed. As Nia dodged another attack, Daisy finally leaped at her. The wands Nia lifted to impale her were cast aside as Daisy latched on and forced her to stare into her black eyes.

Nia was immediately nauseous and gasped for air.

She lifted Nia by the throat until her feet dangled. "So glad you could join us, Nia. I wondered how I was going to make Kai suffer. I think watching you die will work!"

Daisy drew her closer to watch the life waver from her eyes. Human energy was fascinating. Like air and water, it bubbled to the surface when there was nowhere else to go. Daisy smiled as Nia's life spilled out from her pores.

She inhaled this scent until her nose hovered at Nia's gaping mouth. Daisy said, "Time to eat!"

Nia sealed her lips together and turned away. In desperation, she kicked at Daisy's body, but the spirit was relentless and slammed her onto the ground. As Nia gasped for air, long claws curled over her mouth to pry it apart.

"Open wide," Daisy sang.

The Succubus Queen was so engrossed in taunting her prey that she never noticed the shaman sneaking up behind her. By the time she heard the last step, it was too late. Touso threw the hoop rattle over the spirit's head and fell back. The rattle was blessed by Shee Yee and burned like fire against the succubus's throat. She shrieked with rage as Touso dragged her away from Nia. Then he looked for his brother, who was finally pulling himself off the ground.

"Hurry! Get that necklace on Sheng!" he shouted.

Kai nodded, meeting Nia's petrified gaze only briefly before he sprinted toward the girl with the black dress.

When the Succubus Queen thrashed against him, Touso yanked harder to keep her throat locked within the rattle. Even so, she still spoke inside his head.

Why do you protect him? He's only made your life harder!

Touso spun, throwing the spirit face down onto the ground. He turned the hoop so the dagger pressed against her throat but kept her treacherous eyes away from his own.

"He's my brother. We protect each other!" Touso pushed his knees down into her back when she tried to turn.

Daisy laughed. *How sweet. Has it ever occurred to you that family is just a distraction?*

Even as he knew she was toying with his mind, Touso's heart raced.

You're all fools, Touso Khang! Do you really think that Du Yong has gone through all this trouble simply to drain souls? Yes, eating is great. Gaining power is nice! But do you know what he really wants the most?

In his apprehension, Touso's grip was loosening. "What does he want?"

He wants Mossy. And now, she's alone... without you, without her spirit guides, without anyone to protect her!

"It's on!" Kai shouted from a short distance away, but Touso barely heard him.

"What does he want with her?" Touso demanded.

Daisy giggled. *Oh, silly shaman. You know this answer. What does every demon or spirit want that they can't have?*

Touso's eyes grew wide as he realized what she was saying. Mossy had the unique ability to heal. It meant her body could sustain any trauma... even possession.

"She'd have to accept, and she'd never do that!" Even as he said it, he prayed it was the truth.

When Daisy sighed, it was almost sympathetic. *Yes. But one tends to do strange things in the name of love. What would your chosen bride sacrifice to save you, Touso Khang?*

She grinned triumphantly when Touso loosened his grip altogether. Before he realized this mistake, Daisy exploded from the ground. As he fell, she quickly wrapped him with long strands of sticky succubus hair and brought him back so that they faced each other. This time, Touso couldn't avoid those poisonous black eyes.

"Mossy can no longer protect you, Touso Khang... and now you won't be able to protect her!"

As Daisy leaned in to drain the life from him, Touso never moved. He was thinking about his bride, trying to connect to her in the underworld.

Mossy, if you can hear me... Don't do it!

The beasts were close behind. Mossy heard their snarls and smelled the stink of their fur. But when Emma fell, they all stopped to help her.

"Emma! Come on, get up!" Sarah cried. But as she reached to grab her hand, her fingers went right through it.

Emma stared at her fading palm. "I'm disappearing!"

Mossy gasped, "You're going home!"

Emma glanced between Sarah and Mossy. "I'll be waiting for you there—watch out! They're coming!"

In the blink of an eye, Emma was gone. When Sarah and Mossy looked at each other again, it was hard not to cry.

"What do we do now?" Sarah asked.

"We have to find the door!" Mossy grabbed her hand and ran again as the beasts snarled behind them. The Black Door hovered at the front of the school. "Just a little more! We're almost there!"

Just as Mossy and Sarah arrived, the Black Door wavered. Mossy cried out when it disappeared. "No!"

"What happened?" Sarah asked, gawking at the now empty space by the statue.

"I don't know." It didn't make sense. But there was no more time. When Mossy and Sarah turned around, the pit bull beast and its friends were waiting, saliva dripping from razor-sharp teeth.

The silver spoon was getting hot. Just as he began to fear that she was running out of time, Alang felt her spirit—she was close! The spoon rattled like footsteps approaching.

"Come on, Mossy. You're almost home." He continued waving the spoon over the candle, even as it began to burn his fingers. *Just a little more time...*

Alang gasped when the spoon was suddenly knocked from his hand. A moment later, the altar and candle crashed onto the ground. When he looked up, his father faced him.

"You fool!" Seng said, his eyes seething with resentment. "Are you really helping these Khangs against your own father?"

"I'm not helping them. I'm helping my sister!" When Alang reached for the spoon again, Seng kicked it away.

"You're pathetic." Seng spat on the floor. "Your sister doesn't need your help. As we speak, she's already draining the life from the Khang shamans."

"If I don't get that spoon turning, Mossy will be stuck on the other side!" His expression pleaded for his father to let him through, but Seng responded by crushing the candle under his shoe.

"She's where she belongs. With the Khangs gone and Du Yong getting what he wants, I'll finally have everything I've ever wanted!" Seng laughed.

"Dad," Alang said, shaking his head. His father never once spoke a kind word to him. Now, he had sacrificed his daughter and would continue taking more lives to fulfill his greed. He glared at Seng. "When did you become such a monster?"

His father's eyes flashed dangerously, and a cruel smile followed it. "You might say I was born this way, son. I wish you had been born the same. But it doesn't matter. It's almost done!"

Trembling, Alang's eyes trailed the fallen spoon to the broken candle. Finally, he studied the sleeping girl on the bench. Was it just his eyes, or did she seem paler? Without the spoon burning over the fire, Alang knew the Slave Spirit had already abandoned her. Without her spirit guides to help, he didn't know how Mossy would return.

She couldn't.

The pit bull monster only had eyes for the girl who once escaped, but the rest of the beasts were eager to tear apart the other. Sarah's energy exuded terror, and it sent them wild with frenzy. Mossy pushed her cousin protectively behind her.

"Mossy, do you know what you're doing?" Sarah whispered, peeking over her shoulder.

She shook her head. In the past, her spirit guides always protected her. Touso was quick to save her whenever she was in trouble. This time, she was alone. Her heart raced anxiously as the beasts trapped them in a circle. They paced excitedly, slowly torturing their prey with anticipation.

What do I do? Mossy's eyes darted anxiously between the creatures staring at them.

Remember the perfection and peace of your altar no matter where you are. It will help you hone your powers and stay in control... Pahoua's last words blew softly at the burning anxiety in her chest, and the world began to slow. *Think of the soft white paper. The incense is simmering. The flames are burning gently. Everything is calm. This is your place of peace...*

As Mossy pictured all of these things, her soul lifted with not just peace but power. Her spirit guides helped her, but the strength she held was her own.

Remember your purpose... her purpose was to protect herself and those she loved. Mossy's soul filled every pore of her body, reminding her of the many lifetimes in which she'd slayed these same monsters and many more. The old soul within Mossy Cha knew precisely what to do.

When Mossy's eyes started glowing, the beasts sensed a new danger. They growled and snapped their jaws but stayed cautiously away. She lifted a hand glimmering with a ball of purple fire. "Demon beasts. This is your last warning. Leave or perish!"

Sarah stared at her cousin. She was used to a compliant and timid Mossy. This one sounded like she was about to whoop some ass, and she had never felt prouder. Soon, her own courage returned.

"Yeah! What she said! Get out of here!" Sarah shouted.

Mossy didn't know dogs could sneer, but the pit bull beast did precisely that. As the pack charged, Mossy calmly pushed Sarah away. "Wait here."

Sarah watched her cousin approach the snarling monsters. A moment later, she heard only wailing as Mossy Cha tore them apart.

No one could overcome the black eyes of the Succubus Queen. Not even Touso Khang. It was a vortex of death that brought the strongest to their knees. He was paralyzed as she continued ripping the soul from his body. She was killing him.

As Daisy was distracted with this work, the brides along the floor started to stir. A moment later, the shamans awoke from their stupor. Thai was the first to become aware of being at the Shamans' Club. He frowned at the other shamans sitting at the table. Then he recognized a familiar girl in a black dress. As Sheng lifted herself from the ground, he quickly scrambled to help her.

"Sheng!" Thai gasped.

When she looked at him, her pretty eyes sparkled in a way he'd never seen. She surprised him by taking his hand and ripping off the black bracelet. Then she smiled and said, "Call me Emma."

There was no time for questions. Ying and Kou were fighting succubus spirits across the hall. Touso was struggling with the Succubus Queen at the center of the room. Then someone called his name. "Thai!"

He turned to see a young man with blond hair helping a pretty dark-skinned woman to safety. As he ran back toward Touso and the queen, the stranger transitioned into a much more familiar person. "Kai?"

Kai grabbed the wands from the ground and shouted, "There's no time to explain! Grab the others. We need everyone to surround the succubus spirits now!"

Thai turned to meet Emma, who said, "We must combine our powers to eliminate them. I'll get the brides. You get the guys!"

Not a second later, Thai was running from table to table, jostling each man to their feet. Emma gathered all the women, quickly explaining what had to be done. As they worked on this, Kai turned to Ying and Kou and shouted, "Get them closer!"

It was during this time that Kai noticed Nia was missing and scowled. He had hoped to keep her safe at the room's perimeter, but now he feared something else had taken her. Then he saw Nia swinging a chair at a team of relentless spirits. She was leading them to the center of the room! She caught his gaze briefly and grinned before yelling at the spirits coming after her.

Kai shook his head. He loved that crazy woman. As he turned around, he saw everyone was where they needed to be. The shamans and the brides had formed a large circle around Touso, the Queen, and the rest of the spirits. *It was time.*

Kai met each of their gazes. "Brothers and sisters! These spirits have been eating you, draining your life. They are strong and will not stop until we're all dead. But it won't happen. Not if we stand together and send them back to hell. When I sound the gong, call your spirit guides. They will show you exactly what to do."

Daisy released Touso and whirled to face them. "How dare you? I am the queen. You can't hurt me!"

Kai said, "I don't want to hurt you, Daisy. You were my chosen bride. I should have protected you."

Daisy's horrible face twisted in confusion. Her voice almost sounded human when she said, "You changed everything."

"I will always regret not giving you the life you deserved, Daisy. But this—being this monster—you don't deserve that either! Please, let me help you." Kai hoped with his soul that she had enough humanity to forgive him and herself.

For a moment, Daisy was beautiful again, and her dark eyes glistened with tears. She said, "I only ever wanted to feel safe."

Kai held out his hand. "Let me protect you now."

Daisy stared at his fingers, wondering again what their life could have been like had he made the right choice. But he hadn't made the right choice, and she was no longer Daisy Vang, his chosen bride. She was the Succubus Queen!

Instantly, she returned to the horrid face of nightmares. "It's too late for regrets, Kai Khang! Now, there are only consequences."

His eyes crackled with a sharp yellow light. "I'm sorry, Daisy."

He hit the gong with a quick and powerful thrust. He repeated it until all the evil entities wailed in pain. Then he started to chant. When Daisy flew at him, his spirit guides emerged to knock her back into the circle. Soon, the shamans and brides were all chanting, and the circle became a bright orb of power. Spirit warriors from each shaman stepped forward to meet the monsters at the center of the room.

Touso Khang stirred and lifted his eyes just in time to witness something incredible: the union of shamans destroying evil. Everyone held hands. The words they sang gave strength to the spirit guides. And as they tore into the succubus spirits and sent them back to hell, Touso thought of only one person: his bride.

Mossy, come back to me!

Chapter 35

Mossy's fury powered her energy. This strength—this power always turned her into someone else entirely. As she blasted the beasts and tore into their bodies, they dissipated and never returned. But the Pit Bull hated her so much that, for a time, she didn't think he would ever go down. Finally, he sunk his jaws into her shoulder and wouldn't let go. The beast shook her like a piece of meat.

Somehow, Mossy managed to curl an arm around his neck until the pressure forced him to release his jaws. She didn't stop squeezing until the beast finally whimpered. Then his neck snapped. A moment later, the body vanished in a spray of smoke. As Sarah ran forward, Mossy slumped against her. She was drained.

"Mossy!" Sarah gasped. "What the hell—how did you do that?"

Mossy stared in a daze. "Do what?"

"Uh, you just annihilated a pack of monsters. You snapped that one's neck!" Sarah exclaimed.

"I think I'm secretly angry." When Sarah frowned, Mossy added, "Pahoua says there are things we can do in the spirit world that we can't do in our own world. I'm just a little stronger here, I guess."

Sarah scowled. "I'll say. Who's Pahoua?"

"My shaman mentor—and mother-in-law," she answered.

"Mentor? Mother-in-law?" Sarah repeated in distaste. "Don't tell me you're going to go through with this marriage, Mossy. They can't force you to do it!"

"Don't say that." Mossy sat up and rubbed her shoulder. It was still raw from the bite but already healing. "No one's forcing me to marry Touso. I love him, Sarah."

"You don't even know him!" she countered.

"I know him." Mossy's voice was firm.

Sarah stared at her cousin for a long time before sighing. Mossy had made up her mind. She asked, "Does it hurt?

Mossy winced. "A little."

"A little my ass! That monster ate your shoulder. Let me look at it." Sarah carefully pulled back the torn shreds of her shirt. "This is terrible, Mossy. There's so much blood—I can't even see all the damage."

"It's fine," Mossy insisted.

Sarah frowned at her wound. "I don't know how you're still coherent."

'Things always look much worse here than they really are," Mossy said.

Sarah didn't look convinced. "I hope you're right. The ER doesn't get a lot of dog bites from the spirit world."

Mossy shifted her weight to stand. "Let's just focus on getting out of here first."

"Yeah, how do we do that?" Sarah asked. "The other girls had amulets that sucked them right out of this world. What do you and I have?"

"We did have an old lady with a basket, but she left us," Mossy replied.

Sarah frowned. "I'm not even going to ask."

Mossy finally chuckled. "We'll get out of here, Sarah. I don't know how, but we will."

"I could help you with that."

Mossy and Sarah whirled at the familiar voice. Du Yong sat on the edge of the statue, watching them with amusement. If he was mad at all about the brides, he didn't show it.

"How about we make a deal? I send you home, but you take me with you?" He smiled innocently.

Mossy straightened.

"Or you take me with you, and I won't eat you," he modified.

Mossy frowned as she came to her feet. She grabbed her shoulders to control the pain. To her surprise, there was none! She quickly recovered her composure so that Du Yong wouldn't notice. "The only place I want to take you is hell."

"I've already been there. Don't care for it," he replied with a smile. "That was quite impressive, Mossy Cha. You took down my beasts quite efficiently. You continue to surprise me in every way. I don't think I've ever met such a versatile bride. You're fast. You're strong. You learn quickly. You also heal incredibly fast. What can't you do?"

"Cook," Sarah whispered from behind Mossy's back.

Du Yong waved a hand. "New age problems. I can deal with that."

"What do you want, Du Yong?" Mossy finally demanded.

Du Yong was always too fast. She never saw him move until he was directly in front of her. Sarah screamed as he thrust her across the parking lot. "Sorry. This is between me and Mossy."

When he faced her, he said, "I've already told you what I want, Mossy Cha. I want to live."

"I thought you came back to destroy all of Shee Yee's descendants!"

"That was a temper tantrum. I was mad. Shee Yee took it all from me and locked me away for a long time. But, I'm willing to let that go with fair compensation," he offered.

"Just say it!" Mossy snapped.

"I already have!" Du Yong grabbed her by the throat and lifted her to the sky. This monster was the one she knew—scary, not charming like the façade he enjoyed playing. "Let me into your body, Mossy Cha. I can live—through you!"

Mossy stared at him in disbelief. "You're crazy!"

Du Yong grinned. "Am I?"

He tossed her onto the ground. As she quickly turned, he waved a hand into the air. It summoned a window that revealed her world. It was the Shamans' Club, and the Succubus Queen was strangling Touso.

"No!" She scrambled forward, reaching with her hands. "Stop it! She's hurting him!"

Du Yong said, "She's not hurting him. She's killing him."

Mossy sobbed out loud when the Queen pried open his mouth to draw out his soul. He was in a daze and couldn't fight back.

"You were right about one thing," Du Yong said as she watched the horror. "I did learn from our little encounter that I could get to the brides with a third party."

Mossy froze.

"Just like I could hurt you and Touso through a third party." He grinned wickedly. "I'm learning that I don't have to do everything myself. I can delegate. I have plenty of monsters at my disposal. Kai failed to seduce you, but it was through him that I learned more about your unique qualities. And now—well, I had hoped to kill Touso, but when the Queen takes him, she'll share some of that strength with me. Contrary to popular belief, I'm not greedy."

"Please!" Mossy was on her knees. "Don't hurt him."

"I won't hurt him." Du Yong appeared in front of her again. "Not if you give me what I want."

Mossy stared at the image of Touso. She'd never seen him look so pale—so helpless. It made her soul cry. Then she returned her eyes to Du Yong. "If I say yes, you'll leave him alone?"

"Him and the whole damn clan!" Du Yong offered graciously. "I'll be generous with my new lease on life. What do you say?"

Mossy inhaled sharply. He was seeking permission to take possession of her body. Her eyes flickered once more to the window. Touso wasn't just in pain. He was dying, and there was nothing she could do except...

"How do I know you'll keep your word?" Mossy demanded.

"You don't. But I suppose this is where you must exercise faith," he said with a shrug. "Come, come, Mossy Cha. You're running out of time."

Mossy cried as Touso fell on the floor.

"She's taking a break," said Du Yong. "I can tell her to stop if we come to an agreement."

Mossy turned away as Touso's fingers curled against the ground. She never saw him lift his gaze to look for her because she was staring at Du Yong.

"What do you say?" the demon prodded again.

For once, Mossy was glad her spirit guides were not there. Every fiber of her being was screaming "No." She could only imagine what her spirit guides would have done. But she couldn't stand to watch Touso in pain. It was her job to protect him. Finally, Mossy peered into the demon's blood-red eyes.

"Yes or no, Mossy Cha?" Du Yong stared back eagerly.

As Mossy parted her mouth to speak, a shadow took the sky. She looked up to see a blue dragon soar through the clouds. At first, she thought it was Kalia, but soon realized this was a different entity altogether. Kalia was blue and pink. This dragon glittered blue against gold. As it spun in a fury, Mossy knew it was coming directly for them.

Du Yong grabbed Mossy and snarled. "Give me your answer now!"

Something kicked her back. The thing in her pack jumped and struggled like a fish caught in a net. The only thing in there was Mr. Foo! Soon, the bag snapped from her shoulders and fell to the ground. Mossy gasped as a massive panda bear with horns leaped at Du Yong.

Mr. Foo will protect you, Fuechi had insisted.

"Mr. Foo?" Mossy stared as the bear ripped at the surprised demon, tossing him with his horns.

The dragon arrived at that moment. It flashed its black eyes and tossed Mossy onto its back. When it circled, she realized it was going after Sarah. A moment later, her cousin was clinging to her from behind. But the dragon wasn't done. Mossy saw the bear run the demon into a tree. Then it ran toward the dragon, who knew exactly what to do. As the bear leaped into the air, the dragon scooped it up with one long claw.

When Mr. Foo eventually fell into Mossy's hands, he was a toy again. This time, when his eyes glowed, she wasn't scared. Instead, she hugged him. "Thanks, Mr. Foo!"

Sarah gawked at the toy over Mossy's shoulder. "What the hell?"

Below them, Du Yong released a ferocious roar. Even in the sky, they felt the spirit world quiver. But it didn't matter. Kaw was taking them home. They were safe.

As Mossy and Sarah laughed, the dragon glanced back at Mossy. *I told you I wouldn't save you anymore, Maihua. But I lied.*

Chapter 36

Together, the shamans and brides defeated Daisy and her succubus minions. The rightful souls were back with their bodies. What's more, the ailing shamans were safe. They now had their real brides to protect them. The nightmare was over. The only person who didn't come home intact was Mossy.

Mossy Cha had come home, but she wasn't awake. She saved the other brides, but her soul remained somewhere it shouldn't be.

"I'm sorry," Alang said. His voice strained with remorse. "She almost made it back! But my father ruined the ritual. I couldn't get the Slave Spirit to return for her once the candle was broken."

To his surprise, Touso Khang didn't glare or fume. Instead, he said, "You did your best, Alang. Thank you for bringing her home."

After Alang left, Touso remained sitting with Mossy. His mother thought she should stay near her altar, where she would be most connected with her spirit guides.

"She needs all the help she can get," Pahoua insisted.

Fuechi tucked his bear under Mossy's arm and whispered, "Mr. Foo will keep protecting you, Auntie Mossy."

Nia gently guided him away. She stifled her tears as Kai drew her into his arms. She asked, "Is Mossy going to be okay?"

"I don't know." Kai glanced at the young woman sleeping on the couch. Anyone who traveled with the Slave Spirit risked never coming back.

Bao placed a warm cloth over Mossy's head. It was infused with herbs meant to stimulate the body's energy. She smiled. "Emma said Mossy was the only reason they made it out. She kicked ass all the way through!"

Touso stared at his bride, willing her to open her eyes. They had been in this place before, but it felt different this time. Her soul had traveled too far. He wondered if she was in pain.

"Mossy." His voice broke with emotion. "I told you not to be brave! Why don't you ever listen?"

Someone pushed a pair of split horns into his hands. Lihue said, "You must call her."

Touso looked up at his father. "Will she even hear me?"

"You won't know unless you try," Lihue answered, handing him one more thing.

Touso accepted the hoop rattle. With one last look at Mossy, he walked to the front door. A moment later, in a voice strained with tears, he sang, "Mossy Cha, daughter of Keng Cha, wife of Touso Khang, I call you... I'm calling your soul to return home where you belong. Come home where you belong, Mossy, come home!"

As he cried, he hit the split horns against the door frame three times.

"Why are there so many doors?" Mossy counted at least ten floating across the grassland. If it was hard enough to call one, she wondered what she had done to deserve ten. "Will they all take me home?"

Kaw scowled. "There's never ten—only ever one. This isn't good. The Black Door is testing you."

Mossy laughed. They had managed to survive a pack of beasts, lost the Slave Spirit, and narrowly escaped Du Yong. Somehow, the dragon, Kaw, was able to save them. But now, there were ten doors to negotiate before she could return home. Mossy thought for sure the gods were angry with her.

"Can we peek inside each door?" Sarah asked.

Kaw shook his head. "The door you open is the door you choose."

Sarah groaned. "I just want to go home!"

Mossy paced impatiently before the doors, searching for any detail that could matter. But each door was the same, the only difference being what was beyond it. If Kaw was right, and he had proved quite reliable so far, they couldn't afford to make a mistake.

"I don't know how I'm supposed to choose!' Mossy frowned with exasperation.

"Pick the one that feels like home," said Kaw.

Mossy gave him a look that said he was no help, and Kaw shrugged.

"Why did you help us?" Mossy asked.

His midnight eyes grew even darker. Finally, he said, "My sister would throw a fit if she found out I left you there."

Mossy accepted this practical answer. "Thank you. I almost lost myself."

"Don't do it again."

Mossy studied him. The dragon spirit knew she had nearly sold her body to the demon. Suddenly, Mossy remembered precisely why that happened. She turned and quickly pointed at each door.

"What are you doing, Mossy? Are you really going to 'eeny, meeny, miny, moe' it?" Sarah demanded in disbelief.

"Do I really have a choice?" she snapped.

"Mossy," Kaw said finally. She was stunned when his long fingers curled around her arm. The dragon spirit was usually careful not to touch her. "You're a shaman. Use your gifts. Stop acting impulsively."

Mossy glared. "Are you lecturing me?"

Kaw grinned. "Is it helping?"

She narrowed her gaze, grateful that Kalia, instead of Kaw, was her spirit guide. She enjoyed Kalia. She would only fight with Kaw.

Finally, Mossy turned to face the doors again. There were ten doors and only one way home. She closed her eyes and hoped one of them would give her the answer she needed. She thought of her altar and the clean lines of the joss paper. She remembered the purity of the white flowers and the pillars that made up the home of her spirit guides. She saw the wall containing photos of all the people she loved: her parents, siblings, Lihue and Pahoua, Kai, and his family. Finally, she saw Touso. It was the photo of them getting married—the one that hadn't happened yet.

Three loud knocks. *Thump! Thump! Thump!*

"It's the door! It's one of the doors!" Sarah cried.

Mossy gasped.

Thump! Thump! Thump!

It was the eighth door. She was eight years old when she met Touso. The Black Door was located on aisle eight at the store. The door home was number eight!

The sky was darkening, and the wind picked up speed. They were running out of time.

"Sarah, come on!" Mossy grabbed her hands and stopped briefly in front of Kaw. "Thank you. If you hadn't come..."

Kaw nodded without smiling. "Your struggles do not end here, Mossy Cha. Stay vigilant, and do not let the demon sway you again with his lies."

As Mossy stared at him, the shadows in his eyes shifted. She saw images of a boy and girl splashing in a small pond. She had asked him before but felt the need to ask again. "Kaw... do I know you?"

Instantly, the shadows returned. Kaw turned away and said, "Go home, Mossy Cha. The people you love are waiting for you."

"Mossy!" Sarah tugged at her hand. "Come on! We have to go!"

Mossy frowned as Kaw walked away. His blue-black mane waved like curtains hiding a dream. Even the way his body moved stirred distant memories. Thunder rolling across the sky finally snapped Mossy back to reality. As the rain poured, Mossy and Sarah sprinted toward the eighth door. It opened immediately, and then they were gone.

When the door closed, a little girl and boy arrived at the grasslands. They never noticed the doors or the dragon spirit watching.

"Are you really taking me to meet the Thunder God?" Maihua giggled.

"Of course! I told you—he's my cousin!" replied the boy.

"Gods don't have cousins!" Maihua said in disbelief.

Little Kaw stood proudly. "We're the best of cousins. I'll be in his army someday!"

"Can I be in his army, too?" Maihua asked.

He answered, "You'll have to ask him. Come on. We have to hurry. When it stops raining, he'll be too far."

"Okay! Let's run!"

Little Kaw was surprised when Maihua grabbed his hand. She was soft and warm. Her touch reminded him of a beautiful summer day and filled him with joy. Then, they disappeared over the horizon.

This memory was the first mistake he ever made. It was the day he introduced her to the Thunder God and the last time Maihua truly belonged to him.

When Mossy opened her eyes and smelled the faint scents of sandalwood and lavender, she knew she was home. Carefully, she removed Mr. Foo and rose from the couch. Someone was standing by the door, swinging a hoop rattle.

Mossy didn't know how much time had passed. But it was dark, and Touso's voice was strained. Whatever he was doing, he had been doing it for a long time.

"Come home, Mossy. Come home where you belong."

Mossy walked past the bowl of rice and incense. A soft breeze brushed past her before it washed over Touso on the porch. He stopped everything to listen. But why wouldn't he look at her?

Suddenly, Mossy feared it was all a dream—or worse, that she'd returned home as a spirit while her body remained elsewhere.

Mossy curled her fingers around the hand that held the hoop rattle. "Touso. I'm home."

Touso turned slowly. He studied her with glistening golden eyes. Then he touched her face, rubbing her cheek with the base of his thumb. "You're here. You're really here!"

Within seconds, she was in his arms. They cried and laughed together. He buried his nose into her hair, inhaling the energy of life absent while her soul was gone. She dug her fingers into his back as though he, too, might fade away. She was really home!

When they finally parted, Mossy asked, "Is everyone safe?"

Touso studied her with a strange expression. "Yes. Everyone is safe. We've all been waiting for you!"

Mossy burst into tears. "I've been so worried, Touso! I saw her hurting you—I thought you were dying. I thought I was never coming home!"

She was still crying when Touso covered her mouth with a kiss. She leaned into the warmth of his body, savoring the sweet tenderness of his touch. "I'm here. I'm safe, and you're home. I knew that if I kept calling, you'd find your way."

Mossy pressed an ear against his chest, listening to the rhythm of his heartbeat.

Thoom-thoomp! Thoom-thoomp! Thoom-thoomp!

It sounded just like the knocking on the door. "Thank you for calling me home."

Awakening

Mossy received her second welcome when her spirit guides flew out and embraced her. They had missed her just as much as she'd missed them.

Chapter 37

Seng Vang sat at the altar, filling the bowls with fresh wine and fruits. His wife bought fresh flowers to keep the altar especially lovely. But to his dismay, the red flowers—Du Yong's favorite color—were already limp and rotten at the stems. Still, he sat and prayed until something changed in the room. It became so cold that Seng's next breath came in clouds.

He spoke excitedly. "Oh, great demon, thank you for gracing me with your presence! I know you are disappointed with what happened, but I'll find a way to—"

He ceased talking as a serpent's tale slithered around his throat. A moment later, a hideous face glared at him with blood-red eyes.

"There is no such thing as disappointment, Seng—only food!"

Du Yong did not care that the necromancer Seng Vang screamed the entire time. The fact that his mouth was open only made ripping out his soul easier. The screams added to the pleasure of eating him.

Paj Vang

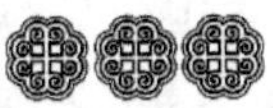

When Alang Vang heard his father scream, he remained unmoved. Seng Vang didn't tolerate failure. Any mistake was met with a punishment cruel enough to ensure it never happened again. It was precisely how Seng had raised his children. After disappointing the demon, Alang was sure his father had suffered the same fate. Du Yong didn't tolerate failure, either.

Alang sat in his sister's room, thinking of better days. While most kids feared the space underneath their bed, it was there that Alang and Daisy had found safety. When Seng was on a rampage about one thing or another, the siblings hid under the bed. Sometimes, Alang would read her a story. Other times, they'd simply lay there and draw. It was easy to pretend they were anywhere else.

Alang was no longer a child but suddenly felt a strong urge to slide under the bed. A moment later, he was on his back, staring at simple drawings against the wooden slats and bed frame. He'd forgotten that they used to forego paper altogether and simply drew on the expensive furniture his mother bought. He smiled as he touched the pink piglet. Daisy once said she'd never become a shaman because she couldn't sacrifice one of her favorite animals.

"They're too cute."

Alang turned to see his sister lying beside him. To his surprise, she looked normal. She wasn't human but was no longer a soul-sucking Succubus Queen.

"Freakin shamans. Why can't they sacrifice something uglier—like an armadillo." Daisy frowned.

Alang chuckled. "I think armadillos run short in Laos. Why do you look like this? Where are you going?" He wanted to say she looked "pretty," but their family had never been good about compliments.

She was even prettier when she was happy. Daisy almost looked human as a smile spread across her face. "I'm going to the afterlife!"

Alang frowned. "Do evil spirits go to the afterlife?"

Daisy laughed. "No, silly! Don't you see? I've changed my wicked ways."

When Alang continued to look confused, Daisy explained, "Kai negotiated with the Gods to redeem my soul. He told them it was his fault—something of a sort. Anyway, I'm pretty sure he'll be punished somehow. But he was able to free my soul from an eternity of demon-like behavior. Wasn't that nice of him?"

It was nice and surprising. He asked, "What are you doing here?"

"Oh, brother! You should already know this! The soul must visit every place it's been to before moving on. I was born here in this house, so this is the last stop before I go to my new home." Daisy was so happy that it felt wrong to be sad for her.

When she looked him straight in the eyes, he was surprised to neither feel nauseous nor afraid. These were not the eyes of the Succubus Queen. She was his sister.

"I also wanted to say goodbye."

"Goodbye?"

"Goodbye and thank you. I'll miss you, Alang. I know you suffered the most with our father. He favored me—I should have helped you more. I spent so much time helping strangers but couldn't help my brother. Do you hate me?" She looked troubled and sad all at once.

Alang felt an unexpected ping of emotion. He looked away and wiped at the tears forming in his eyes. Finally, he said, "I don't hate you. I'm just glad he didn't hurt you like he hurt me."

"He'll never hurt you again." The way she said it was absolute, and Alang believed her.

"You've been a good brother, Alang. I hope we will see each other again someday," she said.

He met her gaze. "Go in peace, little sister. May your next life be a beautiful one."

Daisy smiled, and then she was gone. Alang reached out, expecting to feel warmth where it was now empty. He sighed when it just felt empty.

Alang returned to touching the childish drawings on the wooden bed. His sister was finally at peace, and his father was gone. For the first time in his life, he felt so much relief that he laughed.

He was free.

Chapter 38

They had just returned from a walk through the woods, and Nia was anxious to prepare lunch for Fuechi. She frowned as Kai stopped at the front door and waited.

"What's going on? You know this is your house, right? Just walk in," she said with a teasing grin.

"No. We have to wait," Kai insisted.

"Wait for what?"

The door opened. Her mouth fell in surprise as Lihue walked out with a colorful rooster.

"What is this?" She glanced between her husband and father-in-law.

"Your official initiation!" Kai shouted excitedly.

Before he returned to the spirit world, he had made one request from his father: "She's my wife, and Fuechi is the future. I want our ancestors to know they're Khangs. They're family."

Nia gawked as Lihue sang the "Welcome" song, waving the rooster several times around their heads and at their feet.

"Welcome! Our son has finally brought home our new daughter-in-law, and we are officially welcoming her into the family today." This welcome song continued for several more minutes as he invited their ancestors to bless this union.

Because Nia didn't understand the words, it felt awkward. But she was comforted when Kai held her hands and smiled. "Nia baby, this is your family now. Don't forget."

As Lihue finally released the rooster, the door swung open. The rest of the family—Pahoua, Bao, Touso, and Mossy shouted, "Welcome!"

Fuechi ran out the door and hugged both of his parents. "Yay! Mama and Daddy are Hmong married!"

Everyone laughed. Then, the ladies pulled Nia away so Kai could complete the rest of the ceremony alone. As his ancestral spirits swarmed his home, Kai saw angry faces and sighed. He had earned this disdain by breaking the rules. Now, he faced the consequences of redeeming himself. Kai bowed and prepared himself for a long night.

It was a day like any other. After Kai finished bowing to the ancestors, earned their forgiveness, and received their blessings for his new family, he celebrated. He walked with Fuechi around the pond, telling him about each koi that listened better than most people. He shared his dreams for Fuechi's life with his brother and father. He listened to Bao talk about medical school and reminded her to make room for fun.

"You're always too serious," Kai admonished but said with care. "Don't forget to enjoy this life, Bao. You deserve it."

Bao threw her arms around her oldest brother, knowing they had wasted too much time questioning each other.

"WWKD. What would Kai do?" She grinned.

Kai grimaced. "Sometimes, just do the opposite, okay?"

Bao laughed. Then they discussed the only acceptable attributes of a future brother-in-law—the foremost being: no necromancers.

Kai found his mother putting food away in the kitchen. He frowned and asked, "Mom, when will you finally get a housekeeper?"

She smiled. "I have two daughters-in-law now. I'm optimistic."

"I think they're all watching TV." When he grinned at her, she threw a rag at him.

"Shut up and help your mother, you brat!" As Kai quickly complied, her eyes warmed with tears. It wasn't often that a mother had to say goodbye to her son twice.

After he was done putting the boxes in the fridge, they settled at the counter to drink some tea. She poured him his favorite chamomile and honey, which always helped him rest.

"Are you happy, mom?" Kai asked.

"It's a strange question when my son is leaving me again," Pahoua replied pensively.

Kai said, "Mom, you know better than that. I won't be here, but I won't be gone."

"It won't be the same!" she cried quietly. "It hasn't been the same since you left."

Kai hugged her close. "But it's still going to be a beautiful life. You and this family—this is what my son and Nia need. As long as our family thrives, I'm happy."

"We'll miss you," she whispered.

"I'll miss you, too. But I'll always be watching. You can count on that," he replied.

Pahoua looked at him suspiciously. "Have you seen that future? How do you know you won't forget about us after your dip in the Lake of Life?"

Kai shrugged mysteriously. "Let's just say I've discussed it with upper management."

Pahoua rolled her eyes. "You're right. I won't worry about you. You're too sneaky!"

After a quiet moment, Kai said, "I just want you to forgive yourself. You didn't kill me. I don't want you living that way, Mom."

Pahoua inhaled sharply. "Somethings can't be undone, my son."

"But it can be forgiven." Kai held her hand. "I could not have asked for a better mother in this life or any other. Before I leave, promise you won't hate yourself. Promise me you'll be happy."

Tears fell from her eyes. "Only if you promise you'll be my son again in another life."

Now, Kai was crying, too. "Done! In every one possible."

Kai spent the rest of the evening watching "Paw Patrol" with Fuechi and teaching him how to punch bullies.

He said, "Remember, you're a Khang. Your shame is my shame. Don't let anyone push you around!"

Fuechi nodded. "Yes, Daddy!"

Awakening

When Fuechi punched him in the stomach, Kai dropped to the floor and begged for mercy. And when the little boy kneeled to check on him, his father wrestled him onto the ground. While Fuechi giggled and snuggled into his arms, Kai said, "You know I love you, right, bud?"

"And Fuechi loves you this much, Daddy!" As he stretched his arms wide, Kai broke and embraced him. Fuechi asked, "Why are you crying, Daddy?"

"Because I'm going to miss you so much, bud," he answered.

Fuechi, always too wise for his age, smiled. "Don't worry, Daddy. Fuechi will always find you."

Kai stifled a sob and wiped his eyes. "I hope so!"

Finally, he tucked his son warmly under his blankets and kissed his head. "I love you, Fuechi. We'll find each other again."

Kai found his brother sitting on the porch. Since Touso had no friends, he often sat alone, staring at the stars. Kai used to make fun of him all the time. As he sat next to his brother, he asked, "Are you looking for me in heaven already?"

Touso scowled. "I'm negotiating on your behalf."

Kai snorted. "Appreciate the support as always."

Touso studied him. His brother's soul was strong, but the body was failing him. Dylan was pale and looking frailer by the day. The battle with the succubus was especially draining. Kai Khang needed to move on if Dylan Reed was to survive.

"I'll always take care of them. You know that, right?" Touso looked at him sideways.

"I know." Kai stared up at the stars. "I'll come back if you don't!"

Touso smiled, but they settled into an uneasy silence. Finally, he asked, "What can I do to make this easier, Kai?"

Kai looked away, shaking his head. "Just stay alive. I meant it when I told you—our family only survives, if you do. Don't do anything stupid, okay?"

"I wish you would just tell me what you see," Touso growled in frustration. "Why do you always play so many mind games?"

Kai considered him. "When I go, you'll see everything I see. And you'll understand. Knowing the future is a curse. Telling people about it is even more useless."

"Then why give it to me at all?" Touso demanded.

Kai met his gaze. "Because you need all the monopoly pieces, bro. You don't pick and choose what you want. You gather them all and use what works. It's your only chance."

"I thought it was all supposed to be easier when I found Mossy." Touso shook his head.

"You love her, right?" Kai asked.

"More than I expected." He smiled as he thought about his bride.

Kai studied his brother. "Mossy is different. She's not just a bride. She's a game-changer."

Touso frowned. "What are you saying?"

"What will you do if she picks the wrong side?" Kai asked.

"What wrong side? She's on my side!" When Touso was agitated, sparks flickered around his body. The lights on the porch were flashing as well.

"Chill out—it's just a question!' Kai sunk into the chair. "She's a beast, bro. She'll protect you with her life. I know it. I'm just saying she's young—and a tad idealistic. She might choose the wrong way, thinking it's the right way."

"It won't happen."

"Okay. Just don't say I didn't warn you." As Touso continued to scowl, Kai said, "Look, I'm happy for you. I can see you're crazy about each other."

"But?" Touso arched a brow.

Kai lifted his hands. "No buts. Don't worry. Be happy."

Touso laughed. "That fucking song. Mossy called me old 'cus that's the only song I know."

"She's not wrong, either. You're lame, bro. When I'm gone, please make some friends. Go to a concert. Smoke some weed! But mostly, make friends so Mossy doesn't have to put up with you alone," Kai pleaded.

"I'll take that into consideration." Touso rolled his eyes but smiled. "It's been good having you back. I've missed you."

Kai took a deep breath. "You've always been my best friend, kid. I wanted to protect you until the end, but I'll have to pass the baton to Mossy. Just—try to be happy, okay? I mean it. When this shit all blows over, live a normal life. Don't always worry about the rules. Just be happy."

Touso nodded. "I promise."

As the brothers stared up into the sky, a shooting star appeared. Both made a wish and prayed it would come true.

Nia had folded the same towel a hundred times before Kai finally returned to the room. He walked up behind her, kissed her neck, and ran his hands down the length of her arms. She closed her eyes as he pressed his body against her backside.

"Nia baby," he whispered.

She was already crying by the time she turned to face him. Tears slid from her brown eyes and down her cheeks. "What am I going to do without you?"

He smiled sadly. "Live, baby. Raise Fuechi. Have adventures. Maybe find love again. Just be happy. Don't hold back because of me."

Nia shook her head. "I love you, Kai. I'm always going to love you."

"I'm counting on it."

He gently kissed her head and cheeks before finally lingering on her lips. But some acts weren't meant to stay soft. A hungry and passionate embrace drained her of all rational thought. He was the love of her life—the only man she had ever loved. She didn't want to live without him. As he explored her body, suckled, and lingered on the softest parts of her flesh, she wanted nothing more than to melt into his soul.

"Let me come with you," she pleaded.

Tasting her tears, Kai looked into her eyes. "No, Nia baby. You belong here. But remember me. Because I'm coming for you in our next lifetime."

Nia said, "I'll be waiting!"

Kai brushed his mouth over her quivering lips and pushed her sensually against the wall. "I love you."

"Show me how much," she whispered against his teeth.

Kai grinned, and for the first time in his life, he did exactly as he was told.

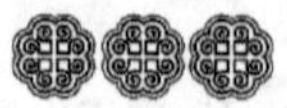

Dylan Reed had waited anxiously for the day when Kai would leave his body, and now that it was happening, he felt torn. Kai was no longer just a lost and angry spirit. He had become the older brother Dylan never had.

"I hate you, but you're all right." Dylan Reed stared into the mirror and wiped away a trail of blood coming from his nose.

Kai chuckled. "I'll miss you, too, bro. Never been much for roommates, but we did well together. By the way, you look like shit."

"My roommate's an ass," Dylan snickered.

"He's leaving soon," Kai promised.

There was a long silence. It wasn't often that two souls shared a body. What was the proper etiquette? Finally, Dylan said, "You were a good dad. Fuechi loves you. Nia loves you. Solid B+. Don't let those do-gooders give you a hard time in heaven."

Kai smirked. "If they do, I'll just beat them up."

Dylan asked, "Was it worth it? Giving it all up for him?"

"If you're asking me if I love my brother more than my wife and son, the answer is 'no.'" Kai shook his head with a laugh. "Life is not about what you want, man. It's about what's best. Fuechi will become who he needs to be because I loved him enough to sacrifice the time I have."

"I think that's bullshit!" Dylan scowled at the mirror. "You're his dad! Who doesn't need their dad?"

Kai met his gaze. "I'll always be his dad. I'm part of him. His thoughts are my thoughts. He'll never be alone. And he has a family to look out for him. I'm letting go because I trust that future. You need to do the same."

Dylan froze. "What does that mean?"

"You and Mossy. That chapter has closed. Du Yong used you because you're a distraction. Don't distract her anymore, bro. She's got things to do—important things. Saving-Fuechi's-life-type things. Get it?"

"She'd be safer with me."

"But she won't be happy. If you love her, don't force her to choose. Just let her be. Half her pain is just wanting to please people. Even you."

Dylan looked away.

"She cares about you, Dylan. And if you care about her, give her peace," Kai said in the kindest way he knew. He was never the one to give dating advice. But he considered this one legit since it was about parting with a girl. "Would it help if I said you could do better?"

Dylan said, "Fuck you, Kai."

Kai laughed. "You'll be all right, bro. Just—don't try to be so serious so soon. You've got a whole life ahead of you. Save all that love bullshit for later."

"Thanks for the advice." Dylan frowned and crossed his arms. "But what if I just save myself for Nia?"

When Kai's eyes flashed electric gold, Dylan laughed. "I'm just kidding, dude! Sheesh!" As Kai relaxed, Dylan's tone became more serious. "I'd like to be her friend, though. Fuechi's, too. Is that okay?"

Kai nodded. Fuechi liked Dylan, even if it was mostly because his father's spirit was inside the man. In the future, he might be able to give

Fuechi the kind of support Kai couldn't. "Thank you. I appreciate that."

"What a fucking life, dude," Dylan sighed.

"Just live it, bro. The best way you know how."

As Dylan nodded, they both heard something. It was the kind of sound that tugged at souls. Kai followed it out into the hallway, where he found Touso standing downstairs. The brothers looked at each other, and Kai noted the lusheng in the other's hands.

"It's time," said Touso.

Kai nodded. He hated goodbyes. But as Touso lifted the lusheng to his lips to play the death song, everyone walked out of their rooms.

"Daddy?" Fuechi looked confused.

Kai's lifting soul immediately ceased. The lusheng, frustrated by this sudden disruption, sent a chord that thrashed at his soul to move. Kai trembled and fell to his knees.

Nia flew to his side. "Kai! What's happening?"

As Touso Khang continued playing the death song, Kai twisted in pain. Nia screamed, "You're hurting him!"

She paused when Kai curled his fingers around her hand. "No. Don't stop it, Nia. It's time for me to go."

Nia sobbed and fell against him.

Soon, Fuechi was crying, too. "Daddy! Please don't go!"

His tears hit him in the chest like daggers, and Kai struggled not to push him away. Instead, he reached for his son and said, "Don't cry. Daddy's just going to work."

Pahoua arrived at Nia's side. "Come, Nia. As long as you hold on to him, he'll be in pain."

Nia shook her head. "I can't. I love him!"

"Daddy!" Fuechi buried his face into his father's neck.

Kai sat up just enough to curl his arms around his wife and son. He didn't want to leave them. He wanted to stay with them forever. And because of this sudden change of heart, his pain grew. Kai began convulsing and fell to the ground again.

"Kai!" Nia screamed.

Lihue Khang touched his son's head. Tears fell as he said, "He's in pain. If he stays, his soul will kill this body. His soul will remain tortured. If we love him, we must send him where he belongs!"

Pahoua and Bao put their arms around Nia.

"Look at him. He's suffering," Bao whispered.

Kai was curled in a fetal position on the ground and held onto Nia's hand.

Pahoua said, "He loves you and Fuechi the most. He'll only go when you permit him."

"Nia," Kai trembled as he looked up at her. "I love you. Every... everything is going to be okay."

His skin felt colder than ice. The next time Kai wailed in agony, Nia couldn't stand it anymore. She pulled Fuechi close and looked into his eyes. "Sweetie, do you want to send Daddy somewhere nice?"

Fuechi stared at his mother. "Where?"

Nia sniffled. "Daddy is very sick right now. If we send Daddy to this nice place, he'll get better. We want Daddy to feel good, right?"

Carefully, Fuechi nodded.

"But Daddy won't go if we don't tell him it's okay. Will you help me tell Daddy it's okay? Because no matter where he goes, we'll always be able to find him, right?"

Despite his tears, Fuechi seemed to understand. Finally, he sunk to the floor. Everyone looked away, stifling tears, when the boy rested his cheek alongside his father's pale face. He whispered, "It's okay, Daddy. You can go to the nice place. Fuechi and Mommy will come find you later."

Almost as soon as Fuechi said this, Kai stopped moving. His body relaxed, and it seemed his father had fallen asleep. Then Fuechi felt a tickle at his ear. When he looked up, his father's soul stared down at him. Kai Khang was no longer Dylan Reed. He looked just as he always had, with a sun on top of his head, jewelry on his face, and koi tattoos along the side of his neck.

"Hey, bud. Don't cry for me. I'm okay," Kai smiled at his son.

Fuechi asked, "Are you going to the nice place now, Daddy?"

Kai nodded. "I have to go so I can stay strong for you. I'm so proud of you, Fuechi. Wherever I go, I'll be watching you. You'll never be alone, okay?"

Fuechi smiled. "Wherever you go, Daddy, Fuechi will find you."

"Kai..."

He turned as his wife approached.

"Don't cry, Nia baby. I hate it when you cry." He traced the curve of her face with his light. "I love you. Remember what I said. In another life, I'll come find you."

"And I'll be ready," she promised. Finally, Nia took their son's hand. "Time to say goodbye to Daddy, baby. Let's send him off to the good place."

When Fuechi reached for his father, Kai sent forward a trail of light that wrapped him in warmth and love.

"Bye, Daddy. I love you."

Kai smiled. "I love you, too, bud. Take care of your mama."

Then he straightened to look at all the people he loved one last time.

"Dad, Mom, I'm going now."

Lihue and Pahoua nodded.

"You've been a good son. I'm sorry if this old fool ever made you feel any other way!" Lihue cried quietly.

"Go safely, Kai. Behave on the other side." Pahoua could hardly see him as she wept.

Kai turned to his sister. "Take care of everyone, sis. I know you always have. Remember, no necromancers!"

Bao laughed despite her own tears.

"Mossy."

She was surprised when Kai Khang's soul called her. He was a son, brother, sister, husband, and father to everyone else. In that respect, Mossy and Kai barely knew each other. So, when he called her name, she felt nervous. As she stepped into the hall, Kai smiled.

"From one protector to another, I leave my brother in your care. As you go forward with your battle, remember: don't save a life if it will destroy a soul."

Mossy's face turned in confusion, but before she could ask anything, the lusheng was already pulling him away.

Kai Khang followed the song of death down the long hallway and over the stairs until he finally arrived at the door. He glanced over at Touso, whose eyes had remained closed while he played. Now he opened them to see his brother one last time.

Kai grinned. "Come on, bro. Take me home."

Awakening

Touso nodded before closing his eyes again. As he blew all his love into the bamboo reeds that spoke the words of the dead, the soul of Kai Khang walked out the door for the last time. He whistled *"Don't Worry, Be Happy"* and hoped they would all remember.

Rest in Peace
Kai Khang

Chapter 39

As Mossy Cha graduated high school, her family was larger than ever. When Mr. Nguyen called her name, her parents and siblings cheered with big "thumbs up" gloves. Aunt May and Uncle Yer held a sign that read, "Too Cool for School! Congrats!" Sarah, Thai, and Emma waved their arms and yelled like crazy people. Lihue and Pahoua looked like jumping carrots in their matching orange shirts. Only Bao managed to stay cool, waving a single hand like a beauty queen. But it was the man watching her silently that took her breath away.

Touso Khang didn't yell, jump, or scream, but she knew he was proud when he smiled. As their eyes met, he put a palm to his heart. She did the same.

After tossing their hats, everyone dispersed to meet their family. But there was one person that Mossy especially wanted to see. As she approached the corner, she saw Dylan Reed hugging his parents. When their eyes met over Dr. Reed's shoulder, a slight scowl came over Dylan's face. Immediately, Mossy's heart fell. He still hated her.

After Kai Khang left his body, Dylan refused to speak to anyone. He finally let Pahoua check his vitals, and when he seemed stable, she drove him home. It was the last time Mossy saw Dylan.

Until now.

Strength and a beautiful tan replaced the gauntness and pale complexion. When he smiled, his blue-green eyes were bright without any strange light. He was normal again.

As she approached, Dr. Reed and Deloris exchanged knowing glances.

They knew.

They smiled and hugged her, anyway. Then they excused themselves, leaving Mossy and Dylan alone.

"Hi," she said when he wouldn't look at her.

"Hey, Moss." Dylan kept his eyes on the floor.

"I've tried calling you."

"I've been busy."

Mossy frowned. "So, I've heard. Dylan, are you ever going to talk to me again?"

When he looked at her for the first time, she inhaled sharply. The pain in his eyes made her feel like a terrible person.

"I've never had an ex-girlfriend I still loved," said Dylan.

Mossy struggled to keep her voice calm. "I'm sorry for everything. I want you to know how much I appreciate what you did. I know it's not easy to sacrifice for the people you care about. Thank you for always giving me your all when I should have given you more."

Dylan pulled her into his arms. He held her so close she felt his heart beat against her chest.

He said, "I'd do it all over again. Be happy, Moss. But if you're not—if you ever need me, if he ever hurts you—I'll be there."

Tears filled her eyes. He was saying goodbye. What's more, he was letting her choose. The only thing she could think to say was, "Thank you."

He smiled. "See you later, Moss."

As Dylan Reed disappeared into the crowd, he took with him a life she would never know. Once upon a time, Mossy would have cried desperately to get it back. It was strange how quickly things changed. But she was grateful that some things would always stay the same.

"We've done it! We're done! We're out of here!" Eva Garcia wrapped her long arms around Mossy and jumped excitedly.

Mossy giggled as she joined this joyful dance. "We survived!"

As the two friends settled into a warm embrace, Eva asked, "How did that go? Are you okay?"

Mossy said, "I think we're all going to be fine now."

"I wish you could come with us today," Eva said with a soft pout. All the seniors were going to celebrate at Tyler's house. Eva didn't like their arrogant classmate, but if she were going to throw up and ruin anyone's furniture, it would be Tyler's.

Mossy smiled. "Me, too. But some things must be done."

Eva's eyes sparkled knowingly. "Get it done, girl. And call me later!"

As Eva ran off to join Jeremy in a round of photos, Mossy felt the arrival of the person she missed the most. Touso Khang slid his arms around her waist and whispered into her ear, "Are you ready?"

She nodded. "Let's do it."

It was their wedding day. Bao felt like she was playing with a doll while brushing Mossy's hair. When she finished tying it into a neat bun, it was Pahoua's turn. Her mother-in-law approached with a long length of deep purple cloth.

She said, "Hold still. This hat represents your new marriage. The ribbon that secures it symbolizes your commitment. It must be perfect!"

There was something beautiful and intimate about wrapping the head of one's future daughter-in-law. And when she was done, the turban looked like a heart around the face of its lovely bride. It was completed with a black and white ribbon along the edges. The crossing ribbons at the front of the turban were two lives becoming one.

Pahoua and Bao appeared beside her as she stared into the mirror. Mossy always considered herself a modern girl stuck in a Hmong world. The person in the mirror was a Hmong woman dressed in a simple black jacket with traditional blue cuffs and a white pleated skirt. Green and pink sashes hugged her tiny waist.

Mossy brushed the hundreds of coins along the blue apron that dangled at the center of the skirt. They matched the bands of silver rings that hung on her chest. She stared at the soul lock beneath the necklace for a long time. Then she gazed into her own eyes, understanding for the first time that she didn't have to abandon the modern girl or tradition.

She could embrace them both.

"You're ready," Pahoua whispered with tears in her eyes.

Mossy smiled. "Yes, I am."

Awakening

The role of maid of honor was reserved for a woman from the groom's family, so Bao was dressed in traditional attire as well. Mossy was grateful for her familiar presence. She didn't want to be alone while Touso tried to win over her family.

The ceremony would begin at her home, where Touso and his groomsmen faced the daunting task of earning their approval. When he wasn't with the *mej koob*—the wedding negotiator—working through the marriage terms, he was expected to socialize.

It worried her. Touso faced demons without hesitation, yet crowds of loud, celebratory relatives unsettled him in ways no spirit could. Accepting blessings meant drinking round after round of beer and liquor from each of her male relatives.

Mossy had many male relatives, and she hoped they would show him kindness.

Escorted downstairs by the Khang women, she found the wedding party waiting by the door. Her gaze went straight to her groom.

Touso looked like a prince, his black-collared jacket fitted to his lean shoulders, dark slacks falling cleanly over long legs. Green and pink sashes echoed her own, tying them together in color and tradition. When he stepped forward to greet her, the coins of his moneybags—symbols of prosperity—jingled softly, bright and sure.

He took her hands. "You look beautiful."

Mossy blushed.

Chief wedding negotiator Wang Meng Khang clapped his hands, his voice ringing out, "If you want to get married, follow me. Let's get this party started!"

As the wedding party filed out the door, Touso turned to her. "Are you ready for a lifetime with me?"

Mossy met his gaze, her eyes glistening. "Always."

He leaned in and kissed her, soft and certain. Relief washed through him as the visions came—quiet, fleeting glimpses of peace. For a little while, they would be spared.

He had promised to fight even the gods, just to give her a few normal days. As they stepped forward to follow the others, both understood: this was one of them.

To be continued...

About the Author

Paj Vang, a writer with a love for romance, fantasy, and a dash of horror, was born in Portland, OR, and grew up in Sacramento, CA. Now settled in the scenic Northcentral Washington, she lives with her husband and four energetic kids. When she's not busy writing, she's likely binge-watching romance or fantasy dramas or making memories with her family. Paj's world is a blend of imagination, family, and a good story—because who doesn't love a great tale?